BLACK HARLEQUIN

By

Paul Boyce

...ooOoo...

 New Generation Publishing

PART 1

Development

Chapter 1

Little Tamm DuHan had been a sickly boy right up until his parents moved away from the damp marshlands to be nearer to the sea air. Although long of body, he was painfully thin virtually from birth and had a pallid appearance. His hair was a sleek black, a legacy from his father and forbears. It was only through sheer hard work by his doting parents and their constant care that he survived through his toddler years. A bronchial complication led to colds and influenza throughout the autumn and winter months every year. *That poor lad,* people would observe, *see how he struggles to keep pace with his peers,* to the point that the other lads would often run off on their mini adventures without him.

Tamm's father, Leage DuHan, eked a meagre living with his crafting of scrimshaw, the intricate carving of models and statuettes from the bones of oxen, goat and sheep. He was fortunate that he was able to sell these to traders and merchants who passed through the village on their way to the markets of town and cities to the east and west.

Leage wasn't much good for anything else; an eye lost in an accident on his small-holding, his lower left leg lost in the goblin raids on their settlement and half an ear lost in a senseless fight with a drunken farmer. He often said that fate was slowly whittling him away. In ten years there would be little of him left at this rate. As a proud one-time swordsman in a town watch it was a devastating way to see out his life. Bones of farm animals were all good and well but they could be brittle and were difficult to work with when using his fine tools. The blades hardly lasted a week and replacing them was expensive. He yearned for the bones of the great fish of the sea having heard how ideal they were for his elaborate style of work.

"We ought to move away from this dampness," he said, not for the first time.

"Then do it, don't talk about it," retorted Luanne, his wife. She was barely tolerating this environment and the effect this was having on Tamm. "Procrastinating will mean we stay here. Tamm needs better air. We all do."

There were two other children aside from Tamm; Hanni and Natti, twin girls two years younger than Tamm but almost old enough to do chores. Both of them displayed a fascination for knowledge; always asking questions, they were. "Why, Mama. How, Mama." They did not suffer through the winters as Tamm did.

There was no learning house for children out here in the soil country. They were teaching Tamm letters and numbers, best they could. Well, Luanne was at least. What little education Leage had was more practical than academic and he could only manipulate numbers, with surprising dexterity, when throwing tiles with the old 'uns in the tavern.

His opportunity came unexpectedly when a merchant passed through the settlement. He had shown interest in Leage's finely detailed scrimshaw and had previously promised to buy anything that he could produce. He recommended the family move to Tranquil Port on the Landsdrop Coast, a little north of Westron Seaport. When Leage protested that he had not the means to travel with his family so great a distance the trader, Ephil Banaman, simply replied "Pack your belongings together on a mule-cart and I shall collect you all in a tenday on my return. Tranquil Port is my home. The air is clean, fisfbones aplenty and a house of learning for your little 'uns."

The little fishing village, fifteen leagues or so north of Westron Seaport, lived true to its name and provided just what the family needed. Banaman rented them a cabin. Within a year Leage had a steady income, an array of good quality tools and a wife more doting than she had ever been. Tamm's health improved and there was a teaching house alongside a little Temple dedicated to Tarne, the god associated with justice, bravery and the rule of law.

During the days that there were no lessons to attend Tamm was out and about with new friends, climbing trees, cliffs and rocks, play-fighting and fashioning swords and bows out of branches or whatever materials were washed up on the beach.

By his twelfth summer, Tamm was tall, lean and very fit. He was mastering his letters and numbers and could recognise the constellations and major stars. His prowess with swordplay was remarkable for one of his age and his father watched with growing pride. With the right training in using balance and dexterity with his feet and body, the lad might one day become a skilled swordsman.

At the end of the second year Leage had saved sufficient money to enable him to buy the cottage.

But then events took a turn for the worse.

...o o O o o...

Hanni and Natti were also enjoying a freedom that they had never before experienced. Mama would take them to the shore once the teaching house was closed. Tamm would occasionally go with them but more often than not would be with his friends. The dunes, cliffs and rocks along the shoreline provided a valuable training ground for his adventurous group of friends. The twins were running through the shallow surf and squealing with delight as the little waves soaked them up to their knees. Mama knitted while keeping an occasional eye on them.

Perhaps it was the warmth of the sun that caught Luanne and caused her to doze, or it may have been because Leage had been up a few times during the night with an upset stomach. Perhaps it was the effect of both. Suddenly a piercing scream cut through her consciousness. She leapt to her feet and squinted across the sand. Hanni was running back and forth along the surf waving her arms and shrieking for her mother.

All of a sudden, Tamm was racing across the sand with his friends some yards behind him. He took hold of Hanni and bellowed at her. The screaming, terrified girl pointed out to a low, smooth rock. Within seconds he was threshing through the waves towards the dark rock. And then there was nothing for a while.

Abruptly there were two heads bobbing in the sea coming from the far side of the rock. Tamm was furiously kicking against the under-current, with Natti lifted onto his chest, while Luanne waded out chest-deep into the sea to intercept them.

In what seemed an age Luanne and Tamm brought Natti to the shore. Despite every effort to revive the little girl, she was already dead, her wet hair plastered across her face. Luanne wailed and clutched the lifeless body to her bosom.

Leage was at the scene within minutes and carried the little body back home. As would be expected, both Luanne and Hanni were inconsolable and remained so for many days. Despite their loss, Tamm was treated as the hero of the hour but this did little to influence his own opinion of himself.

"I should'a been there, Papa," he said over and over again, rocking to and fro with his head buried in his hands.

"You were, lad. You were, thank the gods."

The family never recovered from their loss. Leage held no blame towards Luanne over her moment of lapsed concentration; after all, both girls could swim. Nevertheless, Luanne descended into the depths of abject despair and withered over the next few months. Hanni never spoke again in spite of the amount of attention that both Leage and Tamm gave her. Neither she nor Luanne ever ventured by the beach again. Tamm, however, sat day after day by the shore, staring at the rock from which Natti must have tumbled or been washed against it by a freak wave.

During the next winter Luanne passed away. Grief stricken and wracked in guilt, some said, she had become a shadow of her former self. Hanni continued to live in a silent, closed world. In the following spring, a Priestess of Haeman, dressed in a white gown over which was a lilac robe and mounted on a white horse and accompanied by four similarly-attired acolyte clerics on foot, arrived in the village. Following a long discussion and a generous offering to the Temple of Haeman, which was dedicated to the God of Sun, Fertility, Growth & Renewal, the Priestess took Hanni away to the great temple in Westron Seaport.

Tamm was almost a man now that he was thirteen summers. He had virtually completed his learning and felt ready to make his way in the world. His father presented him with a long, slim sword and a matching dagger. The hilts were wrapped in black leather and the sheaths were black with silver tips. Tamm gasped with bliss.

"This, my boy, was left for me a couple of years ago by an old friend. It is a rapier, long and slim, you see? It is light and fits perfectly in the hand. At least, it will do once you come of age. Look here. The handle is concave, that is, it is narrower in the middle than at each end. It means that when you swing the weapon it is less likely to slip from your hand in the rain or when you sweat. The dagger matches it, you see."

"But Papa, it is yours and I'm not ready yet, am I?"

"You may have use of it one day soon, my lad. I have my *Old Trusty*, the long-sword that has been my friend for many years. I know it well and all its funny ways. A rapier is too light for me and besides, it is the weapon of a real swordsman. Become one with it. Swing it every day, just as when you practised fighting with wooden swords with your friends. But don't carry it about around the village just yet."

Over the next few months, Leage dragged himself out of the grief of losing his wife and one daughter and his other daughter having been taken to the great city for recovery. He now threw himself into his craft and occasionally spoke of training an apprentice.

"It was often my aspiration that you would come into the family business once you finished your learning. But I have seen that you are destined for greater things."

"Papa, but –", Tamm began to protest. "You need me here. Who will help you?"

"Your friend Arash has accepted my offer for an apprenticeship. I shall be well looked after by Arash's mother, Kenna. Take yourself off to the Fighters' Academy in Westron Seaport," said Leage. "You are a year too young but you have been accepted on the evidence of Goodman Banaman and you are expected. He has offered to take you to the Academy on the morrow."

"But – but Papa!" Tamm's mind raced. It was a bittersweet moment for him as he weighed up the thrill of a new future against leaving behind his father and his friends.

Next morning, Tamm clasped his father tightly as

Banaman's wagons rolled into the village.

"Call by the Temple of Haeman," he said. "Look in on Hanni and, if she can hear you, give her my fondest love."

"I will Papa."

It would be some years before he was to meet his father again.

Four days later Tamm stood at the large studded door of the Fighters' Academy and took a deep breath. Tentatively, he tugged at the bell-pull

...o o O o o...

Chapter 2

Tamm did not pick up a sword for two years. His own rapier and dagger, which he prized above any of his other belongings, were taken from him with a promise that they would be returned in time. The first year was gruelling and yet tedious. He fetched and carried. He cleaned and polished. He washed, mopped and swept. He tidied and cleared up behind the other, older students. Tardiness and laziness earned beatings from those older students. He learned quickly that to complain was to invite beatings from the tutors as well as the older students. He wasn't the only trainee of his intake and, although he was the youngest by almost a year, he was the tallest and toughest. It was common for the sons of those in privileged society to undertake the gruelling training offered by the Academy but often, provided that the trainee was adequately sponsored, their background was immaterial.

Tamm did often wonder how it was that his father had been able to afford his training. It was very expensive and far beyond the affordability of the average family. Not once during his first year did he receive a message from his father and neither did he get the opportunity to visit the Temple of Haeman to look in on his sister. Despite the occasional beatings, which Tamm took stoically, his manner and politeness served him better than that of his peers.

The first-year students slept together in a dormitory. Nine other lads shared the dormitory, each had a wooden bed with a straw mattress, a foot locker and a small cupboard. The room itself was built of stone and, with nothing adorning the white-painted walls, it was austere. A small window was at the opposite end of the room to the door. A tutor would enter the room periodically and without prior warning. Cleanliness and tidiness was demanded.

It was a difficult time for Tamm at first. Bullying was commonplace and he received many a beating from two of the boys in the dormitory. All of his fellow students were older them him by about a year. He tolerated their behaviour for a few months by which time he had had enough. He decided to wait until the largest, and most aggressive, tormenter came over to him to intimidate him once again.

Darvan had been fortunate enough to enjoy a privileged upbringing. Everything had been done for him to the point that he had little idea of how to take care of himself, even with the basics of personal hygiene. This did not trouble him the slightest, however. He had selected a slave to do his laundry and cleaning. His target was Tamm.

Tamm had witnessed the wrath of a tutor when Darvan had put a pair of cockroaches inside the bed of another lad. The poor boy, Trevvi, had been marched outside and severely thrashed. Darvan's sidekick, Eston, had sniggered as Trevvi had staggered back into the room in tears and clutching his rear. It wasn't the first occurrence of this kind of behaviour but this was the episode that caused Tamm to plan how he would settle the score.

That evening, Tamm sat next to Trevvi and gave him words of consolation. "I'm going to finish it," growled Tamm. "He ain't doing that to anyone again."

"What are you going to do?" whispered Trevvi.

Just as Tamm whispered "Dunno", Darvan sidled over with Eston close behind him.

"What are you two losers whispering about, eh?"

Tamm rose from the bed and stood up. He was the same height as Darvan although many pounds lighter. He looked Darvan directly in the eye.

"Not your business, Darvan," he replied.

Darvan stretched his right hand forward to push Tamm's chest to force him back onto the bed but Tamm turned his chest to the left causing Darvan's hand to slide past and him to to stumble forwards slightly. Tamm's left elbow flashed up and caught Darvan's nose. There was a nasty crunch and blood poured down Darvan's lips.

An expression of shock was quickly replaced by pain as Darvan let out a yelp. There were gasps of surprise from the other lads who crowded around expecting to see a fight ensue. They were not disappointed.

Darvan leapt forward pushing Tamm backwards and down to the floor. Tamm, however, collided with Trevvi's bedframe causing both of them to turn onto their side. A fist cannoned into Tamm's face, narrowly missing his right eye and he pushed with both his feet against Darvan's hips, effectively pushing the boy partly under an adjacent bed. Tamm twisted onto his hands and feet but as he straightened up his foot slipped on a splash of Darvan's blood and he fell back down to the floor.

Darvan had stretched out his right hand to pull himself out from under the bed. Tamm's knee landed on it with all of his weight above it. There was another sickening crunch as fingers broke. Darvan screamed in agony.

Both boys climbed to their feet.

"Take him to the medic," cried Tamm as Darvan whimpered unintelligibly.

Eston had seen how events were turning and had run out of the dormitory. He was back within a few heartbeats with a tutor, Master Halness Tann, close behing him. This tutor had been the one who had administered the beating to Trevvi. He was dressed in

14

black trousers, soft boots and a grey shirt, the uniform of the tutors.

"There, sir. Look," exclaimed Eston. "DuHan picked on him, sir. For no reason, sir!"

The tutor, one of many in the academy, strode across. "Hmm, I shall see. Wait outside my chamber, DuHan. You, Darvan, can follow me. You too, Trevvi."

Eston was almost dancing from one foot to another. "Saw it all, sir," he shrieked. "I can tell you what happ–"

"Stay here, Eston. I don't need you."

"But–"

Tamm and Trevvi waited by the door to Master Tann's chamber for what seemed like hours. They didn't speak and fidgeted nervously with their fingers. Trevvi gnawed at his fingernails. Tamm rubbed his left side, painful since having crashing into Trevvi's bed. He fully expected there to be a nasty bruise by morning.

They straightened up as Master Tann strode round the corner of the passage. He marched up to his door and wrenched it open.

"Inside," he said, quite calmly.

The lads filed past him and stood in front of his desk. Tann closed his door, went round his desk and sat down. The chamber was quite small but with a high ceiling. The desk faced the door and upon it was a sword, in its ornate scabbard, resting on a mount. The wall to their left had a large tapestry depicting a soldier in full armour standing beside a fine lady dressed in white. Her hair was almost white but her skin was dark, almost black. A sword, identical to that on the desk, hung at the soldier's side. The wall to the right had a set of book shelves stacked with books, scrolls and what seemed to be trophies. A set of scale armour and a helm, again similar to those in the tapestry, were arranged on a stand next to the bookcase. The wall behind the desk was lined with a variety of weapons, a shield and a great bow.

The chamber of a hero, thought Tamm.

"What happened?" Tann asked.

Both boys began speaking at once. The tutor held one hand up to stop them and then pointed at Tamm.

"Well, sir," he began, somewhat nervously. "Darvan has been bullying us since we began and his friend Eston has been too. One of them put the 'roaches in Trevvis bed and he didn't know and he got a beating for it. I was talking to Trevvi and telling him it wasn't his fault and Darvan came over and started on me so I finished it. That's about it really. Er, sir."

Tann leaned back in his chair so that the front legs were raised a little from the floor. He looked at the boys in turn and then let his chair drop back down.

"That is not how he tells it," the tutor said. "He tells me that you went to him and started the fight over nothing at all."

"But sir," began Tamm.

"I know who I believe," interrupted Tann. "However, I know who I should believe. Darvan is the son of a military leader from the neighbouring country of Cascant to the east. This man has paid a lot of money for his son to train here."

Both boys cast their gazes down to the floor expecting the worst.

"I know who I do believe, though," continued the tutor. "We shall give Darvan leave of absence while his hand, and his nose heals. He shall return under serious warning that bullying is not tolerated here. We shall allocate him to another training squad when he comes back."

Tamm and Trevvi exchanged glances, relieved that they had escaped blame.

The tutor continued. "I do give you warning, DuHan, that the taking of this sort of revenge is also not to be tolerated. You will, in future, report problems to the tutors who will take appropriate action if your reports are well-founded. Is that clear?"

"Aye, sir," replied a chastened Tamm.

...o o O o o...

After a year of deferential service he was taken, along with the other first year trainees, through to a training gymnasium. He had only been allowed to enter once before and that was to clear the floor after cadet training using straw dummies. The stale smell of bare feet and sweat had aroused in him a hunger for the training that he hoped would eventually come. Of the original group of fifteen first-years, only six others joined him as they entered through the gymnasium door. Neither Darvan nor Eston were included in the group. Nor was his friend, Trevvi. The door closed behind them with a deep, resonant boom.

...o o O o o...

One man watched Tamm DuHan's development with interest. The Master Tutor, a man of middle years by the name of Yukio Mishima, soon recognised that the boy was quickly leaving his peers behind to the point that when it came to free weapons practice none of them would partner him. He could see that Tamm was feeling isolated but soon realised that by arranging for an assistant tutor to spar with Tamm, there was potential for the boy to develop further and somewhat faster.

Yukio had himself been an adventurer only a decade or so ago. Prior to that however, his past was something that he kept only to himself and his beloved wife, Caeron. The story was rumoured amongst the students that he had returned to consciousness after a powerful storm at sea had propelled him to a strange land, indeed a strange world, for his own home was reputed to be amongst the stars in a land called Nippon. Songs were even sung in taverns and by travelling bards and minstrels telling this story. The *Samurai* skills that he himself had perfected he would now pass onto students in the Academy, the sons, and occasionally the daughters, of the privileged. These students would one day become the captains and generals of the armies of various countries in the Territories and Kingdoms of the West.

Some students, however, progressed even further. These were the elite. The elite were accorded an anonymous existence and their identities would never be spoken of outside of the higher echelons of the Guilds of Protectors and Assassins and in the staterooms of the great palace of Westron Seaport.

Up to now, there was only one student in preparation for the elite service. Yukio Mishima had high hopes that there would soon be another.

...o o **O** o o...

Chapter 3

The next year introduced a strict and rigorous regime to which Tamm thoroughly immersed himself. The students were given separate chambers, which they referred to as cells. These had beds with mattresses that were more comfortable than anything Tamm had ever experienced before. Also in the room was a foot locker and a wardrobe. A window overlooked the training yard where he could watch students training on the rare days that he had to himself.

Although the other youths complained about sprains, strains and the occasional broken digit, Tamm took to it like an eagle soaring into the sky. In his opinion, this was little harder than the play that he and his friends had filled their spare time with in the village of Tranquil Port. They weren't considered ready to use edged weapons but they trained relentlessly with wooden poles, bamboo canes and wooden swords. Within a few weeks not one of the other youths was able to spar with him. Instead, a tutor would be his partner, slapping his legs, back and shoulders until he learned the art of both defence and attack simultaneously.

"You have two eyes, DuHan," said his tutor, a stocky, powerful, grizzled dwarf by the name of Master Stag. "Use them both to look at mine. My eyes will tell you where and when my next attack will come. Watch my shoulders for they will tell you where my feet are."

After four months, Tamm's uncanny balance and dexterity propelled him to the point where there was little to be gained with him continuing to practice with simple wooden weapons.

One morning, before Tamm had a chance to begin his day's exercising, the stocky dwarven tutor beckoned to him. "Pick up your pack and follow me," he said.

He was escorted by Stag along a corridor to a smaller training room to stand before the master tutor. On the way, he was advised by Stag to address the strange-looking warrior, Yukio Mishima, by the title *sensei*. The *sensei* sat cross-legged on the training mat flanked by his two most senior tutors, Master Halness Tann and a half-elven woman he hadn't seen before. She was introduced to him as Mistress Caeron.

As was customary, Tamm dropped to his knees and lowered his hands to the floor and bowed his head.

One of the senior tutors, the woman, called sharply but softly "To your feet, DuHan." Tamm complied.

"You are to be taken out of the current training scheme, Tamm DuHan," said the enigmatic warrior, the Master Tutor, with an almost murmuring voice.

Tamm was shocked. "B – But sensei, I –" he stammered.

"Wait!" The timbre of sensei's voice had not risen by the least amount but Tamm immediately closed his mouth. "I did not say that you have finished your training. You will come with me to the north wing. I myself shall supervise a unique training regime for which I feel you will be more suited."

"Thank you sensei," whispered Tamm as he once again bowed, this time from the waist. His heart hammered behind his ribs. *Surely, sensei can hear my heartbeat,* he thought.

The other tutors rose, and with a bow they all left the gymnasium, leaving only Tamm and the *sensei*. At last, Tamm could quickly look around him at the gymnasium. The walls were lined with many different weapons, some of which he had never seen the like of before. He recognised spears and javelins, pikes and flails, morningstars and war-hammers, swords and axes, bows and crossbows. But there were many more weapons besides. A wooden gallery stretched along one end of the gymnasium, about ten feet or so above the floor.

"Come here, young warrior," said the master tutor. "Sit before me and let us dispense with some of the formalities. Tell me, what qualities does a warrior need to have?"

"Sensei, to fight against injustice, to protect the innocent and downtrodden, to deal justice against the wrong-doers and evil-doers."

"Ah, that is the mantra of a fighter and protector indeed, but a warrior needs an inner strength to ensure his intentions are honourable. What else do you consider?"

Tamm paused for a few heartbeats. "To know when to fight or when not to withdraw your sword," he replied.

Sensei smiled; a rare sign of emotion.

"Now you begin to understand, young warrior. But there are more qualities. Honour and duty are the absolute qualities. The knowing of when to withdraw your sword as a last resort is a sign of the supreme warrior's discipline. Reason and assertiveness will often diffuse a difficult situation. But there are also times when the weapon is needed to fulfil your duty when all other avenues have been exhausted. These avenues may have been travelled by others and your duty is to conduct that last resort. Do you understand?"

"Yes, sensei. I believe I do. But the idea does not seem to suit the rules of battle and fairness."

The *sensei* nodded. "Ah, now you are thinking logically. That is good. You may realise your objective by arriving at your destination but your success is measured by how you made that journey. This new training regime will contribute towards that success but it is you that needs the strength of will to follow the road. It will be a great challenge. Know then, that there are forces that roam the lands that do not feel obliged to follow these rules of fairness in battle. For the good of the society in which you live there are times when it is prudent, if not absolutely necessary, to eliminate evil and only that evil."

"But, sensei, when would we recognise evil?"

"Consider this. Is the snake evil for attacking a child?"

Tamm considered this and replied "Nay, sensei. It protects itself."

"And is the wolf evil for attacking a man?"

"Nay, sensei. It feels the need to feed on the easiest of prey."

"Is the orc evil for ambushing a passer-by?"

For a moment, Tamm furrowed his brow. "Aye, sensei. The orc has the wisdom and ability to hunt for game to eat and it attacks without provocation."

"Ah, young warrior. Your mind goes back to your father, does it not? The orcs brought an end to his fighting ability."

Tamm jerked his head up in surprise. *How did* sensei *know?* He held his tongue back despite his need to ask questions.

Sensei continued. "Evil is the antithesis of goodness. It is by action or intent that evil is recognised, as it is with goodness. Dwell on this as you progress with your training and let it fill your heart and mind. Follow me."

Yukio Mishima, the ultimate warrior, rose to his feet in a seemingly effortless motion, and walked to the rear of the gymnasium, closely followed by a bewildered but elated Tamm DuHan, aged almost fifteen summers.

...ooOoo...

"What are you willing to do to become the best, young warrior?"

The room he had been taken to was less dramatic that the training room they had just left. It was a gymnasium dedicated more to lifting weights, pugilism and personal muscle-building. The walls were of stone blocks painted white and were lined with climbing bars and hanging ropes. The ceiling was probably more than thirty feet above his head.

Tamm hardly hesitated. "To work to the best of my ability, sensei."

"Hah! Even the lowliest sword-hand will do that to achieve his aim. You will have to go further, much further. How far will you go?"

Tamm took a deep breath and, for the first time since being admitted to the Academy, looked the Master Tutor straight in the eye.

"Sensei, I will train night and day if necessary until I can best you!"

Sensei chuckled and shook his head. "Aii, that training will come at a cost to you, perhaps to your sanity. Who knows? Very well. You will be segregated from the other students. Your belongings, including the rapier and dagger that your father gave you, are already in your new chamber. Hai, I know of your father through a mutual friend. Banaman-san, the man who brought you here spoke of your father's wishes and has offered to fund your training here for two years. Since then the burden of payment has fallen to another."

"I had no idea, sensei, that you knew of my father. I do not know if he is alive or dead for I have heard nothing from him in all this time."

"Know him I do. He lives; he prospers; he has someone to dote upon. Banaman tells me that his new lady teaches him writing and numeracy. He has two young men in training for his magnificent carvings, one of which I have in my private chamber. Tomorrow I shall accompany you to the Temple of Haeman. You will hardly recognise your sister Hanni. Like you, she has developed and now she shows all the signs of being a great intellectual."

"She speaks?" he asked, incredulously.

"Hai, she is not so withdrawn. You shall see for yourself. Then, in the afternoon shall your training start in earnest."

...ooOoo...

The two figures whirled in combat. Each wielded a wooden sword, not of the type made and carried by youths playing at adventuring but full-length, slightly-curved weapons crafted from bamboo. The master tutor called them *bokken*. Even without a sharp steel blade, in the hands of an expert this weapon was a lethal killing tool. Thrust, parry, slash, block and swing. Each attack was blocked; each block was turned into an attack. The combat went on for what seemed to the single onlooker to be an age. Time and time again, a charging attack would be heralded by a sharp cry as a pull-stroke caused the tip of the weapon to act as a whip. Neither protagonist had the advantage over the other. Although their strength was waning, neither made a noticeable error.

There must have been an unseen signal because both withdrew instantaneously. They tucked their two-handed *bokken* into their cloth sashes and knelt opposite each other. Placing their hands on the mat, they bowed their heads towards the ground in salutation. Then they rose to their feet, both still sweat-soaked and panting after the exertion.

"I am still unable to best you, sensei," gasped the young man. Similar to his protagonist, he was dressed in a grey, loose-fitting tunic and black hose. A brown fabric sash was tied around his middle. Over his chest he wore flexible protective armour made from lacquered bamboo and wood with black steel plates over the shoulders and upper arms. He removed the helm with its hinged neck guard and held it to his side under his left arm.

"You hesitated and held back when you should have pressed forward your advantage, young warrior," replied the master tutor. "After four years of intensive training almost every morning I expect you to fully commit yourself. You know the basic rules of any hand to hand combat. Focus your *ki*, your inner strength, on my inner core for that is your target. Follow through with every attack. Be aware of your balance and defence when you push forward. Be ready to close your undefended area. Your shield is your ability to move, dodge and avoid while exploiting an opening and taking the opportunity. Your attack is your heart and mind. I am your sensei but that must not stop you taking every opportunity. I shall not hold back on any more attacks on you."

Again, without a signal, they moved towards the centre of the large rush matting that sensei called *tatami*. They stood opposite and bowed to each other from the waist. The *bokken* were withdrawn from their sashes and they circled each other, eyes locked on those of their opponent. Each made a simultaneous attack and each blocked it successfully. Tamm, however, darted his right foot forward and swept the sensei's ankle forwards, pitching the tutor on his back. The young man's bokken slashed down onto the top of his sensei's helmet. He stepped backwards two paces to place himself out of bokken's range and stood at the ready.

The master tutor climbed up off the mat and removed his helm. "There, you have bested me after all."

"You allowed it, sensei," replied Tamm.

"I assure you, I did not, young warrior. You are now ready. I have spoken."

The sound of applause broke through the silence. A warrior with less discipline would have been distracted by the unexpected noise but Tamm kept his eyes locked onto those of his sensei. The Master Tutor looked up over Tamm's head to the gallery that perched above the entry door of the sanctum. He bowed from the waist.

"Honoured Guild Master. I consider the weapons training and that of unarmed fighting techniques to be complete. I therefore commend Master Warrior Tamm DuHan to your service."

A voice sounded. "I accept, Master Tutor." Its timbre was barely more than a murmur but the deep baritone resonance sounded rich as it reverberated off the walls.

Sensei waved a hand to the mat, beckoning Tamm to the kneeling position. The pair bowed formally, with their hands on the mat and their foreheads dipping to just above the mat surface. Then the Master Tutor rose to his feet and quickly strode to the door, closing it behind him.

A bewildered Tamm rose to his feet turned and looked up. He caught the sight of a figure, dressed in black, disappearing through a doorway at the left-hand end of the gallery leaving just one figure standing watching him. A slim warrior dressed much as himself except that instead of a grey, loose-fitting tunic and black hose, it was black throughout. In addition though, there was a turban-style headdress with a piece of fabric pulled loosely across most of the face. As Tamm watched, the figure vaulted over the railing and with a full somersault landed solidly on the floor. The figure raised the arms in a flourish. The rail of the gallery was easily twelve feet above the floor.

The physique of the figure was unmistakable. *A woman?* Tamm was impressed. He would surely break his ankles if he tried such a move.

The figure reached up and removed the headdress. Tamm took a deep breath and his heart skipped a beat. There stood the most beautiful human being he had ever seen in his life. The woman was tall, although not as tall as Tamm. She was also lithe and athletic although this was not immediately obvious to the young man. Copper-coloured hair tumbled over her shoulders, framing a solemn-looking face.

"Don't gawp!" she snapped. "You will be joining me for the next phase of training."

"More?" gasped Tamm. He had been hoping to see something of the outside world. All he had seen so far was the occasional short walk to the Temple of Haeman when visiting his sister, Hanni. She was now very much a grown-up young woman who spoke with confidence and assertiveness that he wouldn't have thought possible a few years ago.

"Now we will learn other skills," she said. "So you are Tamm DuHan."

It was a statement rather than a question. As such, Tamm declined to respond.

"I have heard your name mentioned by sensei. I saw your fight with him. You bested him. It was an unfair attack. You reaped away his ankle while he was advancing in an attack."

Again, Tamm declined to respond.

"Do you not talk?"

Ah, that was a question! "When I am asked a question or when I am engaged in pleasant conversation. Yes I do talk."

"So then, Tamm DuHan, do you consider that win to have been fair?"

"Well, Miss Whoever-You-Are, yes I do. Sensei taught me many fighting skills. When he engaged me in contest today he did not specify which fighting skill I was to use. He left himself wide open to a foot-sweep which I took advantage of. He did not complain when he picked himself up off the floor."

The young lady had reddened appreciably at Tamm's reply. Then she sighed and gave a wide smile.

"It was very good though," she acquiesced. "I am known as Soren-ko, the Little Scorpion, for reasons you will probably find out in due course. My real name is Dellie Starwatcher but I have been told that I shall be leaving that name behind. You may find that the same will happen to you."

"I shall probably find out in a while. Did you train under the Master Tutor?"

"Aye, I did. That training finished yesterday. I could not best the sensei, but then neither did he best me. I wish I had tried your trick. I saw the opening but ignored it. I believe it was his intention for the both of us. That was me giving you the applause, in case you were wondering."

Tamm laughed. "Then you are too kind. I wish I had seen your contest though. Perhaps we will get the opportunity to spar together."

"Of that I have no doubt. It is good to meet with you, Tamm DuHan."

"It is good to meet with you too, Dellie Starwatcher; or would you prefer me to call you by your new name, Soren-ko?"

"Which do you prefer?"

"Dellie is a beautiful name that suits you perfectly. I shall use that one."

Once again, Dellie flushed. But she laughed too.

"Let us go to the new Chambers of Advanced Learning," she said. "We have to meet with a man named Guram Dobethian."

She walked with an athletic grace that Tamm could not resist staring at.

"I do hope you are not watching my bottom, Tamm DuHan," she laughed. This time it was more like a girlie giggle.

Now it was Tamm's turn to flush.

...o o O o o...

Unexpectedly, the next phase of the learning did not involve weapon-training at all. It was to a restricted part of the Academy to an inner sanctum of an alchemist situated in the cellars of the Academy that they were led by an Academy porter. Guram Dobethian was old. Tamm believed he would have been old when his father, Leage DuHan, was born. Two walls of the alchemist's laboratory were lined with tables that rocked on their legs, each ringed by hard stools. Dellie was certain that it made sure that the students would sit only on rare occasions, or more likely would prevent them from falling asleep.

A black-painted board was attached to one wall and on it were many mathematical symbols and equations. At first, both students groaned inwardly at the sight of the glass container, tubes, pipes and phials that covered some of the table-tops. Jars and bottles contained an assortment of chemicals, objects and what appeared to be body parts. One wall was completely line with shelves and racks that were stuffed full of scrolls and books.

Master Dobethian was dressed in a black cape over a grey gown. Both had seen better days. His face was deeply-lined and his white hair was long and unkempt.

"Here you will spend your afternoons learning about —" he began. "Stop fidgeting, young lady!"

"Um – sorry," she murmured.

"As I said, you will learn ab – What is the matter with you, young man? You can stop playing with your testicles. Stop it, I say!"

Dellie strained to hold back an outburst of laughter. Tamm's face was scarlet. Dobethian glared at her, then at Tamm. This was not a good start.

"Now, if you are both ready," said the new tutor in a sarcastic monotone. "We shall continue. I shall teach you the use of chemicals and compounds that will give a bright light to blind an opponent's view of you, that will create smoke to hide your escape, that will cause sickening smells to deter pursuers, that will blow a hole in a wooden door or a cell lock. I can show you the simple mixing of compounds that will help you to light a camp fire. If you want to avoid having the skin on your hand melted by a burning liquid then you must pay attention, Master DuHan, and stop picking at your fingers!"

"Aye, sir!"

"I shall continue. Where was I? I intend to demonstrate for you the properties of a combination of chemicals which, when combined, will produce a blasting compound. You will need to master all of these skills in your future profession and stop trying to stifle a yawn, young lady. If you are tired then stand up."

...ooOoo...

Their morning training, however, was a completely different matter. The routine began with a light dawnfeast well before daybreak. On the first day they were escorted by a Guild porter to a training chamber where they were told to wait for the physical trainer. Set into one of the walls were small recesses and protrusions.

"What do you think that is for?" mused Dellie.

"That is for climbing, I am sure of it," Tamm replied but with a hint of uncertainty in his voice.

Adjacent to another wall hung four thick ropes. They looked well-used and the bottoms of them were frayed.

An array of weights were stacked on racks and in the centre lay a padded mat, similar to others that Tamm had practised unarmed fighting the previous year. Dried bloodstains clearly showed that the mat had hosted many furious training bouts.

They were shocked when a small gnome stepped in through a door at the back of the chamber. Was this their physical trainer? His light orange skin was something rarely seen in the City and was very much unexpected. Although not very tall, he was heavily-muscled.

"I am called Belettanbiele, a gnome in case you 'adn't noticed and as you can no doubt see now I 'ave drawn your attention to it. This place is known as the *muscle factory*. I got two ways o' doin' this. One way is the easy way where you don't work 'ard, you fail to meet the expected level of fitness an' you get kicked out o' the Guild after getting' your mind wiped by a friendly wizard 'cos you know too much. That is easy 'cos it's easy for me. The other way is the 'ard way. You work 'ard 'cos you want to. That's the 'ard way 'cos it means I gotta put extra work an' time in. But I don't care. It's all the same to me, I got nuffin else to do. You might try to outdo each other in a friendly competition. Maybe the winner will get to 'ave some time on the town or somethin'. Which way is the best for you? Missy?"

"I can and will work hard. That is the only way for me." She glanced at Tamm with a raised eyebrow.

"An' you, master?"

"I intend to be the best. I *will* work hard."

"Good answers. You 'ave three weeks in this *muscle factory* an' then you will 'ave finished with both me an' your alchemist. You will be taken out into the lovely countryside to practice living off the land an' surviving off what it can provide for you."

Tamm and Dellie looked at each other and smiled. This sounded good.

The trainer took them around the chamber and showed them the equipment they could use.

"I will give you a task each mornin' an' you will then work towards achievin' it. That means that you will sometimes 'ave quite a few tasks addin' up. Work 'ard for me an' you will be ready to start your field trainin'."

For the first week, they arrived at their alchemy lessons with aching arms, shoulders and legs. At the end of each morning the trainer would appear to review their progress. Rare were the times that he seemed pleased. They practised rope-climbing skills and dragging themselves up the climbing wall. This seemed to be where their tasks were prioritised.

At the end of the three weeks they were required to climb all four ropes to the top, touch the ceiling and climb back down without taking their weight on their feet. Although both proficient it was Dellie who excelled on the ropes. Their other task was to climb the wall from bottom left to top right and then again from bottom right to top left.

Belettanbiele answered the unspoken question from his two students. "This is 'cos you 'ave been climbing straight up the wall from bottom to top an' you know all the easiest climbs. Now you gotta think."

Tamm easily beat Dellie's time with this task but not without drawing blood from the palm of his left hand, the result of a clumsy stretch.

"You done well. Now you go back to your quarters an' pack your travellin' gear ready to move out at midnight. We're goin' out to the wild woods an' countryside where the wild beasties live. Make sure you got your weapons, cloaks an' water. Oh, an' your basic alchemy pack. You won't need much else. Keep it light 'cos you carry it all 'round with you every day. You got any questions?"

Tamm looked up. "Aye, I have. Where are we going?"

"Silly question! You will know when you get there."

"Do we need to take food with us?" asked Dellie.

"You wanna starve afore you get there? Another silly question. Travel rations will be packed an' made ready for you to collect from the kitchen. Enough for six days. After that you catch or dig up your own food."

...ooOoo...

Chapter 4

The ride out through the City took them through the dark alleyways where one might have expected confrontations from drunken revellers and cutthroats. Despite rowdy behaviour in adjacent alleys and streets, there was not as much as a drunken insult. The gnome, Belettanbiele, led them out of the city. Despite the East Gate normally being closed at that time of the night, it was held open for them as they approached. Not a word was spoken between Belettanbiele and the watchmen as he rode past but once the three riders were through the gate was closed behind them. They heard the great bars being slid into place on the inside.

Their ride took them away from the conventional roads and tracks. The darkness proved to be hazardous for Tamm and Dellie and after a while the three of them had to dismount in order to lead the horses over the treacherous ground.

"We gotta keep movin' else we'll be late," grunted Belettanbiele. "Keep the noise down 'cos we don't want to bring attention to ourselves now, do we?"

In the early hours before dawn they stopped for a break. A keen north-westerly wind made it feel cold and they pulled their capes tightly around them. Belettanbiele built a small fire that flared up instantaneously. Both of his companions immediately recognised the alchemical compound that had started it from the pungent odour.

"Two hours sleep," said the gnome. "Make the most of it." He was snoring within moments.

Dellie whispered to Tamm "I'm not really tired but my rump is very sore. This is exciting."

"Same with me," he replied, throwing a small piece of wood onto the fire. Sparks scattered and then the fire settled again.

Tamm started as a cold hand slipped inside his.

"I'm damnably freezing though," she said. "Double-up with the capes?"

The two were shaken awake to see the first light of dawn.

"I do 'ope you two wasn't up to mischief during the night," grunted the gnome.

"It was cold," replied Tamm. "We shared resources."

"Eat some rations, see to the 'orses an' we leave before the sun comes up."

Dellie thought that Belettanbiele would have been horrified if he knew that Tamm had spent part of the short night with his hand exploring her breasts. Where her hand had strayed, at one point, would not even be discussed between the two of them. *He is a big boy though*, she thought to herself with a wry smile, *but he can wait*.

...o o O o o...

The remaining ride took them all day. The wind still blew into their faces but it was not quite as biting as it had been during the night. Both Tamm and Dellie carefully avoided mentioning their closeness during the night but there was no awkward atmosphere between them.

The journey was hard. The gnome did not lead them along recognisable tracks and seemed to change direction at almost random intervals. He had advised that they all keep a vigilant watch when on the tops of hills, amongst trees and behind rocks. At no time did they notice anything threatening. They stopped infrequently and then only to allow the horses to take water or graze for a while. During these times Dellie and Tamm would rest, eat and drink while chatting excitedly about what might happen.

Dusk was approaching when they rode along a chasm between rock faces. Without warning Belettanbiele stood up in his stirrups and called a word in an almost melodious voice. Instantly, three figures stood up from behind rocks and shrubs. Another stood in the road with his arm raised. Neither Dellie nor Tamm had seen them.

Belettanbiele rode up to the sentry and exchanged a few words with him. He gestured to the two riders behind him and the sentry nodded, turned away and beckoned them to follow him. He trotted for almost a mile and led them through a stout gate that stood across the gorge. With a call from the sentry the gate opened to admit the three riders. Belettanbiele instructed the two trainees to wait and then he rode away. A few moments later the two exhausted trainee warriors were led by a caped watchman to a tented area. He indicated a tent which it seemed they would both share and stated that they would be called for the nightfall feast at the campfire by the sounding of a gong.

The tent was barely large enough to stand upright in but contained two light military-type straw-filled mattresses either side of a centre pole. There was no privacy to preserve dignity.

As Tamm stretched out on his mattress, Dellie stood with her back to him and removed her tunic, stretching to relieve her saddle-sore muscles.

"I expect I will have to get used to you watching me as I change my clothes," she said.

"I will look away if you prefer," he muttered.

"Don't expect me to though," she replied with a mischievous grin and a giggle. She turned to face him and laughed as he gave an involuntary gasp.

She looked down to his midriff and said "I see you

approve."

The gong sounded an hour later.

...o o O o o...

They shared the large campsite with many other acolytes who came from a variety of other fighters' schools and academies in other cities from the Landsdrop Coast, Home Territories and small Kingdoms of the West. All of them had arrived that day. Humans, dwarves, elves, and even a Halfling, were sitting on rows of benches arrayed around the large fire.

Beginning the following morning, the training was harsh. By the end of the first ten days, there were twenty-two remaining out of the original thirty-six. The others were taken out of the camp and were assigned to watch rosters. Tamm and Dellie excelled at everything and encourage each other throughout the gruelling regimes.

Not again did they have another private moment as they had had on that first eveing. Aches and tiredness ensured they were almost instantly asleep.

One morning, at the end of the first tenday, Tamm stood waist deep in a river they were fording. He and Dellie were partnered with another young man, Casca, and were in a circle gripping each other's arms and shoulders as they supported each other against the strong current and freezing water. They were the first to cross.

Suddenly, a shriek sounded from the river a little way upstream as another group of three lost their footing and began to be swept away in the current. Without a second thought Tamm, Dellie and Casca waded back out and intercepted each of the other group as they were swept within reach. All three were brought to the river's bank. One of them, the Halfling, had lost his sword. He was immediately returned to the campsite and reassigned to the camp watch, despite his sword turning up further downstream in the shallows.

"This must serve as a lesson to you all," growled the grizzled chief trainer. "Scout along the river to find a suitable crossing point. Secure your pers'nal weapons and make sure they fit properly in their scabbards. It is no use crossing a river if you cannot carry out your mission due to a lost pers'nal weapon. You cannot afford to make these mistakes. That is why we give you no second chance. You got brains; use them. The actions of these three undoubtedly saved the lives of the others. Well done."

From the second tenday, every morning started with a cross-country run. However, they were required to carry a heavy rock for a mile. Day-by-day the distance increased until by the end of twenty more days they would be carrying it for three miles through rough terrain, rivers and densely forested areas. Once again, Tamm and Dellie brought each other through these days by sheer determination, courage and willpower.

By the end of two months there were just ten acolytes remaining. Dellie and Tamm, together with Casca, were still regarded as the most outstanding trainees. The hard physical training was now completed. They still began each day with a hard exercise though. From now they would be taught the use of alchemical compounds to confuse, confound or disable an enemy. They were taught about the arts of survival in many different environments. Hunting, stalking and trapping, preparing game and cooking it would, from now, be the only way they would find food. They were shown methods of lock-breaking, escape, flight and avoidance techniques, rock-climbing and more advanced methods of river-crossing and chasm-crossing.

Each evening they practiced their weapon fighting skills for three hours and learned to specialise with a wide range exotic weapons. They practised horsemanship and riding skills until they were acutely saddle-sore. During the afternoons they were given more training in advanced unarmed fighting styles.

At the end of the five-month intensive training course, there were eight that graduated.

The chief trainer sat them in the campsite and shook each by the hand, giving them a bronze medallion on a stout chain.

"These are badges of your achievement and proof of your achievement. You truly now belong to the most elite warrior class in the Home Territories. You may have already been given a warrior name. If you have, that is the name that you will use from this moment. Leave your family name behind so as never to implicate your family in any exploits that you are engaged upon. With people who know you by your family name, do no disclose your warrior name. Keep the two worlds separate. If you have no warrior name then choose one. Who has a warrior name?"

Dellie raised her hand. She was the only one to reply. "I do, Master."

"You do? What is it?"

"Soren-ko, Master."

"What does it mean?"

"In the tongue of my Master Tutor, it means *Little Scorpion*."

The tutors looked at each other. "Why were you given that name?"

"It is for the sting of the scorpion's tail that I can deliver, Master."

"I am not sure that I understand," replied the tutor. "Are you able to show us?"

"Aye, Master. But I need a padded pole in the ground to simulate a human body."

Within thirty minutes a six-foot pole was embedded deep in the ground. It was wrapped in thick padding and matting.

Dellie stood before it, facing it, and then turned sharply to the left. Her head continued to turn and her right leg whipped around to strike the padded pole in its centre. The stout pole snapped in half. A collective gasp came from the gathered new warriors, none the least Tamm.

Dellie returned to Tamm's side. She quietly said to him "There, Tamm, I told you that you would find out one day, did I not?"

"Aye, lass, you did. That was remarkable."

"Have the rest of you decided upon your warrior names yet?"

Tamm was the first to reply.

"Aye, Master. I have," he replied. He cast a quick glance at Soren-ko and then back to the tutors.

"Are you prepared to tell me?"

"Aye, Master. I wish to be referred to as Black Harlequin, Master."

...o o O o o...

Belettanbiele arrived that evening and in the first light of dawn on the next day they rode back to Westron Seaport.

"I 'ardly recognise you," he said as they rode in the early light of the day. "I 'eard you really done well an' that you now go by your warrior names. I knew o' yours, Soren-ko, but yours now, Black Harlequin. That is a mystery now. Very unusual. I'm tol' that you don't tell anyone why. Is that right?"

"Aye, that it is. I have a plan but to put it into reality

I have to recruit some special followers in such a way that I blend in with them but in the quiet times I can carry out my mission unnoticed and unconnected with them."

Belettanbiele said "It is right that you keep your plans to yourself but when involving the unwitting compliance of others you must take extra care not to place 'em in any danger."

"I am aware of that and have had a few weeks to plan this carefully. I consider that it is easier to hide in a crowd than as an individual and I intend to exploit that."

"The two of you will be presented to the Protectors' Guild Master on the morrow an' 'e will either direct your missions himself or allocate you to your new employers. Black Harlequin is a bit of a mouthful when talking to you though."

"How about Harley," said the newly-named Soren-ko.

"I like it," he replied with a laugh. "I'll be Harley."

...o o O o o...

The Master of the Guild of Protectors rose to his feet and welcomed Harley and Soren-ko into his sanctum. With them were sensei Yukio Mishima and Belettanbiele. Another figure sat almost unnoticed in a corner. A tall man wrapped in a large cape and a wide-brimmed hat pulled down low over his eyes, was not given an introduction. A long, black staff leaned against the back of his chair.

"I salute you both as the newest of the elite warriors of the Guild of Protectors," began the Guild Master. "I have taken much interest in your progress ever since your selection for specialist instruction. I am privileged to receive you now. You must be wondering about your future within the auspices of the Guild."

Harley was about to speak but the Guild master did not wait to see whether they would reply.

"The Guild, you see, is more than just a sponsor for the training establishment for fighters. We are by far the largest Guild in the Home Territories, in fact the largest anywhere on the Continent of Baylea, at least as far as we are aware. The public face, as it were, may just be as a training ground for fighters, soldiers and watchmen. It is also commonly known to be a place where accomplished fighters may live, practice, recuperate and recover. You, however, have had privileged access to areas that are kept undisclosed from the outside world. You have been highly trained for a reason. That reason is to assure the safety and security of the Home Territories and Kingdoms of the West."

The Guild Master paused as if to carefully select his next words. Tamm could think of nothing to say or ask, such was his eagerness to hear what was to be said next.

"From this moment on, you are not referred to by your given family names. These are struck from our records. You have been given, or have selected, pseudonyms to which you will be referred. These will follow you throughout your future involvement with this Guild. You will also no longer be referred to as warriors, fighters or the like. Why should it be of importance to any person on the outside what your profession is?"

Once again, he paused. "No, quite simply, you are *associates*. You may be acting as negotiators, mediators, representatives. In essence, you are our agents. You may be required to advise on and enforce law, give protection, remove obstacles, eliminate injustice, observe nefarious activity and report back, liaise with authority and those in positions of power. Your weapons and training will be your strength. Your dexterity, intelligence and wisdom are your armour. Are you both resolved to give your all into this cause, for the good and benefit of the Guild and of their Mage-Lords of the City of Westron Seaport?"

As one, Harley and Soren-ko both straightened their backs and shoulders and cried "Aye, Guild Master."

"I will tell you one thing that may cause you to change your minds. The Guild has at any one time two-score of associates in the lands. Few are those who know more than one or two of the others. Life expectancy is low. It is known that some have not survived for more than a month but others who were trained five or more years ago still report back and receive new missions. Your rewards will be great as befits those elite associates who operate in the gloom of the shadows. Each task will have its own reward as determined by the challenge. Those rewards will be significant. Do you have questions to ask?"

"Aye, Guild Master," called Soren-ko. "May I assume that any task will be placed upon the Guild by a, er, customer?"

"That is quite correct, Soren-ko."

"Then as identities are protected, I assume there is a token given to the associate that would be recognisable by the customer."

The Guild Master hesitated then smiled faintly. "Again you assume correctly, Soren-ko. This is made quite clear on the onset of a task."

"Guild Master," called Harley. "I have a question."

"Ask it, Black Harlequin."

"I have a plan to hide my true nature within a travelling group that I shall form myself. Should a task take me from place to place and I wish to take this group of people as a veil, so to speak, would this create a problem within the Guild?"

"You already know that you have one world that is your chosen profession. You will travel with a world that belongs to the travelling group. I assume it would be under the guise of merchants, or perhaps musical or acrobatic performers. Am I right?"

Harley smiled and nodded.

The Guild Master raised an eyebrow. "This is an interesting proposition. Then the solution is simple. You keep the two worlds separate. Once one interferes with the other then you will be compromised and will have to perform an unpleasant adjustment. Watch your back and cover your tracks constantly."

The Guild Master looked across at the seated figure who nodded causing the hood to dip almost imperceptibly.

"Soren-ko, I would like you to accompany me and the Master Tutor to the chambers beyond. Black Harlequin, I wish for you to remain here."

Soren-ko followed the Guild Master, the Master Tutor and Belettanbiele out of the chamber. Harley was left alone with the hooded figure. The man slowly rose to his feet and reached up to remove his hat. Harley saw a tall, lean, distinguished man with black hair just beginning to show specks of grey. The thin face had a narrow, straight nose and sported an immaculately trimmed beard, as black as soot. The cape completely covered the man's clothing except for the bottom, which didn't reach far enough to cover a pair of spotlessly polished boots.

"Black Harlequin. That is a rather strange pseudonym which perhaps indicates your choice of future travelling companions. You have done extraordinarily well for one so young. I understand you were the most junior recruit the Guild has ever trained. I have personally selected you for employment by the

City Palace. Your Guild Master has kindly allowed me to take advantage of your skills and capabilities. How does that appeal to you?"

"I am honoured, Good-sir. May I ask if I am replacing a previous incumbent for that post?"

"Ah. As it happens, you are indeed."

"In that case, Good-sir, may I ask what became of that previous incumbent?"

"He perished. A month or more ago. His body was discovered in a well in Grappina, fifty leagues south, on the coast. Does that news cause you to refuse the post?"

"Not one bit, Good-sir. Will you be requiring me to investigate the incident?"

"Black Harlequin, you show very astute thinking. That is to be your first mission. I assume that you will be assembling a troupe of travelling entertainers."

It was a statement rather than a question. Harley nodded.

"In that case I can give you assistance there. Come to the Palace East Gate at around the ninth hour in the morning. You will be met there and escorted within. Be prepared to take up a permanent residence there. I would imagine there are some final activities you will need to finalise here at the Guild. She is very beautiful, is she not?"

Harley was momentarily taken aback. "I beg your–"

"Soren-ko."

"Aye, Good-sir. She is that."

"Farewell until the morning." The figure replaced his hat, took his long, black staff and rapped it on the floor once.

The door through which the Guild Master had left now opened and Belettanbiele walked in. He bowed to the figure. "Back to your quarters, Harley," the gnome said.

Harley bowed and left. *How did the caped man*

know that I favoured Soren-ko? These people don't miss a trick.

He walked through the corridors to his room. Outside his door stood Soren-ko.

"You were not very long. I know my future," she breathed excitedly. "I am to be assigned to the Guild Master for missions on the Landsdrop Coast. I will be informed in depth tomorrow. How about you?"

"I'm being met by someone from the City Palace tomorrow and then I will be off somewhere. It all sounds mysterious, doesn't it?"

"Are you going to invite me in? I've not seen your chamber yet? It may be a long time before we see each other again."

"I very much hope not. The chamber is a bit of a mess," he said guiltily.

"Hah, you should see mine," she replied.

He held the door ajar and she walked in. As he followed behind her she stopped.

"I hope you're not looking at my behind," she said with a huge cheeky grin.

"Most definitely! I can never take my eyes off it!"

She turned, grabbed his shoulders and planted her mouth on his, kissing him furiously.

It was two hours before the gong sounded for evening feast. After the meal they returned to his chamber and stayed together until dawn.

...o o O o o...

PART 2

ASSIGNMENT

48

Chapter 5

His meagre possessions hardly filled the small back-pack. His beloved and precious weapons sat in their plain black scabbards on his belt. He felt very self-conscious that his clothing, shabby and stained from the months of training out in the wilds, would look out of place in the Palace. His heart beat feverishly as he approached the Palace. When he caught sight of the high, smooth stone walls that surrounded it he almost turned about to run back to the Guild. *Deep breath, Tamm! Dammit, I mean Harley,* he chided himself.

He was very early; too early. The east gate of the palace wall was closed but as he drew close it swung open to reveal a palace flunkey. The man was dressed in a ridiculous scarlet tunic with white, bulbous pantaloons and short, black boots.

I have seen performing monkeys dressed in that manner! Harley thought. He could hardly resist a wry smile. He did his utmost to hide it.

"You will be Good-sir Harley," said the man.

There! How did he know my associate *name, her nickname for me?* His heart ached as he thought of his wonderful night with Soren-ko.

"Good-s –? Er, aye, that is me." He had not been addressed as *Good-sir* before, ever.

The flunkey looked at Harley's attire from bottom to top. His face showed slight distaste. "Follow me, sir. I shall take you to your quarters. His Excellency will meet with you at noon."

"His Excellency?"

"Yes, sir. I am instructed to inform you that this gate will be the one that you should always use. It is under constant watch and no doubt you will become known in time."

Harley was led into a side entrance of the palace. He need not have been concerned with his appearance because they met no others. He was taken up a flight of marble stars to a wide corridor with a row of doors along the right-hand side. The opposite wall was festooned with pictures and tapestries and with small alcoves, each with a statuette or an exquisite pottery vase. Globes, placed in sconces on the wall, gave a strange soft light. *Magical, surely,* he mused.

The manservant stopped outside the third door. It had a cartouche, the size of the palm of a hand, showing the bust of a harlequin dressed in black clothing with a similarly black face mask.

The man unlocked the door with a key and passed it to Harley. He opened it and beckoned Harley inside. Following him in. the Flunkey showed him a small door. Harley opened it and was taken aback by the clothing contained inside.

"These were made especially for you Good-sir. They should fit perfectly. There are two that should interest you, though."

The man removed two carefully-folded sets of clothing and placed them on the bed. He turned to go but stopped and turned back towards Harley.

"Good-sir, should you require anything at all, drinks, something to eat, laundry, your chamber pot emptying, anything at all, just pull on this cord and a chamber maid will be along swiftly. Female company can also be arranged, just ask the maids and they will arrange something for you. My name is Arfan. A gong is sounded for all meals, dawn, midday and evening."

"My thanks, Arfan. I shall surely do that."

Once Arfan had left, Harley looked at the two piles of clothes. One looked to be a formal set, almost a uniform, while the other would suffice were he to leave the confines of the palace grounds.

Arfan collected Harley before midday and led him through the palace. Harley felt much more confident now that he could dress in a presentable manner. He wore a light, tan, leather tabard over a white shirt and black hose. Arfan had confirmed that it would not contravene etiquette for him to wear his weapons in front of His Excellency so he had strapped his sword belt over his tabard. He wore a pair of soft leather riding boots that had been polished until they shone.

At exactly midday, marked by a bell elsewhere in the palace, Arfan knocked on a exquisitely-carved door. A voice from inside called "Enter!"

The caped man that Harley had seen at the Guild now stood to welcome his guest. This time however, the man was casually attired with a loose-fitting, flamboyant, white silk blouse tucked into black hose. He wore a small, narrow-bladed dagger in a sheath on his belt. Harley guessed from its ostentatious construct that it was more a ceremonial accoutrement, rather than serving any practical purpose.

"Black Harlequin," the man stated, as he had previously. "Welcome. I understand you are called by the epithet Harley."

Her nickname for me.

"For the sake of expediency I hope you are happy that we refer to you by that name?"

"Aye, er, Your Excellency."

"Ah, yes. I am referred to by that title usually by official visitors, members of Their Magelords' court and the staff. I would be pleased if you would call me by something a little less pretentious, such as *Commander*. Will that suit, do you think?"

"Aye, Commander. I believe that would suit us both." Harley felt immediately at ease in this man's presence.

"I was purposefully not introduced yesterday in the Guild Master's chamber. I am Trowban Huntinghorn, often called The Trollbane. You see I was once like you, an elite *associate*. I retired almost twenty years ago. My position here now is Chamberlain to Their Magelords. I organise and oversee the business of court and ensure Their Magelords' directives are passed into the city for the local governors to administer. I spend many hours in the City Halls. Consequently, I am one of the very few who have access to The Magelords of Westron Seaport. They keep themselves closeted in a large suite of chambers at the top of this palace and are rarely seen outside of it. Their identities are kept a secret from the public world. Were you to encounter one of them it is because they have willed it."

"But, Commander, do they never leave the confines of their chambers? Are they forever prisoners within their own chambers?"

Trowban laughed softly. "Nay, Harley. They have their own ways of leaving and entering the palace and no doubt are often away on business of their own. Often, their business will result in the tasks that are passed on to you, and the two other elite associates who reside in this palace from time to time. You may meet them; you may not."

"Commander, you mentioned yesterday that you would be able to give me some assistance in putting together a travelling group."

Trowban, the Commander, paused for a brief moment. "Their Magelords use many agents and operatives throughout the Home Territories and Western Kingdoms, Harley. There is, however, one group in particular that will be well suited for you. They should, at this moment in time, be on their way back from Northwald City with a certain brigand locked and hidden from view in a small cage. I shall introduce you to them when they arrive here in the city but only tell them what we believe they need to know. Better still, perhaps you would like to ride north and meet up with them. I shall give you a message for one Boulaye, their leader, which will introduce you. You have a few days, up to ten days I expect, in which to do what you need for yourself. I would suggest you take yourself out into the City and get to know it. Perhaps call in on your sister in the Temple of Haeman."

Is there nothing these people do not know about me? he thought. "I shall, Commander."

"A word of advice for you, Harley. Make you appearance match the part of the city that you go into. Dress roughly and take an old, battered sword if you go into the Docks Quarter, the shanty town outside the walls or into the dark alleyways. Keep your wits about you. People will rob you for your boots and the shirt off your back, and they will not be polite about it. You may wear the palace tabard, it earns enormous respect from the populace, but do not wear it in the more insalubrious areas of the city. Have you been into the Palace training arena yet? No, of course you won't have. There is an armourer's store there. Take yourself a sword and leave your own in your chamber. The armourer is expecting you, by the way. A very pleasant man named Oggie Doob." He chuckled and shook his head as if in response to a silent joke.

...o o O o o...

Harley's first duty in the city would be to call in at the Temple of Heaman and ask to see his sister, Hanni. He felt proud to be dressed in his palace tabard and people treated him with respect and deference. Even the uncouth sword-men and burly thugs stepped aside as he strode purposefully through the multitude. He had asked the manservant, Arfan, if he would arrange for his sword and dagger sheaths to be polished. They now gleamed at his side. *Damn, how shall I introduce myself at the temple?*

Notwithstanding his dilemma with the name he should call himself, he strode confidently through the gates of the Temple compound, up the wide marble steps and in through the open great doors into the marble-floored hallway. At once, a young acolyte priest walked up to him and dipped his head in a deferential bow.

"Greeting and welcome to you, Good-sir." The acolyte, probably no more than fourteen summers, called in a polite, sing-song voice. "Do you come to pray, or perhaps, repose in silent contemplation?" At Harley's shake of his head, the young lad continued. "Perhaps to speak with a cleric for enlightenment or inner-healing?"

"None of those, thank you," he answered.

The acolyte looked puzzled. "Then how may I be of service?"

"I have actually come here to ask if I may speak with my sister, Hanni DuHan. I have been remiss in not having seen her for a few years. I would be grateful if I may have an audience with her."

The young lad looked delighted. "I know her well, sire. She graduates this very day and is at the celebratory service in the main Chamber of Prayer. I am sure you will be most welcome to attend. Please come with me."

He did not ask me to identify myself. Phew!

The large hall was filled with priests of Haeman, dressed in White gowns beneath lilac robes, but a few of those of many other faiths were seated at the sides of the chamber. Twenty, or perhaps a few more, acolyte priest, dressed in long, cream-coloured vestments with a lilac sash around the waist, sat in a line in front of an ageing High Priest, a wizened, elderly man dressed in a cream-coloured robe. He was flanked by two other senior priests, a woman and a man, both of middle-age and similarly attired to the High Priest.

A eulogy followed a sequence of prayers and responses from the congregation. In it, the High Priest spoke of the immense training that had been undertaken by the acolytes and their collective achievements. He then spoke of the challenges that would face many of them as they went out into the Home Territories to spread the divine grace of the Lord Haeman, to offer divine inspiration, protection, advice and healing to the community and to conduct instruction of basic skills, philosophical schooling and mentoring to young people as they approached adulthood.

Then he called each acolyte in turn. Warmth and a feeling of well-being filled the hall as each acolyte was blessed. The purple sash was removed and a light-coloured purple vestment was handed, neatly-folded to each one of them. Hanni was the last to be called. The High Priest read her testimonial. It was glowing. Her highest commitment to theological studies had earned her the Scroll of Achievement. She would be a natural teacher. Her healing abilities, in particular the Laying on of Healing Hands and drawing upon her faith, were exemplary. Her abilities to turn away, and even destroy undead, was an example to all. He predicted that she would go far in her service to Lord Haeman and to the greater community.

Harley was astounded. He had been told some years before that she was an academic. The fact that she had achieved so much despite the terrible events many years ago was so unexpected. How proud their mother would have been had she lived to see it. Would Natti have achieved such greatness too? Probably; they had been so alike. Their father, Leage DuHan would be puffing his chest with admiration too.

The elderly High Priest addressed the assembled new Priests of Haeman, the God of Fairness and Law.

"You will be going forth into the world and spread the word of peace to the populace. Be of good courage and strength and hold fast to that which is good and just. Give no evil to those that are evil for you must be an example to all, good and evil alike. Strengthen the faint of heart and support the weak for they may not be able to face those of greater power. Help the distressed and the suffering. Spread the word and love of the Lord Haeman and converse with Him daily, giving thanks for His aid and guidance. In this way His divine magic will constantly be made available for you."

More blessings were bestowed on the congregation and the High Priest and his assistants bowed to the Holy Shrine and closed the service. People rose to their feet and made their way to the two exit doorways. Harley left before the crowd hemmed him in but from the top of the sloping floor he saw Hanni making for the other exit.

He slipped out and made for the other door and was there waiting as Hanni left surrounded by other newly-created priests.

"Hanni," he called.

She looked up and saw his beaming face. It took a few heartbeats as recognition dawned.

"Tamm? Is it you?" she cried. "Is it really you? Haeman be praised!"

"Aye, it is, little sister," he responded, his arms outstretched.

She jumped into his arms, laughing and crying at the same time.

"Where have you been, big brother? And look at

you, in the service of the Palace. Not a watchmen though. What post do you hold?"

He was pleased that he had anticipated this question.

"I am a special envoy to the Chamberlain to Their Magelords. I mediate with people from across Baylea and rectify problems. Or rather, that is my new position. I have had to do much training to ensure I do things properly and within the rule of law."

"You sound very important, Tamm," she mused.

"No more than you, dear Hanni. Have you heard from father?"

"Er, I have, he's –"

"Right behind you," added a gruff voice.

Harley spun around. His father stood behind him, a wide grin on his ruddy face. His eyepatch gave him an almost piratical countenance.

"Father," Harley whispered.

"Well, well. Look at my two children, how well you have done."

"And you, father? How goes the trade?" asked Harley.

"From strength to strength, lad. I have the finger-knots now. Look at my knuckles. But I am dextrous enough to train the youngsters. You remember your friend Arash? He is a business partner now and has good skill with the tools. He lacks finesse and is somewhat abstract with his craft but his models sell well. I make a good living now and with training scrimshaw to a new apprentice, I have earned sufficient to build a small teaching school for scrimshaw. I am to wed Arash's mother, Kenna, in the mid-summer."

"She is a good lady, Dada," said Hanni. "I wish you peace and happiness."

"And I too," added Harley. "Wish Arash well for me."

"Aye, I will that. I have seen what Hanni has

57

become, what about you, Tamm. Is this the livery of the Palace?"

Harley did not see the need to correct his sister and father over his change of name. "Aye, Father. I am now employed as a Palace envoy. I am to travel the Home Territories, and perhaps beyond, to foster peace and bring troubles to an end." In a way, he felt that this was a truthful response to his father's question.

"Take care on the journey back to Tranquil Port, Dada," advised Hanni. "I am told that there are troubles to the north of here."

"Aye, Father," agreed Harley. "Do you travel alone?"

"Nay lad, I shall act as sword-man for a merchants' caravan heading north through Northwald City to Icedge. It is barely six days to Tranquil Port and there are a few of us escorts. Enough of us to scare off a warband of orcs or goblins, anyway. We leave at dawn and I am missing Kenna."

"Perhaps I shall ride with you part of the way, Father. I have to guide in another party that is travelling south to Westron Seaport. I am not sure where they are but they are due here within eight or ten days."

"I am very pleased, my son. Then we shall meet by the North Gate before dawn. Perhaps you can walk with me there shortly. Hah! They have food in yonder chamber."

Leage turned and stomped towards the side room.

Hanni hugged her brother. "You have changed much, Tamm. Look at your muscles. That beautiful sword. That was Dada's, was it not? But you whole demeanour has changed. You are confident but your eyes miss nothing. I would not be surprised if you could tell me about the small man behind you."

"You mean the man with the multi-coloured cape over the green silk robe and the desert-type slippers?

The one wearing the white turban with the little gold pin on the side? With the little white beard and the scar over his nose and above his right eye? The one who hides a small thin dagger up his left sleeve?"

"Ha-ha-ha!" she laughed. "No, I mean the other one! Take care of yourself, Tamm, and look after Dada on the journey home. It has been wonderful to see you today. How did you know I was to be celebrated today?"

"I truly did not know, I asked the door warden and he said you were on this special ceremony." *Did the Commander know? Probably.*

"Well, big brother, it was an amazing coincidence. You must come and see me before you leave on your first adventure."

"I shall of course. Congratulations, little sister. Take care."

Harley kissed her on the cheek and made his way over to the small chamber where food and wine was being distributed to the visitors. Leage was there which a large chunk of bread and a piece of cheese. After a small tankard of wine they left the temple and walked along the busy street towards the North gate. It was almost two hours later when they arrived. Leage approached the caravan's team-master and introduced his son, as Tamm, to the rugged, burly man.

"I can't pay for another sword, even a Palace sword," said the team-master. "The merchant gives me one purse of gold and that's already spoken for."

"I travel that way regardless," answered Harley. "I will be happy to share some food and the warm fire for a few days in payment for me being another pair of eyes for you and to stand watch when needed. Will that be acceptable?"

"Aye, that is acceptable." The team-master spat into his right hand and held it out for the clasp. Harley took it but the man's grip began to tighten. *He is playing me for a fool!* Harley's grip tightened in turn. It took a few moments but it was the team-master that conceded. He grinned at Harley.

"Aye, lad. You will do nicely!"

...o o O o o...

It was still dark when Harley met his father at the North Gate. He had dressed in the clothing he had been wearing when he had left the Guild for the Palace. During the previous evening he had left a message with Arfan for the Commander that he would like to borrow a horse, with a saddle, from the stable-hand and ride north, to accompany his father with the merchant's caravan, to meet the party coming south from Northwald City. He had received word from the Commander within the hour agreeing to his request. Harley had spent the rest of the evening attending to his sword and dagger and readying his equipment. *My first expedition!* He thought excitedly.

Leage DuHan was already astride a saddle when Harley rode out through the North gate. In the light of burning torches Harley saw his father waving at him.

"Well met, Tamm. We are in for bad weather, mark well my words," said Leage, sniffing the air. "The wind is up and it feels chilled."

"But the stars are out," replied Harley. "How many wagons, Father?"

"Oh, nigh on a score. There are more than twenty outriders to provide protection, including ourselves. That is a lot of money for protection. The cargo must be worth something."

"It looks like furs, pelts, fabrics, leather and carpets," answered Harley. "Where has it all come from?"

"Leather from Gorador, I believe, and the rest from Qoratt and Lopastor."

"But Gorador is across the sea to the south, is it not?"

"These leathers are special. It is said that they are the skin of fearsome animals with extremely long noses and tusks as long as a man is tall. They are traded for by the barbarians of the northern ice lands. They have copper and tin in exchange."

"And I believe that we have military difficulties with Lopastor too," Harley reminded his father.

Lopastor and the Home Territories, along with some of the minor Western Kindoms shared a common border a couple of hundred leagues to the south. It was common knowledge that the armies of the Home Territories had bolstered those of the Western Kingdoms along the border forts.

"Ah but we are not at open war with Lopastor, lad," responded Leage. "Their armies are hopelessly outnumbered and already have Qoratt baying at their own southern borders for access to the lakes. Water is scarce in Qoratt."

The lead wagons were already starting to pull away and the pair took up positions either side of a wagon near the rear of the train. Dawn was late in appearing. Leaden clouds threatened rain as the light grew and before long large spots of rain spattered on the road, their clothing and the horses and wagons. Within an hour the rain had turned into a cloudburst driven by a strong wind blowing in from the ocean to the west. The team-master rode back from the merchant's coach giving instructions for every person to take shelter beneath their wagons.

An hour passed before the rain dropped sufficiently for the wagons to resume the slow journey. The road was wide enough for the wagons and their outriders to move comfortably but there were many times that they encountered traffic coming the other way. It was convention that the smaller caravan would give way by pulling in to one of the occasional passing places. The rain continued all through the first day.

The second day dawned as dark, wet and miserable as the first. The other outriders seemed to tolerate this as part of everyday conditions. All riders, including Leage, and the wagon drovers were well-protected by hooded *baladranas*, the waxed, close-weaved cloaks worn by travellers that kept out the worst of the downpour. As a student warrior, Harley had seen little of an adventuring life and despite having spent more than four months field training he had seen little severe weather. On the odd day that there had been showers, he had trained hard and accepted the slight difficulty.

This was different. He had little or nothing to distract him from the driving squalls that were battering his left side and soaking him to the skin. Unfortunately, Harley's inexperience showed. He had no rain-proof cape as the others had. He was permanently soaked to the skin and had spent the previous night huddled shivering and cold to the marrow beneath a wagon.

"Cold, son?" asked Leage.

"I was not expecting this weather, Father. In all those years as a child in the marshes and in Tranquil Port I don't remember rain like this."

"Ah, but we did. It is just that when it did rain heavily, we ran inside our homes. Perhaps this will serve as a lesson. There is no such thing as being cold, but there is such a thing as being inadequately dressed. The weather improves now and perhaps it will stay fine until we return to our homes."

Harley almost whooped for joy when the caravan pulled to a stop close to a little market town. It was midday and the rain still lashed at his face, filled his left ear and had made his journey miserable. He tied his mount onto the wagon that he and his father had been escorting and splashed through the slippery mud. He did not hear his father calling to him to ask him where he was going. The enclosure wall around the settlement was little above head height, not uncommon for isolated settlements, and had a single gate. The watchman allowed Harley entry without hindrance. Within an hour Harley had spent half the money he had to his name and strode out of the village wearing a new baladrana.

An hour later the rain stopped and the skies began to clear.

By mid afternoon the caravan had left the village a couple of miles behind. The sun had burned off the remaining clouds and Harley's new cloak was rolled up behind his saddle.

"Any sign of the group you are looking for, son?" asked Leage.

"None as yet, father. Perhaps it is a few day's early yet and they may also have been held up by the weather. Look at the animals!"

The horses, mules and oxen drawing the wagons were steaming in the sun and Harley felt warm at last. He had no doubt that, with the coming winter, he would have use of his new cape.

However, Leage's hopes of fine weather were dashed. The next day the rains came again. The road was already ankle deep in mud and it was worse for the wagons at the rear of the caravan. The merchant would allow no stopping. Spare oxen from the front wagons were taken to aid those at the rear and this helped for a while. A wagon's yoke broke under the strain and would have to be repaired. This would probably hold up the last seven wagons for two hours.

The team-master was furious as he rode up to them

through the mud and he berated the drover for having placed the progress of the caravan at risk.

"You will have to repair that and catch up," growled the team-master. "We cannot afford to stop the team for you all. I suggest you all lend a hand to this fool so the rest of you can be on your way. Be at the next stopping place as quickly as you can or you will not be in time to eat."

Leage's practical skills were invaluable as he fashioned a new yoke from a sapling. He had all seven drovers and six outriders struggling to help. Within an hour the last wagons were on their way.

They had hardly started on their way when a sudden yell came from their right. A flurry of arrows whistled from the hill to their right.

...o o O o o...

Chapter 6

Two outriders fell from their saddles and one drover yelled in agony as the first few arrows struck. A second flurry of arrows followed quickly and Leage fell from his horse. He had the presence of mind to retain his grip on the reins and he managed to coax his mount to the ground to give him some cover.

Eight dark, swarthy, squat figures broke cover and rushed down the slope towards them, whirling short, wide, hooked blades and screaming ferociously.

"Orcs!" cried one fighter. "Here they come!"

Harley was the first to react to this new threat. Even as the second wave of arrows sped towards them, he was leaping down from his horse. He slapped its rump, causing it to gallop away. His sword was ready in his hand within a heartbeat and he ran towards his father just as he saw his father's horse drop beside him.

Good!

The other horsemen followed Harley's lead. Almost immediately three of them were engaging in swordplay. Long-swords rang against the vicious blades. Loose horses stampeded between the orcs and fighters throwing up mud from their hooves.

Harley engaged one orc, its foul odour assailing his senses. He parried an attack and swung his own rapier in a swipe that cut the beast's throat to its spine. He ran towards another and was about to thrust his blade into it when it dropped at his feet. A crossbow bolt had embedded itself in its side. Looking up to his left he noticed a drover standing atop his wagon, his mouth agape and a crossbow held in readiness but without a bolt.

"Load it, man!" Harley screamed at the top of his voice.

The drover came to his senses and, with some effort, pulled the thick cord.

"Father!" called Harley, panic rising in his voice.

"I am fine," called Leage. "Do not worry."

Another outrider had fallen; his body was being searched by an orc. A crossbow bolt, and then another, struck the beast in the chest and head. It fell across the body of the fighter.

Two orcs advanced on Harley. One of them charged at him but he sidestepped, turned and slashed it below its ribs. He did not wait to see if it had fallen but, with a battle-cry he launched himself at the other orc and felled it with the tip of his blade through its eye. Only now did he glance down to see that the first of the pair was clearly dead with its entrails spilling out through the wide gash in its belly.

Two orcs remained. They turned and fled. One was brought down with a crossbow bolt. Two of the outriders chased after the last one on foot. They disappeared over the brow of the hill despite protests from Harley and the others. He breathed a sigh of relief when they returned with grim faces and brandishing a right ear, festooned with iron rings, from the orc.

Leage's horse struggled upright but now he was unable to control it. Harley rushed over and slid in the mud to drop beside his father. He heard, from across the road, an outrider calling for the right ears of the orcs to be removed. *Is this a bounty?*

"Papa," he called.

"It bleeds greatly, son." He removed his hands from his thigh, the one which had already lost the lower part of the leg, where the stub of an arrow protruded, and the blood flowed freely.

"Put your hand back on there, Papa and press hard." Harley reached into his belt-pack and searched for the rolls of clean cloth that he kept for use as bandages.

They were there, wrapped in waxed parchment. Using his dagger he slit Leage's hose leg and squeezed his fingers over the stub.

"It is in deep, Father. Wait, it starts to come out the other side; I can push it right through. Can you let me?"

"Oh Gods, I don't know," gasped Leage. "It hurts me already."

"I'll turn you on your side first. Then we'll prepare for it. I must take it out, Father."

With a little effort, for Leage was quite a large man now that he was in middle years, Harley turned him so that the stump of his left leg was uppermost and supported on his right thigh.

"I'll push through from the back and pull through from the front," said Harley, softly.

His father closed his eyes and held his breath. "Do it quick, son. Count down, or up, whichever, so I know when you will do it."

"I will count down from three then I will do it," whispered Harley. *I hope my hands are steady and do not shake.*

"No, no! Tamm, wait. On one or on zero?"

It will not matter. "On zero."

He took a firm grip on the blood-soaked arrow-head and placed the palm of his hand a few inches away from the broken stump of the shaft.

He began to count. "Three!"

Immediately he slammed the palm of his hand on the shaft, feeling it move through his father's thigh, and pulled hard on the arrow-head.

His fingers slipped on the blood. Leage screamed in agony and the stump of his leg jerked upwards. Immediately, Harley gripped again and pulled hard. The broken arrow came free. Leage yelled once more. Blood poured out of the exit wound but merely trickled from the entry wound. Harley ripped the waxed parchment off one of the cloth bandages and wrapped it around the thigh. He then unwrapped another bandage, folded it into a pad and placed it on the exit wound. He unrolled a third bandage and wrapped it tightly around the thigh so the pad was firmly pressed onto the exit wound.

Leage was soaked through with sweat. Two of the drovers helped him up onto the board of a wagon, passed up the wooden leg and Harley instructed him not to move.

"Aye lad," croaked his father. "You forgot to say *two* and *one!*" He was clearly fatigued and in immense pain.

Three of the outriders had gone down but although one still lived, within a short while the man has also perished, his lungs having filled with blood from a devastating chest wound.

The three bodies were loaded onto another wagon for burial later. The bodies of the orcs were searched but they yielded little of value.

"Take their weapons," growled one of the outriders. "No more of the bastards will be able to use 'em. We'll bury them too."

The wagons resumed their laborious journey. In places they found it was easier to drive the wagons off the road, despite the shrubs and long grass. Harley rode next to the wagon to keep an eye on his father, who slept fitfully. It was after nightfall when they pulled into the camp with the main wagon train.

"You took your time," grunted the team-master.

"We were attacked by orcs," replied one of the surviving outriders. "We finished 'em off but you've lost three of your escort."

"Hah! A likely story. They've hightailed it off back to Westron Seaport, most like," the man retorted.

"Listen," replied another outrider. "Their bodies are

here and we've got eight ears to prove it. You ass-holes left us behind and vulnerable and you lost us three good men. It's your damned fault. If you leave a wagon behind once more you had best stay with it yourself if you know what's good for you. We'll be taking their pay for their families."

The team-master reddened and stood square on to the others. "Do not threaten me. We have a schedule and we are already a day late. I'll pay you what you –"

"What is going on here?" called a voice. It sounded foreign.

The team-master looked over his shoulder. Behind him stood an opulently-dressed man with a silk, quilted robe of many shimmering colours about which was wound a wide, light blue silk sash. On his head was a similarly-coloured luxurious silk turban in the centre of which was a tall black cone. It was the merchant, a man rarely seen since he generally rode in his coach.

"Sir," replied the team-master. His manner had suddenly turned sycophantic. "I am admonishing these drovers, and their escort, for having delayed on the road. They took two hours to repair a breakage and they got themselves in a fight with a few orcs."

"I am sure you underestimate the situation, Bratten. See that they are given hot food and some of the ale you have hidden in your wagon. Make them comfortable."

"We have three bodies to bury, sir," called Harley.

"Then the team-master will provide a party of men to do this task while you eat. Please see to it, Bratten."

"Aye, sir," replied the team-master.

The Merchant turned and strode off to his coach, taking care to avoid the pools of mud.

Bratten stood almost nose-to-nose with the leader of the small escort. "You shall have your men but you will all be on watch this night, including you, boy." He directed the last comment at Harley. "Where is your father?"

"He is on the wagon, badly wounded," answered Harley.

"We shall drop him off at the next village tomorrow morning. We cannot take wounded with us."

Then you shall lose me too! "You will pay him his two day's pay though," replied Harley. "He was wounded trying to protect your wagons."

"We shall see."

...ooOoo...

Leage suffered during the night. He awoke frequently and was bathed in sweat. By the early hours he shook with cold even though his brow showed that he was feverish. In the morning, he was placed on the rearmost wagon with a dour and anger-filled Harley riding close by. Leage's horse was tethered to the rear of the wagon.

A long slope led down to a small community, a collection of huts to the east side of the roadside where people scratched a meagre living by providing food supplies, clean water and wagon repairs for passing traders and caravans.

The wagon-train stopped, stretched along more than the full length of the hamlet. Stalls stocked with fish, cheeses, meats and bread had already been set out for the passing trade of the day and wagon drovers began to queue at each on of them. The usual arguments about prices sprang up, as they always did, and the art of haggling was soon in full sway.

The team-master, Bratten, trotted his mount up to the last wagon. Harley rode over to him, ready for confrontation.

"Is he able to ride as an outrider today?" Bratten bellowed.

70

"He is not. I shall take him to the healer. You owe him three day's pay."

"I owe him nothing. He is leaving us partly unprotected."

"You left us vulnerable when you did not stop," roared Harley. "Pay up or I shall become unreasonable."

"How dare you speak to me like that, you whelp? You shall face my sword."

He leapt down from his horse, withdrew a wide longsword and advanced on Harley. Immediately, Harley dismounted and pulled his rapier. Bratten chopped in a downwards motion which Harley easily parried. A second attack, a backhand swing, from the team-master resulted in his sword being flicked from his grip by Harley. For the first time, the team-master showed fear on his face. The young lad had hardly flicked his wrist.

"I have no desire to hurt you," said Harley, in an almost benign manner. "I shall ask you politely just once more. Please pay my father what you owe him."

"What is going on here?" called a voice. It was the Merchant.

The team master screeched "I have been attacked by this –"

"Not true," called four or five voices simultaneously.

One man, one of the outriders who had helped overcome the orc attack, spoke up. "Your team-master refuses to pay Leage DuHan for his three days, sir, and is leaving him here."

"Is this true, Bratten?"

"Aye, sir, but –"

"Pay him, then. Give him double for he was hurt while protecting those you had left behind. Give me the purse and leave the team. Ride away."

71

"B-But –"

The merchant turned his back.

"I suggest you take your father to the cleric at the end of the village," the merchant said. His immense bulk caused him to wheeze and his multiple chins wobbled as he spoke. "It is probably too dangerous to transport him on the wagons to his home village – where is it?"

"Tranquil Port, sir" answered Harley.

"Ah, less than a tenday at the rate we move. Take this to pay for his care. I would have lost a lot of valuable goods had you all not have protected the wagons. I shall ask someone to find the cleric and send her up here forthwith."

He passed a small bag of coins to Harley, turned and strode away. Harley pulled the drawstring and peered inside. In there were probably a dozen or more gold crowns.

The dark-skinned outrider who had spoken on Leage's behalf stepped over to Harley, his hand outstretched.

"We have not had a chance to speak much," he said. "I am called Kasidian. I come from Kamambia originally. You are impressive with that sword."

"I practised regularly with friends. My father gave me the sword and its matching dagger many years ago. I used it in anger for the first time yesterday."

"Ah, your first kill. That is always the one that causes the most anguish. But as it was an orc, no more than a feral beast, perhaps it was not so?"

"I just thought about protecting my father. I was taught that to take a life would be the final resort unless you needed to kill to save another life."

Kasidian laughed. "A just sentiment, er, Tamm are you called?"

"Aye, that I am. I travel with my father only so that

I can meet with a travelling group who comes this way from Northwald City. Then I am supposed to lead them to Westron Seaport."

"It may be a few days before your father is well enough to travel but it will not be good for him to do so alone. Perhaps I shall take him to Tranquil Port for you. You see, there is a lady there, a widow with hair as black as a raven, her eyes beautiful and dark like those of a doe, and breasts as firm as a melon." His eyes took on a faraway look as he spoke. "Jenatha, she is called. I intend to ask for her hand in marriage."

"Then I wish you joy and good fortune," laughed Harley. "Take this purse on behalf of my father. Share the coins between yourself and him."

The cleric, an ageing Reverend of Cahuhl, approached them a short while later.

"I am Reverend Catilla," she called, in a soft voice.

Although short in stature, she looked sturdy and walked without a staff.

"I believe you have a wounded man with you." It was a statement rather than a query. "Do I assume he is to be made ready for passing into the afterlife?"

Harley looked horrified. "He just needs healing," he replied tersely. He led her over to the wagon where Leage slept fitfully. The Reverend looked at the blood-soaked bandage and at the skin to either side of it.

"So he has already lost the leg. The wound has become infected but it was well-bandaged. There is little blood loss. Bring the wagon over to my hut."

The drover took the wagon, passing most of the others in the train, and pulled up outside what was one of the grandest huts in the community. The jolting of the wagon had brought Leage to a rude awakening and he moaned with the movement. Together, the drover, Harley and Kasidian took Leage inside the hut. The Priestess ushered them back out again instructing that

73

they return at noon of the next day.

"You can sleep in the stable at the back of my little temple." She added. "I hope you have your own food for I have little. I have no ale either."

Harley and Kasidian looked at each other and walked towards the market stalls. Within a short while they returned to the cleric's hut with a sack of cheese, salted goat-meat and bread, and a small barrel of ale. The cleric accepted them without a word and closed her door.

"There's gratitude for you," laughed Kasidian. "I think we should return to the market for a feast for the two of us!"

...o o O o o...

Malevolence festered in the mind of Bratten and he was determined to rid himself of the young man who had humiliated him and engineered his dismissal from his post as team-master. An ex-convict, he had the scars of the scourge on his back. That alone had taught him hatred of those in authority. He had used deceit to get himself on the escort party; ex-convicts were rarely given a position which entrusted them with the protection of others. By connivance and further untruths, he had soon risen to the position of team-master. That had allowed him to be given the purse used to pay the drovers and outriders. With careful planning, he had been able to skim off a tidy amount for his own purse. After two years, he had earned himself a large amount of money which, when the opportunity arose, he converted into gemstones for the convenience of carrying.

Now this source of income had been wrenched away from him and he wanted revenge. *I'll have that lame man and then his son. If the damned outrider, Kasidian, gets in my way, I'll finish him off too.*

He had watched as the three men had taken Leage into the cleric's hut. She would be easy to deal with.

...ooOoo...

Harley & Kasidian settled down in the stable with sacks of food and two small barrels, one of ale and the other mead. They told each other tales of their lives although Harley purposely omitted to speak of his years at the Fighters' Academy and the special training that he had been given. Kasidian spoke of his years as a soldier in the Kamambian militias and their struggles in one border dispute after another, each of them short, each of them pointless.

"We gained nothing," he explained. "We gained no extra land nor did we lose any. We gained no gold, no livestock only a few slaves. We lost some people who undoubtedly became slaves. It was just to satisfy the egos of our lords who each bragged as being better at warfare than their neighbours. They boasted as to who had the better army or the best weapons. It is like boys who brag about who has the biggest cock! I left the militia and moved west. I am happy to be a sell-sword and it earns me enough money to live well when I choose. But now I hope to spend the rest of my days with the lovely Jenatha. Do you have a woman that you are drawn to?"

Harley smiled and looked down at the ground. "Nay, Kasidian, but there was one recently. She too was beautiful and I was privileged to spend some wonderful hours with just a few days ago. She is red-haired, tall, lithe and supple with a perfect body. She is very fit and very athletic, in many ways. Copper coloured hair that ran down her shoulders like a waterfall. Her name is Dellie and she gave me the

75

nickname *Harley*."

"She sounds like she was very special to you."

"Aye, Kasidian, she was, for a while at least. She still is, in my mind."

"Life moves on, my young friend. You must grasp at life and take the opportunities that arise. I should have offered my life to Jenatha a few years ago but she is very strong-willed and I think I was afraid of rejection. I had little to offer but now I have more. I shall not be so fearful now."

They sat on bales of straw, feasting, drinking the ale and chatting about their future aspirations. Of course, Harley made up the picture of his future, not knowing what it held for him. After a while he rose to his feet, slightly unsteadily.

"Excuse me, I really need to piss," he mumbled.

Kasidian laughed. "Do one for me while you are out there!" he joked.

Just as Harley stepped outside the door to the stable, he heard a muffled cry and the sound of a pot falling to the floor in the cleric's hut. His head suddenly cleared and he was focussed on the sounds from within. He tore over to the hut, dagger in hand.

Bursting inside, he saw two figures in the gloom of a single candle flame, just as the taller figure seemed about to strike down the other with a heavy sword.

He hurled his dagger and heard a grunt as the dagger struck home, followed by the noise of the sword being dropped.

Immediately a chant issued from the mouth of the cleric and the larger figure lifted his hands to clasp at his head. The figure, clearly now a man, issued a sound as of a person in torment and he slumped to the floor, writhing and groaning. Within a few heartbeats the figure quietened but continued to cradle his head inside the protectiveness of his arms.

76

The cleric rose to her feet and lit another candle. "I am unharmed but his fist has hurt my head. See to your father."

Harley rushed over to a cot in the corner and knelt by his father's side. "He is unharmed and still sleeping," he said, relief coursing through his body.

The door to the hut was still open from where Harley had crashed in. It now framed the large figure of Kasidian.

"What goes here?" growled the fighter, his large sword held at the ready.

"This person came in to do my father, and the cleric, harm. What did you do to him, Lady Reverend? Is the man dying?"

"I have weakened his mind. Do not kill him. He shall now do service to this community and shall sleep in the stable until I think he has learned to live a decent life. Would you take him out to the stable?"

"Aye, lady," replied Kasidian. "It would be for the best."

Between the pair of them they lifted the compliant form of the figure to his feet and led him out of the hut. In the moonlight, the features of the man became clear.

"By the gods! It is Bratten!" gasped Kasidian.

The one-time team-leader did not resist in the slightest as he was led in to the stable. He was unmistakably confused and struggled to speak coherently.

"N–n , no!" he murmured. "I, mm –"

"Aye. Come and eat," said Harley, almost benevolently.

"What's that gods-awful smell?" gasped Kasidian. "He's only gone and shit himself!"

Bratten seemed confused; he realised that the new contents of his hose were strange but appeared to have little idea of what to do about it.

"We had better get him outside and strip him off," suggested Harley.

Kasidian sighed. "Aye. You do that and I'll fill a pail of water from the trough to soak him with."

Harley led him outside the stable. Bratten began to wander away, unsure of what was expected of him.

"Come here, big boy!" laughed Harley and began to strip the man off.

As Bratten's belt fell to the ground, there was an almost insignificant clinking sound. Harley stooped and picked up the belt. Hanging from it were two bags attached by their thongs. *Feels like coins. I'll take a look in a while.* He tossed the belt inside the stable door.

It took a while to clean the miserable wretch and his clothing but, once finished, they had to dress him in the soaking hose. They led him into the corner of the stable where he would be able to settle down to sleep. Harley retrieved the belt and opened one of the bags.

"Ye gods!" he exclaimed. "There is a fortune in precious stones here. Look, Kasidian."

"By the nine Hells!" gasped Kasidian. "There is more than enough here to buy a whole village. This could set you and me up for years."

Harley looked puzzled at the gems. "What shall we do with them?"

"Let us see what is in the other purse, first," suggested Kasidian. "Here, hold these."

Harley's hands grasped the purse and gems so he passed the other purse to his companion.

Kasidian looked incredulous. "There must be two dozen gold. This is more money than I have seen for ages. What to do with it all though."

They sat in silence. Bratten sat in a corner and rocked to and fro. Harley reached for the beer keg. It was now half-full. He pulled the cork and took a draught and passed it across to Kasidiam.

After a short pause, they both began to speak together. Harley waited while his companion gathered his thoughts.

"Tamm, I think we should give a few gold to the Priestess. Some of this may truly belong rightfully to Bratten, but not all of it, I am certain."

"Aye, I agree with that," answered Harley.

"Give the rest to your father as a wedding present?"

"Aye, sounds good."

"Share the gems for our own future. What say you to that, Tamm."

"Well, Kasidian, we will never know who might have been the real owners of those gems, and the gold coins, but perhaps we can put the treasure to good use while mayhap giving generously to worthwhile causes. I shall need to lodge my share with the Moneylenders' Guild in Westron Seaport because I shall not need to use it right now and it is said that the money grows with time."

"Aye lad, that is what they say. I have ofttimes considered doing the same but, well, the coinage seems to burn a hole in my purse already and I have many time found solace at the bottom of a tankard or a whore's bed. That is long behind me now, I am pleased to say, and I hope to have a future, as I hope will you too, one day."

Harley's thoughts immediately turned to Dellie, or Soren-ko as she would now be known. He missed her terribly and occasionally wondered if she missed him too. She had always seemed so full of confidence, so in control, and so eager to be sent out on her first mission. He had little doubt that she would soon forget him. Perhaps he would begin to forget her too. *I don't think so, not really.*

"Perhaps I shall, Kasidian, perhaps," he replied.

The next morning, soon after dawn, Harley knocked on the door of the cleric's home. She answered before the echo had subsided.

"Your father is awake and his fever has passed," she said as she stepped out through her door. "He should be able to travel in two days. I have to perform some rites in the temple. A Farmer's child died of consumption. A few townsfolk come in for a blessing before they get to their day's work. There is little enough room for them all, especially when it rains here, and that is often. If you could see your way to providing a small donation before you leave? A few coppers, a silver or two? Please come inside."

Harley stepped inside. Immediately, there was an overpowering, heady aroma of fresh herbs, incense and spices in the stuffy air inside the hut. He coughed a couple of times to clear his throat. She had tidied up the debris caused by Bratten's iniquitous visit the previous evening.

Leage propped himself up on his right elbow and smiled at his son.

"Good to see you son," he said. "I understand there was a bit of a fuss in here last night."

"Aye, Father. Bratten tried to do some mischief but he has seen the error of his ways and now does simple chores for the community."

"That does not seem like him. How did you encourage him to do that?"

"Ah that was quite simple. Something the cleric said made him change his mind!"

Leage smiled and shook his head. "All to the good. She says I may be fit to travel tomorrow. She will make me up a poultice that I can change every day on our journey."

"Father, I shall not be travelling very far with you. As soon as I meet up with the group I shall be turning back towards Westron Seaport. But Kasidian will be riding with you all the way."

"Ah, Kasidian. He is a good man. I believe he wants to stop at Tranquil Port for reasons of his own. I reckon he has a sweetheart in the village."

"Aye, he has that, Father."

"We need a man of his stature there. The village has a watch but they are undisciplined and lazy. I shall speak with him. After all, I have been asked If I would take the position as the village patron. It is a big responsibility"

"Father, I had no idea. I am so pleased for you."

"Ah, do not be, Tamm. It was only offered to me because nobody else wanted the responsibility and those who have been there all their lives were either too old or were out fishing day after day. I have years left in me yet and a wonderful woman to support me."

"I shall come by and see you from time to time father. I do wish you all the happiness in the world with your new lady."

"That is good of you, son. Now, I must sleep because the lady said I must, and I am a little tired."

"I shall call by later, Father."

...o o O o o ...

With some assistance from Kasidian, Leage managed to get astride his horse. A small but adequately-protected wagon train prepared to leave the village soon after sun-up. Kasidian reckoned they would be overtaking the other great wagon train in about two days.

Harley pressed a small purse into his friend's hand and winked, glancing surreptitiously towards his father.

Kasidian smiled back, nodded and swung up onto his own mount. The wagons slowly began to move northwards on the road. Harley thought how awkward his father looked on horseback, not having ever seen him astride a horse when he was growing up.

"Five days to Tranquil Port," said Harley. "I just need to see the Lady Priestess right now and then I'll catch you up. Just a few moments."

He walked over to the cleric's hut and she opened the door just as he was about to rap his knuckles upon it.

"I have a donation for your temple," he said.

She held out a silver platter and he placed a small pouch onto it. She bowed in gratitude; Harley gave his appreciation for her hard work in looking after his father and walked away, a wry smile on his face.

...ooOoo...

Reverend Catilla, the Priestess of Cahuhl, moved her aching jaw from side to side. Her hand reached for the left side of her cheek and gingerly felt just beneath the left cheekbone. There was definitely something not quite right; her jaw clicked as it moved to the left and a lance of pain shot up the side of her face, making her wince. She had looked at her reflection in the horse trough and was sure a bruise was forming. A swelling was forming too. That would need some work along with some intercession from her beloved deity, Cahuhl.

Damn that man, Bratten; or damn the man that he had once been. He had the mind of a child now and he would gradually be retrained to become a more useful member of the village. That would be a challenge that would take time and discipline but from it would spring an income for the temple as she hired him out to carry out simple chores around the village. She would be the one to mete out the discipline when required.

She reached for the silver platter and fumbled opened the purse, spilling its contents out onto her left hand. She fully expected to see a few copper coins and, if lucky, one or more silver coins. She gasped in surprise as a pile of gold coins, easily distinguishable from silver, and six precious gems spread across her palm. She paused to regain her breath. This was a fortune indeed.

She offered a short prayer to her deity and lifted her hand, now closed around the coins and gems, to her forehead. Cahuhl had answered every one of her hopes and prayers. This fortune would pay for the rebuilding of the temple and more besides.

She counted the coins slowly, hardly believing what she had. Twelve gold coins. The gems surely must be worth a hundred gold or more. The High Priest would be passing through any day now on his three-monthly circuit and she could discuss it with him and mayhap exchange the gems for gold and silver coins. But he would demand the majority of the money for the great Temple in Nasteed, in the neighbouring country of Shordrun. It would be better served here. But few were the people, even wealthy merchants and traders, who would deal in gems. Gold and silver were the preferred currency. Copper coins were used mostly by the deprived and unfortunate, beggars and vagrants. A journey to the city of Westron Seaport was needed, either by her or a trustworthy friend. But who?

As for Bratten, there was possibly another use for which he could be put. She would look into this the next time she stripped him down for washing. She wasn't so old that she didn't have needs of her own.

...o o O o o...

It was another four days before Harley, riding with his father and Kasidian, met with a group coming towards them from the north. Harley spurred his mount forwards to intercept them before they approached too close to the wagons.

"Hail, stranger," cried the lead rider. "Do you wish to speak?"

"Well met. Am I addressing the leader of a travelling troupe of performers?"

The rider laughed. "I am not the leader of this merry band of entertainers, you will need to speak with another. Is there anything I can assist you with?"

"I have been asked to pass on a message of greetings from one person in the fair city of Westron Seaport."

The rider, dressed in a brightly-coloured doublet over tight-fitting yellow hose, turned in his saddle and called out a name. A man dropped down from a small wagon and strode forwards to Harley.

"Greetings, young stranger. I am Boulaye, the leader of this band of nuisance-makers. How may I help you?"

Harley eased his mount across to meet the man. He leaned forward so as to lower his voice. "I bring a word of greeting from the *Commander*. He sends his kindest regards and requests that I join you on the journey to Westron Seaport."

"The Commander, eh? And where did you meet this man?"

Harley had expected probing questions and was prepared. "In a building of the finest quality, full of formality, art, fine decorations and the best food and wine that may be found anywhere in the Home Territories."

"How would a visitor address this man?" asked Boulaye, his lip curling with a smile full of cheek and mirth.

"Your Excellency applies to this man although in private he is less formal."

"And who was your personal manservant?"

Damn, what is his name? "Oh, aye, that was Arfan."

"A good man to know, especially if you want some extra company during the dark hours! Not that I do, of course, on account that I have a wife who attends to all my needs."

Harley laughed. "I am told that you bring a miscreant with you," he added.

"In a cage, trussed up, locked up and arse-up! Are you leading us in though the city?"

"Aye, Goodman Boulaye. The, er, package is to be delivered straight to the watch-house of the previously-mentioned fine building."

"Boulaye, just call me Boulaye. And never call me by my given name."

Harley looked puzzled. "What is it?"

Boulaye looked slyly and wagged a finger at Harley. "Aha, haha!"

Harley stopped talking as the wagons, with his father and Kasidian, drew close. The three of them bade fond farewells.

"I shall look in on you all one day," called Harley as Leage and Kasidian turned their mounts after the wagons.

...o o O o o...

Chapter 7

The return to Westron Seaport was uneventful with very few of the Company of performers talking with him. The twelve members either rode on horseback or on one if the four wagons loaded with their performance equipment. The rearmost wagon, however, carried something more sinister. The occupant of the cage that it carried slept throughout the daytime but during the night it was awake assailing the ears of the company with the foulest language that Harley had ever heard.

The rider who had first welcomed Harley introduced himself as Gandar and would speak with Harley about the journeys that the Company undertook and the peoples they met.

"We are making our way down to the southern lands, young 'un," he explained. "We give performances and the people throw coims our way. It is a grand life. Oh, my brother, Undar, is the one who drives the rear wagon."

Another member of the travelling troupe who spoke with him from time to time was a woman by the name of Olwetta Makkadan, a tall, Barbarian woman with long blond hair in thick braids and breathtaking features. Harley noticed immediately that she walked with a dignified air notwithstanding her athletic physique.

The Company entered the city after a week of riding. Harley led Undar's wagon, with Gandar as escort, to the East Gate of the city palace.

...o o O o o...

Harley answered a knock on his chamber door. He had

just had time to change out of his travelling clothes and into the Palace tabard and hose. He hoped to look in on the bath-house where, by all accounts, he would be able to relax in hot water while being bathed by the Palace bathers. This sounded like a wonderful experience. *Would they be naked like me? Would I disgrace myself by, well –*

The manservant, Arfan, stood outside his door. "His Excellency requires that you attend to him in his quarters, sir. Would you please follow me?"

Harley took the time to strap on his sword belt and straighten his lengthening hair. It felt filthy.

"Harley!" boomed the *Commander*. "Welcome. Sit with us at the table."

With him was Boulaye.

"Good afternoon, sir, er, Commander," said Harley. He pulled a chair, wincing as it screeched across the floor.

The *Commander* pulled his chair and, to Harley's relief, it created a similar noise on the polished wooden floor. For some strange reason, Boulaye's chair was almost silent as he half-lifted it away from the dark-oak table.

In the centre of the tables were platters filled with fruits, bread, cheeses and meat. Flagons filled with wine and mead, with pewter tankards were placed to one end of the table. Harley offered to fill them for the Commander and Boulaye.

"I am pleased you have already met," started the Commander. "You shall be seeing much of each other from now on. Harley, as you know, Boulaye here is the leader of the travelling group of entertainers. What do you call yourselves at the moment, Boulaye?"

"We are the Blue Sky Spectacular Company, at present, Commander."

"You travel under a new name each time I see you.

Is this a ruse?"

"A subterfuge, Commander, that allows us to travel about and makes it difficult for others to trace our movements. This is especially so, when we leave behind certain changes to the landscape. There are many travelling groups but we consider ourselves to be better than most and no worse than the best."

The Commander grsticulated while chewing a morsel of cheese. "Umm, Boulaye, tell Harley how you travel with your troupe and how you operate within it."

Boulaye wiped the froth of his ale from his mouth and leaned across the table towards Harley.

"I keep my true purpose separate from the rest of my troupe, even from my wife although I am certain one other in the Company has her suspicions. Harley, I am the eyes and ears for the Commander but the troupe has no knowledge of this. Indeed, nobody suspects a jester that sits foolishly juggling and balancing balls on his fingertips, nose and feet, or who falls clumsily off a broken stool. I, young Harley, am a collector of information. I have informants who do not know my identity. I have been far too dextrous for anybody to try following me. The problem is I am getting too old and my joints begin to fail me when I need them the most. It will soon be time for me to hand over the reins to a new jester, a troubadour, a fool!"

"I do hope you are not suggesting I am a fool!" laughed Harley.

"Hah! You come highly recommended, young Harley. I suspect that the Commander has some other purpose for you though."

The Commander leaned forward in his chair as if to emphasise his response.

"He may be given special tasks on my behalf but in essence Harley will carry on, eventually, with your good work, Boulaye. By the way, at the very most, the others in your troupe must only know that he acts as a messenger for the Merchants' Guilds of the City of Westrun Seaport."

"Goes without saying, Commander."

"Yes, yes, of course, Boulaye. But with another in the group, a new face as it were, there are bound to be questions asked."

"I've sorted that one," Boulaye said, with a wink at Harley. "I told 'em earlier that I'm getting a bit long in the tooth for acting the fool and jesting. Throwing myself about starts to get painful and picking myself up off the ground makes me realise just bow many corners my ageing body has got! Another thing, people will ask where these messages are being taken."

The Commander folded his arms and looked up to the ornately-decorated ceiling for a few moments. "Then say that they are taken, by word of mouth to civil and military, or militia, dignitaries. Or say that you are prearranging your vivits to the next town. I don't know; just spin a yarn but make it feasible. Do not say that they are something of a confidential nature."

Boulaye nodded his head. "He will have to learn some special skills," suggested Boulaye. "I would –"

"Hey, just a moment!" interrupted Harly. "I am here you know. I can be a part of this conversation, particularly as it is all about me!"

"What clowning skills do you have?" asked Boulaye.

"Well, er, I can tumble, er somersault, you know what I mean."

Boulaye frowned and rubbed his chin. "Hmm. Can you fall over?"

"What? Can I –? What sort of question is that? Of course I can!"

Boulaye sighed and shook his head. "Nay, lad. I

mean, can you fall over and make it look hilarious? Stagger about, trip over something that is not there and get back up with a straight face? Can you do it without hurting yourself and make it look convincing?"

"You want me to demonstrate that? Right now?"

"Gentlemen," said the Commander, his hands raised. "Perhaps now is not the time. Suffice to say there are tasks for you both to address in preparation for your journey. I would suggest the Blue Sky Spectacular Company makes ready for a long ride to Casparsport quite soon."

"That iniquitous thieves' den!" exclaimed Boulaye.

"Indeed," responded the Commander as he nodded in acquiescence. "But I will also have a mission for Harley to undertake. I will need you, Boulaye, to give him support to aid him in his success. Return in three days, by the midday, and I shall brief you further. You will, however, travel by way of Grappina. Again, there is a mission that may suit the two of you. As I say, back here three days hence."

The Commander rose to his feet and pushed back the chair with his legs. Once again it screeched on the wooden floor. Despite Harley trying to lift some of his chair's weight, he could not prevent the same deafening shriek. As before, Boulaye's chair made barely a sound. *How did he do that?* he thought.

Boulaye spent the next two days coaching Harley in the finer arts of jesting, buffoonery and slapstick entertainment. Harley's specialised abilities benefitted him immensely, much to Boulaye's interest.

During the first evening, Harley had asked Arfan to take him to the Palace tailor. As they entered the workshop, his breath caught in his throat. The tailor, a wonderfully attractive, slender, half-elven female of relatively young years, asked no questions as Harley gave her specific instructions although she did raise an eyebrow. She also gave him a sardonic smile as he went through his list of requirements. Her two, thick braids of brown hair hung down well below her narrow waist.

She took his measurements, taking a little more time than he might have considered necessary. He could feel his face flushing and his heartbeat quickening as her arms encircled him or probed into his armpits. When the back of her hand reached towards his croth to measure the length of his inner leg, he felt his knees weaken. She gave a little giggle.

Is she teasing me? he pondered.

He specified his requirements and asked for two costumes to be fashioned.

"In two days, at midday, I shall bring them to your chamber to see if they fit well," she said. "You can try them on while I am there so I can make any changes."

"Is there a cost?"

"None. You said want all black for the second one; are you sure?"

"Aye, black but not shiny. And strong; hard-wearing. No pockets except for the long one in the right leg."

The young woman gave a slight nod and a mischievous grin. "For your very special weapon?"

Harley felt himself blushing even more. "What? Er, aye."

She gave a little giggle at his discomfort. "We shall have to see how well it fits then, won't we?"

Harley had intended to ask Arfan to collect the costumes but now he would not have to. *It could be interesting though!*

"Mid – midday then," he stammered. He hoped another, more physical, reaction to his predicament was not too obvious.

"I'm looking forward to it," she replied with a

demure smile. "I am Trenisse, by the way."

Harley almost stumbled out of the tailor's chambers, colliding with the half-open door as he did so. *Damn it! I am acting like a humiliated juvenile. What must she be thinking?* He heard a little chuckle from behind him as he closed the door and couldn't resist raising a little smirk despite his acute embarrassment.

...ooOoo...

He found the buffoonery more difficult than he had imagined. It was not that easy to stagger about while pulling an idiotic expression; falling about in an exaggerated fashion caused him to sustain many bruises but Boulaye, in between fits of laughter, showed him how to fall practically and without injury.

"You are a natural clown, young Harley. With your face painted, your costume and this new talent, you will fit in well with the troupe while they are performing their own special skills. You need to use your voice a little more; a shriek here, a long moan or cry of anguish. Lay it on thick for it will entertain children and grown-ups alike."

At midday on the third day, Harley waited in his chamber. His door was a little open, intentionally. His heart leapt when he heard a soft knock. He called for the visitor to enter; Trenisse stepped in with two rolls of clothing under her arm.

"Your costumes," she said. "You need to try them on."

He dithered a little and she giggled. Its sound reminded him of a tinkling stream.

"Yes, you need to take your other clothes off to put these on. Do not be shy, I shall turn away if you really prefer."

He didn't reply but just began to remove his tunic

92

and hose. She didn't avert her eyes.

It was early evening when he woke up. Trenisse' head lay on his shoulder; her long braids across his chest. He eased his leg a little and she reached an arm across his shoulders. He couldn't resist gently stroking the side of her face.

Her large dark eyes opened. "You want more?" she purred. "You are insatiable."

He didn't know what the word meant but supposed it was something good. Another hour passed before Trenisse finally left his chamber. She stood outside his door for a while, her heart beating furiously. She then walked down the corridor with a contented smile with the hope that he would soon invite her back. *If he were a few years older,* she thought.

...ooOoo...

Harley was exhausted. By the gods, she had been so energetic! *She is one that I would like to see again!*

He looked at his costumes. One, a fairly tight-fitting, multi-coloured costume would be his performing clothes. With it was a stiff face-mask of the same colours and pattern. The leggings, however, were loose-fitting to give the impression of fluid movement as he sailed through the air while performing the long, graceful tumbles. He had white footwear, soft ankle-length boots which suited the costume perfectly.

His other costume was similar in design. The difference, however, was that instead of being a two-piece outfit, as was the former, this was a one-piece, full-length attire with tighter leggings. It had no open pockets that would have snagged on protrusions and obstacles. There was a long, narrow pocket however, that would take his sheathed dagger so that it would be completely concealed. Another set of small pockets on the inside of the costume leggings, would take other small objects that he might need. This costume also had a full-face mask which had been moulded to his features from a piece of leather. It was completely black, fitted with a tightly-fitting hood which could be tightened with a draw-string and would be finished off with his pair of soft, black boots.

He tried both costumes on once more, wincing as he dragged them across bruises he had taken while practising with Boulaye. He nodded with satisfaction. Each would be perfectly suited to his needs.

He was ready.

...ooOoo...

"What do you know of the city of Grappina?"

Harley had been shown in to the Commander's inner sanctum. This was a chamber he knew of but would never have expected to be given admittance to. The Commander had risen to his feet as soon as Arfan opened the door to let Harley in.

Another figure, that of a tall, dark-haired woman, opulently dressed, sat at a large table upon which were scattered scrolls, parchments, quills and bottles of ink. Another item, as large as a family meat loaf, sat in the centre of the table, wrapped in a midnight blue, shimmering cloth, probably silk.

He looked at the Commander, then at the woman, half expecting an introduction. None came. He looked at the woman or rather, he tried to. Oddly, he couldn't discern her features. He blinked and tried to focus. It was if she were covered with flowing water with her face constantly rippling with tiny waves.

"Er, very little, sir. I gather it is a lawless city frequented by outlaws, adventurers, slavers and, I believe, a great many pirates."

The Commander turned to face the woman.

"You are quite correct to some extent," she said. "But that was its reputation in days past. There has been rule of law to some extent and it improved year by year. I placed my own adventuring group in there a few years back to recruit and train a force of disciplined watchmen and thereby reduce that lawlessness. They succeeded and a temporary peace force patrolled the entire city while a City Watch was recruited and trained."

Similar to her features, Harley had difficulty in focussing on her voice. It seemed distant, with a faint distortion. He felt slightly uncomfortable in her presence.

The woman leaned back in her chair and looked up to the Commander. He continued the discourse.

"As with any force providing law and protection, there is corruption. Reports reached this citadel a year ago of random tolls and taxes being imposed on traders and merchants. There had been beatings and some people thrown in gaol until they, or their families or colleagues, paid these tolls. You are correct about the pirates; I also believe that the City Watch is either ineffective in curtailing their activities or may even be involved with them. I sent in an agent to investigate the top tiers of the City Watch. This was six months ago. I have had no word from him at all and I fear the worst. In essence, Harley, I need you, with Boulaye's advice and assistance, to try to find my agent or look into what happened to him, to carry on where he left off, to eliminate the root, at its highest level, of any corruption in whichever way you consider the most expedient and then to quietly leave the city."

"Aye, sir," replied Harley. "It seems simple in the idea. I shall send reports as often as I may."

"It is a challenging mission for your first time,

Harley. I have a small scroll with the name and description of my missing agent, a contact who will pass messages back to me and the names of the three senior officers of the Watch. They will be your primary targets for observation. Boulaye knows a little of your mission but not the final act; he would probably not approve. Do you have any questions?"

Harley felt breathless with the excitement and the apprehension of this, his first mission.

"I expect I shall have many questions sir, but these will come after I have left the city and am on the way to Grappina."

The lady laughed; a light sound that made Harley catch his breath.

The Commander gave a wry grin. "Boulaye and the company will be on the road sometime after dawn tomorrow. They will meet with you at the South Gate at sunrise. Take utmost care, young man. Rely on your wits and remember your training. Do you still practice?"

"Every day, sir. Without fail."

The lady rose to her feet, dipped her head at Harley and smiled at the Commander. She left through a small door hidden behind a tapestry at the back of the chamber.

Harley gave a quizzical look at the Commander.

"I cannot identify her to you, Harley. She is a Magelord of Westron Seaport and is personally tied to this undertaking of yours. Suffice to say that success in this venture will likely net you more favours, if you know what I mean, than you will probably have ever seen but you will earn them at great risk to yourself and perhaps the others you travel with. Boulaye holds your working money with which you may buy what necessities you need as well as the comfort of inns. I believe that travelling companies like the Blue Sky

Spectacular Company like to live comfortably when they can. Take care, young Harley. Travel well."

"Thank you Commander. Farewell."

...ooOoo...

Harley felt excited but not without some anxiety. He now had the advantage of a long road journey to get to know the company. The ride into Westron Seaport with them had not really given him that opportunity, partly because of the state of the road and the constant fatigue of the troupe members. Boulaye had introduced Harley to each member of the company, saying that Harley would be joining them in the near future. This raised a few eyebrows and more than one suspicious glance. Harley had shrugged it off and kept himself to himself for the remainder of the journey, speaking only with Gandar Bakaril and his brother Undar, the statuesque barbarian Olwetta Makkadan and, of course, Boulaye.

This morning, the troupe had set up a small circular arena just outside the City's South Gate. A ring of gaily-coloured flags on poles marked the area. Two Halflings, a male and female, were practicing acrobatic somersaults and tumbling while, to one side, a pair of muscular barbarians each lifted an anvil up to shoulder height. Harley remembered that one, the massive male, was called Ragdan Makkadan, the spouse of Olwetta. Despite her well-defined muscles, Harley found her incredibly attractive although she towered over him by a full foot and a little more. It had been the two Halflings, though, who had given him suspicious glances during that ride. The pair placed the anvils on the ground and approached each other.

Harley watched as Olwetta placed her hands in those of her kneeling husband and kicked her legs behind her. She inverted herself into a hand-stand position and Ragdan rose to his feet while lifting Olwetta above him at full stretch. His muscles bulged as he gritted his teeth. They remained in this position for a few moments before Olwetta swung back down to the ground.

A few onlooking travellers applauded at the display and Harley joined in.

Ragdan smiled mirthlessly and walked over to Harley. "Ah, you are Harley. What will you bring to the company, young man?"

"I am not as skilled as you and your wife," replied Harley. "I can do a few silly tumbles but Boulaye has coached me on the wondrous joys of being the buffoon. At other times I shall act as a guard and escort while we travel, a particular skill that I have been endowed with so I am informed."

"I hope your informant was himself reliably informed."

Harley was tempted to retort but Olwetta spoke from the arena. "Will that little sword be adequate for the task?"

"I believe so. It has a capable master of that you may be sure."

"Perhaps we should see," said a voice from behind him.

Harley turned. The owner of the voice gave him a warm smile. It was Gandar, the brother of Undar the fire-eater. Harley had got on with Gandar quite well during the trip to Westron Seaport.

"Perhaps we may get the opportunity during our travels," Harley replied. "Although I hope not."

"Then perhaps we may practice together in the evenings."

"Aye, that would be of benefit to us both."

Gandar walked away and started packing away the flags. Olwetta approached Harley.

"You need to know that Gandar has set his cap towards Tishia," she said quietly. "He can be very possessive although Tishia has yet to respond to his advances. I believe she will soon although she shows little sign at the moment. Tishia can be a tease and she may make advances to you to make Gandar jealous. It happened once before, in Northwald City. Gandar beat the poor young man to a pulp. I had to step in to save the boy's life for Gandar would have killed him. Boulaye said that if it happened again he would cast Gandar from the company, and Tishia too although she is his wife's sister."

"Thank you," said Harley. "I shall take care. It would be a shame to lose anyone from the company."

"That is good. Somebody else has taken quite a shine to you though."

"Really? Who?"

Olwetta laughed, a deep resonating, almost masculine chuckle. "Ah, no doubt you shall see, Harley, in time. Do not fear, it is not one of the males in our group."

"I am gratified to hear it," laughed Harley. *There is only one lady it can be, the little mage that rarely speaks. I cannot even remember her name. She hides her face under her hood; I have not seen her face. Rett, or something. I shall ask Gandar.*

Gandar and Jetti, Boulaye's spouse, rode in soon after and chivvied the company to make ready.

"Load up, my lovelies," roared Gandar. "Time to make way!"

Four brightly-painted covered wagons, each one pulled by two heavy horses and driven by one of the women, began to trundle towards the great Trade Road from the South Gate of the city of Westron Seaport. Ahead of them was a long Journey to the city of Grappina. Although the roads were generally busy, attacks by brigands were not unusual on the smaller caravans. These days, smaller groups of travellers, traders and merchants banded together for mutual protection, often picking up stragglers on the way. In the Home Territories, forts and fortified trading posts were situated every few miles and armed militia patrolled the Trade Road and the adjacent areas. However, all caravans took liability for their own protection very seriously.

Olwetta and Ragdan, the barbarian couple, wore breastplates and helms and carried huge weapons, greatswords and battleaxes. They rode at the vanguard of the caravan, causing oncoming travellers to baulk at the sight of them. The remaining males of the company acted as outriders with Gandar Bakaril riding loosely back and forth to advise where necessary.

Harley had asked Gandar for the name of the quiet girl on the wagon.

"Treat her gently, lad," Gandar had replied. "I believe she has suffered tragedy and she speaks rarely to us. But she is worth her weight in gold for the added protection she can give us."

Riette Seawind, the little mage, hid her face partially beneath her hood and blushed each time that Harley approached her. She spoke quietly in response to his questions, offering little about herself. She drove the second wagon, occasionally reading from a large leather-bound tome, often murmuring as though performing some verse or poem.

It took three or four days for Harley to win Riette's confidence so that he could speak easily with her. At the campfire one evening, she inadvertently pulled back her hood and Harley quickly suppressed a gasp as he saw the scars of a vicious burn on her left cheek. He decided immediately not to mention it. The time might come when she would speak of it.

"Did I tell you about my days fishing in the village stream?" he asked her late one evening, long after the late meal. The company had stopped close to a way station but no accommodation had been available. They had set up camp in a small area at the edge of a little forest.

"No, tell me," she answered. "What went wrong?"

"What makes you think something went wrong?" he replied with a hurt expression.

She laughed, hiding her mouth behind her hand. "In all your stories, everything goes wrong."

"Well, this day, me and a friend went fishing. All we had was a long pole and my Papa lent me a length of fishing line and a fishbone as a hook. We were after this great big carp, you see, and nobody could catch it. It was far too canny and had survived many attempts for years. We were determined to get it. I swung out the line and all looked good and what do you think happened next?"

"I don't know. Er, the fish jumped up and bit you?" She giggled.

"No; that happened the next time."

Riette laughed. "What then?"

"I caught a duck!"

"What?" she exclaimed, laughing almost uncontrollably.

"Aye, it made a fearful noise and tore the rod out of my hands and dumped it in the river. I couldn't even catch that duck because it flew off and never came back. I had to jump into the river to retrieve the rod and the line because papa would have taken my hide off if I lost it."

"What happened then?"

"Papa took the hide off me anyway because I came home soaked and covered is stinking river weed. I couldn't win!"

101

"You are so funny, Harley."

"Have you got any stories from your days?"

The mirth faded and she turned her head to one side. "No, nothing like yours. I love your stories. Have you got any brothers or sisters?"

Harley was quiet for a few seconds. Riette suddenly wondered whether she had said something wrong.

"I have one sister, Hanni, a little younger than me. She is a newly fledged Priestess of Haeman. She had a twin but she died. Her name was Natti. I shall tell you about it sometime; I cannot right now."

Riette placed a hand on top of his. "Oh, Harley. I am so sorry. Have I upset you? Are you angry with me?"

"No Riette, I cannot be angry with you. I do not think I could ever be angry with you. You are so, er, sweet."

"I can be nasty when I want to be. Look."

She screwed up her face and stuck out her tongue. Harley giggled and turned his hand to hold hers.

"Do you call that nasty? That wasn't a nasty face. It was far too, er, beautiful to be nasty."

She abandoned the expression. Harley laughed again.

"I am not beautiful," she said. "I will never be that."

"Aye, you are. Anyway, get that look back on your face. I prefer it as it was," he said with a mischievous grin.

She punched him on his arm but didn't release the grip on his hand. She was instantly surprised at the rigidity of the muscles beneath the sleeves of his tunic.

"I like you, master Harley," she said, her face almost scarlet and she turned her head to one side. "I shouldn't say that, should I?"

"Yes you should," he replied quietly. "I am pleased that you said that." *It is something to build on anyway,* he considered quietly.

She kissed him on the cheek. "I must sleep and you are on watch soon."

"Aye, lass. More tomorrow. Sleep well. I shall keep a special watch over you."

Riette smiled at him, rose to her feet and walked over to her bedroll. As she closed her eyes her thoughts immediately turned to the young man. His confidence and strength of character appealed to her. She had watched him training with the long, light sword and was astounded at the speed at which he made it move; the precision at which it sliced through an acorn thrown by Gandar. She felt her heart race as she remembered the taut muscles in his arm and wondered if she would ever be able to experience that moment again. Perhaps next time he would kiss her, but only on the cheek. Nothing else; not yet. She was not ready and wondered if she ever would be. She was ugly and would never know love. But Harley was different. Her thoughts made her feel warm but then other thoughts followed which gave her icy fingers of fear down her spine. *No, not yet.* She pushed those thoughts from her mind and soon fell asleep and as such was unaware of the snake that slowly slithered its way beneath her thick blanket.

...o o O o o...

Chapter 8

"You have discovered who it was that had her eye on you, Harley."

Harley had watched the young mage intently as she returned to her bedroll. He was a little perturbed that she kept herself so far from the fire. Most of the others either slept inside or under their wagons or next to the fire, not only for warmth but so that creatures kept their distance during the night.

Harley rose and approached Olwetta, the tall, very attractive barbarian woman. As usual, she showed a cautious stance as Harley approached, relaxing only when he called his name to warn her of his approach.

"Aye, Lady Olwetta. That I have."

She laughed at his comment. He had called her by that name a couple of times, firstly because he had heard her spouse say it and secondly, because he recognised something about her that emanated a high-born radiance. Her commanding presence exuded authority and he was certain that he had seen Ragdan give a slight bow when he approached her.

"You are the only person who has made her laugh so freely in this company," she said. "She is shy and I believe there is something that troubles her. Take my advice and give her time to know you well before going further. I am not sure at all about the troubles she has but she has woken in the night with very bad dreams. Something evil has traumatised her."

"I shall take every precaution with her, Lady Olwetta, and be content just to be her friend. If, one day, she gives me a sign that she wants to progress with our friendship, I shall be watchful."

"You have a wise head on your –"

A piercing scream split the night.

...o o **O** o o...

"Riette!" cried Harley and Olwetta in unison.

Figures leapt in the darkness from wagons and bedrolls and the sounds of weapons being drawn accompanied the calls for explanation.

They rushed to Riette's bedside in time to see the banded snake slink away from beneath the blanket. Olwetta slammed her fist down on the snake's head, crushing it to a pulp. The long body squirmed and coiled for a few heartbeats and Harley threw it away into the nearby bushes.

"She has been bitten, I am certain," hissed Olwetta.

Jetti Boulaye appeared from the darkness and pitched her healers' case onto the ground.

"Find the bite wound, now!" she commanded.

The other members of the company gathered around, some with weapons drawn. "Step back and give some air," Boulaye growled.

"I have a remedy that may help," cried Harley. "It is something I was given by my master in the training school."

He felt an elbow in his ribs from Boulaye. Immediately, Harley realised he had said too much but he rummaged in his leather belt pack and brought out a familiar phial, handing it to Jetti. She raised a quizzical eyebrow but said nothing. Riette was screaming with agony as the poison made itself felt and she groped for her lower leg.

"Here," cried Olwetta. "Above the right ankle."

"Tie a belt around the leg, above the knee," commanded Jetti. "Make it very tight. Hopefully the poison has not travelled far. How do we use this, Harley?"

"Pour half of it on the wound and get her to drink the rest with water."

105

Somebody handed a small knife to Jetti. "No, no!" she yelled. "That will do more harm than good. It will allow the poison to get in more blood vessels. The poison has to be squeezed out by hand, taking with it as much poisoned blood as we can. Would you do this, Harley? Start from the knee and squeeze down towards the wound. Squeeze hard, mind."

There were tears in his eyes as Harley pressed and wrung at the leg. He was amazed at the way the blood flowed out at first but it soon slowed. Riette continued to yell with the pain.

"Keep doing it until I tell you to stop," Jetti ordered.

For what seemed a long while, Harley continued to expel the blood from Riette's leg until sweat began to run down his face and back. Soon, Riette responded only to each of Harley's squeezing actions and no more blood flowed.

"Release the belt, now," said Jetti. "Stop working Harley and pour over some of your fluid. Slowly, very slowly now."

Harley scraped of the wax coating from the neck of the phial and bit at the hard cork stopper. He dripped some of the pungent liquid directly onto the wound.

"That is good," said Jetti. "The clean blood will take some of it around the body. A cup, somebody, with water?"

Gandar handed a cup to Harley who added the remaining fluid from the phial into the water.

"Drink it, lovely girl," whispered Harley. "Drink it all. I want my new friend to be well by the morning."

In the light from the campfire, Harley saw her eyes look into his. Tears had been streaming from her eyes. He put one arm around her shoulder and half-lifted her, ignoring the snot that had run down her upper lip. Slowly, her trembling hands lifted the cup to her lips. She took one mouthful and almost gagged.

"That tastes like you got it from the back-end of a horse!" she gasped. "No more."

"I shall be very upset with you if you don't," he responded. "All of it, quickly now, and you will not notice it. Do not waste it for it is the only one I have. I will never be able to afford another were I to live for a hundred years."

She gulped the rest down and he used his hand to remove the snot from her face. She tried to shake him off, albeit half-heartedly.

"Time for her to sleep," said Jetti. "Carry her to the first wagon, Harley. I shall watch over her this night."

Harley continued his watch until an hour after midnight. He roused Bajari Lightfoot, the quiet Halfling. Bajari looked at the moon and stars and shook his head.

"You should have woken me an hour ago, young 'un."

"I am not tired and only now feel ready to rest."

"You are keen on her, are you not?"

"She is fast becoming a good friend. Is it that obvious?"

"Aye, lad. As obvious as singing it aloud to thousands," laughed Bajari. "Go and sleep. She will be well. After all, you have saved her life this day."

Harley lay in his bed but he hardly slept. What little sleep he did have was filled with scenes of snakes, sometimes covering him and at others, covering Riette. One nightmare saw his sister, Natti, drowning in the waves and covered with great, writhing snakes. He awoke bathed in sweat and slept no more. He rose from his blanket and strode over to speak with wwhoever was on watch. It was Ragdan.

"Good morning, young hero," whispered the barbarian. "You did well. She will probably have died had you not worked so hard."

"Well met, Ragdan. Nay, I do not feel like a hero. I am just relieved that she will live."

Harley and Ragdan spoke until dawn. Boulaye and Solarin Fleet, the Halfling bard, complained that they had not been called for their turn to take watch. Jetti came over to them saying that Riette was well although complaining of stomach cramps. Her lower leg had swelled but was not burning with a feverish infection. She would ride in a wagon and sleep when she needed to. Jetti asked if Harley would drive the wagon but he replied saying that he knew not how to. Solarin Fleet offered to do that instead owing to the fact that his ageing posterior was ill-suited to horseback and the saddle chafed his meagrely upholstered rump.

...ooOoo...

After another day of travel, the Company arrived at a walled trading post in the late afternoon. It boasted a number of tented huts each with a wooden floor and double-tiered cots. Two of these huts were available for the troupe to use. The operators of the post stated that with the number of patrons staying at the trading post, the company could sleep at no cost provided they put on a show that night. Boulaye spoke with the others who enthusiastically agreed.

It was to be Harley's first performance as the troupe's buffoon. He had dressed in his new gaudily-coloured harlequin costume, complete with the mask and had never felt so nervous. More than once he tripped or collided with obstacles quite by accident but it fitted so well with his act that the crowd roared with laughter.

Riette's act was a little different however. For the children she performed cantrips, these being little spells with dancing lights and coloured bubbles that would burst with a *pop*! She kept glancing across at Harley, somewhat surprised at his athletic physique. In fact, on one occasion she seemed so distracted that her cantrip, glowing bluebirds flying in circles, faded to nothing much to the puzzlement of the children.

After the performance, Boulaye came up to Harley with a beaming smile on his face.

"Well done, Harley. You were outstanding. You have certainly earned a place in this Company."

"I thought I had done badly," answered Harley. "I could not see through my mask properly and kept tripping over things and bumping into the others."

"It was hilarious," yelled Tinnisse Lightfoot, Balari's Halfling spouse. "You tripped over me just as I was about to juggle the ox-bones and then Balari threw me his bone and it bounced off my head. I could not stop laughing. It still hurts though. I have a lump here. Feel it."

She indicated a place on the top of her head. Harley touched it gingerly.

She jumped. "Ouch!"

Harley began to apologise and Tinnisse laughed. Balari, her husband, roared with laughter.

"She jests with you, Harley," he called. "She jests with the jester!"

Harley gave a look of mock anguish and began to laugh. Tinnisse and Balari strode away.

Olwetta stepped over and bent down to speak in Harley's ear. "Someone is waiting to talk to you," she whispered and pointed to the other side of the arena.

Harley crossed over to Riette, waved and gave her a broad smile.

"How are you, lovely girl?"

"Am I forever to remind you that I am not lovely? I am much improved thanks to you, Harley. They tell me that I might have died if you had not given me that treatment and forced the poison out of my leg."

"It was not just me, you know. Jetti took control. It was she more than me."

She smiled at him. "You are just being modest. I do not know how to thank you."

"Ah, that will be easy." *Oh, how lovely was that smile.*

"Oh," she answered, her face losing the smile and replacing it with a look somewhere between disappointment and fear. Harley caught the look immediately.

"Aye. Just give me that beautiful smile every time you look at me and I shall be happy thereafter. Nothing more. That will be payment in full. . And I must retell, you *are* lovely so let us hear no more about it!"

She smiled broadly again. "You are a good friend to me, Harley," she said, softly. "Others would have asked for something more and that is something I cannot give just yet. Not yet. I am sorry."

"Lovely girl, There is nothing for you to be sorry for. I ask for nothing from you that you would not want to give. Just to have you as a good friend. And that smile; oh, and that nasty face you pulled yester-eve. It is the perfect you!"

"Hahaha! You are such a fool, Harley the harlequin. Oh! Is that where your name comes from? Or is that a mere coincidence?" She reached out and held his hand. Hers was warm, gentle and soft.

"Just a coincidence. Nothing more than that. I have been called Harley since I don't know when. Another story for another day, lovely girl."

"You have many stories, Harley. I hope one day you will feel you can tell me them all. I will speak to you one day of my past, too, but I cannot just yet. We are two poor souls together, are we not? But I think you may well be the one who I will be able to pour out my heart too. I love you calling me by that name."

Harley moved around to stand in front of her, gently pulled her close and held her for a very long time. She put her head on his shoulder. When he finally released her she stood on tip-toes and kissed him briefly on the lips.

He smiled as she leaned back on the straw bale.

"Did I ever tell you the story about how we sent a wagon train in the wrong direction?" he asked.

She laughed. "Another mishap?"

"As it turned out, aye, it was," he replied. "We were just youngsters, me and my friend Arash. Long merchant trains of ox-drawn wagons would come through our village. Even at night. The oxen would just keep moving in a straight line while the drivers and merchants slept on the wagons."

"I think I know where this story is going," laughed Riette.

"Well, it was like this. Me and Arash figured out that if the front wagon went a different way then the others would follow. So we thought we would give it a go. We waited at the village crossroads after midnight and along came this train of wagons. We led the lead oxen to turn left instead of going right and, sure enough, all the wagons went down the hill and onto the beach. Luckily they stopped before they reached the middle of the ocean."

Riette looked horrified. "What happened? Did you follow them?"

"Are you mad? Nay. We ran for it back to our homes. Apparently, it took all day to get the wagons off the sand where they had bogged down. The merchants were in a fearful choler too. The good thing was that me and Arash, and a few more of the village lads, got a silver coin each for helping untangle all the oxes. What a mess. It was chaos."

"Did you not get into trouble?" asked Riette. The horrified expression had given way to a grin and then a laugh.

"Papa suspected that I had something to do with it. Me and Arash wanted to do it again but the drivers were always awake during the night after that when they came to our village. By the time things got back to normal I left for the city to learn my new trade. Arash promised he would do it again and let me know how he got on."

"And did he?" asked Riette.

"Nay. I have heard nothing from him since I left. I do know he is apprenticed to my father."

"That is rather sad," she responded. Then her eyes opened wide and she put a hand to her mouth. "Nay, not that he is apprenticed, but because you haven't heard from him."

"I was probably where he could not find me. I shall tell you all about it sometime soon."

"Good, I hope so," she whispered. "I am tired. I must sleep or collapse here and my leg is painful. Will you walk me to my tent?"

He took her hand in his arm and led her across to her tent. It was not far.

"Sleep well, lovely girl."

"And you, master Harley." Then she was gone. Harley strode away, his mind whirling.

He walked over to the corner of a corral and leaned against the post.

"You are playing that to perfection, Harley," said a hushed voice behind him.

Harley whirled about. Olwetta stood a few yards away, arm in arm with Ragdan. "I am pleased for both you and her. All of us in the company have seen that the two are close friends. She values you as someone she can trust, you know."

112

"Has it really been that obvious? Aye, I think perhaps it has. I am pleased because I feel the same for her. I am somewhat confused for it is something I am not used to. You are quite correct that she has a, er, difficulty. She admitted to it without saying what it is. Perhaps she will tell me one day. I will not press her nor will I pressure her for anything else. You know, Lady Olwetta, for the first time ever, I feel that there is someone worth waiting for. No matter how long it takes."

Ragdan had laughed at Harley's use of the term *Lady Olwetta*. The pair of barbarians turned and strode towards their wagon. Obviously, the cots in the tents would have been to small for them.

Harley was asleep as soon as his head hit the straw paliasse.

...ooOoo...

Chapter 9

The company travelled further southward for many days. The roads improved and the days became warmer. What breeze there was kicked the dust from the roads and into their mouths, noses and eyes. The landscape changed too. The countryside was a little more barren with wide areas of bare hillsides with occasional lone trees that looked to Harley like flat canopies. There were few farms except for some smallholdings close to the way-stations.

"It is the *umbrella tree*," said Ragdan. He had noticed Harley looking at the surrounding landscape. "My lady tells me that some large deer-like creatures will feed from its bark. Its real name is acacia. Far to the south there are huge beasts, twice the height of me. They have great tusks that grow from their mouths and long noses that they use as arms. They feed from trees too, pulling down branches and pushing them straight into their mouths. Those are the *munina-kamba* acacia trees, with massive, long branches. That bark is supposed to be able to treat your stomach if you suffer from severe shits and the people there have skin burnt black by the sun. They use the branches of the *kamba* tree for firewood and to build cattle sheds. That is a very strange land in the far south. You see, my lady teaches me much."

Harley turned in the saddle and looked back at Ragdan. "You are indeed a fortunate man," he said. "By what name is that great beast known?"

"Aye, Harley. I am privileged indeed. As for the beast, I know not."

Water was not so plentiful and was increasingly expensive to buy from the trading posts and settlements. Of course, lack of fresh, flowing water meant that there was little game for hunting and fresh meat was scarce.

"It is always the same in these parts," Boulaye had explained. "We spend more money than we earn. In two weeks, perhaps a little more, we pass an area of salt and freshwater marshes. We will be plagued by midges and worse for three days, probably. Those are the Grappin Marshes that give the name to the city we are travelling to."

Harley was quiet for a while as he rode next to Boulaye. Then he turned in his saddle to look at Riette behind him. She had recovered completely from the snake's bite and had been driving the wagon for two weeks.

Boulaye chuckled gently. "She is still there, Harley. She has not ridden off. When will you tell her '*I love you, Riette. I love you*!'?" His last words were uttered in a high falsetto voice that made Harley cringe. He shifted in the saddle and felt his cheeks redden.

"When I know she will accept it from me," he replied.

"Grab life by the balls, young man. She may be wondering why you haven't yet. She may think you are not interested and may fall in love with another. Or perhaps she will think you have other preferences."

"What? Hey, no! Do you think so?" Harley looked horrified.

"Hahaha! No, dear boy. I do not! But you should, you know. You may be surprised at her response."

"Or disappointed," murmured Harley, a crestfallen expression on his face.

"To business, Harley. I am to assist you in Grappina but it is to be you that makes the request and gives me the information so that I can be of help. Ah, look ahead. Graban Hills. We shall be stopping here this evening."

A large fortified way-station lay to the west-side of

the road. They tagged on to the end of another group of wagons that was queuing to gain entry to the stockade.

Harley looked behind him once again. Riette smiled coyly and gave a little wave. He said "Boulaye, I have a message from the Commander that I must study, then I should like to discuss that with you. Perhaps, in a couple of days?"

"Aye, lad," replied Boulaye. "When you are ready. Remember what I say about the young lady."

...o o O o o...

The way-station was situated on a rise that would give the occupants, or defenders, a commanding view over the local area. As they drew nearer they could clearly see that it was a well-defended, oblong-shaped fortress encircled by a thick, wooden rampart that was constructed of upright logs with sharpened points built on raised earthworks. A wooden tower in each corner provided the watch with vantage points. Two concentric, deep ditches surrounded the earthworks inside which were wickedly-sharp poles sticking out of the inner slopes of each of the ditches. The single gate was reached by a narrow causeway with a bridge over the outer ditch and a drawbridge over the inner.

The Blue Sky Spectacular Company approached the Graban Hills Way Station. Smoke from cooking fires inside the way station curled thinly into the sky until higher breezes wafted them away. Burly and heavily-armed mercenaries guarded the ramparts and gates.

"Goods here are dearly bought," advised Boulaye. "Not to mention, of course, the costly toll for entry to the way-station and the toll for using the road just to pass by it. Apparently, it pays for the protection we get."

"The mercenaries must be well paid," mused

Harley.

"Or the money goes into the coffer of the rogue who runs it," replied Boulaye. "His name is Hanuta. Rumour has it that he was once a very nasty individual but everyone likes a rumour, do they not?" Harley grinned in response.

It seemed to take ages for the queue to pass through but eventually their wagons and horses trundled onto the drawbridge. Boulaye stated that they required staying for two days in order to replenish food and water and rest themselves and the horses and mules. The two guards insisted on searching some of the crates carried on the wagons and looked suspiciously at the array of weapons carried by the members of the Company.

"We travel the length and breadth of the Landsdrop Coast," boomed Boulaye in an exaggerated manner, "Generally unescorted. We must protect ourselves at all times."

"Keep your weapons stowed while you are inside this station. We do not tolerate swords being drawn and arrows readied within the confines of these walls. We shall be watching you."

Boulaye scowled, turned in his saddle without a word and led the company through the gates. A station guide, a young lad of probably thirteen summers or so, led them to an area of the courtyard and they started to make camp.

Boulaye was seething as they dismounted and started uloading their tents and crates. "Sixty gold crowns it has cost us to stay here. Scandalous!"

Gandar took their mules and horses to a small corral allocated specifically for them and handed them over to a young lad who rubbed his chin and used a string of beads to count the fee.

"Two days, four mules and ten mounts. Goin' ter

cost yer fifty-six gold to be paid in at the trading office," he said.

Gandar shook his head in shocked disbelief and strode over to Boulaye. The latter erupted with barely-restrained fury. "Outrageous!" he exclaimed as he stamped away.

Harley looked around. He was determined to talk with Riette. He would have to tell her how he felt for he was now concerned that he would lose her otherwise. He ambled over to the wagon she had been driving and found her perusing her leather-bound book. He cleared his throat and she looked up at him. The scars on her cheek were quite plain to see but still his heart leapt as her eyes met his. His throat was suddenly dry and his palms felt damp. She rose to her feet.

He took a deep breath. "R–Riette," he stammered. "Um, I need to, er, I want to tell you something."

Her gaze momentarily flicked past him. Without warning, her hand came up to her face and she gasped with shock. Harley took an involuntary step backwards.

"It's him!" she whispered. "Bastard!" She sunk down to the ground and her hands grasped at the sand and rubble. Her breathing became laboured.

"What? Who?" he gasped.

Harley dropped to his knees and gently held Riette's shoulders. "What is it?" he asked.

She seemed to withdraw into herself and then suddenly she began to sob. It was a while before she began to breathe properly. She shook her head and pulled her hood forward.

"I am sorry. You wanted to tell me something, Harley?"

"Aye, but it can wait for now. What came over you? You looked as though you had seen a ghost, or worse."

She paused as if considering her next words. "Worse, believe me," she whispered. "Perhaps I should tell you my story. But I want to hear yours first."

"Mine? Oh, um, that's straightforward enough. I just wanted to tell you that, er, well, to say that I, um, I love you, Riette." A new confidence surged through him as he finally made the admission. "I really do. But I will understand if you think I've gone too far and if you think I am being silly, or something."

With the tears that had streaked through the dust on her face, she looked almost comical. Harley had no cloth with which to dab her tears away. He felt awkward, helpless.

She took a deep breath and released it. Harley felt apprehensive and a little embarrassed, thoroughly believing he had made a complete fool of himself.

Her voice caught and she cleared her throat. "Well, Harley," she began and then sniffed. With a nervous and quavering voice she responded. "Buy why? My face – it looks terrible!"

"Not to me it doesn't. I mean it, you know."

"I have been waiting for you to say that for days but I didn't think you would want to. Now to my business. Can we go somewhere a bit quiet? I do not really want anyone else listening in."

Many travellers and merchants were setting up their camps in the courtyard and there was a lot of noise. Harley led her by the hand to a spot towards the rear ramparts.

"I have not told anyone else about my past, Harley," she began, haltingly. "It hurts. I lived with my parents and older sisters in a village to the south of the Home Territories. It all ended when a large band of bandits raided our village for food and slaves just before winter came. It was getting dark and they came with fire and murder in their hearts. My father joined with the menfolk to fight them off but they were not enough. When the gang finished them off they came looking for

119

the women. I was little and my mother hid me under the tool shed."

Riette began to cry, sobbing.

Harley held her close. He could feel the heat from her face on his and the wetness of her tears as they dripped down his own cheek. "You do not need to say more, lovely girl," he whispered.

She sniffed again and wiped her sleeve across he face. She coughed and continued. "Then, they found mother. The leader pushed her on the ground and –"

She sniffed again. "Then my sisters came at them with farm tools. One of the gang had a sickle through his throat and mother was covered in his blood. Then the bastards killed them; my sisters and then my mother, right there. They killed them, Harley. Then they burned the village. The leader laughed all the time. He had a scar across his forehead; it was a vivid red. They did not find me. But the tool shed burned and I was burnt too. But they did not find me because I did not scream. I was lucky because they rode out and then I could scream, and scream, and scream." She sobbed again, her eyes closed as if she were in a nightmare. "But I had seen their leader's face and I have searched for it ever since. I saw it again just now, when you began to talk to me. He is here, Harley, the leader with the scar. He is up there by the blockhouse."

"By the gods!" exclaimed Harley. He released Riette and she leaned away from him.

...o o O o o...

"I have been looking for you."

Riette's breathing had become ragged, erratic, and her hands shook violently as she once more scraped up grit with her fingertips. Harley reached for her but she held back. They both looked up as Olwetta strode up to them, looking beautiful, powerful, imposing. And deadly.

"What is wrong, Riette? Harley?" Her expression was a mixture of concern and suspicion as she towered over them.

Riette said nothing but kept her head bowed down.

Harley asked of Riette "May I tell her?"

"Tell me what," said Olwetta, her face creased by a frown.

Riette nodded slowly then lifted her head. "Nobody else, not yet, Harley. I do not think I am ready at this time."

Olwetta stooped down but then adopted a cross-legged sitting position. She placed a hand over Riette's fidgeting hands.

Harley recounted Riette's tragic story and ended saying that she had seen that leader in this very way-station.

...o o O o o...

He was a wealthy man and he had used much of that wealth in buying this way-station from its aging owner. It had been subjected to regular raids by a myriad of foes. Mostly, these were gangs of deserters, insurgents from neighbouring lands, and even Kobolds, small dog-like bipeds that would kill much larger humanoids simple by overwhelming them. The fortress had been badly in need of repair at that time; he had his own gang and he had a plan.

Many years of raiding in the Home Territories had forced the Lords of Westron Seaport to raise an army to root out the trouble and end the slaughter. The raids came to an end but those that had caused them then moved south.

With his new-found wealth and his new name,

Hanuta, he began to rebuild the Graban Hills way-station. This would cost a lot of money but he would soon claw it all back – from tolls for those using the road or fees for those using the facilities. In six years he had built up the business of the way-station.

The only problem he had was that damned scar across his forehead. This had been the result of a skirmish with a village sentry. Despite his eyes being bathed in his own blood, he had ensured that the sentry had died slowly. After procuring the way-station, Hanuta had sought the services of the best healers in an attempt to expunge the scar, all to no avail. The damage had been caused too long ago for even divine healing to be effective. The severe-looking redness of the scar did fade, however.

Today, he was pleased to see the influx of travellers coming into the way-station. The income would be most welcome. Most welcome indeed. There was even a Company of travelling performers that would provide some interesting entertainment. They had passed through here before and were damned good.

He now had a taste for flamboyance. His clothing, although functional, was ostentatious. His boots were the best that he could buy in Grappina, a few days' ride away. His sword-belt, with its scabbard, was beautifully engraved with woodland animals. His sword was decorated with silver and gold filigree. These items had been incredibly expensive and he had been reliably informed that they had once been owned by a long-dead king. He thought that was a sack of cack! A leather bag full of precious gems hung constantly from his belt. This appealed to his arrogance and vanity.

Hanuta was a heavily-built man but his one-time muscular physique had become flabby through laziness and strong liquor. He had not been able to wear his armour for three years because of the flab that now sat around his body; it was high time that he addressed this crisis. He could still wield his sword with skill nevertheless. He wore a trimmed beard and kept his blond hair quite short.

The sun had almost set on this profitable day and his guards were now setting the torches alight in the courtyard. As expected, the performers were beginning their show. The laughter of the onlookers trickled in through his open window. He paced over to the great oak table and picked up his goblet of wine. He took a long draught and replaced the goblet next to the half-empty bottle.

Two minutes later he emitted a pitiful wail of pain and anguish. He raised his arms up to his head and dropped to his knees. Saliva dribbled from his mouth and he descended into a world of confusion and madness from which there could be no return. The leather bag had mysteriously disappeared.

...o o O o o...

Chapter 10

A hush descended on the activities in the courtyard. The pathetic cry froze everybody in mid-motion. The two Halflings, Tinnisse and Balari Lightfoot, were balancing, one atop the other. Tinnisse tumbled to the ground but landed harmlessly. Way-station guards ran to the blockhouse, yelling for assistance.

Boulaye strolled over to the group. "Something is going on in the blockhouse. Are we all here?" he asked. He glanced about him as if counting heads. "Where is Harley?"

"I am here," Harley replied. Olwetta looked at him with a raised eyebrow. Harley gave an almost imperceptible nod and she returned a faint, wry smile.

A guard came out of the blockhouse door and called for a cleric. An elderly man dressed in a threadbare robe walked over, leaning on a staff.

"The overseer has taken ill. We cannot understand what has become of him. He burbles like a new-born infant. Would you help?"

The cleric nodded and went inside, bidding the guard to follow him.

"Hanuta is ailing, by the looks of it," said Olwetta.

Before long, the cleric exited followed by the guard.

"I have already told you, I can do nothing," insisted the cleric assertively. "His mind has gone. He will not be able to feed himself, dress himself or clean himself. It is now up to yourselves to decide what will become of him."

The guard shrugged his shoulders and walked away.

"He'll have his throat cut and be buried before this night is out," muttered Boulaye to whoever would be listening. "I suggest we close down and get some rest. We shall keep a watch this night. Gandar, I shall leave those arrangements to you."

The Company cleared away the equipment and settled down. Harley, Riette, Olwetta and her husband, Ragdan, sat together on bales of straw. Riette sat beside Harley and gripped his arm, an act that did not escape Olwetta's attention.

"How did you do it, Harley," she asked. "Hanuta. It was you, was it not?"

He looked alarmingly at Ragdan.

"I have told him the very basics," she whispered.

"Lady Olwetta," responded Harley. "What makes you think I had anything to do with this?"

She gave a knowing wink and smiled at him. "Own up, Harley. We are not stupid. It will go no further and it seems like he has been given just punishment."

"I added a substance to his wine. It was intended to cause his mind to imagine visions of terror. I may have put in a little too much."

Ragdan leaned forward. "How did you manage to gain entry, unseen, into his chamber? He has been in there all day."

"I was very quiet!"

Olwetta put a hand on Harley's arm. "There is more to you than meets the eye, young man. We shall speak of this to no other person and shall mention it no more. Sleep well."

Olwetta and Ragdan rose up and walked away arm-in-arm. Riette shivered. Harley placed his arm around her shoulders.

"Thank you Harley."

"You were chilled, it is the least I could do."

"No, I mean thank you for what you did to that monster. I have wanted to find him for a few years but had no plan of what to do once I discovered him."

...ooOoo...

During the night, Harley was still awake. The memory of the kiss that Riette and he had shared before they went to their tents stayed with him for ages. Suddenly, he was alerted by a dull sound, a soft thud. He held his breath and focussed his senses. There it was again. A careless footfall. Then a door banging shut and footsteps on a wooden platform. He faintly heard hushed voices and a *sushing* noise.

He climbed up from his blankets onto all fours and moved over to the tent flap. He shifted it slightly to one side and peeked out.

In the dim light from the braziers he discerned three figures struggling with a large object between them. He had no doubt at all as to exactly what that object was.

The small group disappeared from his view as they made their way towards the main gate. He returned to his bed and, with all thoughts of Riette out of his mind, for a while, was soon asleep.

...ooOoo...

Harley awoke in the early morning, just after dawn. People were moving about and some travellers and merchants were beginning to prepare to move out. He hadn't slept well, not because of his drugging of Hanuta, whom he knew to have been a murderous rogue, but because of the callous way in which the dead man's own men had seemed to despatch the wretched man. Harley crawled out of his tent and rose to his feet. Yawning, he arched his aching back and stretched his arms. Boulaye was already up.

He asked Harley whether or not he had been involved in the activity the previous evening.

"Aye, Boulaye. I was involved. There was a rightful reason for it."

"Harley, I trust to your judgement. Do you want to

126

talk about it?"

"I shall do but I cannot right now, better when we are clear of this place."

"Any other person from our Company involved?"

Harley looked him straight in the eye as he answered. "No other person from our group was involved in this act, I swear it. I shall speak with you when I can but now is not the time."

"I am putting my faith in you, lad. I hope there will be no repercussions from the action. Did you take anything out from his chambers?"

"Aye, a bag of gems. It is hidden but I shall give it to you for the benefit of the Company once we leave here."

Boulaye nodded and clapped Harley on the shoulder. "That is well. Come, my young friend, we have our practising to do. Will you be training with Gandar, Olwetta and Ragdan again today?"

"Aye, that is the plan."

"Then we had best inform the way-station authorities. I wonder what has become of Hanuta."

"I think I may know," Harley said quietly. He wanted to make sure that he would not be overheard.

The pair wandered over to the straw bales where Harley had sat last night with Riette and Olwetta. They lowered themselves down and he told Boulaye of the movement he had seen during the night. Boulaye thought quietly for a while.

"If the large object was Hanuta," he said, "then I expect there has been a change of management this morning. We may have to tread carefully but I daresay that with so many travellers here, we are unlikely to be at any risk. Let us speak with the administrator."

They strode over to the blockhouse. On entering through the main doorway, they approached a long table but there was nobody in attendance. They could hear a lot of movement of people and furnishings from the upper storey and some shouted commands or instructions.

"Sounds like they are searching for something," whispered Harley. "If it is what I think it is then they won't find 'em."

"I would think that unlikely; it is probable that they don't even know of their existence. We had better announce our presence."

Harley yelled "Hello!" Almost immediately a guard thundered down some stairs and ran into the official's chamber.

"What do you want?" he asked, clearly agitated.

Boulaye replied. "We just wanted to let you know that we will be doing a bit of swordplay this morning."

"Well, just get on with it then. Er, let the wall sentries know. Is that all?"

"Aye, that is all. Oh, we are just curious, how is Goodman Hanuta today? Is he recovering?"

"Er, aye, he is. Er, we took him to Grappina during the night. Someone will be caring for him there. If there is nothing else, I have work to do." He tramped away without waiting for another word.

Boulaye and Harley left and returned to their camp.

On the way, Harley said "I think I was correct in my assumption; they finished off Hanuta and are now looking for the gems."

"I think we should rally the company and keep a watch through the day and night and be on our way as soon as we can in the morning. Time for our morning feast. Come on."

...ooOoo...

Harley had sat outside in the group of tents for a short while during the early hours of the morning. Individual guards patrolled the courtyard and seemed to him to be more interested in the wagons and containers belonging to the Company and the other travellers than in the security of the way-station. Other guards maintained watch on the surrounding areas from their vantage points in the four watch-towers.

Undar Bakaril, their sword-swallowing and fire-eating performer, woke them all just before dawn. They prepared to leave so that they could be on the road as the sun began to rise. They would eat their morning meal once they had cleared the way-station.

They had not even begun to pull away when raised voices showed that the main gate was locked and a large group of mercenary guards, all armed to the teeth, was barking orders at the three travelling groups in front of the Company. They promptly commenced searching every trader's wagon and pack-horse as the travellers made ready to leave. Goods were unceremoniously piled or scattered on the ground. The merchants and traders were protesting heatedly, their arms waving in disapproval, but with no effect.

They had been queuing for almost an hour by the time the Company was in position to have their baggage and wagons searched.

An angry Boulaye yelled at the leader. "What is the purpose of this intrusion? How dare you treat us in this way?"

"We dare!" barked the man who was apparently the leader. "Items of great value have been stolen from the Master's chambers. We are searching everyone so you will have to wait until we have finished. Only when we have completed our search of your baggage can you go, unless, of course – "

"Unless what?" boomed Boulay.

"Unless we find what was taken in your wagons or chests."

"I shall report your behaviour to the authorities in Grappina!"

"Hah! What authorities? There is no law in Grappina that has juris – jurisdiction here!"

Despite a thorough search through the wagons, crates and baggage, and with even their clothing and belongings scattered on the ground, the mercenaries found nothing. There were questions asked when some items were considered dubious.

The company was finally allowed to leave.

It was a mile or two before Boulaye chuckled.

Gandar asked "What is funny about that? You were all worked-up and furious."

"That was an act, my friend. If we had stood by and said nothing, they would have been even more suspicious and may have ripped everything apart. That might have been catastrophic."

Gandar gave a puzzled look but rode away without further comment.

A little while later Boulaye pulled Harley aside. "Hey, young man," he whispered. "Tell me, what did you do with them?"

"With what?"

"Dammit, Harley, you know what I mean. The gods-damned bag of gems!"

Harley grinned and winked. "Ah, now that is a tale to tell. I have left it behind me. I shall show you when we next stop."

"For your cheek, Harley, you may ride back and inform all that we shall stop in the mid-day for a break. We cross a wide ford, if my memory serves me correctly, and once we have done with that it will be a good opportunity to eat."

. . o o O o o . . .

PART 3
MISSION

Chapter 11

"Hahaha, I see what you mean by a *tale to tell*; you have *left it behind you*!"

The river was wide where it crossed the Trade Road and, being at the foot of a valley, it was quite heavily forested.

The fording had been more difficult than Boulaye had envisaged. One wagon, that which was driven by the two Halfings, had wallowed in the fast-flowing water when the horse had stumbled on the river bed. Two crates had torn loose, one of which had tumbled into the river. Ragdan and Gandar had retrieved it with some effort. The Company stopped on the far bank to secure the wagon and its freight.

Harley led Boulaye to his horse and lifted its tail. He parted the tail hair. Tied with thin thongs deep within the soiled tail hairs was the leather purse. Harley handed it to Boulaye who threw his head back with gales of laughter.

"I would never have thought of hiding it there. It shall be divided equally between us, if you are happy with that."

"Aye. It will make each of us quite wealthy, I would imagine. I have never seen such a fortune."

"Right now Hanuta's men will be tearing the Graban Hills way-station apart looking for that treasure. They had already started during the night once they had gotten rid of Hanuta. If they fail to find it, they may decide to come looking for us, maybe the other travellers too. Whether they do or not, it would not surprise me if we find the way-station under new management when we come back this way. If they do come after us then we had better be ready. I do suggest we keep a watch behind us. Do you fancy the job for a day or two?"

"Aye, I can do that. I'll stay on foot and travel light. I just want to talk with Riette for a few minutes and then I'll hang back."

"Then I shall get Gandar to accompany you. Four eyes will be better than two."

By now, many of the other members of the Company had begun gathering around them to see what was causing the hubbub between Boulaye and Harley.

"My friends," cried Boulaye. "I suggest we keep a watch open for our safety. I have reason to believe the thugs from the way-station will be looking for trouble. They said we had taken something of value from the recently-demised Hanuta. Well, we now know that Hanuta and his brutes have had a history of violence. The man's death was no accident. The item of value they seek will be used to put right some of the wrongs that they have perpetrated. This is that item."

He pulled out the leather pouch; it still carried some of the soiling from its recent hiding place.

He continued. "If you believe we should hand this over to those ruffians then perhaps we should. Please say so."

There was some shuffling and muted discussion while the Company considered this proposal.

"Nay. We keep it," called a voice. Balari Lightfoot, the Halfling tumbler stepped forward with his wife, Tinnisse, beside him.

"Aye, he's right," cried Ragdan, the barbarian strongman.

The call was taken up by the entire group except for Riette who remained silent.

Jetti Boulaye, their leader's spouse, stepped over to her husband. "Just how much treasure are we talking about here," she asked.

Boulaye loosened the cord around the neck of the

pouch. The group closed in on him as he tipped the contents onto the palm of his hand. Even he looked shocked as he watched the contents fall from the pouch.

There was a collective gasp as they looked at the pile of precious gems that glittered in his hand.

Undar gave a whistle. "We could take a rest for a year," he whispered, loud enough for them all to hear.

"You will end up drunk in a tavern somewhere," laughed Gandar.

"Aye, with you aside me!" retorted his brother amid laughter from the Company.

Harley watched as Riette slowly stepped away. He turned from the group and went after her.

He softly called her. "Lovely girl?"

She turned to face him, tears rolling down her face.

"Thank you Harley. Now get over here and give me a hug," she said softly.

He held her tightly and moved his head forward to kiss her cheek. She turned her head so her lips met his.

A few heartbeats later they heard Boulaye's voice. "Come on, you two. We have to move out. It's two days' ride to Grappina and this is a dangerous road. You and Gandar have a task to do, Harley."

Riette pulled away from him sharply. "What task?"

"I'll be keeping a watch behind us. If we see anything coming we'll rush back here and let the company know so we can defend ourselves."

"It sounds dangerous. Take care and come back safely to me."

"I will, beautiful girl. I promise."

Boulay held out a pack of arrows which Harley took with a nod of gratitude.

Harley and Riette kissed once again and, armed with his precious rapier and longbow, Harley trotted back towards the ford where Gandar was waiting.

"I love you Harley," she called out.

He stopped, turned and waved back with a boyish smile. Then he turned back and was gone from view.

... o o O o o ...

Gandar was surprised at how silently and effortlessly Harley moved through the scrub and undergrowth of the forested areas to the eastern side of the road. They trotted out of sight of other travellers on the road as they made their way back towards the high ground. They intended to use the terrain to observe any fast riders who might be pursuing them.

They had jogged for almost half a league uphill and Gandar, carrying his great bow and with his heavy sword thumping against his left thigh, was panting and wheezing with the effort of keeping up with the young man.

They reached the summit although Gandar was a hundred paces behind Harley. He wheezed up to the younger man, dropped his bow and flopped down onto the ground. His face was bathed in sweat.

"Gods dammit, lad. I'm getting too old for this!"

...o o O o o ...

It was now almost midday and the sun beat down remorselessly. They lay unmoving amongst the bracken and undergrowth to watch the road back towards the way-station. The hilltop gave them a commanding view in all directions. They both took off their travelling cloaks and spread them on the ground to lie on.

A league to the south, the direction that the company now ponderously trundled, the river meandered from the east towards the ocean in the west. With his keen eyesight Harley could see the way-station in the distance, almost two leagues to the north.

Unusually, other travellers on the road appeared to be passing by without stopping to rest or replenish, as might have been expected.

"They must have shut the gate," pondered Harley, shading his eyes from the sun as he looked.

"Obviously to allow them to search the buildings for the jewels," offered Gandar. "They won't want interruptions from merchants and traders now, will they?"

Harley turned onto his back with a dried grass stem in his mouth. He spat it out. "Question is, will they just come after us or will they be stopping the other traders too? You know, the ones who were in the queue to leave before us."

"Probably all of 'em," grunted Gandar. "That is if they come at all. But if they do, we are the largest and slowest of them and were the last to leave so they will come onto our Company first."

"For the best then. We should be able to offer some good resistance and not suffer too many injuries if we are prepared and ready. The other traders are ill-prepared to defend themselves."

The sun was powerful as it continued to beat down upon the back of their necks. Buzzards circled high above them, looking for smaller, more manageable prey; their hoarse calls barely audible from their great height. Harley shifted a little and tugged at the corner of his cloak to cover his head and neck. Gandar looked across at him and smiled.

"A damn hot one," he murmured. "Want a drink?"

Harley took the offered flask and took a single gulp, washing the warm water around his mouth to gain the maximum benefit from it.

It was mid-afternoon before anything happened to grab their attention. Harley pointed out the cloud of dust thrown up from the dry road that had appeared by the way-station.

"Riders," muttered Harley. "Coming this way. I cannot tell how many just now but it may be eight or ten judging by the dust cloud. They will probably be upon us before we catch up with the others. I reckon we have half an hour, maybe less."

"Then we must set a trap to slow 'em down," growled Gandar. "Let us get to the ford. Quick now!" He leapt to his feet, grabbing his cloak and bow, and sped off down the hillside.

Harley was just a couple of paces behind him as they reached the ford. A wagon, drawn by two large horses and with three traders sitting on top, had just crossed the river heading north and was painstakingly entering the narrow gulley through which the road passed up the slope. Another small cart, loaded with cabbages and root vegetables, was being driven by a pair of farmers from the south towards the ford. They moved at a snail's pace and were still a couple of hundred yards away from the river.

"Damn! These farmers will be in the gods-damned way if they don't get a move on," grunted Gandar. "We need to stop 'em where they are. Then we need to get into a position of concealment."

Harley wasted no time. Handing his bow and the pack of arrows to Gandar, he sprinted off up the slope towards the approaching farmers. Already tired from tearing down the hill from their vantage point, he puffed and panted the last few yards to the farmers.

"You must stop," he yelled, holding up his hands. The looked suspiciously at him.

One of the famers had stood upright on the cart as Harley had approached and was now wielding a rusty sword.

"What are you about?" he called, somewhat gruffly.

"There is about to be a problem on this crossing.

Some ruffians are robbing travellers and they are coming this way. We shall try to stop them but you must stay clear."

The farmer nodded and sat back down, lowering his sword. Harley nodded to them and tore off back down the road to where Gandar was waiting, somewhat agitated. Harley was sweating profusely as he reached his friend. Gandar had opened the pack of arrows and took half of them, giving the rest to Harley, along with his bow. They took up positions of concealment, Gandar to the left side of the road and Harley to the right. Harley readied some of his arrows, point down in the ground.

The large wagon was moving laboriously up the slope on the opposite side. It was little more than a hundred yards from the ford. Harley saw the group of riders suddenly appear over the crest of the hill about a quarter of a mile away. He quickly counted them. Eleven riders. He made ready his first arrow.

The riders approached the wagon. Curses were shouted by the horsemen at the drovers and they were forced to slow their horse's pace to pass the wagon through the narrow space. One of the drovers, a young, muscle-bound man, stood up to remonstrate with the first rider and was cut down with a sword thrust. He toppled from the wagon and narrowly avoided being trampled by other riders. He struggled to get between the wheels of the wagon.

Harley nodded in satisfaction. This would help with picking them off.

...o o O o o...

The first three riders were now in the middle of the ford. Most of the others had only just entered the ford, the water splashing from the hooves.

Harley loosed his first arrow. He immediately nocked another and loosed that to. Gandar had simultaneously shot his first arrow. Each of them sent arrow after arrow streaking towards the riders.

After many arrows, Harley paused long enough to take stock. Five horsemen had fallen from their mounts and the river clouded red with their blood. Four other riders had been hit. Some mounts had taken arrows and were rearing and screaming in pain and fear. A couple of them bolted downstream. Gandar was still pouring arrows at the riders. Harley and Gandar broke cover and stepped onto the road with bows ready. Three of the riders were galloping back up the slope away from the ambush.

Suddenly Riette appeared in front of them. And another Riette! And more. Harley looked at them in shock. Four images of her stood with staff raised and wand pointed. This had an immediate effect. The horsemen wheeled their mounts around and rode furiously back down the slope towards the ford. They were met with arrow after arrow from Harley and Gandar. One of the horsemen fell, bristling with arrows.

The two remaining riders, both wounded, rode at Harley and Gandar with their swords raised. Both together, Harley and Gandar dropped their bows and withdrew their swords.

The first rider approached Gandar and gave a vicious swing with his blade. Gandar reacted by turning and shoulder-barging the horse. The rider barely managed to stay in the saddle but Gandar gripped the man's tunic and wrenched hard. The rider toppled and fell into the water. Gandar stamped his foot onto the man's sword-arm and placed his hands around the exposed throat.

The other horseman rode straight for Harley, his

mount's hooves churning the water. Unexpectedly, a large eagle swooped in front, causing the horse to rear up and throw its rider. Harley splashed through the water and was upon him immediately, driving the point of his sword through the man's chest. The eagle had gone.

Harley looked across at Gandar. His friend rose up from the water and a body floated away from him. All of the horsemen were dead. Three of their mounts were dead and three others had arrows protruding from them. The others had galloped a short way downstream.

"Riette!" Harley gasped. He called her name again, this time louder. He looked up the slope at the images of Riette but they were all gone, except one. She was grinning at him as she walked down the slope towards him. He sauntered through the water over to her and she rushed into his arms.

"What are you doing here, you sill girl?" Harley gasped. "You might have been killed."

She looked up at him. "I just wanted to help. Some of them may have attacked my village and, well, you know. I said to Boulaye that I would be fine and would stay out of the way. I was hiding when you ran up the road to the farmers on the cart. You didn't see me. I must say that was very exciting but quite tiring. Using spells does that to you sometimes, you know." Her eyes widened. "Are you hurt?"

"Oh, no. That is not my blood; someone else's. I am well. There were so many of you. One of your spells?"

"It was. And the eagle too. I haven't done one of those before. Was it good? That took some concentrating, I can tell you. I needed to stop the riders getting away because we would not want them coming upon us in the dark, would we? And I needed to distract the rider who was coming for you. It is what I can do. Illusions. Good, eh?"

141

"Amazingly good, lovely girl."

Gandar joined them and passed Harley the bow the young man had hurriedly discarded. "Young lady, you probably saved our lives there," he said.

"Really? I did?"

"Aye, you certainly did," replied Harley.

Gandar interrupted. "We should grab some horses and get on back to the Company," he advised.

"We must check the merchant drover," replied Riette.

"He was hit by a sword as the riders came past," stated Harley. "Look, he is climbing back up onto the wagon."

Gandar trotted up the slope towards the drover's wagon. He was relieved to see that the sword-thrust to the drover had struck his belt buckle. The man had suffered little more than a shallow cut to his abdomen. This was hastily patched up by his colleagues.

Harley and Riette searched the bodies. There was little of value except for the weapons. These he gave to the farmers who ponderously trundled down to the ford. The farmers happily helped to move the bodies of the riders away from the road and down the river. Harley turned a blind eye to their removal of boots , belts and other items from the bodies.

Two hours later, Riette, Gandar and Harley rode into the next traders' post. The post was smaller than that at the Graban Hills but was similarly protected. The stockade was set in a square with a wooden rampart mounted on earthworks. The deep ditch that surrounded the earthworks had sharply- pointed wooden stakes pointing outwards in its inner wall.

Boulaye was pacing back and forth outside a hut that he had arranged for the Company for the night. His relief at seeing them unharmed was clearly evident. The others of the Company were also pleased to see them and they crowded around to hear the story.

"I shall pen a song to celebrate your battle," cried Solarin, the Halfling bard. "The three heroes of Graban Hills!"

They put on a show, one of their best ever performances, that night. Harley felt relaxed and jested with the onlookers, acting with tomfoolery. As he expected, Riette laughed at his antics and delighted children with her illusionary tricks.

They returned to their hut. There were no separate chambers. However, Harley and Riette slept together that night, tucked tightly beneath blankets.

...o o O o o...

"Seven leagues," said Boulaye. "We can do it this day if we start early and keep a steady pace."

It was early dawn and the sun had yet to appear above the low hills in the distant east. Dawn seemed late in coming; perhaps they would not see the sun today. Riette's head had been nestled in his left shoulder for most of the night and now he had a numb arm. He gently nudged Riette and she stirred. A few minutes later they joined the others outside. Courteously, nobody had mentioned the fact that Harley and Riette had spent the night together although Tinnisse and Tishia smiled at them both as they made their appearance.

Boulaye continued his address. "Gandar and I shall ride ahead to Grappina and secure lodgings. With luck, we shall have somewhere this coming night. Ragdan will lead the company in my stead. We shall meet outside the city gate at sundown. Travel well. Farewell." He embraced his spouse, Jetti, and kissed her on the cheek. A couple of minutes later they rode out of the gate of the trading post.

The skies were grey and a fresh wind blew through the courtyard of the post. This was a rather refreshing change after so many days of hot and dry weather. However, as the troupe prepared to pull out, dark and heavy clouds amassed on the western horizon. This did not bode well.

"We shall need our rainproof cloaks," bellowed the massive Ragdan. At over seven feet in height and a heavily muscled stature, the Barbarian was an imposing figure. His wife, Olwetta, was just a couple of inches shorter than he, with a breathtaking beauty but with an athletic physique.

Covers were erected over the four wagons to protect the cargoes and drivers. An hour after pulling out through the gate the rain started. It was gentle at first but it gradually grew in ferocity. Balari Lightfoot, the Halfling performer, shouted that it was probably a short squall coming in from the sea.

"This looks like being more than a short squall," yelled Undar after they had progressed barely a mile. He was riding in the saddle in protection of the lead wagon. Already the dray horse was struggling to pull the heavy load through the deep mud. The lead wagon served only to churn the mud, making it all the more difficult for the following wagons.

The driving rain rammed straight into their faces, trickling down inside their tightly-wrapped cloaks and soaking them to the skin.

It was fortunate that the warm climate did not freeze them to the bone. Undar led them into a passing bay where the ground was much firmer. Ragdan stated that they would tarry here until the storm abated. The rain continued to lash down until midday when it ceased almost instantly. Pools of water, often a foot or more deep, lay in the depressions and wheel ruts in the road. It was another two hours before the company resumed their journey, occasionally passing other travellers and merchants who struggled to make their own way.

It was two hours after sundown when the company finally arrived before the single, iron-clad, oak gate into Grappina. They were wet, hungry and totally exhausted. Boulaye and Gandar were waiting anxiously and were very relieved to see them. Although the gate had been shut, a shout from Boulaye to the watchman on the parapet had them opened. He led the wagon into the city.

Although it was now dark, braziers, suspended from tall posts spaced along the narrow streets, provided an adequate amount of light for them to see their way. Despite the lateness of the day, mud and dung-spattered children ran squealing and laughing between the wagons and horses. Many of them begged for coppers, encouraged by their older peers.

They progressed through busy streets but on passing through the Impoverished Quarter which consisted of little more than rough shanties and huts, the reek assailed their nostrils.

"This part of the city is filthy," called Olwetta, holding her cloak across her face. "Do they still have no dung collection? No dungsweepers' guild?"

"Aye, they do, Olwetta," replied Boulaye. "But they probably don't venture into this Quarter, even at night."

Rotting carcasses of dogs, fowl and other animals littered the streets. Putrid fish, meat and vegetation, horse dung and, worst of all, human body waste was ankle-deep in the centre of the road and in the gutters. The smell was overpowering and caused some of them to gag. Riette and Tinnisse barely avoided retching. Faeces and urine, as well as horse and cattle dung, was not unusual in any street, in any town or city, but putrid carcasses were. They had to tolerate this for half a mile before they passed through a gateway in a tall stone wall. The watchmen allowed them to pass through with a nod and on receipt of a handful of coins from Boulaye.

It was with palpable relief that they left the foul stench behind them as they entered the Mercantile Quarter. Olwetta was riding her great warhorse beside her husband on one side and Harley on the other.

"If I ran this damned town," she said, "I would have them clearing the shit from the streets, guild or no guild."

"It is not that easy," replied Ragdan. "They would replace it with new shit and it would always be the same."

Harley scratched at something that was moving about in his hair. He looked at his fingernails but the offending bug was not there. "They would have to change the way they live but I suspect that sort of society will not take change," he said.

"Perhaps," she answered. "I certainly would not allow the watchmen to profit from the passage of travellers. They are corrupt. I wonder if they all are."

Harley nodded and thought about the task he had to undertake while in the city. He was here. This would be his first assignment; his first test.

He hoped it would not be his last.

...o o O o o...

Chapter 12

Boulaye led the company to a large tavern, three storeys in height and with a large corral and stables. The sign hanging in front of it, and the large statue outside the main doorway, identified the establishment as the Silver Raven Inn.

Opposite the tavern was large park with a small circular arena in its centre. This was surrounded by four rows of wooden, tiered seating that was used for public performances, orations, plays and occasional travelling entertainers.

The wagons were led into the corral by Gandar. Astride his horse, he held open the gate as they all filed through. They unhitched the horses and mules from the wagons and, with their mounts, led them into the many stalls in the stable. A burly but pleasant and polite stable attendant stated that their horses, mounts and wagons would be well cared for but at a cost of twelve gold coins per day.

There were gasps of surprise from many in the company but Boulaye said that this was a worthwhile cost.

"But we do not have the gold to pay for ten days of caring for the horses and wagons and the cost of our chambers in the tavern," complained Solarin Fleet, the bard. He was not normally a talker unless he had a crowd of people sitting about him listening to his storytelling and songs of deeds by great heroes.

"We do have more than enough," responded Gandar. "What do you think we came out of Graban Hills way-station with? I intend to convert some of them into cash."

There was much nodding and acquiescence from the Company.

"Besides," added Boulaye, "we deserve good lodgings, food and ale for once. Follow me. Oh, and try not to show surprise when you meet the proprieter of this establishment."

He led the company in through a rear door of the tavern and into a large ante-room. An ornately-dressed, portly Gnome sat at a long table on which were scattered piles of documents and scrolls and a small pewter pitcher of what seemed to be wine or mead. He rose to his feet and introduced himself as Niebelittin Bellpealer. His dark orange skin colouring did not hide the deeply-etched lines of age and the hair that they could see beneath his wide, black, velvet cap was white. Gnomes were uncommon in the lands on the Landsdrop Coast, often venturing no further westwards than the Dragons' Teeth Mountains.

"I am the owner of this establishment," he began, offering his arm to Boulaye for the formal clasp. Harley was watching intently, this being the first time he had set eyes on a Gnome. He was surprised at the firm muscle-structure on Bellpealer's arm.

The Gnome nodded at the other members of the company in turn as Boulaye introduced them all. "Well met. I also serve on the council of this city," he continued. "I am sure that when you travelled through the city to get here, you will have seen the deprivations in the poor quarter. No matter what encouragement we give the people there, it counts for nothing with them. Murder and disease are commonplace there. The city council members are constantly trying to figure out what is best action to take." Bellpealer shook his head in frustration. "We have even considered moving the people out of that Quarter and burning it all to the ground."

Ragdan leaned forward with his hands on the table. "But that would only serve to drive them out into the wilds where they would become bandits. Travellers would not be safe."

"Indeed," agreed Bellpealer. "We could clear the Quarter area by area but in a year it would return to the state it is now. We shall find an answer to it one day."

The innkeeper was very articulately spoken. With his opulent clothing, he had an aristocratic air about him.

"Oh, I also sing ballads and tells stories in the taproom," Bellpealer added. "Providing, of course, I have taken a quart of ale first! Now, before I arrange your chambers, I must tell you that I run this tavern with a set of rules. Note that there is a curfew in this part of the city, the Mercantile Quarter, from midnight until dawn. The tavern doors are closed and locked at midnight although ales will still be available for patrons that stay here. Food is served up till midnight. However, if you are gambling, the tap-room is to be quiet from midnight. There will be no fighting and you should know that troublesome drinkers will be thrown out into the street no matter what the time. No weapons are allowed in the tap-room unless you are walking straight through to the street. No whores from the street are allowed into the tavern but for those with needs we do have willing tavern wenches who are to be treated kindly. The gambling tables are run by my own people so you can be assured that there is no deception. Oh, keep your shutters closed during the night; thieves flouting the curfew are known to creep around this Quarter during the night. There is a bounty paid on thieves who are caught. That is about all."

He stated that he had six available chambers on the topmost storey. "Two have single cots," he said. "The rest have twin cots. Take it or leave it; that is all that is available at the time. There is some space in the stable if there are not enough chambers."

They began to climb the stairs weighed down with their packs, weapons and other equipment.

Boulaye called out to them. "I have already arranged a chamber for Jetti and me. It's at the end of the passage on the right. There is enough room for us all to meet in there in a few minutes. The room opposite is for Olwetta and Ragdan; the beds are more suited to them. The two individual chambers are next to these. The rest are for you pairs. A few minutes, everybody. We have flagons of wine and mead and a huge bowl of oatcakes in Jetti's and my chamber."

There was a murmur of approval at this. The members of the company had eaten little all day and they were hungry.

Olwetta had a mischievous grin on her face: "Who will sleep with whom?"

There was an awkward moment as they realised the number of rooms may be insufficient for many of them to be alone. Harley, red-faced, offered to sleep in the stable.

"I am sure that will not be necessary," said Boulaye. "Foolish lad!"

Riette pouted, folded her arms across her chest and said "The solution is obvious. I shall have to share a room with someone else of course."

Jetti responded. "Ah, of course. Tishia."

Tishia laughed and raised her eyes to the ceiling. "Oh for the gods' sake," she cried. "As much as Tishia and me are good friends, that is not quite what you had in mind, was it Riette?."

There was a silence, but with a few titters, as they all paused on the stairs.

Riette continued. "Do I really have to draw diagrams? Look everybody, I shared a bed last night. We can do the same while we are here! *Can't* we, Harley?"

Harley, his face scarlet, cleared his throat. "Aye, lovely girl. Of course we can. Did you have to make it so obvious?"

There were guffaws of laughter as Undar put his hand on Harley's shoulder. "We all know, lad. Now get on with it and don't keep us awake all night with your chamber activities!"

There were shaking of heads and a collective sigh from the whole Company and murmurs of "Obvious!" from Gandar, "Slow on the uptake, ain't he?" from Balari and "At last he gets the idea!" from a giggling Tishia.

Harley and Riette entered their chamber and closed the door behind them. The windows had shutters and the door had an iron lock with a key. The two cots, a little wider than those usually found in a tavern, were on either side of the chamber and had mattresses which, from the fresh smell, had recently been filled with new straw. Thick blankets were already laid out and fine feather-filled bolsters, such as those that Harley had used during his stay at the Westron Seaport Palace, were at the head of the cots. There was a table holding a water-filled pitcher with a washbowl and two chests, also with locks, at the foot of each cot. From the aroma, the room was well cared for.

Riette lowered her head. "Each of these cots is big enough for the two of us, if you have a mind to share." She blushed and put a hand to her mouth. "Oh, do you think I am being a bit forward?"

Harley: "Nay, lovely girl. Not at all. We are important to each other now, are we not?"

Riette whispered: "I don't think I am really ready to, well, you know. But I would love to be hugged. Is that alright with you?"

Harley smiled and placed his hands on her shoulders: "Of course it is. There is no hurry. I shall not pressure you and I really do love cuddles with you too. Come, lets us go to see what the talk is to be about."

The door to Boulaye's chamber was slightly ajar. Harley knocked softly and Jetti's voice responded with "Enter."

Almost everybody was there and seated. The chamber was large enough to have a great square oak table with many wooden chairs surrounding it. A tray with earthenware cups sat in the centre of the table. Next to it was another tray with four large pewter pitchers. A great bowl, filled with warm oatcakes, had been placed on another little table close by.

Tinnisse and Balari were the last to enter.

Boulaye rose to his feet and outlined the plans for the next few days. "We shall stay here and rest for two days. We can spend another three days practising our skills, perhaps learning new ones. Another day rehearsing our shows and distributing notices of our forthcoming performances. Then come the performances for another few days. We now have an opportunity to make some good money while we are here. I expect us to remain here for ten days at least and then another two days of rest and preparation for our journey to Casparsport, about ten days' ride south from here."

They spent a couple of hours chatting, eating and drinking before going off to their own chambers for the night. As he rose to go, Harley was stopped by Boulaye who whispered to him. "We need to talk in the morning about your plans to carry out your task."

"Aye, we had better. I need to know the city. I will need help with that."

"Just after dawn then, before morning meal. What does Riette know?"

"Absolutely nothing. I will not tell her. I shall have to come up with an excuse to explain my disappearances during the next couple of days. She says she will be spending time in study to improve her spell-knowledge. I need to find an apothecary too."

Boulaye scratched the bristles on his chin. "I shall think of something. Sleep well. Look after Riette, she is very vulnerable."

"Aye, I shall."

...ooOoo...

Just after dawn next morning, the streets below were coming into life. Carts trundled to and fro and a few dogs were barking. Men shouted at each other, exchanging pleasantries or curses, and women yelled at their children. Harley sat up in the cot and placed his hand on Riette's cheek. She stirred and opened her eyes. It had been late indeed when they finally dropped off to sleep.

Harley sat with her at a table in the quiet taproom. It seemed they had been the first to rise from their cot. Boulaye appeared very soon after, with Jetti close behind him.

"Did you both sleep well?" he asked, a glint in his eye.

"Aye, we did, thank you," answered Harley.

"Actually, no," said Riette with a faint smile. "Tell the truth, Harley. We kept each other awake for hours, it seems."

Jetti chuckled and promised "We shall stay quiet about this, won't we Falarr?"

He briefly winced at her use of his given name. "Of course, m'dear." He raised his eyes skywards. "Now, Harley. I need you to do a job for me that will take you away from your beloved for a day, perhaps two."

Riette's eyes widened. "Will it be dangerous?" she asked, crestfallen.

153

Boulaye gave a brief chuckle. "Nay lass. I just need him to ride out of the city and check the next few trading posts or way-stations to see what sort of management they have. We won't want a repeat of the last problem. Just look, Harley. Don't do anything rash."

"Got that," he answered. "I will need a quiet chat with you before I leave though."

A little later, while Riette, Jetti and Tishia were in the taproom chatting and giggling, Harley spoke with Boulaye in his and Riette's chamber. Boulaye suggested that they ask Bellpealer, the proprieter, for advice.

"He is a good man, er, Gnome," corrected Boulaye. "He has a lot of influence in this city. I don't really want him to know what your task is just in case he thinks we are getting in the way of Council business."

They descended the stairs and knocked on the door to the Gnome's chamber, the ante-room where they had met with him the previous evening. The stocky little Gnome was dressed in a crimson velvet cloak richly decorated with gold frogging. A scabbarded slim sabre, befitting his size, hung from his left hip. He carried a small silver mace, a symbol of his official status, tucked into the crimson silk sash that was wound about his waist.

"You have just caught me moments before I leave for the City Meeting Hall," he said. "How can I be of help?"

Boulaye briefly said that he and Harley needed to meet with people, old acquaintances, in the Foot 'n' Mouth Tavern and they either needed directions to find the place or an escort to take them there.

Bellpealer paused and looked up to study Boulaye's face. "I do think there is something that you are not telling me," he said. "I fully understand that corruption exists within the city. This tavern, similar to many other establishments in the Poor Quarter is habitually the haunt of some of the worst of humanity in the city of Grappina. I know the owner. His ale is poor but in that Quarter it is better than the water." He shuddered at the thought.

"The first place," he said. "The Foot 'n' Mouth Tavern is situated on the very edge of the Impoverished Quarter but you can ride around through this part of the city to save getting filthy. Leave your horse in the livery stable on this side of the barrier because in the time you take to speak to the one you seek, your mount will have been taken, cut up, cooked and eaten. Beware the owner of the tavern for he is a bad-tempered dwarf by the name of Koagar. He lost an ear in a riot in his establishment two or three years ago."

Harley glanced over at Boulaye. "Sounds thoroughly unpleasant," he murmured.

Bellpealer nodded in agreement. "If you must go there, do so there looking and acting mean. It will probably result in you getting into a fight but something about you tells me you can handle yourself, young man. It shows in the way you carry yourself. If you finish it quick and clean, your reputation will be assured. Koagar will be impressed. That is when you will want to ask him whatever, or whoever, you are seeking. Just say that you are the brother of the man's woman and he left her penniless and destitute. As a dwarf, Koagar will be angered by that and will be keen to collaborate with you."

"Aye, that sounds like a good idea," said Harley. "What can you tell me of the Brothel of Six Seraphs?"

"Ah, the delightful palace of recumbent bliss!" laughed Bellpealer. "That establishment is one of the few well-operated brothels in this Quarter of the city. It is more than just a whore-house. It is a dance-hall too, with scantily-garbed ladies singing and kicking their legs high. Similarly-dressed girls perform acrobatic tricks high up on suspended ropes and swinging bars, above the tables. The brothel produces some of the best food in the city and their wines are of the highest quality. But you would pay the highest prices for it all. Now, there you would have to dress well otherwise they would not let you in. I go there from time to time. Are you looking for a certain person there too?"

"Aye, I am," Harley answered.

"We cannot say much at this time but may be able to be more forthcoming once we have concluded our business," Boulaye assured him.

"I understand. You do not say it but I suspect the involvement of the Magelords in this matter. It is high time that the tree was shaken in this city such that the rotten apples fall out. If you need any *special* assistance, please come and talk to me."

They took their leave and Harley went up to his room to dress in his most common of clothes. He then walked to the corral. Boulaye followed him out. "Why ride, Harley? Walk to the tavern."

"Nay, it is best to ride if only to show that I have made a long journey. If the others see me without a horse, they will suspect that I have stayed in the city and will be wondering why and where."

"Take care, young man. Come back safely. You know, the whole of the company is pleased about the special friendship between you and Riette. She rarely spoke and hid her face. Now she is open, laughing and chatting to us all. If we hear nothing of you by dusk tomorrow I shall have to consult with Niebelittin Bellpealer."

Harley trotted out of the corral and joined the throng of citizens on the main thoroughfares.

...ooOoo...

It hadn't taken Harley very long before spotting the tavern. It was a low, wooden, single-storey building that probably saw better days forty years ago. Most of its timbers were decaying with gaps between the planks of its walls and roof. There was no glass in its windows, just slatted, wooden shutters, one of which hung at a jaunty angle on one of its two remaining original leather hinges. A burly tough-looking man, probably half-hobgoblin if his appearance was anything to go by, stood as sentry at the front door. He glared at Harley as he approached.

Harley had left his pack of decent clothes with the gate warden as he left the city Quarter. He changed his mind and left his horse there too, taking only his saddlebags with him. It had cost him a silver piece but he considered it worthwhile as it would also secure his return with a pre-arranged spoken keyword. He had left his main weapons at the Silver Raven but carried his dagger on his right hip, another hidden, and had taken the time to sprinkle road dust on his clothing. He smeared some on his face and hands; it might help to convince Koagar that he had only just ridden into the city.

Harley barged past the door sentry who spat an obscenity at his back. Harley ignored it; he may have to leave promptly and would not want another obstacle to deal with.

There were a few drinkers in the taproom. Two were very drunk and were trying to out-brag each other in a corner. He would not be surprised if it turned into a scuffle.

The stench in the taproom was unbelievable. He almost gagged with the stink of stale smoke weed, added with that of stale ale, urine, sweat and vomit. His eyes were watering as he approached the bar and he suppressed a cough with some willpower. He made his way over towards the bar while his eyes adjusted to the murk and the atmosphere.

In the gloom he collided with a chair. Its occupant spun round with a curse and leapt to its feet.

"Bastard! You spilled my beer!" yelled the man. He was tall, lithe and had whipped out a slim dagger, the type an assassin might carry. Harley had one himself; it was strapped to his left forearm.

"Your pot was already empty," growled Harley.

"Hear that everybody?" sneered the man. "This weasel is calling me a liar," he cried.

A few disinterested heads turned round to see what was happening.

"Aye, you're a liar!" replied Harley with a sneer.

The taproom hushed. Even the two drunkards had stopped quarrelling. The lanky individual seemed surprised as Harley, with no drawn weapon, confidently stood his ground.

His companion, a man of advanced years compared to the lanky one, called "Stick him one, Jagg. He's just a scrote."

"Aye, stick me one, Jagg!" prompted Harley, still sneering. "Get to it!" *Scrote indeed!*

The man was in a quandary as he hesitated. His greasy black hair had fallen across one of his eyes and he brushed it aside with his left hand. This was all the distraction Harley needed. Now was the time to make an impression.

He lashed out with his left hand, its edge striking the man's right wrist. The dagger dropped to the filthy floor. He closed his hand around the wrist and twisted, forcing Jagg to lean, off balance, to his right. Harley kicked his right knee hard up to Jagg's left ear and the man slumped to the soiled floor, out cold.

Harley picked up the slim dagger, wiped it on the unconscious man's jerkin and stabbed it, point down, into a table. With a sideways swing of his forearm against the hilt, he snapped the blade. He used the hilt to knock the blade to the floor.

With a derisive look at Jagg, and a huff of satisfaction, Harley turned to face the other drinkers in the tap room. "Who is next?" he growled.

There was a silence and one by one, they turned to look down into their ale pots, the man who had encouraged Jagg amongst them.

"Who are yuh, boy?" a gravelly voice enquired.

Harley turned. Behind the bar stood a Dwarf. His beard was long, thick and greying. It was also matted with grease. His hair was long and similarly filthy.

"I am Tamm DuHan." *Might as well give my original name.*

"Not from this area, are yuh?"

"Nay. Up north."

The dwarf nodded. "Handles yusself good in a fight, boy."

"Aye. He was a fool."

The dwarf seemed to be searching for something to say. "Ale, Tamm DuHan?"

"Aye. But a good 'un."

The bar-keeper glanced around the taproom as if to ensure none of his other patrons was watching, reached below the top of his bar and filled a quart pot. He passed it up to Harley and received a few coppers in return. The dward raised an eyebrow at his visitor's generosity.

"I am called Koagar. I run this shit-hole. I would prefer nice tavern in the clean part of the city but it aren't right for a dwarf there. Nobody come in – har har! But *this* is my shit-hole. Not like the Drunken Urchin Inn on the other side of this Quarter. Ankus

Akalvin is a elf, skin is dark a bit like a Dark One. He is the owner of the Drunken Urchin and we fight sometimes."

Harley listened to this with interest and downed half of the contents his pot. Doing so was out of character for him but unexpectedly, the ale was quite good. He did so intentionally for the effect on Koagar.

"Why yuh come here, boy?"

"I seek someone. A man. A bastard. Searched for two years."

"Uh-huh?" grunted Koagar. He was now showing ardent interest. "What he do?"

"He married my sister, Lotti. Then I heard that he beat her and left her. She was destitute when I found her and she was close to starvation. I got there just short of too late. He has got to pay."

Koagar was visibly angered by Harley's story. "Who is he?" be grunted.

"His name is Rautha Adras. Also known as *the shit!*"

"What yuh do with him when yuh find him?"

Harley gave an evil expression. "Do not ask!"

Koagar grinned. "I only askin' becoss I think I know him. He ain't drunk in here for long time."

Harley glanced around the taproom as if looking for Adras. "Where is he?"

"He were here every night then watchmen came and took him 'way. Months ago. He din't come back."

"Watchmen? Why? What did he do?"

Koagar leaned forward, looked around the taproom again, and spoke softly. "One of 'em said he asking too many questions. That is all I know."

Harley forced a smile despite the feeling of dread that coursed through his gut. "Maybe the watch have done my job or me."

"It was Khargal Tron." Koagar whispered the name

160

is if it were that of the dread God, Killik the Beast Master, himself.

"Who?"

"Khargal Tron. He is Commander of the City Watch and, it is said, Traviss Hartimmer's right-hand man and chief inquisitor. Tron is a hard man. Zheulin was there. A dwarf, though it pains me to the sayin' of it. Spiteful and nasty. He a torturer. You don't care about that Rautha Adras no more. He be dead now. You tell your sister he won't do her no more trouble. What her name?"

"Lotti," replied Harley. "Then all is well. Who is this Traviss Hartimmer?"

"Ah, he is aristocrat. Old family. He look after city watch and the city gaol. You say bad word 'bout how they do things and they do bad things to you. Best keepin' quiet."

Harley nodded. "Now to some drinking!" he announced.

And to planning.

...o o O o o...

Chapter 13

The evening approached and Harley left the Foot 'n' Mouth Inn. He had carefully drunk the ale in a way that gave the impression he was drinking copiously, tipping some out of the adjacent window when attention was diverted elsewhere. Jagg, in a bad way, had been helped out of the tavern by his companion and another man. Harley was careful to watch for a reprisal attack as he made his way back to the gate into the Mercantile Quarter.

The warden was more than happy to allow Harley to use a chamber in the gatehouse to change into his best clothing and clean himself up. Harley passed over the necessary silver piece. He would need to look his best to get into the Brothel of Six Seraphs.

Following the directions given by the gate warden, he easily found the Brothel despite the increasing darkness. He looked up in wonder as he got closer to the building.

Apart from the City Council's Halls, it was probably the grandest building in the Mercantile Quarter. A smartly-dressed stable lad took his horse, after demanding a gold coin. Harley was shocked at the price.

Wide marble steps, with rows of miniature trees on either side, led up to a grand entrance that was framed between two tall pillars carved with the likenesses of elegant women in provocative poses. The two great wooden doors were also carved but with winged angelic figures. *Are these seraphs?* he wondered.

A pair of smartly dressed doormen stood there to welcome, or reject, prospective customers. Fortunately, Harley was welcomed with a smile, mainly resulting from the gold coin he passed to one of them.

Once inside the door he gaped at the opulence. Statues of semi-naked women graced the short hallway and paintings, framed in gold-coloured frames showed fully naked ladies in audacious postures. A deeply-piled red carpet with gold edging covered the hall floor. Ornate sofas lined the walls. The smell of incense filled the air.

A few men, and a couple of scantily-clad ladies, sat on the sofas laughing, drinking wine and chatting. One of the ladies winked at Harley and he smiled in response.

There were four wide doors, each with a pictogram which, he guessed, showed the activities beyond them. Harley paused and studied the first door on the left; it showed piles of coins and gambling tiles.

The girl who had smiled at him glided over to him. She was very pretty indeed but he was somewhat taken aback by the amount of bosom she was displaying. He had to tear his gaze away from her ample cleavage to look up at her face. Very long blond hair, tied with a blue ribbon behind her head, hung to her waist. She was completely unabashed.

"Hello handsome boy," she purred. "I would say that you are new here, right? That door will take you into the gambling hall." She put her right arm through his left and led him to the second door, a dozen paces further along, which showed a bowl, spoon and knife.

"This is the feasting hall. The best food you will ever have had. Can you smell the spices from all over the realms and sauces galore?"

Harley could indeed determine the abundance of glorious smells. However, she led him over to a door on the opposite side of the hall. This showed a bed with tall posts at each corner.

She leaned over to him and nuzzled his ear and giggled. The sound of it was like a delicate waterfall. "I think you can guess what goes on in there," she said.

"Aye. People sleep?"

"Eventually," she replied and giggled again. "The bed-chambers. Now let us go to the last door."

The door at the end of the hall displayed a lute and musical pipes. The sound of people singing a well-known ballad came from beyond the door.

"That is where I work," she said. "I am just a dancer on the stage and will be going to perform after this singing. I do hope to see you in there. We are not busy yet for it is still early. Inside each of these doors is a desk. Just book in there and they will tell you what to do."

She gently placed the palm of her hand on his face, winked and then turned away. She opened the door to the dance hall and passed through, closing the door behind her. *Gods! She smells good*! he thought.

A few more men had arrived at the Brothel. Some went straight through the doors to one or other of the attractions while others sat on the sofas in the hall. Harley remembered from the Commander's scroll that Pretteen was a dancer in the dance hall. He needed to find her and speak to her. He opened the door and entered. He had been so shocked by the effect the girl had had on him on the hallway that he hadn't thought to ask her about Pretteen. *Dammit!*

He stopped at a desk on the left hand side. A heavy dark curtain closed off the dance hall from its entrance. He could hear the ripple of applause from the other side of the curtain. A woman dressed in an ornate violet gown sat behind the desk. She held a short pipe of smoke weed in one hand.

"Hello dear," she said. "You are new face. You are just in time for the dancers. Two gold coins if you please."

He reached into his money purse, withdrew coins

and handed them to the woman.

"Oh, a question for you," he said. "A good friend of mine suggested that I chat for a while with Pretteen. Is she available tonight?"

"Who is this friend of yours, dear?"

"Ah, that is Niebelittin Bellpealer. I know he is a Gnome but he was quite taken by Preteen and recommended her to me. I am staying in his tavern."

"Ah, Cityman Bellpealer; a valued and generous customer. You have already met Pretteen, I think. She was in the hall and came in here a little before you. I am sure that if she wishes to speak with you, or do even more, she will be agreeable. I do request that you make it worth her time, if you comprehend me."

"Aye, ma'am, I do."

The woman smiled, obviously charmed by his politeness. "She and the other dancers will come out into the audience after her dance act. It is customary for people to give them silver coins in appreciation for their dancing. Call her then. In you go, dear."

Harley went through the curtains and stared amazed by the opulence. The well-upholstered chairs were placed around tables. Each table had a small but ornate candlestick with two lit candles in them. One table, at the front but to the left-hand side of the auditorium, was unoccupied but all of the others had two or more men, some with ladies from the establishment. Smoke from pipe smoke-weed hung in the air but it competed with the smell of incense for dominance.

Harley made his way to the table, pulled out a chair and sat down facing the stage. A smartly-dressed man, a flunkey, came over and asked whether he would like something to drink.

"Aye, a wine if you please." He reached for his purse but the man shook his head and said that the first drink was included in the cost of entry.

The wine, in a small jug with a little glass on top of it, appeared just as a row of five girls and three musicians appeared on the stage. The music started and the girls danced in a skilful, energetic and slightly provocative dance routine. A few whistles and catcalls came from some men, a little the worse for the drink but it soon faded.

Harley recognised Pretteen immediately. She was easily the most attractive girl in the group and she gave him a little smile when she glanced over at him. He smiled back in return.

A second dance began after a brief applause. The music was slower and somewhat haunting, designed to arouse emotion from the audience. The dancers moved together in a slow and graceful flow that brought a great ovation at its completion. The dancers and musicians came to the front of the stage and bowed in appreciation. The woman from the entrance desk called out for the audience to show generosity when the dancers came out into the auditorium.

Pretteen came straight over to him. He handed her a few silver coins and she beamed with delight.

"Would you sit with me?" he asked her.

She nodded saying "I must just go through the tables. Won't be long."

In a few moments she returned and took a chair next to Harley. The flunkey appeared and Harley ordered a flagon of wine. That cost him two gold coins. *Outrageous*! It was placed on the table with two small glass tumblers.

"Do you just want to talk?" she asked him, with the hint of suspicion in her face.

"Aye, that is all. Really. But it is very important and I would rather we did not speak here. My name is Harley. I am told yours is Pretteen. Very appropriate, if you don't mind me saying."

"I do not mind at all. I hear it all the time and I do not notice it after a while. Have you got a woman?"

Harley thought about his answer for a moment. He did not want to say too much about Riette; she was too special to him. "Aye, lass. I do. That is why I would just like to talk with you."

She smiled broadly. "That is so nice. Most men who talk to me want a lot more. I don't usually do that – well, I do sometimes. I can get a bed-chamber for the night if you want but it will cost you – "

Harley laughed. "Don't tell me! A gold coin? More?"

She giggled in response, a sweet, tinkling sound. "A lot more if you are taking me with you, even for talking. More like twelve. Two of them will come to me. But you do get the most comfortable beds and you will have morning feast brought to the chamber for the two of us, if I am still with you that is. We can take the wine with us too if you want."

Harley nodded and said "Let us go then, if you are happy to, that is."

She rose to her feet and started towards the way out. Harley grabbed the wine jug in one hand and the glasses in another, and followed close behind her. There were some envious glances from a few men around the tables.

The bed chamber was sumptuous. Two gold-painted chairs, with scarlet upholstery, were arranged beside a mahogany table. The iron-framed bed had silk sheets and velvet blankets and looked incredibly comfortable. A soft, thick-piled carpet covered the floor. Oils and perfumes were placed next to a pitcher and bowl on a stand. This room was far better than any that he had seen before; better even than his chamber at their Magelords' Palace in Westron Seaport.

Harley placed the wine and glasses on the table.

Pretteen sat on the edge of the bed and sank down a little way into the soft mattress. Harley sat on a chair at the table.

"I shan't bite, you know," she said.

Harley smiled but ignored the comment. He took a deep breath. "I am aware of a job you used to carry out for a certain person. Carrying certain messages and leaving them for others to collect."

Her face betrayed shock, then fear, and she raised her hand to her face.

"Do not be alarmed, Pretteen. I am trying to find out what happened to one of the people who left you the messages. Do you know who I am talking about?"

"Rautha Adras," she whispered. "I think Khargal Tron, the City Watch commander and his gaoler, Zheulin, might have taken him. Gods know what they will have done to him."

"Do you know why?"

She seemed to sag on the bed. "Rautha had said that he thought he was being watched and was beginning to worry. I told him I didn't want to know, that it was nothing to do with me so he didn't say any more. He didn't leave any more messages after that."

"Does anyone else leave messages for you to deliver?"

"Michan Garand did until last Yule but I heard that he rode away and never came back. I was scared, Harley. I feared that they would come for me too."

"Pretteen, do you know who it was that collected the messages?"

"Nay. I was told never to stay once I dropped the messages off."

Harley poured some wine into one of the glasses and handed it to Pretteen. She received it and took a large gulp. He poured a little more for himself but placed the glass on the table. He sat next to her on the

168

bed. *Damn, she smells good!*

"Look," he said. "I'm staying here tonight. Please stay here too but I must not let my lady down, although if it was not for that..."

"Enough said, Harley," she replied. "I shall sleep on the other side of the bed."

She was naked when she slipped between the cool silk sheets but Harley was true to his word, despite the temptation. He did not sleep well for a while. He was extremely aware of Pretteen sleeping beside him and the thought at the forefront of his mind was that he needed to find out about the city's gaol.

...o o O o o...

The sun was quite high in the sky when Harley was woken by a polite tap on the door. A flunkey stood there with a large tray.

"What time of day is it?" he asked.

"It is mid-morning, goodsir. It was thought that you might not want to be roused too early."

Morning feast was a wonderful experience for Harley. He lifted the lids off silver containers, discovering meats in aromatic sauces, warm bread, porridge with honey, a mixture of chopped fruits in warm honey and mulled wine.

He shook Pretteen awake and she lifted her head. Her hair was matted on one side. *But she still looks dazzling!*

Pretteen washed and dressed after they had eaten. Harley splashed water on his face and dressed back into his travelling clothes. It was just before midday when he made ready to leave. They stood together in the entrance hall.

"Will you come back, Harley," she asked.

"Perhaps. I am spoken for, remember. But I am

pleased to consider you a friend."

She smiled, kissed him tenderly on the cheek and was gone. Harley left and collected his horse, surprised at the excellent condition of its coat. His saddle had been highly polished and his stirrups were gleaming. That had been a gold coin well spent.

He rode into the corral of the Silver Raven in the early afternoon and immediately went in search of Riette. Boulaye could wait a while, a short while at least.

... o o O o o ...

"No real surprise there, lad. You did well in the Foot 'n' Mouth. And in the, er, other establishment. What did the dancer have to say?"

On arrival at the inn, Harley had searched for the Company only to be told that they were in the park rehearsing and practising in the display arena. He had walked over and Riette ran out to meet him.

"I missed you. You smell nice," she had said.

"I was filthy after the ride and I had a bowl and pitcher of warm water with oils prepared for me. Niebelittin Bellpealer is a great host. I missed you too, lovely girl. You cannot begin to imagine the sacrifices I make by being away from you." *But you are worth it.*

Now though, he stood aside with Boulaye and described the conversation he had had with Koagar, and later with Pretteen.

"I feel I should try to get inside the gaol," he said. "But that is a challenge easier spoken of than done."

Boulaye scratched the stubble on his his chin. "Zheulin and Tron will have a host of city watchmen at their beck and call. But then again, perhaps not."

"What do you mean?" asked Harley, suspiciously.

"What I mean, lad, is that should something happen

170

in the city, the watch may be called out to sort it out. Give me a while to think about it. I may have to involve some of the Company though. Can it wait 'til the morning?"

"Aye, of course."

"In that case, lad, we have a performance to rehearse. You need to polish up your jesting and pratfalls. I have suggested a new routine for you and me. It will require some help from Riette too; distracting the crowd you see. We will be busy 'til sundown."

The new routines were tough and complex. Harley spent much of his involvement in being at the right position on cue. It would be another day before he started putting in his tumbles and trips. Similarly, Riette planned her cantrips such that the attention of the audience would be drawn at the right moments.

By evening, the routine was taking shape. The other members of the troupe had also been busy. Undar and Gandar practised with knife and axe-throwing against thick planks of timber. Tinnisse and her husband, Balari, tried new forms of tightrope walking, tumbling and juggling, often integrating one with another. Ragdan and Olwetta performed new feats of strength with their athletic displays and balancing acts. Jetti and Tishia, with Solarin in tow, took themselves off to Bellpealer's tavern to practice new exotic dances to the bard's music.

After a while, Harley took himself aside and practised sword techniques. He also tried out some unarmed fighting moves although he felt this exercise was incomplete without another person to grapple with. This gave him cause to think. *Perhaps if I spoke with Gandar.*

Niebelittin Bellpealer had set aside a large dining chamber for the company. Ale, mead and wine were provided after the feast. Boulaye rose to his feet with his mug of wine and complimented them on their efforts during the day. He advised them that they would be putting all the individual acts together as a complete performance over the next couple of days. After the evening feast they all retired to their sleeping chambers.

Harley and Riette hugged for ages before the fell asleep locked in each other's arms. They woke during the night. It was an hour later that they drifted off to sleep again, Harley was somewhat pleasantly surprised; Riette had been more insistent than he would have imagined possible, given her earlier misgivings.

...ooOoo...

They continued rehearsing again next morning. Grey clouds covered the sky. This was good because the sun would not burn so much and cause them to sweat; a hazard when carrying out some balancing acts and feats of strength. A performance was now beginning to take shape but Boulaye was a perfectionist and not easy to please. He harangued and chided them all.

"Timing is crucial," he yelled. "You must be professional, look professional and act professional. Think of where we are now. These people of Grappina are not simple folk that we will be performing to." He knew only too well that a handful of hecklers could easily destroy a show not only for that day but probably for the time they were in one place.

Harley had noticed two men lounging beneath a tree. He had not seen them before but they looked incongruous when compared to other citizens who often casually observed the company. For one thing, they were trying to look inconspicuous, hiding in the shadow of a great copper beech. Most other city folk would walk by, stop to observe for a while, applaud politely and then move on.

He moved from one end of the arena to the other. Sure enough, their gazes followed him. *Now I have somebody's attention! Good.* He was thankful that Riette was still in the tavern with the two dancers. He didn't want people watching her too. *She was too vulnerable.* He casually ambled across to Boulaye who was sitting on the low stone wall that surrounded the arena.

Boulaye glanced over to the two figures. "What do you want to do about them?" he asked.

"It may be nothing at all. But I want to follow them to see where they go. I shall quickly go and change my clothes."

He wandered over to one of their wagons and climbed inside. A few minutes later, dressed in plain grey clothing that he hoped would make him virtually unnoticeable, he waited for some traffic to trundle past and he leapt out of the wagon to merge with it. A few more minutes later he had positioned himself behind the watchers. *This is too easy!*

They were noticeably relaxed at first, still watching the wagon on the far side of the arena, but were increasingly agitated when their quarry failed to appear. After a while they began to shift uneasily from one leg to another; they became quarrelsome and then moved away from their vantage point. Harley followed them at a distance.

...ooOoo...

Chapter 14

Sankie was anxious. It was not like Pretteen to let the dancing group down like this. She was their principal lead. She hadn't appeared for their show review this afternoon. Kassa hadn't turned up either. She was another dancer who shared a couple of rooms with Pretteen. That young man was to blame, surely, the lean athletic youth who had come in to talk with Pretteen last night. Hadlee, or some such name; the friend of Niebelittin Bellpealer so he claimed. Well, if Pretteen didn't appear within the next half hour, she would jolly well go over to the Silver Raven and speak with Bellpealer with a couple of their Brothel heavies in tow.

Sankie Meadowroot was the woman who sat at the front desk of the dance hall, collecting the entrance fees from the revellers. Her duties also included announcing the acts and checking attendance of the performers. She had just heard that a troupe of travelling performers had arrived at the town. This would not be good for her business but, no doubt, they would be gone in a few days.

That lad she had spoken with last night had seemed so nice. He had been polite to her, unusual with men at that time of the night. Many of them were a little drunk when they arrived at the establishment to indulge in whatever vices took their fancy. But the young man, Haplee, or whatever, was sober and quiet, certainly well-dressed and with a scrubbed face. Apparently, he even took a room at the establishment so he was not short of a gold coin or two.

As she was deep in her thoughts, the door to the dance hall swung open. A young lady stood there, tears streaming down her face. A purple bruise was beginning to close her left eye and her blouse was torn. She held it tightly across her chest with one hand.

"What in the nine hells –?" began Sankie. "Kassa, what has happened. How can you go on stage like tha – ?"

"Th – they've taken Pretteen, Sankie," blubbered the young girl. "They took her away."

"Who did? The young man?"

"What? No, no!" Kassa was almost hysterical now but her speech was slurring. "The watch. It was that dwarf, Zheulin, Tron's gaoler. He hit me, Sankie. He punched my face. He took Pretteen."

"My gods! Why would they do that? What do they think she has done? Is it something to do with that young man?"

Kassa wailed and shook almost uncontrollably. Her dark hair had matted against her face and snot, mixed with blood, ran down her upper lip. Her cheek was swelling more and more as Sankie looked on. Kassa raised a hand to her cheek but could not touch it and she gingerly tried to clear the bloodied snot from her mouth.

"He said something about questions," she sobbed. "Pretteen was terrified. Zheulin will kill her, Sankie. People don't come back from him."

"We must get you to a healer without delay," said Sankie, a tight-lipped and determined expression on her face. "Then I shall go to see somebody."

...o o O o o...

Harley kept a good distance from the pair. They strutted along the street through the City Quarter for half a mile, with a belligerence that forced other people to take a wide berth, and then turned up a short road. There was very little activity on this roadway with just

175

a couple of cheap boarding houses on one side and small storage sheds on the other. The building at the end of the road, however, was of a much different appearance.

It was a large, single-storey, grey stone structure. There were very few windows in this building; those that he could see were barred. Two steps led up to a large iron-banded door which stood open. A pair of uniformed watchmen stood outside, pipes of smoke-weed in their hands. Harley assumed that this would be the city gaol although no sign or notice as to the function of the building.

The two men Harley had followed approached the watchmen. Only now that he was closer to them could be see their features a little more clearly. They were almost identical with blond hair and beards. Each of the watchmen snapped to attention. Harley squatted behind a broken wagon and nodded to himself. He turned away, his wide-brimmed hat pulled low over his eyes. He hadn't gone far when, without warning, a black coach with its windows covered, drawn by two black horses, sped by him and turned into the road.

Harley sped back the few yards to the corner of the road and peeped round. The coach had pulled up by the steps to the building and three figures climbed out, a dwarf and two watchmen. A fourth figure, covered in a hood or blanket, was dragged out, struggling and screaming. *Damn, a woman!*

He turned away and made his way quickly back to the tavern. When he arrived he was greeted by a commotion.

...ooOoo...

It was just before midday when Harley strode into the tavern; he could see Niebelittin Bellpealer trying to

176

placate the woman. The woman turned and spotted Harley. He recognised her immediately. It was the woman from the dance hall. He looked about the taproom. Boulaye, Gandar, Ragdan and Olwetta were also there. The woman turned to face him, a face full of anger and anxiety.

"What did you involve Pretteen in?" she yelled at Harley. "She has been arrested."

"What do you mean," replied Harley. "I have no idea what you are talking about." But he had a sick feeling in the pit of his stomach. *The woman in the carriage?*

Boulaye grabbed Harley's sleeve and took him aside. "They must have been watching her in the, er, dance hall," he whispered. "When they saw her with you they obviously decided to watch you too and to take her in for questioning."

"Damn!" exclaimed Harley. "I had better do something. Look, can you arrange that diversion for tonight?"

"It doesn't give me much time, lad. But I have an idea. I may need to bring in some of the group with this. Gandar, Ragdan and Olwetta. That is all. We might have to leave the city afterwards though."

"I would think not," said Harley. "What these bastards want her for is not official city business. It is to cover their own corruptness. That is why she will disappear just as Rautha Adras has if we are too tardy."

Boulaye strode back over to Niebelittin Bellpealer and the woman, one Sankie Meadowroot.

"Fear not, good lady," he said. "We shall endeavour to return her to freedom. It may mean that she will need to leave the city though."

Sankie was clearly unhappy with that. "She is my principal dancer," she whined. "I shall want her back on the stage."

"In which case it may well put her back in danger," yelled Bellpealer. "Train another to take her place, Madam. Now, leave us to sort it out and return to your Bordello!"

With a strut, she spat "Bordello indeed!" She sped off, her clothing flapping about her like a ship under full sail.

There was silence for a few heartbeats as they looked at each other.

"What is going on, Boulaye?" asked Olwetta. "Why does something like this concern us?"

Ragdan stepped to the side of his wife. "We do not usually get involved with politics or the city watches," he said with his deep voice resonating through the otherwise empty taproom. "Why did that woman come to speak with us?"

Boulaye was about to speak when Gandar cut him short. "It seems that you have some part to play in this, young Harley. Just where did you go yesterday?"

Boulaye stopped the questions with his hand held high. "Harley and me cannot involve the rest of the company in this. Yes, there is something happening in this city that him and me have been tasked to look into."

He asked them all to sit down but with one or two patrons now coming into the tavern, Bellpealer offered them all the sanctuary of his private chambers. They followed each other in and took a seat around the table.

"Where shall I begin?" sighed Boulaye. "You must understand that the more I tell you, the more it could pose a potential risk to your safety as well as Harley's and mine."

Olwetta, Ragdan and Gandar looked at each other once again, puzzlement still etched on their faces.

"We have all noticed that there is more to our young friend, Harley, than meets the eye," offered Gandar.

"He continually bests me with his sword, much to my vexation! In fact if I had my sword and he was armed with a feather I feel he would still best me!"

They all began to speak at once but as soon as Olwetta spoke, they all seemed to defer to her.

"I agree with you, Gandar," she said. "Your weapon skills are remarkable, Harley. But you have other fighting abilities too, do you not?"

"A couple, Lady Olwetta," he agreed.

"And, what is more," interjected Gandar, "I saw the skill with which you saved Riette when she was bitten by the snake. That is not something that an aspiring jester would generally know."

There was a ripple of laughter from around the table.

"And how did you manage to sneak in on that oaf, Hanuta, and take his bag of jewels?" asked Ragdan.

Harley just shrugged his shoulders. "I have not been very cautious, have I?" he mumbled.

"I ask again, what is going on, Boulaye?" enquired Olwetta, somewhat forcefully this time. "Just who or what are you, Harley?"

Boulaye looked at Harley, eyebrow raised. The young man nodded.

"I have been asked by a certain person in Westron Seaport to look into the disappearance of an agent here in Grappina. The young lady who has now been abducted is also involved in this business. The people who seized her are those who are being investigated for corruption."

Bellpealer leaned forward. "You mean Khargal Tron, the Commander of the City Watch and his lackey, Zheulin, the Commander of the Town Hall Guard, do you not?"

Harley nodded and Bellpealer continued. "We in the Council have known for a long time that they are fraudulent but we cannot prove it much less do anything about it. Tron commands a large contingent of City Watchmen, almost sixty I believe. There would be little we could do to overthrow them from their employment."

"I need to get into that gaol," said Harley. "To do that I need get as many of the City Watchmen out of the building as can be done. Then I can enter using those skills you seem to think I have."

Once again, there was another ripple of laughter.

Bellpealer stood up and walked over to a side table upon which there was a pitcher of water. He poured a little into an earthenware cup and returned to his seat. "Be wary though, young Harley. There is one nasty piece of work in there, known as Samsan, called *The Redbearded* by some. He is of human descent but probably has just as much orcan blood in him. He is the Warden of Grappina Gaol and is known to be as cruel, if not more so, than Zheulin. He works directly for Zheulin. When Samsan finds out there is a woman in the gaol, he will hurry down to take full advantage of her. Be wary of him; he is known to be virtually invincible."

"He has yet to meet me," growled Harley.

"He has other, nasty characters in his pocket," Bellpealer continued. "The four Massbourg brothers, villains and rogues the lot of them. They are all tanners, sawfish-boys and slaughterhouse workers. It is rumoured that they act as his spies and, on occasions, his assassins."

"I shall watch for them. I may have seen two of them already. Do they have blond hair and beards?"

"Indeed they do," replied Bellpealer.

"What are your plans, Harley?" asked Gandar. "What can we do to help?"

"You can help by creating a major diversion that

will call out as many of the City Watch as are on duty. That will help me get into the gaol. That is all I ask. I cannot ask you to help me with what I have to do. I shall need to find an apothecary first. Oh, and I shall need some gold coins too, Boulaye."

"Consider it done, lad," replied Boulaye. "By the way, Niebelittin, what part in this will the Grappina Militia play?"

Bellpealer smiled, sat back in his chair and put both his hands behind his head. "The City militia is separate and I have complete faith in Florian Quellivar, a man with elven blood in his veins. He is the Commander of the Marshwatch Towers and of the Grappina Militia. He and I are very old friends. I shall go to him immediately and request that his men take no active part tonight. He will need no encouragement at all with this for he and Tron have an intense dislike of each other."

"When will you need the diversion, Harley," asked Gandar.

"Soon after dark." Harley suddenly snapped his fingers. "Hah! I have an idea that is bound to work," he exclaimed.

...o o O o o...

Dusk was barely falling as Harley watched the short road to the City gaol. From his vantage point at a window in a nearby inn, he saw a squad of about two dozen men mounted in three wagons and being driven into the city. They appeared fully armed and wore breastplates and helms.

The wagons headed east towards the Impoverished Quarter. He finished his cup of mead and stepped into the street. He was wearing loose, dark clothing over his black harlequin costume. He looked in the direction that the wagons were taking and could see black smoke curling up into the sky. *Now that is a serious diversion!*

He strode briskly down the road to the gaol and noted that there were no sentries at the door. The door was open just a crack. Mounting the two steps he flitted to the opening in the doorway and listened. There was some sound of movement from inside but not close to the entrance. He opened the door and walked straight in. He closed the door tightly behind him.

A gaoler or watchman was sitting on a wooden chair drinking from an earthenware mug. He looked up in surprise as Harley stepped up to him.

"What do you want?" asked the man.

"Good evening," said Harley. "I am here to kill Zheulin and release his prisoner! Where are the cells?"

The guard was dumbfounded. "What? Ah, of course, you jest, haha! That was a good one! Hahaha! In the usual place, where it always is." He pointed to a stairway leading down.

"No, I am serious," Harley replied and struck the watchman just below his left ear just as the man reached for his sword. The hapless guard slumped to the floor, unconscious.

He took off his top clothing and placed them, folded, in a corner of the hallway behind the door. He pulled up his tight-fitting hood and face mask. A slim sword and matching dagger hung at his hip. On his belt were three pouches made of stiff leather. He glided noiselessly on his soft leather shoes towards the stairway, listening constantly for other sounds. He suspected that there would still be a few watchmen remaining somewhere in the gaol.

He descended a little way down the steps and stopped to listen. He could hear sobbing from below. He descended a little way further. A scream, such as may be heard from an animal in distress, brought a chill to his bones. A man's voice shouted above the anguish.

"Tell me, bitch, or Samsan Redbeard will have you while I watch."

There was another scream.

A coarse voice sounded. "You will get nothin' more from 'er, Zheulin. Yuh might as well give 'er to me."

An incoherent babble sounded and Harley dropped silently to the floor. A corridor stretched ahead of him. It was lit at three points by burning torches mounted in sconces. The air was foul with the smell of the torches, sweat and human waste. Following the sound along the stone slabs of the gloomy passage, he passed by three closed cell doors in his right and arrived at the fourth. It was open. He risked a glance around the door frame. The cell was dimly lit by a burning torch on the opposite wall. What he saw sickened and angered him.

A huge half-goblin sat on a stool. Next to him squatted a dwarf who was studying his handiwork in front of him. Harley knew it was Pretteen by the long blond hair. Her hands were tied with a rope fed through a ring on the wall. Her face was a mess. She was covered in her own blood. Harley was furious but he took a calming breath.

He quietly withdrew his sword and dagger and leapt into the cell. With a lunge, he thrust his blade through the back of his most dangerous adversary, the half-orcan. As the man's back arched, Harley drew the blade of his dagger across his throat. Dark blood fountained across the cell and the half-orcan slumped to the floor.

The dwarf spun around lashing out with a small cudgel. Although missing him, it took Harley by surprise and he stumbled backwards out of the cell door. The dwarf rose from his crouch and lurched after him.

Harley's left hand dropped the dagger to the floor, where it clattered, and flashed to his middle pouch. He withdrew a small object and threw it to the floor. There was a blinding flash and a cloud of white smoke.

Harley reopened his eyes and immediately saw Zheulin stumbling around, blinded. He thrust his sword into the dwarf's throat and then again into his chest. He retrieved his dagger and studied the bodies. Redbeard was clearly dead but Zheulin gurgled through the blood flowing in his throat.

"Rautha Adras. Where is he?" growled Harley. "Dead?"

Zheulin's eyes opened wide in fear as Harley's totally black form appeared in the dwarf's recovering eyesight.

"Is he dead," yelled Harley. "Nod for *yes*, shake for *no!*"

Zheulin gave a barely noticeable nod. That was enough. Harley thrust his dagger through the dwarf's heart.

Pretteen's head hung down lifelessly. He checked her for signs of life and was rewarded by shallow and erratic breathing. She had fainted. He cut through the rope and lowered her gently. *Now to get the two of us out of this place.*

He lifted her carefully over his left shoulder and made his way along the passage towards the stairway, sword ready in his right hand. Moans came from other cells. He ignored them and carried on. As he neared the top of the stairs he stopped to listen once again. He heard nothing, surprised that the gaol was virtually empty of watchmen and gaolers. The unconscious watchman was still on the floor where Harley had left him. He strode over to his pile of clothing and placed Pretteen carefully on the floor.

He clumsily pulled the smock that he had worn, over her body and pulled the voluminous hose over his costume. He rolled down his face mask and hood.

Picking up Pretteen again, he stepped out of the gaol. Two large figures approached him and he held his sword in readiness.

"Fear not, Harley," called a familiar voice.

He breathed a sigh of relief. Olwetta and Ragdan were smiling. They also had fearsome-looking weapons at the ready. Olwetta took the still form of Pretteen from him and they walked to the end of the road onto the main street where a small dog-cart and pony were waiting. Olwetta cautiously laid Pretteen in the back and Ragdan led the cart back to the Silver Raven.

...ooOoo...

PART 4

RECOVERY

Chapter 15

"She was badly beaten and had the little finger of her left hand cut off. She lost quite a lot of blood. It looks like her nose is broken, her lips are torn and her face will bear the scars if a Cleric cannot perform a miracle rapidly. Her body is a mass of bruises. Fortunately, thay had not assaulted her in a sexual manner. The good news is that she will live thanks to your intervention, Harley."

Harley, Ragdan and Olwetta had arrived at the tavern just as the wagons carrying the city watchmen rattled by in the opposite direction. The passengers were laughing and merry. They were followed by a large number of citizens who had been to see what the disorder had been about.

They had taken Pretteen in through the back of the tavern and up the stairs to a small chamber. A healer from the Temple dedicated to the God Haeman, the Life-Giver, had been sent for.

With Boulaye and Gandar, they sat in Bellpealer's chamber and drank the wine and mead that he had generously provided.

A beaming Ragdan had clasped Harley's wrists and clapped him on the back, almost knocking him off balance, and Gandar laughed, saying "Knew you could do it, young 'un!"

Olwetta hugged him so tightly he thought his ribs might crack.

Bellpealer strode in a little later and brought them all back to a more sombre mood, telling them of Pretteen's condition. "I have called for the best healer in the nearby Temple and she arrived a few moments ago. Her skills are formidable. It is too soon to predict the young lady's recovery. Time will tell."

Boulaye leaned forward and put his hands flat on the table top. "I must ask that we be guarded in what we tell the others in the company. As much as we would like to sing Harley's praises, they must remain unspoken. That does include our partners or spouses."

The others nodded in agreement.

"My Jetti will have to be told a little of what has occurred," explained Boulaye. "Well, enough to explain Pretteen's arrival in the little chamber adjacent to our own, because she will be carrying on with some healing. Niebelittin, what will her future be?"

Bellpealer shrugged his shoulders. "With Pretteen's features likely to be scarred, I would expect that Sankie Meadowroot will cut her out of the dance troupe. She will most probably be reduced to being a whore in the ordinary part of the brothel or out on the street in the Impoverished Quarter. Perhaps the Blue Sky Spectacular Company can employ another dancer."

"I shall make no promises there," said Boulaye. "Perhaps we should speak with this Sankie Meadowroot first. The Brothel of the Six Seraphs is too influential an establishment for us to become embroiled with, even if it is just over who wants this dancer. Let us call this woman in. The company will also need to agree if Preteen were to join with us."

"I shall send a message for her to come here. Now, when do you think you will be able to give a performance to the good citizens of the Mercantile Quarter?"

"Three days," replied Boulaye. "Two days to perfect the performance and then we shall be ready."

"Excellent. I shall spread the word. Now, it is late and time to retire for the night. I bid you all a good night."

Harley went into the taproom and joined the rest of the Company. Riette rose up from her seat and hugged

190

him.

"Hello, lovely girl," he said as he squeezed her tight.

"Where have you been?" she asked. "I missed you. Gandar, Ragdan and Olwetta disappeared too. And Boulaye, I think. Were you all together?"

An explanation had already been agreed between himself, Bellpealer, Boulaye, Gandar, Ragdan and Olwetta in case someone in the company was to ask.

"Aye, we were. There was a riot by the gate into the Impoverished Quarter. Fires were raised in two of the taverns, the Foot 'n' Mouth and the Drunken Urchin. The Urchin burnt to the ground apparently. The gangs from each tavern met near to the gate and fights broke out. Bellpealer asked us to escort him to the gate so he could monitor the situation himself. A young girl was badly injured and she is upstairs now being cared for by a Priest of Haeman."

Riette raised her hand to her mouth in horror. "The poor girl. What was she doing there?"

He scratched his head. "She's a dancer I think. I went through the gate to drag her out. Ragdan and lady Olwetta helped me."

She giggled.

"What is funny?" he enquired.

"It is the way you always call her Lady Olwetta. Why is that?"

"There is something about her, Riette. She has the air of command. Ragdan bobs his head when he greets her. It is in the way she holds herself; her poise and wisdom. She is almost regal in a way. It would not surprise me if she were a barbarian noblewoman."

"She seems to like it and Ragdan seems pleased too."

At that moment, Boulaye and Jetti joined them. He explained to them the agreed story of all that had happened and the appearance of the young girl, a dancer called Pretteen.

"She is very badly hurt and is being attended to by a very accomplished priest from a local Temple. When she recovers we will return her to the Impoverished Quarter."

There was a murmur of dissent from around the table.

Tishia gasped. "Back to that crap-hole? You cannot do that! We could really use another dancer, couldn't we Jetti? Tell him, Jetti."

Jetti chuckled. "We could, really. It will have to be her choice though."

"I am making no promises about this," said Boulaye. "We will all need to agree and she may not want to."

It was an hour before midnight when they climbed the stairs and went into their chambers. It was an hour past midnight when Harley and Riette fell asleep.

...ooOoo...

Bellpealer summoned Boulaye, Gandar and Harley into his chambers just after morning feast. They waited for Olwetta and Ragdan to join them.

"Rumour has it that a prisoner, a small woman by all accounts, escaped from the City gaol last night," said Bellpealer. "It all seems rather implausible to me, particularly as both Zheulin, the Commander of the Town Hall Guard and Samsan Red bearded, the bestial Warden of Grappina Gaol, were killed. It appears that these two were known to be fearsome fighters so it comes as a surprise that a woman was responsible for the killings. They were, um, thoroughly despatched. Very interesting indeed."

"Was any other gaoler attacked," enquired Harley.

"Strange that you should ask that," replied

Bellpealer. Gandar suppressed a laugh. "A sentry reported a fleet shadow passed across his vision and struck him with a tentacle. Pure nonsense of course. The poor man has been sent home for a day."

Gandar was now struggling to conceal his mounting hysteria.

"What are the authorities doing about it all?" asked Harley.

"The Council is rather divided on this matter. Some members want a scrupulous investigation while others have said that their excesses in the dungeons have resulted in their just demise. A decision will be made as to the course of action to be taken when we next meet. That will be in about ten days."

Boulaye smiled. "One can only hope that wrongdoers will be punished."

"They probably already have," muttered Gandar, the laughter finally bursting from him. "Ohh, gods!" he gasped.

Bellpealer shook his head. "Now, tell me of the diversion."

$$...\,o\,o\,O\,o\,o\,...$$

Earlier that afternoon, Boulaye had gathered Gandar, Ragdan and Undar together in a quiet corner of the Taproom in the Silver Raven. Undar had no inkling of what was about to be discussed between them and was taken aback when Boulaye swore him to secrecy, saying only that a request had been made from a higher authority. He asked Undar if he was happy to volunteer for a special task. He agreed without hesitation but could not hide the uncertainty in his face.

Boulaye explained the plan. The four of them were to split into two pairs and each pair was to make their way on horseback, and by stealth as much as possible, towards one of two taverns in the Impoverished Quarter. One of the pair would care for the horses while the other was carrying out the task. They were to ensure they had a clear escape route back to the Mercantile Quarter.

"At precisely the time the sun goes down," directed Boulaye, "I want you to start a fire in any outbuilding belonging to the two taverns so that the fires start simultaneously. Before the fire fully catches, you are to go to the tavern door or entrance and yell that you have a gift from the other tavern. Then you run like crazy down your escape routes to the horses and ride back to safety. Provided you do not gallop too madly through the gate you will be let through. Bellpealer will see to that."

"What is this all for?" enquired Undar. "Have the tavern owners complained about our performance abilities?"

"No, it is to create a diversion so as to bring out the City Watch. As I have said, it is a directive from a higher authority. Please do not ask whom. I cannot tell you."

Undar looked uncomfortable as he squirmed in his seat. "Then why is the Company involved. We never usually get involved with politics."

Boulaye thought for a few seconds. "It is a favour for which we will be very well compensated. If you would rather not do this, Undar, I will understand. It is for justifiable reasons which I promise will be made clear in time."

"Nay, Boulaye, I am happy to do this. It takes me back to a time when I did more of this sort of thing for reasons that were totally unjustifiable. This should be fun." Undar then gave a vicious grin. "Will I get to fight anyone?"

Boulaye smiled. "Probably not but take a couple of

small weapons with you just in case somebody gets unreasonable."

...ooOoo...

Ragdan and Undar were given directions on how to find the Drunken Urchin tavern. It was barely more than a quarter of a mile from the Foot 'n' Mouth but on a parallel road. They were to ride on a circular course, memorising the escape route, to ensure they kept clear of the other tavern, the Foot 'n' Mouth.

Undar accepted the job of setting the fire and shouting the threat through the front entrance to the tavern while Ragdan remained with the horses, about a hundred yards distant from the tavern. Undar, the company's fire-eater, sword-swallower and knife-thrower generally acted as a guard and escort while the company was travelling. Being lean and athletic, he was regarded as being the fastest runner in the troupe and was a natural choice for the task.

Dressed in pauper's attire and riding with the shabbiest saddles in the Silver Raven's stable, they drew few stares as they picked their way through the debris and refuse that littered the streets. They halted at the chosen place, a gap between two old and dilapidated timber sheds.

Undar knew he would cover the remaining distance to the tavern in a couple of minutes and he now had a few more minutes in hand before the sun dropped. He checked his tinderbox and satisfied himself that everything inside it was ready and in a dry condition, including the tinder. He checked also that his two daggers and his throwing axe were ready for use should he have need of them.

Ragdan scanned the rooftops and nodded to Undar. The latter gave an evil grin and set off.

Undar rounded a corner and saw the Drunken Urchin ahead. A small area that might have once been a corral was to the right side of the battered-looking building. Part of the front wall must have been destroyed, or it had just decayed away, because it was now just a sheet of sailcloth stretched and affixed to the corner-posts and eaves of the wall.

A small wooden structure, likely a privy, stood in the area close to the tavern. He saw this as an ideal place to set his fire.

He strode casually across to it, pulling a scarf across his face.

As he reached the wooden structure, two drunken men lurched out of the Urchin. They stopped by the privy and pissed against it.

Undar grimaced and moved round the other side. He was not in anybody's view here. He loosely rammed some thin oil-soaked twigs into a gap in the structure and scraped his flint down the steel.

A shower of sparks flew onto the tinder but it did not flare. He tried a few more before, at last, an ember grew into a flame. He breathed a sigh of relief, almost choking on the white smoke. The oiled twigs caught and the flames spread quickly - too quickly!

He leapt around the privy. The two drunks were still there, their job unfinished. Undar bashed one of them on the back of the head and the man head-butted the privy wall. He fell groaning onto the piss-soaked ground. The second man cursed and quickly tried to tuck himself away but Undar kicked him on the back of the legs. He too, collapsed on the ground, the piss stain growing down his leg.

Undar raced to the door of the tavern. Wrenching it open, he yelled at the top of his voice. "A present for you from the Hoof! Oh dear! FIRE!"

Then he sprinted away.

Boulaye and Gandar, meanwhile, rode a pair of rangy-looking mules to the gate leading to the Impoverished Quarter.

They had agreed that Boulaye, dressed in the attire of a blacksmith, would wait with the mounts in an adjacent road to that with the Foot 'n' Mouth while Gandar, dressed in a torn leather jerkin and worn hose, would carry out the raid on the Hoof's outbuildings.

They guided their mules through the grubby roads and attracted some interest, mostly from drunks who were forced to dodge out of the way as they rode through. The pair was forced to stop as two men with a carthorse dragged the dead carcass of a horse into a side alley, the very alley where Boulaye had hoped to wait for Gandar. The reek coming from the rotting carcass almost made them retch although the two men seemed to be unaffected by it.

"No matter," grunted Gandar. "The next alley will suffice."

He was feeling very much at home with this mission, after all, he had some experience with this way of life in his younger days, just like his brother Undar. He had a short-sword tucked inside his jerkin and a hunting knife in a sheath at his hip. He carried his tinderbox in his left hand and a wad of tinder and twigs inside his jerkin pocket.

He dismounted and handed the reins to Boulaye. It was almost time for him to play his part in this new performance. He was very excited and could feel his heart beating furiously. He checked his breathing and felt the exhilaration subside. Now he was ready. He winked at Boulaye and sidled away down a narrow passageway.

Gandar crept through narrow passages. There were

*a few people, beggars, whores and drunks mostly, but
he virtually blended in with them and they barely gave
him a second glance as he passed between them.*

*He crossed a road and entered another alley. A
figure stepped out in front of him, knife in hand and
pointed at his chest. The knife looked like it had dried
blood caked around the hilt and guard.*

*"Money! Give me money," said the man. He had a
thick accent that Gandar could not place.*

*He reached for a little pouch hanging at his belt but,
instead of unhooking it, he flashed his fist upwards,
catching the man under the chin. Opening his hand,
palm outwards, he struck the man's chin again, this
time with the heel of his hand. Blood and shattered
teeth sprayed out from the man's mouth and he
dropped like a stone.*

*Gandar didn't give him a second glance but moved
on. He came out onto the road, the Foot 'n' Mouth on
his left.*

*He crossed along the front of the tavern and was
rewarded by an empty woodshed by the side of the
building. There was no door, shards of rotting timber
on the ground had probably once been used to secure
the shed.*

*It took a few heartbeats for the fire to spread. He
rushed out and made for the door to the tavern. A
drunken wretch coming out collided with him and
careened back inside, tripping over a stool and
crashing to the floor. His companions laughed
drunkenly. Gandar could not resist a chuckle.*

*He shouted to the crowd. "Your attention please!
You have a fire in your woodshed courtesy of the
Drunken Urchin. I believe they are on their way here
now. You had better drink up! Good evening!" He
laughed again, turned and trotted off. He was some
distance away before the shocked revellers reacted.*

198

...o o O o o...

Boulaye, Gandar, Ragdan and Undar arrived at the gate at the same time, all roaring with laughter. Black smoke was already rising over the rooftops of the hovels and sheds in the Impoverished Quarter. The Gate Wardens let them pass through without a glance.

Bellpealer's face momentarily peeped out from behind the curtain of a small, black coach.

...o o O o o...

Chapter 16

Later that morning, Bellpealer summoned Boulaye and Harley to his chamber. The rest of the Company was perfecting the performance. With a performance scheduled for the evening of the next day, Boulaye was anxious that the performers would not be ready. They all insisted they would be; after all, they had never let him down yet.

Bellpealer informed them that the City Council was still divided as to whether the excesses of Tron and Zheulin should be examined but then evidence had been found in the gaol to prove that they had been engaged in fraudulent activities.

He explained that one of those Council members who had originally advocated that the investigations were unnecessary, was now himself the subject of an investigation.

"Traviss Hartimmer, of one of the old aristocratic families, a cleric, I understand, disappeared during the night. We are hunting him right now. The four Massbourg brothers, thugs to a man, appear have fled with him. Possibly some members of the watch too."

Harley smirked. "They will have left the city as soon as the gates opened," he alleged.

Boulaye leaned across the table. "With Tron and Zheulin dead, who will take over the command of the City Watch?"

"And how many of the watch can be trusted?" asked Harley.

Niebelittin Bellpealer leaned back in his chair and clasped his hands behind his head. "I sent couriers out at midnight last night to call in Captain Largo 'Stallion' Charget, the City Militia Commander of the Northentry Citadel and Captain Maud Orrenti, the Militia

Commander of the Southentry Citadel. I requested that they take over control of the City Watch until a senior member of the watch can be promoted by the City Council to take over Tron's post. They are taking a roll-call to ascertain whether or not any members of the City Watch have gone with Hartimmer and the Massbourgs."

"What about Harley's question about the city watch members' trustworthiness," prompted Boulaye.

"As to that, from now, no individual will have the authority to do anything without detailed records being kept for perusal by the City Council. Prisoners in the gaol will be processed through the City Assizes within a day of them being arrested. The use of torture will only be countenanced by the full membership of the Council and a healer of high ranking is to be in attendance."

"One thing I forgot to mention," said Harley. "There were some prisoners being held in the gaol when I got out but I left them where they were in case they had committed foul crimes."

"Three of the dozen prisoners in the city gaol have now been freed," said Bellpealer. "One of them, Tyson Kashtillan, a Priest from the Temple of Diette in the Docks Quarter of the city, had been missing for some months. It has been thought by some that he was among the number of people who had been abducted by, or for, one Larenz Korbirre , a foul and evil Lich."

"A lich?" asked Harley. "I seem to recognise the word but what is a lich?"

"It is an undead mage," replied the stocky Gnome. "Korbirre is said to have haunted the Bourgin Manor for a couple of centuries. Citizens dread the manor and many will avert their eyes rather than glance at its dark windows. Personally, I have my doubts about it all but I would still decline any invitation to visit the great house. Something has caused the grass to stop growing there and for the birds and beasts to shun the grounds around it."

"Gods! I can understand that!" exclaimed Harley. "But what about this Kastillan?"

"Ah, poor Kashtillan," sighed Bellpealer. "Surprisingly, he had not been taken by the Lich at all. He had actually been held hostage in an effort by the criminals, including Traviss Hartimmer it seems, to reveal the whereabouts of the legendary treasures of the infamous Ignacia Karouche, a Pirate King from four centuries ago."

Boulaye immediately sat up straight in his chair. "A treasure, you say?"

Bellpealer laughed. "I did indeed! I thought this would interest you. This is a story with ancient beginnings but the other prisoners seem to think that Hartimmer believed Kashtillan to be a descendant of Karouche. He may well be because one of his ancestors on his mother's side shared the same family name. Unfortunately, Kashtillan has been losing his mind since the dreadful treatment by Zheulin in the gaol. Believing him lost to the vampire, a new priest was brought in to the Temple of Diette. Kashtillan is now in the capable hands of the new priest, actually a priestess, called Akea Wulder."

"Who does the treasure belong to," asked Boulaye. "Were it to be found, who would have claim to it?"

Bellpealer chuckled again. He could see where this conversation was going. "It depends where it is found. A share of it would go to the owner of the property where it is found, or their family, and the rest to the finder." His demeanour became sombre. "If you do decide to speak with the poor man, be gentle with him. His mind wanders; he is very unwell and has lost some fingers from one hand and all of the toes on one foot.

Zheulin could be very cruel."

"Not any more, he isn't," murmured Harley.

"Aye, thanks to you, lad," said Boulaye. "Have there been any clues as to what this fortune is, Councillor?"

"No, but if it was a cache that came to the interest of a notorious self-styled Pirate King, I would suggest it may be a quantity of gold, jewels, precious stones, valuable weapons and armour, religious artefacts or magical items. A pirate, particularly one with the vicious reputation of Ignacia Karouche, would have little use for scrolls or books of knowledge, science or learning. In fact, he was known to burn them, along with their owners, including clerics and mages."

"What became of him?" enquired Boulaye.

Bellpealer slumped a little in his chair. "It ended in a farcical scandal. He was vanquished in a battle at sea where ships of the Westron Seaport Royal Flotilla engaged him in a hail of flaming missiles and crossbow bolts. As his ship burned, he ran it aground and he, along with his surviving men, was taken. He bargained for a full pardon and it was accepted on the proviso that he identified all members of his network on land and at sea. Many people, men and women, were executed on his evidence. It is said that some of them were innocent, having been branded by Karouche in revenge for past difficulties. Committed to exile, Karouche sailed away to one of the Westwind Isles, Ledeira I believe, where it is said he lived for many years as a pauper unlike the king he had always pretended to have been. He faded from history."

"Perhaps the treasure is on his island to this day," mused Harley.

"It is unlikely that anyone will ever find out. That Isle is shunned by sailors, adventurers and all folk on the sea, whether of good or evil intent. It is said to be the lair of werewolves and undead of every description. An army of clerics and paladins would not dare to venture even to the shallows of its shores. Forget it, good men. It would be a fool's errand." Bellpealer shook his head and laughed softly.

"But you said *pauper*," mumbled Harley. "How do people know? What about his treasure?"

"Sailing men would call on him and some of his surviving buccaneers to deliver him his victuals. He had no need of treasure on that island for he had nowhere to spend it. It is believed he left it somewhere in this very city so he could return to it in the future. The Pirate King had a woman in Casparsport. She had a son, possibly with the Pirate King. I cannot remember his name, no matter. It was said that he was sent to a Temple to study and since then his offspring have carried on the religious tradition. Perhaps that is a good place to find the treasure. If you are to go fortune hunting then please let me know."

...ooOoo...

A while later, as Harley and Riette walked to their bed-chamber hand in hand, Boulaye poked his head out through his chamber door.

"I hate to break up you lovebirds," he said. "I need a quick word with you, lad. Just a few minutes?"

Harley kissed Riette's cheek and said "Won't be long, lovely girl." He stepped through Boulaye's door.

In Boulaye's sleeping chamber, Harley whispered "We are going to Casparsport soon, are we not?"

Boulaye nodded. "Aye, lad. We are. Take a seat. This could be very interesting, especially if you are considering looking for Ignacia Karouche's treasure. Look, lad, you may be on a fool's errand, you know, as Bellpealer said. There may be nothing left. It may have been found centuries ago."

"Aye, I know. But that poor man, Tyson Kashtillan, will be entitled to some of it to make his last years more comfortable. They tortured him, Boulaye. They ruined his hands and feet. Some of that treasure should be his."

"Mayhap you are right, lad. It pleases me that you are not looking for it for yourself, or even for the Company. But Casparsport now; it is a lawless city but there probably will be areas where we should be able to search."

"You said we! Do you intend to help me search too?"

"Perhaps it would be better for you and me, perhaps Gandar too. That is if we decide it is a good idea to do so. I would not be a bit surprised if somebody else would also be looking for this treasure."

"You – you mean Hartimmer and the Massbourgs?"

Boulaye took a deep breath and let it out slowly. "Aye, I do. It stands to reason, does it not? They tortured him to try to get him to talk about it. They got nothing from him because he knows nothing."

"So they are likely to be on their way to Casparsport. It has a bad reputation. Is it justified? What can you tell me about it?"

"Aye, it is partly warranted. What is more, part of Casparsport is almost a lawless town just like this one, excepting for the mercantile areas of each of them, of course. Like Grappina, there is a guarded wall that surrounds the municipality, this being the more lawful mercantile, religious, commercial and residential inner city. One part of that is the docks area which spawned the walled city of Casparsport many centuries ago although even that has its disorder with drunken sailors. Then, apparently because the mercantile area provided work, along with other more nefarious activities and opportunities, the outer city grew up slowly over the last couple of centuries. It is there where the main lawlessness exists."

"What peacekeeping does the city have?" asked Harley. "Do the old city, I mean the municipality, and the outer exist separately?"

"Ah, this is where Casparsport remains effectively two cities. The municipality is policed by organised groups of well-paid mercenaries who are very loyal to the Guild-controlled regime. In turn, the Guilds are supported and well-financed, by all accounts, by the dock's Merchants' Federation. A vast amount of cargo is unloaded at the harbours. To ensure it passes safely through the outer city and into the wilds, a veritable army of steadfast mercenaries guards the caravans too, as they take their cargoes to all corners of the western lands and realms, as you have seen on our own journey here."

"Aye, I certainly have. How safe are folks riding through the outer city to get to the Municipality?"

Boulaye laughed. "It takes gold! Simple as that. We shall have to hire a group of mercenary thugs to escort us through."

Harley's face fell and his mouth hung open. "Thugs? Do we need to? I mean, can we not protect ourselves?"

Boulaye shook his head solemnly. "Too risky, lad. A dozen guards who know the outer city will cost us a gold coin for each of 'em. I could not take us on the right road through to the municipality gates. We would have a hundred filthy urchins clambering all over our wagons. We would be stripped before we got half a mile. A dozen armed men with weapons drawn or with whips cracking will ensure we get through unhindered. Money well spent, lad. You will see. We always make a good income from Casparsport, enough to see us through the summer back in Westron Seaport."

Harley scratched at his stubble. Riette had been trying to encourage him to trim it back for a couple of days.

"Back to Hartimmer and the Massbourgs then," he said. "They will also be hunting the treasure of Karouche, won't they?"

"Aye, lad. As we are certain, Hartimmer believes the priest Kashtillan to be Karouche's descendant and so they will be looking for the treasure for sure. They may even be looking out for us too, because in the end we were involved in turning their world upside down."

"Hmph! I am not afraid of them," murmured Harley.

"You should be, lad. The Massbourg brothers are nasty, spiteful and cruel. Tron and Zheulin used them to spy and assassinate. They work as a team just as hyenas do to bring down their prey. Watch for them."

"How would we recognise them?"

"I don't know for certain but you have seen two of them, I understand. We shall have to ask Niebelittin Bellpealer."

Harley raised an eyebrow and nodded slowly. "What about the Kashtillan residence? Is it still there?"

"I have no idea. I suspect that there is no person in the city who would know where it is. There may be ways we can find out when we get there."

"So what do we do now?"

"Now, young man, we need to concentrate on the practises for the performance. I am considering taking the company on a parade through the Mercantile Quarter this evening to bring the attention of people to the show. Perhaps we shall do another tomorrow afternoon."

...ooOoo...

The performers of the Blue Sky Spectacular Company were in full costume as Boulaye led them through the streets of the Mercantile Quarter.

Acting on a request from Boulaye, Niebelittin Bellpealer had already negotiated a price with the Master of the Dungsweepers' Guild for the streets to be cleaned during the previous hours of darkness. Harley, Gandar, Undar and Ragdan had pasted posters on strategic walls around the quarter that afternoon while Jetti, Tishia and Olwetta trod together around the streets spreading the news of the forthcoming performances.

Solarin Fleet, the bard, storyteller and musician, played the flute as Harley banged a large drum in time to the song. Balari and Tinnisse turned summersaults as Undar blew great gouts of flame from a lit torch. Jetti and Tishia, dressed in flamboyant costumes, danced in synchronisation to Solarin's music and Harley's drum beat. Ragdan held Olwetta aloft, balanced on just his hands, as she changed from one posture to another. The powerful muscles in both their arms bulged impressively. Crowds of onlookers began to line the streets as the company passed along. Boulaye showed the appreciation of the company as the onlookers applauded and children squealed with delight.

The only member of the company missing from the parade was Riette. She rarely took part mainly because of her self-consciousness over her scarred face. This time however, she had another task – looking after Pretteen.

By midday the following day, the performance rehearsals were taking shape and Boulaye was less demanding.

"Tomorrow is our first performance to the public, my dear friends," he boomed. "We have a few wrinkles to smooth out but we are just about ready. Three evenings of performances will be hard work. This will provide enough of an income for us to repair our wagons and renew some of our display boards. I'm damned proud of you all. Tonight we relax but I do not want to see anybody drunk tonight or with aching heads in the morning."

...o o O o o...

On the third evening performance to the public, Harley's antics and tomfoolery delighted the crowd. By now, he could tumble, fall, trip and stagger about with almost magnificent timing. The crowd gasped at the shows of strength, balance, juggling and skill. Gandar drew massive applause as he split six apples with six separately-thrown hand-axes. Tinnisse and Balari performed juggling skills while balanced on a rope tightly-stretched between two trees.

Solarin, meanwhile, entertained children with a puppet show which involved them squealing as one puppet crept up on another from behind. Jetti and Tishia danced exquisitely in time to a haunting melody played on a harp by Solarin. Ragdan used brute strength to straighten horseshoes and Olwetta challenged any member of the audience to arm-wrestling.

Two robed and hooded figures sat to one side and watched the performance. Beneath one hood was Pretteen. Despite her left hand being bound in clean cloths, she was now out of her sickbed and had asked to watch the Company's show. Beside her sat Riette who laughed at every stumble and trip that Harley did. She lifted her right hand to her mouth in horror and fear when, in a simulated blow from Gandar's arm on the back of his head, he flipped head over heels and landed flat on his back. There was a gasp from the crowd as

209

Harley lay still. Then he flipped up onto his feet with a wide grin on his painted face. This earned a cheer from the audience and a sigh of relief from Riette. She resolved to talk to him about it later.

Tishia and Jetti collected coins from the audience before the conclusion and, with the ovation ringing in their ears, the Company gave their final bow.

Two other pairs of eyes, not so thrilled with the performance, had also been intently watching. One of them focussed fixedly on Harley.

Later, once their equipment and props had been cleared away, Boulaye led them back to the Silver Raven. Bellpealer had already provided a sumptuous feast for them. A large table groaned under the weight of meats and fish, vegetables, fruit, bread and rich sauces. Another table held barrels of ale, mead and wine.

Riette walked in on Harley's arm followed with Solarin and Pretteen. The others had already arrived. Niebelittin Bellpealer arrived soon after and sat in a chair at the head of the table.

"Dig in, my people," Boulaye called. "You have earned it. Tishia and Jetti have counted our takings for these three days. They come to just over seven hundred gold. A hundred of that will go to our esteemed host; he has said that is acceptable."

Bellpealer nodded. "This has been an auspicious event for the Mercantile Quarter. It has been an honour to have you here too. There have been a few changes to the hierarchy of the city during this time but it hopefully has not affected you."

Some of the members of the Company looked around each other in puzzlement at this last statement but this dissipated as Bellpealer continued.

"Please eat, drink and make merry. I understand you leave this city in two days. Craftsmen will be made available for the repairs you need on your wagons and equipment. When you leave, a troop from the City Watch will escort you through the Impoverished Quarter. I shall take my leave now for in the morning I will take my place on the City Council. We have much to discuss and it may take some days. I eagerly await your return in the future. Farewell, dear friends."

He rose from his seat and left the chamber. On the way, he reached to clasp Boulaye's arm. As Boulaye clasped it, he felt the purse that Bellpealer placed there.

"Not needed, my friend. Account has been paid in full by the City Council. Farewell."

Sometime later, as the company ate, drank and joked with each other, Riette looked at Harley and he nodded and rose to his feet. He held out his arm and to her and she rose as well. As they left, Harley just caught Gandar's wink.

It was some hours later that the couple finally fell asleep.

"Do you trust your gut feelings, Boulaye?" Harley asked next morning.

"Over the years, lad, my sixth sense and I have become close friends. Why do you ask? Do you feel something awry?"

Harley shrugged his shoulders. "Ah, I do not know for sure. It was more like a shiver down my back. It was like the feeling you get when you think there is something nasty behind your door. Or someone with ill will watching you."

"There are two possibilities, lad. One is that your imagination is fooling you or the other is that somebody actually *was* watching you – apart from three or four hundred in the audience, that is!"

"Is it likely that Hartimmer could have left his spies behind to watch me, or us?"

Boulaye furrowed his brow as if in thought. "Aye, it

is possible indeed. Ah, that reminds me. Bellpealer says that the Massbourg brothers are easily recognisable by their height being in excess of six feet, all of them. Long blond hair and beards too. Watch for 'em, lad. You did come out of the City Gaol with bodies behind you and Pretteen in your arms. Somebody may have been watching. Remember, you were picked up by Ragdan and Olwetta so if someone was observing they will know of the connection with the Company. We must keep vigilant."

...ooOoo...

Chapter 17

The drowsy company rode out of the city very early the following day, leaving before dawn in the first rains for almost a month. Surrounding them were more than twenty grim, lightly-armoured but well-armed members of the City Watch. As they rode through the Impoverished Quarter, the watchmen drew their swords and carried them at the ready. The sun would have just been rising above the eastern horizon as they turned southwards on the Trade Route but the rain-laden clouds delayed the dawn this morning. The Company huddled inside their hooded cloaks to keep out the rain. The armed escort had avoided any potential trouble.

Harley rode his horse close to the wagon being driven by Riette. Pretteen sat beside her carrying a light crossbow and with a pack of bolts tucked down beside her. She had insisted that she had some proficiency with the weapon, despite having lost the finger of her left hand, and indeed carried and handled it with noticeable familiarity. She still carried herself stiffly as a result of the beatings she had received at the hands of Zheulin and Tron. She would have scars around her eyes and mouth to remind her and her nose now turned slightly to the left. No amount of divine healing could have avoided that.

Without a farewell the watchmen turned back towards the city. There were a few early travellers on the road. It was wide enough to allow passage in both directions and wagons to overtake others. Most wagon caravans were merchant-owned and all had armed outriders as escorts. Progress was slow and just the few hours of rain had been sufficient to cause the road surface to be churned into slick mud by wagon wheels and horse's hooves.

The rain eased off by mid-morning and after a while breaks appeared in the clouds. They were relieved to take off their heavy cloaks as steam rose from their horses in the day's humid heat. Midges and mosquitoes ravaged them during the afternoon. Some of them took to their smoke-weed pipes in an effort to keep the insects away from their faces, with minimal success. The marshes lay to the west of the road. A fetid stink emanated from the swamps.

"These damn marshes!" complained Undar. "It's a breeding ground for insects that look to feed on you."

Boulaye brought his mount over to him. "It's your sweat that attracts them. You can't do much about it."

In front of them Ragdan and Olwetta rode each side of Jetti's wagon. Ragdan turned in his saddle. Both of the barbarians appeared unaffected by the insects which collected in clouds around all of the others. "Aye, you can do something," he said. "Smear a little mud across the back of your necks and your faces and hands. They will not be able to detect your sweat. No horse-shit though for it will attract flies."

By the time they pulled up to stop for the night, the sun was dropping behind the low hills to the west. Coolness descended and the buzzing insects abandoned their greed for sweat and human blood. The Company lined up their four wagons and unhitched the heavy horses.

"Does anyone feel like hunting for meat?" called Boulaye. "We have trail rations of oatcakes and cheese but I want to make these last a couple of days. There is no way-station for another two days at the rate we are moving. Fresh meat would be good."

Gandar, his brother Undar, and Harley stepped forward with bows at their sides. Boulaye nodded, saying "Keep close by each other, lads. Take care."

The trio trotted off. They crossed the road heading

eastwards and disappeared from view through the trees and scrub.

They moved stealthily for a while, keeping about twenty paces apart while maintaining line abreast. Gandar was in the centre while Harley took the right flank and Undar the left.

A hiss from Undar alerted them and all three crouched low. Undar pointed ahead and slightly to the left. In the increasing gloom Gandar spotted a grey shape passing behind a small bush. It was a few seconds more before Harley saw it. A small antelope stepped delicately towards Undar. Behind his small patch of scrub, he silently put an arrow onto his bowstring, straightened up and aimed carefully at the animal. It was barely twenty paces away. He could not miss.

Gandar also readied an arrow so that his would fly a split second after Undar's.

Undar rose up steadily. An arrow, streaking out of the stand of hawthorns, struck him high in the chest. His own arrow flew into the ground as he yelled in shock and pain. His bow dropped and he crashed to the ground beside it.

Gandar looked across in horror. His mouth tried to form words as he attempted to focus his mind. Harley sped in front of him and he dropped down beside Undar.

"Assassin! In the trees yonder!" he yelled. "Get down, Gandar!"

As Gandar came to his senses, he began to rush over just as another arrow sped towards him. It passed straight through his tunic although the arrowhead glanced across the side of his chest. He gasped and dropped flat beside Undar and Harley.

"Wait here!" hissed Harley.

Gandar reached out a hand to catch the young man's

tunic. "Where – where are you going?"

"To try to catch the bastards who hide in shadows," murmured Harley.

"Be careful, boy. I'll try to get Undar back to the camp."

Undar, gritting his teeth, gasped "I am not too badly hurt. I can walk I think."

"Give me a couple of minutes in case the archer is still waiting for us," said Harley. "Break off the arrow but leave the point in his chest until you get back."

Harley rose swiftly to his feet and was gone in a flash.

...ooOoo...

He did not head straight for the hawthorn thicket but veered to the right of it and then looped around to the left so as to approach it from the far side. He used every available patch of scrub and bush as cover.

As he drew close he slowed down, all his sensed focussed of the thicket. A shadow carrying a bow separated from it, swiftly moving to another patch of trees a hundred yards away. Crouching low, Harley moved parallel to the running figure, a burly man by the looks of it. He heard the snicker of a horse and the stamping of its hooves as the dark figure approached it. Harley sped up and ran at full speed towards it.

As the figure mounted the horse, he spotted Harley coming straight at him and dug his heels into his mount's flanks. Harley leapt into the air. He collided with the rider, knocking it from the saddle, before the horse galloped away. There was a sickening crunch of a breaking limb and a low scream as the figure landed hard.

Harley leapt atop the figure with his knees slamming into the man's chest. With the breath

216

knocked out of him and his right arm clearly broken, Harley was satisfied that he posed little threat. He was wrong. The man whipped his left hand across to his right side and snatched a dagger from its sheath. At the same time he rolled to his feet. In the fading light, Harley saw that the man had long blond hair hanging loose except for two braids at each side. A thick blond beard hung down the man's chest. He held his dagger so the blade protruded downwards instead of extending from between his thumb and forefinger. Harley was surprised at this awkward style, particularly as the man was using his left hand.

The man took a vicious downward slash at Harley but the young man deftly stepped to his right. The blade passed harmlessly by but Harley threw his right arm over and trapped the assassin's blade arm. He knew he didn't have to worry about the other hand. With a sharp twist of his body to the left, he caused the man to stagger forwards, almost tripping to the ground. With a jerk, the man tried to free his arm but to no avail. Harley spun back to his right and gripped the man's wrist with his right hand. Bringing his left hand across, he gripped with that too. Turning his body back to the left he twisted the man's wrist and locked it against the elbow joint. The man gasped and dropped the dagger.

With his left foot, Harley kicked the man's head and was rewarded with the crack of breaking bone. He still had hold of the man's wrist. He twisted it sharply to the left. The man cried out in agony but jerked his hand away. As he scrambled for his dagger, Harley brought his right heel down hard on the man's fingers, crunching them underfoot. The man screamed again, his face turned up towards Harley with an expression of hatred and anguish.

"Aii! Bastard!" the man wheezed. "You piece of shit!"

217

"Who are you?" asked Harley, unmoved by the insult and his voice calm.

The man spat at him. It was thick with blood.

With the heel of his right palm, Harley struck the man's nose hard. The bone crunched and the man screamed again, fresh blood gushing down over his mouth.

"Why did you attack us?" Again his voice was calm.

The man shook his head.

Harley sighed. His hand shot out again, catching the man's throat. The man gagged and choked. Blood splashed out splattering across Harley's tunic.

"If I have to ask again, I shall break all of the fingers on your right hand. Who are you and why did you attack us?"

"Go and fu–"

Harley's hand once again shot out, its heel catching the man's left eye. The man screamed and collapsed to the ground.

"Is your name Massbourg?"

The man rolled up into a sitting position, nodded and gave a pained grin, blood still flowing from his shattered nose and staining his teeth red.

Harley reached down and picked up the dagger. He plunged it into the man's chest. The stricken man's eyes bulged in shock as he collapsed back onto the ground and moved no more.

With a grim expression, Harley picked up his bow and walked over to the man's horse. He mounted it and sped off after the two brothers. He saw them in the distance and galloped towards them calling Gandar by name so as not to alarm them.

Together, they helped Undar into the saddle and made their way back to the camp. On the way, Harley briefly told Gandar what had happened, without going into the detail of the man's demise. Gandar did not ask.

...ooOoo...

Jetti and Riette worked tirelessly all night to heal Undar. The arrow had entered his chest above the right lung and caused an appreciable amount of bleeding.

"We must remain here for a day, perhaps two," said Jetti.

Riette nodded in agreement. "Undar cannot move just yet," she said.

"Can he not lie in a wagon?" asked Boulaye. "We have to reach Casparsport in twelve days and we have already lost a day because of the slow going."

"Which wagon, Falarr?" she replied. "There is no room. They are all fully loaded."

Boulaye winced at the sound of his givenname. Jetti was the only one to call him that and then only when he exasperated her.

"He is very weak and has lost much blood," explained Riette. "Too much movement will open his wound and could cause him to lose much more. You do not really want his death on your conscience, do you?"

Everybody looked at her. It was unusual for her to speak assertively to anyone.

"What have you done to Riette, Harley?" grunted Boulaye. "She is usually a little more polite to me." He huffed and walked over to his bedroll. "We have to get some sleep, you people. Who is taking first watch? Keep a sharp look out. The rest of the Massbourgs may come calling on us at any time. They may be feeling a little pissed off because Harley has killed one of them."

Jetti stood and shook her head. "Never mind Master Grumpy!" she laughed. "He will feel better in the morning."

"I heard that, my dear wife!" Boulaye responded.

"Another day in this swamp," groaned Solarin. "Bugs, mosquitoes and gods know what else."

219

The others ignored him.

The night passed by and Ragdan roused them soon after dawn. Olwetta had prepared a dawnfeast of oat cakes, cheese and bread. Pretteen was sitting up next to a sleeping Undar. She looked very tired as she held one of his hands.

"How does he fare?" Gandar asked.

"He sleeps badly," replied Pretteen. "The pain. I think the wound becomes infected. It is much swelled."

"Did you stay up with him all night?"

She nodded. Her face looked drawn and dark rings encircled her eyes. "I did because Jetti and Riette worked hard to care for him and they were tired so I sat with him."

Gandar smiled, patted her on the shoulder and nodded. He strode away.

The company stayed the whole day by the side of the road. Undar was very unsettled during the next night and was bathed in sweat. Once again Pretteen sat up with him while he mumbled and occasionally yelled. She soaked his face and chest with water to keep him cool but ensured he was fully covered by the blankets.

Next morning they were passed by a long caravan of merchant wagons. With them were two priests dressed in the vestments of the god Cahuhl. On payment of a not so modest fee, they applied divine healing to Undar. By noon he had noticeably improved and by the following morning he felt ready to ride on the wagon next to Jetti. The muddy road had dried in the heat of the last two days and they were now able to make good speed.

Two days later, during the early evening as the sun began to drop towards the western horizon, Gandar eased his horse next to Harley and leaned across to him. They had left the marshes behind them and had stayed at a way-station the previous night.

"Riders, lad, to the left side about a half mile off," he said, with a half-smile on his face. "Three of 'em. Some men searching for a lost brother perhaps?"

"Aye. I saw them once this morning and again a few times during the afternoon. I believe they have been shadowing us most of the day."

Gandar laughed. "They are not very subtle about it, are they? Would you like to go a-hunting again this evening?"

Harley's hand reached down to his grumbling stomach. "Aye, I wouldn't mind," he replied. "Boulaye has suggested we hunt some meat for our supper but with the noise that these traders' wagons make any quarry will scatter far and wide."

Harley waved at Riette and rode forward with Gandar to meet up with Boulaye at the vanguard of the Company. Before either of them had a chance to speak to him, Boulaye sad "Have you seen 'em too?"

Harley answered "Aye" and Gandar nodded.

"I reckon it's the three other Massbourgs. They're like an itch I can't scratch. Either of you got any ideas?"

"We could try hunting again," suggested Harley. "This time we will try to bring back something we can all eat instead of buying meat from the traders."

"We will stop here for the night. I shall double the watch. They'll all complain but it's nothing unusual for these parts."

...o o O o o...

Gandar and Harley strode off into the surrounding hills. As they began the gradual climb upwards, the slope became increasingly devoid of the patchy shrubs and vegetation. They broke into trot.

As they ran, they considered their plan. Harley

221

suggested that they split up, one of them circling to the left and the other to the right.

"Can't say I'm happy about that, young 'un," responded Gandar. They puffed and panted up a particularly steep incline and slowed to a walk near the top. "They are most likely to ride off to the south but three mounted horsemen will be too much for either one of us to handle if they decide to make a break for it. I reckon we both circle to the right and try to get in front of them so we take them down as they ride."

Harley nodded in agreement. "Hopefully we come upon on the riders unawares."

They crossed a wide stream at a fast pace, the water bubbling softly over gravel and pebbles. Animal tracks had scarred the sward and droppings on the short grass were visible near the water's edge. The hillsides rose in front of them a little more steeply which forced them to slow their pace a little.

Without warning, Gandar slowed to a halt and held up his hand. "A raised voice, somewhere over the hill ahead," he said quietly.

Harley raised an eyebrow in mild surprise. He hadn't heard a thing. They moved quickly but cautiously up the slope. As they trotted towards the crest of the low hillock they clearly heard a yell from the other side.

Without warning, an arrow flew harmlessly over their heads and they dived to the ground. The sound of a voice barking orders was followed by two more arrows, one thudded into the ground within an inch of Gandar's head and the other swished over Harley's flattened body close enough for him to feel his hair ruffle.

Harley put a hand to his ear. "They saw us or heard us coming, Gandar. It sounds like they are riding out, Gods-dammit!"

They heard the thunder of hooves as the riders galloped away into the falling darkness. The pair leapt to their feet and each of them managed to loose off an arrow at the fleeing horsemen but none of the horsemen fell.

"It is too dark to follow them on foot," grumbled Gandar. The near miss with the arrow had shaken him and he felt angry with himself at having almost taken a hit.

"Aye, we had better make our way back to camp. Perhaps we will find some game down by the stream."

Descending the hillside they could just make out the glint of the last light on the stream in the distance. Movement in between some of the bushes indicated that others were taking water. They both dropped to one knee to reduce their profiles on the slope. The moon had appeared from behind the patchy cloud and its light bathed the ground in a silver glow for a while.

"Looks like deer or antelope," whispered Harley. "Two arrows each should be sufficient but we will need to get closer."

"You have keen eyes, young 'un," he chuckled. "It's a pity your ears did not catch the sound from the riders when mine did." He saw Harley's expression. "I jest with you lad."

Gandar smiled and nodded. Silently, they moved forward in a slow crouch so as to approach unseen and unheard to within thirty yards of their quarry. They each cautiously withdrew two arrows from their quivers and placed one of them point-down in the ground.

Noiselessly, they readied their arrows on their bowstrings and took aim. Harley's heart was thumping in his ears as his arrow was the first to fly, almost immediately followed by Gandar's. While their arrows were still in flight, their second was also on its way.

The antelope staggered away from the stream for

about twenty yards and then collapsed onto the grass. Other animals had immediately scattered into the surrounding countryside. The pair ran to the downed antelope. All four arrows protruded from its slender neck.

"Nicely brought down, I must say," said Gandar. "The company will be delighted to get fresh meat." He took out his hunting knife and slit the beast's underside from groin to neck. He deftly removed the innards and tossed them into the stream. Wildlife would soon remove all traces of the offal. He washed his hands in the stream and walked back to Harley.

With help from his friend, Harley hefted the carcass over his shoulders and, with Gandar carrying both bows, they sauntered together back to the camp.

Boulaye sighed with relief as they called a warning the camp and strode in, Gandar in the lead. A small fire lit the faces of their companions.

"We shall need a bigger fire than that," laughed Gandar. "Look what we have for you!"

Harley dropped the carcass of the antelope onto the ground, flexed his aching shoulder muscles and joined Gandar and Boulaye.

"There were three of them," said Harley, softly so as not to let the others hear. "They had the same long blond hair and beards that the other one had the other day."

"The Massbourgs," whispered Boulaye. "We shall have to be vigilant during the night. I think that tomorrow we seek to join up with another travelling group and offer our services. There will be safety in greater numbers."

It was approaching midnight before the antelope was ready to eat. Olwetta reduced the fire so as to improve their night vision and the company sat together, except for Riette and Harley who sat a little apart from the others. A little while later, Undar and Pretteen moved away too. Olwetta nudged her husband and he nodded.

Gandar announced that the watch was to be doubled during the night. This drew exchanges of glances between many in the company but nobody spoke up. Pretteen offered to share the watch with Undar, or with anybody else who would be happy to, but Boulaye was sceptical.

"I am not certain that you would be well suited to standing watch, young lass, as good as your intentions are."

"She can share watch with me," called Olwetta. "I shall instruct her on the finer points of standing watch. She will have her crossbow as she does know how to use it."

"But can she shoot with it?" called Gandar.

"I can remove your sweetmeats with a single bolt," she cried with indignation. "Would you like me to prove it?"

"Nay lass," Gandar laughed. "Perhaps a few of us also have things to prove. Soon maybe."

"I agree with Lady Olwetta," said Harley. "We need as many eyes as we can set to watch."

The night proved to be uneventful and they rose from their bedrolls as the sun began to rise in the east. Soon, they hitched the heavy horses to the wagons and continued their journey.

They waited for a train of a dozen heavily-loaded wagons to trundle laboriously by before pulling onto the road behind it. Boulaye rode up to the lead wagon. On it sat a portly trader dressed in lavish attire with a silk turban wrapped around his head. The man's neatly clipped beard and flowing moustaches wagged with the movement of his wagon on the uneven road surface.

Boulaye doffed his cap and offered greetings on

behalf of the Blue Sky Spectacular Company. He asked if the trader would mind the company joining the caravan. "We would be more than happy to share escort, protection, night watch and hunting on the long ride to Casparsport.

"Greeting to yourself," boomed the trader. "By all means, dear man. How many wagons are you and how many of you are proficient with weaponry?" From his appearance and dress, he originated from the southern lands, probably Calimshan.

"In all, I would say seven of us are most proficient in a variety of close quarter and ranged weapons. We have to be, particularly when we travel on our own. There are many hazards in these lands, not least here in the north of Lopastor where protection to travellers and the law is virtually non-existent. We are a travelling company of acrobatic performers and bring four wagons and a number of mounted escorts with us. Three of us are seasoned hunters, mostly of animals suitable for the campfire but of other two-legged quarry if need arises."

The merchant laughed. "Admirable, dear man," he cried. "Then I shall say that your company is welcome indeed. Tuck your wagons in behind ours but tomorrow you should put them in amongst my own. I am Tallhuli Ben-Hadath, deputy proprietor of the Rising Golden Moon Commercial Society."

The speed at which they travelled was less than they had hoped but with the threat posed by the Massbourgs, their safety would be improved if not assured.

However, Undar, Gandar, Boulaye or Harley would point out riders on the horizon almost every day.

...o o O o o...

PART 5

SEARCH

Chapter 18

The Company turned onto the road leading west towards Casparsport fifteen days later. The caravan left the road and formed up in a defensive square as they always did. The city was a day's ride at the rate of the great train of wagons.

Cooking fires were lit and the gathering sat around them to eat; game had been plentiful on the plains through which the road took them and hunting had been profitable. As darkness fell, some of the Company gathered in closer to Boulaye. This was not customary; usually they drifted away to their wagons or bedrolls once the watch had been set.

"Ho there, what is this?" said Boulaye softly. "Do you have the need to parley?"

Uncharacteristically, it was Solarin, the ageing Halfling bard, who was the first to speak out. "Aye, Boulaye. Some of us has been speakin'. We wants to know what is going on. There's bin riders shadowing us for two weeks or more. Aye, we seen 'em too. There was some goin's-on in Grappina. An' what was that up in the hills when Harley came back with blood all over his tunic and Undar was hurt? An arrow wound that was. An' what *really* happened to Pretteen?"

Boulaye had never heard Solarin put so many words together in a speech at one time before, except perhaps in song or storytelling.

Balari and Tinnisse Lightfoot, the Halfling jugglers, nodded in agreement. "If there is something you and the others are doing, then it affects the Company," said Tinnisse, "you need to tell us what it is or something otherwise you will lose our trust."

Balari, also normally very quiet, rose to his feet and scratched at his scalp. He drew his hand away, looked at his fingernails and wiped then down his tunic. "Look, the way we see it is, if it is something you are doing that is secret then at the very least you need to tell us if you are placing the rest of us in danger. An' if it is illegal or immoral we should 'ave the option of pulling out. Even more, if there is something the whole Company can assist you with then tell us what we can do. But, look, don't just ignore us and think we don't know. Not only will you lose our trust, as Tinnisse said, you may also lose us."

Boulaye leaned back and looked up to the stars as is searching for inspiration. He sighed and looked at the Halflings. "Gather the rest of the Company together," he directed. "Bring them all here."

Solarin jumped up to his feet and called for the others. Within a short time, they had all gathered around, sitting around the fire. Only Undar maintained vigilance around the perimeter of their Company's area of the camp.

Boulaye cleared his throat. "My friends," he began, "some of you are aware of the events at Grappina and why they happened. Please forgive me when I say that I can't tell you all of the background – I am under some restriction myself. I was asked to help find a person, an agent, in Grappina. Harley was also asked mostly because of his own fighting skills. You have seen how he practises with his sword every night."

"Who asked you to do this?" asked Olwetta.

"As I said, there are a few things on which we are sworn to silence. I really shouldn't say, and I ask you to keep it secret but it comes from people of power in Westron Seaport. Harley asked Niebelittin Bellpealer for help and he gave it. Some of you helped by causing a diversion in the Impoverished Quarter; remember the fires? The agent we sought had been murdered some time ago but we had another. Harley was able to rescue

Pretteen. I am pleased she has recovered so well and my lovely lady, Jetti, says she is learning the dances well."

"I done some dancing before," said Pretteen. "Why was Undar hit?" It was no secret that she and Undar had become very close over the last few days.

Boulaye nodded his head. "Ah yes. That is a bit of a long story really. A man by the name of Traviss Hartimmer was a leading aristocrat in the city. When Harley stormed the city gaol, he killed Zheulin the gaoler. This was the dwarf that caused so much suffering. Khargal Tron, the leader of the city watch was also killed by you, wasn't he?" Harley nodded. Boulaye continued. "Hartimmer escaped the city with four brothers by the name of Massbourg and possibly a few others as well. I believe that the three surviving Massbourgs have been shadowing us. It was the fourth that Harley killed when the man put an arrow into Undar."

"So why were they following us in the first place?" asked Jetti. "I can understand that they will want to avenge their brother's death."

Boulaye rubbed his chin but it was Harley who answered. He stood up beside Riette who looked up at him. "Because we upset their position of importance and because we, Boulaye and me, think we know what they are up to next."

Boulaye interrupted him with a wave of his hand. "They are looking for a treasure, a fortune that was once amassed by one Ignacia Karouche."

The Pirate King from centuries ago?" gasped an incredulous Solarin Fleet. "I used to sing a song about him, it was rather rude!" he added with a chuckle.

"Aye, the very same," replied Boulaye. "Zheulin tortured a Priest of Diette by the name of Tyson Kashtillan to tell him where the treasure was. As far as is known the priest either said nothing or he didn't know. But Traviss Hartimmer believes the priest to be a descendant of the Pirate King and is probably already on his way to Casparsport where the priest was born and did his learning. He has probably tasked the Massbourgs with removing the threat of Harley, Gandar and myself."

Riette took a sharp intake of breath and looked up to Harley with her hand to her mouth.

"And you did not want to tell us any of this?" whispered Jetti. "How foolish is that?"

Boulaye shook his head and sighed. Her whisper could well have been a screech for it jarred on his bones just the same. "I know, beloved. I should have told you all but you would have fretted. I do apologise."

"Olwetta and I are also curious," said Ragdan. His voice was deep but soft. "We both have said that there is more to you, Harley, than meets the eye. Your swordsmanship is no natural skill, is it? You practice and move in a way that I have only ever seen once before. At that time it was a man who came from afar, from beyond the stars it was said. His name was Yukio Mishima. Did he teach you?"

Harley was astonished. He didn't expect that the middle-aged warrior teacher from the Guild would have been known by others outside of the Guild itself. But, of course, Yukio will have made his name known before becoming a master swordsman and teacher. "Aye, he taught me. I was privileged to learn from him for a time."

"Wait! I know that name," said Solarin. "I have sung the verses of the Lay of the Companions of the Forest of Gloomshade many times over the years. He is one of those names that are revered. It is not sung so often these days but it describes the terror of the undead

232

that they finally destroyed. They killed a white dragon. Did you know that?"

Harley's head whipped up from looking at Riette. "I have not heard of *that* exploit," he said. "I must get you to tell me more some time."

"Well, it was all –"

"What happened at the way-station, Graban Hills, before we arrived at Grappina?" interrupted Olwetta. "Did you have anything to do with the death of the leader there?"

"Nay, he was killed by his own people," answered Harley.

"Then why did they think we took something of value?" she persisted.

Harley felt a little uncomfortable at this questioning but before he could answer, Boulaye stood up and rummaged in a belt-pouch.

"It is because of these," he replied, holding in his hand a large black velvet bag. He pulled open the neck of the bag and emptied the contents into his hand. Large precious stones glistened there in the light from their campfire. He placed them back in the bag and put it back inside his belt-pouch.

"Were you were intending to keep this from us?" asked Olwetta angrily. There were murmurs of discontent among some of the companions.

"Nay, he was not," said Gandar sternly. "Harley and me knew of it and it was agreed that they would be equally shared between us all when we got back to Northwald City."

After a few more murmurs the company quietened down.

"Well, we know a bit more now than we did a while ago," said Tishia a little nervously. "What are *we all* going to do when we get to Casparsport?" Her emphasis made it plain that the Company was now committing themselves to acting together to address the next dilemma.

Boulaye felt that he had put himself into a tight spot through his mis-managment of the whole of the mission that had been given to him and Harley by the Commander in Westron Seaport so many weeks ago. He looked at each of them in turn as if assessing their individual resolve. They all gazed at him expectantly. His gaze finally rested on Jetti who scowled at him but raised an eyebrow questioningly.

He coughed and waved a hand as a cloud of smoke blew into his face from the fire. "I am considering that we enter Casparsport and embark on a treasure hunt."

...ooOoo...

The company followed in the wake of the procession of the wagons of the Rising Golden Moon Commercial Society as they entered through the huge iron-bound gates in the wall that encircled Casparsport. The wall itself was not particularly high but it had buttresses against its face to provide strength to the walls. A wooden palisade stretched across the whole length of its top as far as the eye could see. There seemed to be pitifully few sentries on watch.

The gates were in a woefully poor state of repair with their worn hinges, which caused one of the gates to sag against the ground, and their loose upright beams which clattered as two young boys kicked them obstinately. A watchman chased them off but they turned and gave him a torrent of verbal abuse.

The area outside the walls swarmed with shacks and shanties made from whatever materials could be salvaged by their inhabitants. This included broken wagons, pieces of other buildings from inside the city and from the city's dumps, tree branches and using wattle and daub walls that were made by the paupers, beggars and refugees themselves. Here and there they could see the shells of burnt-out shanties, any salvageable materials having been taken from them probably even before the flames had died down.

The smell of poverty, excrement, dung and decay filled the air, causing the merchant's people and those of the Company to cover their noses and mouths with their sleeves or hems of their cloaks. Dogs scampered around the hovels barking and snarling. A pair of men, drunk and aggressive, roared at the dogs for peace, lashed out with their feet and lifted earthenware bottles to their mouths. One of the dogs yelped and fled.

People sat in the doorways, what skin they had exposed being grimed and covered with suppurating sores. Children shrieked and chased after the wagons, clamouring around the wheels and riders and begging for coppers or food. Some of these children were clothed in ill-fitting rags and none had footwear. All were filthy, mud, dung and grime covered. Harley would never have believed that such abject impoverishment could exist so close to a large city; or anywhere else for that matter.

Two foul-smelling urchins climbed onto the wagon driven by Riette. Pretteen sat beside her, her face a visage of distaste. The brats immediately started folding back the tarpaulin. Pretteen yelled at them to get down but Riette scattered a few copper coins on the ground. The young children instantly leapt down and scrabbled in the dusty wheel ruts for the coins. Pretteen shrugged and smiled and Riette winked in return. Before the wagons could be invaded again, they were all at the gate.

Tallhuli Ben-Hadath, the owner of the Rising Golden Moon Commercial Society caravan, had directed his escort riders to lead their wagons to a large assembly area to the right as they filed through the gates. The city excise men would soon begin to randomly search through them to evaluate the amount of entry tolls that would have to be paid.

Boulaye similarly directed the Company to line up their wagons on an assemble area to the left side. A young, bored-looking official, flanked by two assistants, dragged himself over to the Company.

"Who's your leader?" the official asked in an almost disinterested manner.

"That will be me, I suppose," responded Boulaye, equally nonchalantly.

"What trade goods do you carry?"

"What, including juggling balls?"

"I beg your –" The official looked mystified.

Ragdan strode over to Boulaye and the official and loomed over the pair of them. The official paled.

"We are a travelling troupe of acrobatic performers, young man!" rasped Boulaye. "The only goods we carry are for our performances and our personal belongings. We are not here to trade. We are here to delight and entertain, a delight that I have no doubt you would benefit from. Now, you are free to check in whatever wagon you choose or even all of them if you are as bored as you look."

"I, er, I –. You are cleared to proceed. You will find accommodation hard to come by. Look, er, I know of a newly constructed livery stable in a corral. It was built for a trader and blacksmith but they were, er, they died unexpectedly. Er, just up the road, yonder, to its end. Tur - turn right and pass the Temple of Cahuhl, then next left and it faces you at the end. Er, speak to Adanshi, the caretaker, and give him my name. T - tell him you have paid Cityman Muggtin to use the stable, er, that's me. If you give me twenty gold crowns it's yours for a week. Is that fair?"

"Is there hay, straw, corn for the horses and water?" asked Gandar.

Muggtin shook his head vigorously. "Er, no. We didn't get around, er, to arranging that just now."

"Then I think ten gold would be preferable, don't you?"

"I think, er, t-ten gold, er, I think, er, aye Goodsir. Aye. I shall write out a, er, reckoning for you. Er, right now."

As the company trundled onwards in the direction given by Muggtin, Gandar and Harley rode with Boulaye. The road they were advised to take bypassed the Underprivileged Quarter, generally referred to as the *Shanty Town*.

"Damned Muggtin! What a fart!" said Boulaye. "With Ragdan standing next to me I could have had that prick giving me money for the privilege of us staying in the stable. That man we have to meet, what;s his name?"

"Adanshi," replied Harley. "He is the caretaker it seems."

"Aye, Adanshi," grunted Boulaye. "Let us hope he does not try to part me from our money."

Gandar looked irritated. "If Muggtin has been feeding us crap, I shall feed him his favourite little toy with a side plate of his own sweetmeats!"

Many eyes were watching them as they made ready to move their wagons. One watcher observed them closely, his single eye looking more intently at Boulaye.

Harley rode forward with Ragdan and soon located the corral. An elderly man sat atop the gate with a pipe of smoke-weed.

Harley approached him and spoke to him sternly. "Are you Adanshi? We have just now come to a financial arrangement with one Cityman Muggtin and shall be staying here for a period of up to a week. Our wagons and riders will appear momentarily. I wish to open the gate to allow them access!"

"I suppose you meaning you wants to come in," wheezed the old man through a cloud of pipe-smoke. "Why di'nt you say so?"

Adanshi climbed down gingerly from the gate and rubbed the back of his legs. "Looks after the place, does I," he grumbled. "No fires in the stable, use the forge. You will have to get the straw and stuff yerself. I'll be back in a week for more money if yous stayin' longer."

Without another word, Adanshi strolled off muttering to himself though his pipe-smoke.

Ragdan reached over and pulled the gate open. Harley rode up to him and pointed across the road.

"There is a very nice tavern there," he said. "I would hope we can make use of that from time to time."

A large flat-bed wagon had just arrived outside the tavern, pulled by four very large dray horses. The wagon was loaded with hogshead barrels of ale. A number of barkeepers and flunkeys filed out of the tavern and rolled four of the barrels off the wagon and down a ramp.

Minutes later, Boulaye led the company up the road and into the corral. Riette had vomited over the side of her wagon but some of it had gone down the wheel. Tishia and Balari had also vomited, so offensive was the reek to their nostrils as they had entered the city.

"Unload the wagons and clean up," ordered Boulaye. "We are going to need some hay and straw. Let's all get to it. Nobody to go to the tavern until I say you can. Riette, get some water and clean that sick off the wheel; it stinks!"

Their arrival had triggered a lot of interest. A few drinkers had stepped out of the tavern opposite, mugs of ale in one hand and pipes in the other as they leaned against the corral fence. A number of children, better dressed and presented than those they had seen earlier, climbed the fence and sat atop it.

Boulaye sauntered across to a group of older youngsters and offered a few coppers to them with the promise of a silver coin to each afterwards, if they could arrange delivery of a wagonload of straw, another of hay and a third of sacks of horse-feed. The three boys and one girl rushed off.

It took the remainder of the afternoon for the Company's equipment to be unloaded and the horses to be cleaned and brushed down. Balari had checked the wagons and greased the axles and the traces were rolled up and stored in the stable. The wagons of straw, hay and horse feed arrived in the early evening and the youngsters were rewarded. They spent an hour unloading the wagons with unexpected help from Riette who used a newly-discovered magical spell to assist lifting the straw bales through the loft opening with a spell of levitation. Night had fallen by the time Boulaye gave them leave to go off to the tavern. Undar, Pretteen and an exhausted Riette offered to stay in the stable to keep watch on their equipment.

They sat around a large trestle table and waited for a bartender to appear. Despite the large number of patrons, unlike many taverns, the air was not so thick with smoke-weed because the window shutters had been opened. A barman appeared, dragging a lame leg as he walked over. Boulaye asked to see the innkeeper.

"The proprietor of this establishment is indisposed at this moment, Goodsir," said the barman with a sanctimonious air. "I shall ask him to come over to you when he appears. Meanwhile, how may we be of service?"

"Pitchers of ales and mead and a large bowl of your

best stew with large hunks of bread and a similar order for three people in the livery stable opposite, if you please!"

"Pitchers, goodsir?" he replied with a sneer of antipathy.

"You do have such a thing, do you not?" responded Olwetta with an imperious, almost regal, expression. "Mugs for all and clean spoons all round."

The barman's face dropped and he scuttled off.

"*The proprietor of this establishment is indisposed!*" echoed Solarin, with a slight emphasis on a higher pitch in his voice.

The others laughed and the mood softened. Ales, mead and mugs were soon deposited and mugs were filled. Boulaye, Gandar, Ragdan and Solarin filled pipes with smoke-weed and sat back wreathing curls of smoke about them. It was a while before a large iron pot full of stew and a basket of bread appeared. Clean bowls and spoons were placed in the centre of the table.

Olwetta picked up a spoon and looked at each side of it. "Clean! Very impressive," she mumbled.

Harley looked at her closely. *There is much more to lady Olwetta than people say, I am certain.*

"This stew is actually very good," gasped Tinnisse. "I can taste herbs and spice. Is this a fungus? Ugh! How strange!"

"Do you know," began Gandar while chewing a morsel of bread. "You are able to eat almost half of all fungus that grows in the wild. Some of them are nutritious but others are not. Many sorts of fungus are highly poisonous. The rule is that if you do not know which is good then leave it where it is."

"Well, I am happy with big lumps of meat," muttered Ragdan. "And ale!"

The proprietor walked over to them during their meal. "Welcome, sirs and ladies, welcome to the Star of Caspar Tavern." He wheezed as he spoke and wiped his brow with a silk kerchief. "I trust the meal is good; it is our best stew with the meat of cow and mutton with the freshest of vegetables."

They nodded to confirm it was good and the innkeeper beamed with obsequious delight. He was short and extremely fat. His greying hair was tied in a tail and he wore a colourful flamboyant gown tied at the waist by a red sash. His grey beard was braided with a red bow at its tip.

"I am Arnan Ben-Harami. I own this establishment. My man over there says that you would like to speak with me. Are you happy to chat while you eat?"

"Aye. We can do that," answered Boulaye. "My name is Boulaye." He gestured to a stool at the end of the table and, with effort, Ben-Harani lowered himself onto it.

"You came here at a bad time. The trade fleet is in the port. They'll be off soon, in less than a week. Then you'll find many of the inns and taverns will have sleeping chambers available."

"No matter. We should be fine in the livery stable," Boulaye stated. The others nodded in assent. "I have no wish to split up the company into two or three different taverns around the city."

"That is good; that is good!" wheezed Ben-Harami, "particularly as I am today engaged in negotiation to purchase the corral and livery stable to extend my business interests in the city. I hope to conclude them tomorrow. Perhaps I shall be able to make your stay more comfortable. Straw palliasses, blankets, water facilities, for example. How do you maintain a watch over your equipment?"

Boulaye glanced at the others. "We all take our turn in standing watch day and night. We are accustomed to it."

241

"I can provide for you a squad of watchmen day and night at a modest cost of, perhaps, four gold crowns per day. They will be well-trained and loyal to me. That means they will be loyal to you too."

"Why?" asked Ragdan. "Why would you do this for us?"

"A good question, Goodsir," wheezed Ben-Harami. He held a silk handkerchief to his mouth and coughed heavily into it. "I sit on the City Council with the responsibility for internal law-keeping and safety of its inhabitants – *cough* – which means that our valued visitors are given protection too. I am just keen to be of assistance. Think about it and talk to me soon. Is there any other service I can offer you?"

"Aye, there is one," replied Boulaye. "A morning feast to be brought over to the livery stable each day."

"Such a trivial request! It shall be done." With supreme effort, Ben-Harami heaved himself off the stool, gave them a curt bow and waddled away.

"I've never heard so much crap!" laughed Olwetta. "These watchmen are not offered to us for our protection. They are to watch us."

The group murmured their agreement.

Boulaye nodded and scratched at his scalp. "We really don't need that right now with what we plan to do. We can keep that as an option though."

Tishia leaned forward with a hand raised timidly. "Er, what shall we do when there are chambers available in the taverns?"

Gandar placed his hands together on the table as he leaned forward. "Assuming the taverns have chambers, I doubt there will be enough for us all to stay together."

It was a moment before Boulaye responded. "I don't want to split us up because anybody who is isolated will be vulnerable. Things may get messy and we should be together."

242

"I still like the idea of having our own guards though," suggested Harley. "It should give us freedom to do what we need to do."

...ooOoo...

Chapter 19

It was the early hours of the morning before the exhausted company finally settled down for the night. Harley, Undar, Gandar and Ragdan provided the night watch. It was approaching midday before all of them were awake and fed. With Olwetta, Pretteen and Riette providing sentry patrols, the others gathered in one of the stalls. Straw bales were set up in a tight circle and a folding table erected in the centre.

Boulaye stood in the centre. He cleared his throat, still hoarse from the smoky tavern the previous night. "We must discuss what we need to do and agree on the next move. We have some options that will help us discover the whereabouts of this treasure. As I see it, we can talk to the High Priest of the Temple of Diette. We can see if the city has a historic journal or office of municipal records and we can see if there are any surviving descendants of the Pirate King's woman all those centuries ago. We shall have to discover what her name was first though. Anyone else got any suggestions?"

"Aye, I have one," replied Gandar: "We shall also need to find out if there has been any other interest in these investigations."

Ragdan's deep voice responded: "Aye. It may indicate that Traviss Hartimmer is in the city and you can be assured he won't be prepared to share the spoils."

"I agree with that," said Boulaye. "Although some of us have been here in Casparsport before, I suggest we walk together round the city so as to get to know our way round. Keep it casual as if we are sightseers. Perhaps we may be able to find more suitable lodgings. After all, we may be here for some time."

Harley sighed. "Look, I still think perhaps we should buy ourselves some fighting men. This looks like the place where we will have the need because Hartimmer's men will undoubtedly be snooping around here soon and this is also the place to find some."

"You may be right, lad," responded Boulaye. "I thought about what you said last night. Trouble is you don't know what you're getting and who you can trust. They may say the right things to you and stab you in the back when you turn it towards them."

"Got to agree with Harley, boss," said Solarin. "Put money on it that who'sit, Hartimmer, will buy hisself some muscle. He's prob'ly got people looking for this treasure right now. He'll have friends in low places, mark well my words."

"Very well, we'll see about that."

Abruptly, Riette poked her head through the door. "Boulaye, there is someone here who says he knows you and wants to see you."

Boulaye looked up sharply. "What's his name?"

"Didn't say."

Boulaye huffed. "What does he look like?"

"Eye-patch, a big scar on his face." She indicated a slash down her own right cheek, itself disfigured by a scar.

"Rax! I'll come out." A grin spread across his face.

He leapt to his feet and tore out of the door. A few moments later he came back in with another figure. This man, very tall, very lean, stood before them smiling broadly.

"Everybody, this is Rax Starwatcher, an old friend of mine from years ago! Godsdammit, Rax, not seen you for, how long has it been?"

"Almost twenty years ago, Falarr, when I pulled you out from the dungeon in Cascant. That was a shit-hole"

Boulaye winced at the sound of his first name. "Aye

Rax. You saved my life that day."

"Just payin' you back for draggin' me out of the burning temple. They took my eye but you saved my life that day."

The man had long black wavy hair that flowed down over his shoulders. A brown leather eye-patch was affixed over his right eye and a vivid scar slashed beneath the eye-patch from forehead to chin. He had a clipped beard and a long moustache which drooped below his chin. He wore a light-weight chainmail surcoat underneath a sheepskin jacket. He had a matched pair of sabres, one hanging from each of his hips, and carried a pair of throwing daggers across his chest. His tanned face only served to emphasise his white teeth as he smiled. He waved jovially.

"How do you come to know each other?" asked Harley.

"Ah, we journeyed together many years ago," replied the stranger. "We fought in the Cascantan goblin wars and wenched and drank ourselves blind. Then he went and found a lovely lady – ah, there I see her; sweet Jetti!"

Jetti blushed and laughed. Boulaye said "Hah! You always were sweet on Jetti, were you not, Rax?"

"Aye, Falarr, that I was but I soon found my own love. Remember her?"

"Aye, I remember her well. Lovely Aleene. How does she fare?"

Rax's face fell. For a brief moment sadness befell him. "She died, my friend. She died having my daughter many years ago. My daughter went to Westron Seaport, oh, three years or more ago to study and learn. I have not heard from Dellie in all that time but she continues to send money to her destitute father."

Harley's head shot up. "Wait a moment. Your name

is Starwatcher?"

Rax looked at him and nodded.

"And your daughter is Dellie?"

"Aye," replied Rax. "Why?"

"Then I do believe I know her," gasped Harley excitedly. "She used to practice with me in fighting and sword-play skills. She was regarded as the best ever female student to ever come out of the Fighters' Academy of the Guilds of Protectors of Westron Seaport. Be proud of her. She obviously has remembered you if she sent money back to you."

Once again, Rax smiled broadly. Well, I'll be gods-damned." He turned back to Boulaye. "I saw you arrive through the shanty town. You are late this year. Look Falarr, I should like to speak with you urgently on a delicate matter concerning your arrival. That is why I have come to you now."

Once again, Boulaye grimaced at the mention of his first name. He beckoned to Harley and Gandar led them to the back of the livery stable.

"Falarr, you were being closely watched by five riders when you came to the gate. Two were dark-skinned, probably Wildings from Chult. The other three were like peas from a single pod with blond hair and beards. They all look like they know how to fight. Have you upset somebody with your absurd ravings during your public performances?"

Boulaye chuckled. "We have indeed, Rax. We all know about these three blond men. There were four but Harley here took one out more than a fourteen-day ago. This man had put an arrow into the shoulder of one of my team. I've had to tell them all what Harley and I were up to because they had their suspicions."

Rax furrowed his brow. "What *are* you up to?"

"All will be made clear. Let us go back."

The group listened attentively to Rax's descriptions

of the watchers. Boulaye sat down on one of the straw bales and told him of some of the events at Grappina without going into detail about the Pirate King's treasure. He spoke of the treachery of Traviss Hartimmer and the likelihood that he was in Casparsport.

"Aye, but why are you here?" asked Rax. "What are you not tellin' me? Don't tell me you are here to do performances to your adorin' public."

There was a silence as everybody looked from Rax to Boulaye.

Boulaye stood up and stretched his back and shoulders. Sitting on bales of straw was not comfortable. "Hartimmer had somebody cruelly tortured to reveal the whereabouts of items of great value. What they are I do not know but it could be manuscripts, scrolls history or religious writings. Damn, it may even be a treasure hoard for all I know."

"And you think that Hartimmer and these ruffians are here lookin' for it?"

"Aye, that is what we think. The fact that you have seen these men virtually confirms it." There was a murmur of agreement from around the table.

Rax smiled again. "So what you need is some ruffians of your own to keep you safe while you start your own searchin', right?"

Boulaye sat back down and shrugged his shoulders. It was Gandar who rose to his feet. "Aye, we discussed using half a dozen reliable and loyal men but I'm not so sure. This was to be a covert activity and now it is growing like a field of mushrooms."

"I can get you the right men," responded Rax. "Ex-soldiers like you 'n' me. They won't ask questions if you pay 'em fair."

From the stable doors, Olwetta called. "Boulaye is right but if we are to split up the company to wander around the city to search for information, the small groups are going to be vulnerable, as we have already said. It will cost us to protect ourselves but it will be worthwhile. We can just about afford it."

"Acceptable," sighed Boulaye, throwing up his hands in defeat. "We shall pay a fair reward and if we find articles of value we shall pay out a share."

Rax nodded his head and gave a wide grin. "I shall find the ideal men but I shall pick them myself, Falarr. They will come from the shanty town but don't let that put you off. They will be reliable, tough and steadfast. As I said, they are ex-soldiers and damned good with their weapons. You need not tell them everything. If you trust me to do this, you will not be disappointed, I swear it. Either myself or they shall name the price and agree it with you. Give me a day; in fact I'll bring them here tomorrow just before dawn."

...ooOoo...

It was still dark when Rax Starwatcher and six broad-shouldered men stood outside the livery stable. All seven of them were fully-armed, wearing an assortment of light armour. Undar, now virtually recovered from his shoulder wound and having insisted on standing his share of the night watch, led them all into the building. Most of the company were still sleeping but awoke instantly on hearing the heavy footsteps of the new arrivals.

The six had the dark hair and eyes of men of the eastern lands. Rax introduced them one by one. LeDuc, Carerre, DuPrenne, Capalle, Merrello and Pallenne.

"The names sound Cascantan," suggested Undar.

"Aye," agreed LeDuc, clearly their leader. "Each one of us served the Dar-Cascan Royal Family in the *Corps of Foresters*. The situations changed in Cascant

249

after the fall of Triosande to the goblin hordes many years ago. The rule of law changed too and the *Foresters* have been exiled and are scattered over the realms."

The story of the fall of the Dar-Cascan dynasty, a generation ago, and the exile of the surviving nobles to neighbouring realms was well known in the western lands.

Gandar and Boulaye started to speak together but it was Gandar who had the edge. "I understand that the vast majority of Foresters managed to leave the country with most of the surviving Dar-Cascan royal family."

"It did indeed. The nobles were scattered, each with a contingent of *Foresters*. Now some of us are here in Lopastor raising funds and fighting support for a return to Cascant. It will happen; very soon."

"What became, then, of the royal fortune?" asked Boulaye. "Can that not be used to buy soldiers, weapons, armour and everything else you need."

"We only just managed to escape with the lives of our nobles and ourselves intact. Most of the royal treasures were hidden, we hope it still is, but much of it was taken. We raise funds in many ways, even by hiring ourselves out as mercenaries. I will tell you that we do not come cheap."

Boulaye looked from LeDuc to Rax and then across the faces of the company. "What do you suggest?" he asked falteringly.

LeDuc had no hesitation in responding. "Two gold crowns for each of us per day, including Rax. That includes food and lodging space in this stable." He smiled broadly as he spoke. "We shall not drink anything but water while we are on active duties. After all, water is drunk by lions so it cannot be that bad, can it?"

"Aye! But lions would drink ale if they could get

250

it!" suggested Gandar.

Similarly, Boulaye did not now falter as he answered. "Hah, I wish the members of my Company thought the same way about their liquid intake as you do! Acceptable," he said, extending his arm towards LeDuc.

A knock at the door brought them all to alertness. Ragdan lurched over and tore open the door. An astonished face looked back at him. A well-groomed servant from the tavern stood there with a two-wheeled trolley of platters of food and pitchers of mulled ales. His eyes looked up at the imposing appearance of the great barbarian and his white face fell.

"Um, m-morn feast. Good – er – sir! Morn feast?" He rushed away as soon as Ragdan relieved him of the trolley.

...o o O o o...

The elegantly-dressed man paced back and forth across the room. His face bore the expression of angered exasperation. Although he could have been described as well-dressed, his clothing showed signs of recent hard wearing, travel-stains and damage. His black hair had once been short and his long moustaches drooped down below his jawline. Six others sat in the austere chamber, two on plain, battered wooden chairs and the others arranged on two similarly battered benches. The small, plain wooden table held a single earthenware flask and atop it, a leather ale-mug.

"Dammit!" gasped the figure. "We risk being identified with the travelling clowns being in the city. Not to mention other travellers and merchants that I have had the misfortune to encounter in recent years. Should I, or yourselves for that matter, be recognised then we all risk being arrested and being carted in chains back to Grappina. We may be able to fight our way out but that could be perilous."

One of the listeners, a tall wiry man with a short, black and unkempt beard that had once been carefully tended and clipped, placed both hands carefully on the table. He began to speak in a slow and cautious manner.

"M'Lord," he began cautiously. "They are travelling minstrels and performers and not warriors. They probably do not have more than two or three among them that can raise, let alone wield, a sharp weapon."

Another blond-haired man played with a narrow-bladed dagger. "One of 'em, the young one what acts like a jester, killed me bruvver, Crand, out there in the long grass. An' he did it easy too. I was too far away to do anythin' about it. He's good wiv his hands an' wiv his blade. We gotta watch 'im!"

The pacing man paused and glared at the latest speaker. "You see, this is your first problem. You Massbourgs are immediately recognisable not only by the authorities and any bounty hunters that are looking for us but with this young jester too. You all look the gods-damned same with your long blond hair in braids and your long beards too. If the word goes out describing you then we're all in danger of getting caught. I suggest you take blades to your hair and your beards too, while you're at it. There could be a fortune at stake here and I don't want it compromised just because you want to look like dwarves!"

The three Massbourg brothers looked at each other and fingered their beards.

"Er, how much fortune?" asked one.

"How much?" roared the speaker. He slammed his fist down hard on the table. "Karouche was a Pirate King, for the gods' sake. It will be a vast amount. How much? How long is a piece of rope? Answer me that!"

The Massbourgs looked at each other again, this time with puzzled expressions. One shrugged and the other two shook their heads. The first replied "Don't know, fifty f–, um, M' Lord."

"You really do not appreciate the finer arts of rhetoric, do you?"

A confused silence descended across the table. The standing man dragged a chair across and sat down on it. It creaked noticeably even under his slim frame.

"M'Lord Hartimmer," a voice said. It was spoken with more confidence than the Massbourg voice.

Traviss Hartimmer, the former aristocratic Town Councillor from Grappina, now on the run with the three remaining Massbourg brothers and three former members of the Grappina Town Hall Guard, jerked his head up. "What is it?"

"The Blue Sky Spectacular Company now has hired help. Seven well-armed and professional-looking fighters turned up at their stable before dawn this morning. These men have the look of ex-soldiers about them. They look tough and are wearing armour too."

Hartimmer leaned back in his chair as he pushed it onto its back legs. It creaked precariously and he wisely dropped it back down again.

"Shit!" he spat. "This puts a very different slant on things. Going in there and wiping them out in one single attack, as I had hoped, is not such a good idea now."

"Perhaps we could consider picking them off in ones and twos," suggested one of the ex-guards.

Hartimmer looked up towards the dingy ceiling and then closed his eyes. "That idea, while manageable, will only cause them to be on their guard even more. If they will be looking for the Pirate King's treasure, as I believe they will, it will make it all the more difficult for us to do the same. We shall let them do the hard work. I want them followed wherever they go. I want you to follow covertly. Use stealth. Use other resources. Young kids may follow them for a few coppers and will be less noticeable than you. Change your appearance. Swop over followers so you don't arouse their suspicions. Report back to me on everything they do. Understand?"

They all nodded and rose to leave.

"And another thing," growled Hartimmer. "Chop off those beards and shorten your hair! You look like damned dwarves! You smell worse!"

...o o O o o...

Chapter 20

"What is the plan, Boulaye?" asked Harley.

The Morn feast had been simply extraordinary. They had expected little more than a basket of bread and chunks of meat, if they were fortunate, or cheese. Instead, they were treated to an array of pieces of meat, goat probably, dipped in a mixture of honey and spices, a variety of cheeses, bread, fruit and oatcakes. To drink they had a beef tea and mulled ale. The company and their team of guards were silent as they devoured the meal.

Boulaye had spent a while on one side talking with Rax Starwatcher. Harley and Gandar had also attended. Rax offered his assistance to the company while arranging the six Cascantans into a watch roster. Boulaye then gathered the whole company together and they sat on the straw bales.

"We need to split into three groups, I would say," suggested Boulaye. "One group to go over to the Temple of Diette to see if they have any knowledge of the family history of their priest, Kashtillan. I would like to see if there are any records going back as far as the original woman who was courted by Ignacia Karouche, that Pirate King."

"That would have been during the time of the so-called god-war," suggested the ageing Halfling, Solarin. "I was a mere stripling of a brat when the skies darkened and thunderous storms of the warring gods and demigods blackened the skies. It was fearful. The winds, hurricanes and tornadoes, the constant lightning and the driving hail and rain, laid waste the lands and flattened or burned the towns and cities to the north. That was barely sixty years past. If what you say about Kashtillan being the latest of a long family line of priests, they might have been in different temples then."

"By the gods!" exclaimed Boulaye as he clapped a hand to his forehead. "I hadn't thought of that. That will give us another question to ask the High Priest I suppose."

"What of the other two groups?" asked Undar.

"Another group can go to the city's records office or registry, if they have one; they may have some records there going back to the time of Ignacia Karouche. We need to try to find the name of the woman he had, for the want of a better term, bedded. We will need to find where her home was.

"And the third group?" prompted Olwetta.

Boulaye paused for a few moments. "I suggest we keep one group here at the stable. During our journeys into the city we can take two of Rax's guards with each group and have the other two here to protect the third group. We can swop group members around to give all of us a chance to get out of the stable if they want to do that. How does that appeal to everyone?"

Nods and murmurs of assent came from around the table.

"Er, there is still a danger from Hartimmer and his men," said Riette nervously. It was unusual for her to speak but with Harley sitting next to her she clearly felt more confident. She still raised her hand to cover the scars on her face however, probably more from habit.

"Aye lass," replied Boulaye. "That there is. It is worth saying that should Hartimmer and his cronies, the Massbourgs, try to do something like that, it would raise a hue and cry that would compromise their own safety. I do strongly recommend caution and vigilance nonetheless. I wouldn't put it past them to try something stupid. I hear tell that the Massbourgs are not the cleverest monkeys in the tree and we still don't know what other men are with Hartimmer."

Harley raised his hand in a gesture of warning. "It may be that they will be content to watch us so we must ourselves be watchful. We still have no knowledge of just how many other men came with Hartimmer when he absconded from Grappina."

Heads nodded again in agreement.

"The City Watch here is apparently keeping an eye open for Hartimmer," said Rax. "But it will be a lazy eye, particularly if he crossed their palms with gold. I wouldn't put that trick past him. Those lazy eyes will be turned away."

Gandar sat back and smiled. "I have an idea," he began slowly. "Look, if we are expecting to be watched, they won't be expecting us to be looking out for them, will they?"

"I rather like that idea," said Rax, a vicious glint in his one eye and a manic smile on his face.

"Let us think about this with a bit of logic," responded Harley. "If we were to watch or follow people who are known to us, it would be quite obvious, would it not?"

Boulaye nodded his head. "So what you are saying is, if I have this aright, they will get others to watch us, or to follow us. That is what I would do."

"And you would use the service of people who would blend in and look like they belong there," exclaimed Harley.

Gandar slapped a hand on the table. "By the gods! Of course! Beggars, youths, children, vagrants."

Boulaye turned to Rax. "Could you muster a group of lads? They should have cunning and guile. This would just be for a few days. I want to know if our people are being followed or watched. They should take no action but follow them unseen to find out where the watchers report back to. Can you arrange that?"

Rax threw his head back and laughed. His long, black hair swayed as he chuckled. "Hah! I love the idea and know just the ne'er-do-well lads who could do that for us. The promise of silver coins will ensure they perform well. Leave it to me; I'll bring some of the lads in the morning."

Boulaye leapt to his feet just as Harley did the same. It was Harley, however, who spoke first. "No! No, do not bring them here! We must not associate these lads with our group. Keep them separated from us and have them report through to you through another intermediary."

"Aye, good thinking, Lad," replied Boulaye.

Leaving Undar and the Halfling tumblers, Balari and Tinnisse, under the protective eyes of Rax and two of the guards to watch the livery stable, the others split up into two groups to go into the city to gather information. It was agreed that they would all carry their weapons so as to meet any potential threat from Hartimmer or the Massbourgs.

Boulaye also suggested that they would all meet up during the day to discuss their progress once they had all returned to the livery stable.

...o o O o o...

They all rose before dawn. Rax brought in the two guards, Carerre and LeDuc, from their patrolling outside the stable. Merrello and Pallenne strapped on their weapons and took over. Boulaye divided them all into the teams that would either carry out investigations around the city or look after the stable and their equipment. The stable and corral would be looked after by Undar, Solarin, Balari and Tinnisse. Rax, along with Merrello and Pallenne, would provide their additional protection.

"Keep a good eye open for people following you. You know what the Massbourgs look like, of course, but you don't know what others Hartimmer has working for him. What do you think, Harley? What would you do if you were him?"

"He won't do any of the dirty work himself. He would get the Massbourgs to do the muscle work, perhaps try to remove us one by one. So we must not get ourselves separated from our teams or leave the safety of the stable and corral alone. As we said yesterday, he would probably recruit a group of boys or youths to watch and follow us. They know the city and will be almost invisible. They will be harmless but will report our movements."

"So what can we do about them?" asked Pretteen.

"Well, we can't kill 'em" chortled Solarin as he puffed on a pipe of smoke-weed. Tishia, sitting alongside him, finally gave up suppressing a cough and moved away from him. He cocked an eyebrow but made no comment.

"Their mamas would probably complain," joked Balari.

"All humour aside," grunted Boulaye. "What can we do, Harley?"

"It may be possible to follow them but these are their streets and if they are sharp, we will be spotted. They will juat run off knowing that we can't chase them without causing a fuss. I suggest we ignore them for now but see what we can do after a couple of days. They may get complacent and not notice somebody watching them. That, of course, assumes that we spot them."

Boulaye rose to his feet and held his arms out sideways. "Into your teams," he said. "Time for us all to go. Stay together in your teams. Keep your weapons handy and keep your guards close."

Boulaye led his team, comprised of Harley, Jetti, Riette and Tishia, along quiet streets. They were supported by LeDuc and Capalle who shadowed them on either side of the street. Traders were at work leading pack donkeys or handcarts loaded with goods but, apart from then, the city was quiet. Casparsport City was only now waking up to a new day. Although the rising sun had yet to appear over the buildings, towers and minarets of the city, the heat of the day was already making itself felt.

It took almost half an hour to find the Temple of Diette, the God of Law and Justice. The temple itself was a tall, round, grey stone tower with a wooden hoarding around its rampart, reminiscent of defensive crenellations and typical of temples dedicated to Diette. The heavy wooden doors were just being opened by a pair of young priests, resplendent in their green and grey robes, tied around their waists by white ropes.

Surprisingly, it was Riette who stepped forward and asked the temple door warden, a young acolyte of little more than twelve summers, to speak with someone who could help them with their historical research.

"Hail, and I bid you welcome," the lad intoned, the first line of a common prayer to Diette. "Lady Mage, I am Tolladin. You will want the Master of Religious Histories." He bowed respectfully and bade them to follow him.

"There seems to be a surprising number of wizards here, Riette," said Harley.

Mages were strolling with their heads buried in parchments and books or walking with the temple priests. Strangely, very few mages were engaged in conversation with other mages.

"Diette is one of the gods of Lawful Magic," she

replied. "There are other gods of magic too but they are dark gods. Diette is not. He is also the God of Protection for the Defemceless. These two portfolios complement each other."

LeDuc and Capalle agreed to wait in the temple lobby while Boulaye and the team were taken along a short, wide hallway floored with gleaming marble. Divine and arcane symbols adorned the walls although predominant among these was the holy symbol of Diette, a pentagon within which was the device of an eye mounted on a small set of scales. Most of the clerics carried with them a highly-polished quarterstaff, said to be the favoured weapon of the God himself. They were taken over to an elderly cleric Tolladin had spotted shuffling across the hall.

"Hail, and I bid you welcome," the cleric chanted.

Riette returned the greeting and explained the purpose of their request.

The cleric, Jeellan, spoke softly with a dry, husky voice. "I can instigate a search for you. I cannot guarantee success and I shall have to ask for a donation for the Temple."

Boulaye had prudently predicted this and he passed a gold crown over to the priest.

The man's eyes widened. "Goodsir is *most* generous. I shall begin immediately. Please follow me to my library and take a seat."

Jeellan shuffled out and led them slowly up two flights of stone stairs, along a short passage and into an austere chamber crammed with shelves and bookcases, trunks and crates. There seemed to be little order with the stacks of ledgers, books and scrolls but he went immediately to a shelf in the furthest right-hand corner of the chamber and searched through scrolls and ancient books for information.

"Tell me again who it is I am searching for?" the

ageing cleric asked.

Boulaye was about to respond but Jetti interrupted her husband. She seemed impatient and Boulaye suppressed his irritation. "We seek information of a Cleric or Priest called Kashtillan from before the time of the first god-war and the emergence of the new order."

"Oh dear! Our records may not go back that far. That was four centuries ago. I believe the best information held in those times was kept by other Temples of the dead gods. He rummaged through a shelf of boxes of dusty scrolls but to no avail.

How about the name of Karouche?" suggested Harley. He wrote the name on a scrap of parchment with a stick of charcoal.

"Karouche? That name sounds vaguely familiar," Jeellan murmured. "Return on the morrow." He suggested they try the Temple of Cahuhl which was close by. "They are not the most helpful of people though. Meanwhile, I shall continue with the search for the Cleric, er, Kashtillan."

They collected LeDuc and Capalle in the lobby and left the temple. The march to their next destination took them to the very edge of the city of Casparsport, through an impoverished area.

Suspicious eyes watched them as they picked their way through poorly-kept streets. The once cobbled surfaces were now covered with filth, horse manure and the dead carcasses of dogs, birds and more besides. The stench was overpowering. The poverty here was worse than they had seen and there was no evidence of city watch or other law enforcement. The team closed up together and their two guards ensured they walked through the area without fear of confrontation by the local people.

The Temple of Cahuhl was a dark, squat building

that, to Boulaye's eyes and those of the others, resembled a great mausoleum. They approached the main entrance, heavy black oak doors with iron banding, that were only slightly ajar.

They were suddenly challenged by an armed priest, dressed in purple robes. "What is your business in the Temple of The Severe Reaper?" he uttered in a customary challenge. His priestly robes were dark grey, almost black, with purple edging.

This time it was Boulaye himself who stepped forward. "We seek knowledge on the history of a cleric a few hundred years ago. Is there one here who can help us? We shall be generous with a donation."

The priest did not introduce himself or offer polite words of greeting but, with a curt gesture, led them across an austere foyer to a door in a corner. He knocked on the door but did not wait to be asked inside, instead walking straight in. "Visitors!" he grunted, then turned on his heel walked out without another word or even a glance at the visitors.

The painfully thin cleric sat on a padded stool and looked over his shoulder at them. His skin appeared stretched across his skull-like face emphasising his rheumy eyes. "Er, What-? I am the Cleric of Historical Records. What do you want with me?" His unpleasant manner prophesised an unhelpful attitude.

The chamber was chaotic with scrolls scattered across tables, the floor and a single wooden rack. The fetid stink of the chamber, the disarrayed cot in a corner and a wooden bucket covered with a grey cloth showed that the cleric spent his life in this one room.

Boulaye spoke boldly and with authority. "We are seeking any records you may have on a Cleric by the name of Kashtillan. It was many, many years ago, before the the first god-war."

The cleric was clearly on the defensive. "I, er, I am

still sorting out these scrolls. As you can see –". He gestured with a sweep of his arm at the piles of scrolls. They had obviously been poorly kept and many were disintegrating.

"Look," he said. "We don't have anything here which goes back that far. A lot of historical scrolls went over to the Temple of Clamberhan or the High Temple of Haeman. These are said to have the most extensive Libraries of City History in Casparsport."

The group turned and made to go. A soft cough from the cleric turned them back. "Look, can you see your way to a donation. Just a modest sum otherwise the next funeral rite performed here may be mine. The Loremaster is very intolerant these days."

Boulaye rummaged in a belt pouch and slipped a small pile of silver coins into the cleric's outstretched hand. The day was unusually hot and humid and the group was feeling its effects. By the time they stopped in a tavern and fought their way through the crowded taproom, Boulaye conceded that it would probably be too late in the day for them to try their investigations elsewhere. Almost two hours later they followed Boulaye outside the entrance to the temple and, with LeDuc and Capalle leading the way, they returned back to the more salubrious part of the city.

Each of them had been vigilant during the day but there had been no obvious sign of followers although with the streets and pathways thronged with citizens, traders, watchmen, and with children darting about and squealing, any watchers would have been difficult to spot.

They finally arrived at the corral, weary, hungry and footsore. Gandar's team was already back. The first bit of news they heard was not good.

...ooOoo...

Gandar and Olwetta jointly led the second team; whichever of them would be determined on the people they would be speaking with. They made ready to leave the stable. They were accompanied by Ragdan and Pretteen and the guards, Carerre and DuPrenne. Their first task, as had been directed by Boulaye, was to find the Guild of Chroniclers.

Ragdan was pacing the slate floor impatiently when, after a wait of almost two hours in the entrance hall of the guild building, they were approached by a bureaucratic official. The man peered at them through a pair of glass lenses perched in a frame at the top of his nose.

Gandar asked to speak with the keeper of historical chronicles or archives. The subordinate stated that the Master Archivist was already preoccupied with other patrons and advised they return in the early-afternoon. They left and waited in a local hostelry two streets away.

"This is damned irritating!" complained Ragdan, his deep voice resonating above the hubbub of the taproom. He scratched at his rough beard and folded his arms across his chest. "Is there anything we can be doing? Boulaye will wonder what we have been up to."

"Patience, husband dear," chided Olwetta. "Two hours and we should go back in there a little more assertively."

They returned soon after midday. Carerre and DuPrenne, their two guards, shadowed them to the Guild but waited outside.

The myopic underling peered haughtily at Gandar as he stood at the front desk.

"We seek any historical information you may have on –" started Gandar.

"We *only* deal with historical records here!" interrupted the man imperiously.

Olwetta stepped forward and placed her large hands flat on the desk. She leaned toward the official, looming over him. The timid man blanched.

"We are well aware of that, underling!" she rasped. "This is why we are here. As my friend was about to say, we seek information on a certain Cleric by the name of Kashtillan, and his mother who may probably have had the same name but we do not know this for certain. We also want anything you may have on the Pirate King –"

"Ah, y-yes," the official stammered, his eyes wide open. "Ig –, um, Ignacia Karouche. We had someone in here yesterday asking for details about this infamous character. We expect the man back early this evening." His lenses looked slightly askew as his head jerked backwards.

"Did this man give you his name?" asked Gandar.

"Er, Kamann, that was it."

"Red hair and beard?" prompted Gandar. The others looked at him in perplexity.

"Nay, unkempt black hair and long moustaches."

"That is him," said Ragdan. Pretteen nodded.

Gandar squared his shoulders and looked the official in the eye. "This man is a renegade aristocrat Councillor from the city of Grappina and is now on the run from the authorities. There is a significant bounty on his head for the successful arrest or demise of this man, one Traviss Hartimmer. He is a dangerous man so if he does come back I suggest you either tell him you are still looking or that you have found nothing. Do not attempt to capture him yourselves."

The official blanched again, his mouth opening and closing in silent astonishment. However, he wrote down the names requested.

"Hartimmer, I um, we are aware of this man absconding. There is a rumour. I, er, we shall conduct a search and have an answer for you by tomorrow at noon. I, er, I am almost certain we will have something on Karouche but the cleric could be a problem. I shall see to it myself immediately. There is a charge for the search. A, er, modest fee. Two, um, t–two silver."

Gandar handed over two bright coins. "There will be another silver piece for your personal trouble if you find us the information," Gandar added softly. His face showed a mirthless smile.

A short while after, as they sat around a board suspended across two battered old casks and sipped their warm ales whilst they pondered on their next move.

"Where else can we ask?" piped Pretteen.

Silence again settled around the makeshift table. Raised voices from across the taproom abruptly caught their attention.

Three drunken gamblers were arguing around another table. They gesticulated wildly and the dispute became more heated. Other drinkers placed their ale pots on their tables, stopped talking and turned to stare.

An earthenware ale pot was swung catching the most vociferous of the trio on the side of the head. The man went down to the filthy floor, catching the edge of the table. Ale, gambling tiles and coins scattered across the floor. The other two grabbed at as many of the coins as they could and tore out of the tavern as fast as their feet would carry them. Meanwhile, Carerre and DuPrenne had already risen to their feet with their hands at the hilts of their swords.

The tavern-keeper, a huge, bald-headed, man, strode over to the unconscious man and tipped a pot of ale over the man's head. The luckless man began to stir, shook his head and let out a bellow. The tavern-keeper reached down, lifted the drunkard and dragged him outside onto the street. Normality fell on the tavern as

267

the tavern-keeper re-entered and strode back to the bar.

"What if we go to the city assizes?" asked Olwetta, continuing the suspended conversation.

Gandar leaned back on his stool, looked blankly at her and then laughed. "You're right!" he exclaimed. "Come on, all of you, drink up." He tossed a few coins on the bar, beckoned to the two guards and together they filed out of the tavern.

The City Assizes were housed in a building constructed of stone on its ground storey and a wooden upper floor. Two uniformed guards stood sentry outside the main entrance and another guard stood inside. All of them were armed with a gleaming *guisarme*, a seven-foot long spear-like weapon with a curved blade at its tip which acted almost as an axe-head.

The Assize manager, a stout and formidable woman of middle years, peered up at them as they entered. Olwetta loomed over the meticulously tidy desk but smiled sweetly at her.

Although somewhat taken aback, the woman held her composure; this barbarian woman's demeanour immediately identified her as someone with authority and standing.

"Do you keep historical assize records, journals, archives or publications?" Olwetta asked.

"Yes, we do Goodlady, but not here. They are in the Citadel."

"And who do we speak to for access to them."

"Ah, I can arrange that for you but you cannot handle the documents yourself for many are old and fragile. What is it you seek?"

"We are investigating anything you may have on one Ignacia Karouche, the so-called Pirate King from four centuries ago. We also seek anything that may be recorded on his woman that he left behind when he left these lands after his incarceration."

"So you are treasure hunters then." It was a statement, more like an accusation, rather than a question.

"Partly perhaps, I must admit," replied Olwetta. "However, there is much more at stake than merely hunting for a long-lost treasure." Olwetta's articulation was having the desired effect on the matronly assize manager. "There is a group of wanted criminals also searching for this information one of whom, a traitorous aristocrat named Traviss Hartimmer, he once served the Grappina town council. He is now on the run, probably somewhere here in Casparsport, and will also be searching for the treasure. We hunt him and his gang, primarily, and the information that he acquires will hopefully lead him to us, or us to him."

"I know the name Hartimmer," responded the woman with more than a little disdain on ther face. "He has had a questionable reputation even here in Casparsport. We had heard rumours of him fleeing the city of Grappina. So you believe him to be here?"

"Aye, ma'am, we do. With at least three other men, all of them known felons. He may have picked up more cohorts on the way here too."

Gandar interjected with a description of the aristocrat and of the three Massbourg brothers.

"I shall inform the authorities today to be on their lookout for these men," she replied. "I assure you he will get no co-operation from this establishment. Return here tomorrow afternoon and I shall be able to let you know how we are progressing. There is a fee for searching through the records though. A gold crown."

Olwetta delved into her belt purse and brought out a cold coin.

"Your name?" she asked the woman.

"I am Meena Kandar, Goodlady."

They rejoined Carerre and DuPrenne in the entrance

hall to the assizes. DuPrenne looked agitated. "There's bin a coupla kids watching us from across the street," he said. "No, don't look. They're still there. Two of 'em. Ragamuffin ne'er-do-wells. Behind the pile of crates and casks."

"Give me a few minutes," said Pretteen. "Then start walking back to the stables."

"What – where are you going?" asked Gandar. "Get back here, young lady!"

"Take care lass," warned Ragdan. "Do not get –"

But she had already slipped away down the side of the assize building.

A short while later Gandar and the team followed Carerre and DuPrenne along the street back towards the corral. There was no sign of Pretteen.

"What did she think she was doing?" hissed a furious Gandar. "Gods! Boulaye made it *quite* clear that we have to keep together! Damned stupid! He'll rip our sweetmeats off!"

"Noth mine though!" sniggered Olwetta. "She is trying to prove herself useful. Did you never do anything reckless?"

"Yes I did!" he responded angrily. "But by then I knew how to wield a sharp weapon! I shall boil her!"

The rest of the team were very anxious by the time they arrived at the gate to the corral. Rax, Merrello and Pallenne were on watch outside the stable and they clasped arms with Carerre and DuPrenne.

They all looked back towards the direction they had walked but there was no sign of Pretteen.

"Undar will be furious too," muttered Gandar. "Not to mention extremely worried. We had better get inside."

Ragdan and Olwetta exchanged glances. Carerre offered to wait by the gate. The others entered the livery stable.

Boulaye's team had yet to return but Undar rose from a milking stool and craned his head. "Where is Pretteen?" he murmured. "Is she not with you?"

Olwetta stepped over to him. "She took it upon herself to follow two boys who were observing us. She was off before we could talk her out of it."

"What?" he roared. "Why in the nine hells of the Void did she do that? Why did you not go after her and stop her?"

"Look Undar," said his brother Gandar. "She wants to prove herself valuable to us. We must give her the opportunity. She will be back soon. Fear not."

$$\ldots o o O o o \ldots$$

She had circled around the back of the Assizes and entered the street forty yards further on. Pretteen crossed over the street and stepped onto the wooden porch that ran along the front of a row of clothiers and an alchemist's shop. The smell from the latter was not strong but acrid nonetheless.

She could clearly see the two young lads, probably no more than fifteen summers although one might have been a little younger, as they stooped behind the crates. They were dressed in grey hose and tunics and their feet were bare, typical of youths of their age if they were born of pauper families.

Pretteen flattened herself against a shopfront, partly hidden by a stout pillar. Hopefully, her own simple clothing would not make her stand out in a crowd but, to help change her appearance, she reached inside her day sack and withdrew a brown woollen jerkin. She pulled it over her head just as Gandar's band started striding away. It had a hood; it would hide her long hair. Her dagger, given to her by Undar, was within easy reach under the jerkin.

She observed the two lads as one flicked the other on the shoulder and pointed across the road. Once Gandar's team had strode about forty yards the boys rose up and began to follow, one each side of the street but one lagging about ten paces behind the other.

Pretteen smiled. *Clever!* she thought. She was enjoying herself. Predictably, Gandar's team returned directly to the corral and after looking back up the street, presumably for her, they went into the stable. The two youths hung around for a while in an alleyway close to the Star of Caspar Tavern. Pretteen waited in the shadow of a doorway not twenty paces from them. She almost laughed with the fun she was having. Her heart raced with the excitement of the task she had set herself.

Suddenly, she thought about how silent she needed to be. A tickle formed on the side of her face. It seemed to jump from place to place as she raised her hand to scratch it. An insect probably. She ignored it. Her injured left hand itched and she had an overwhelming desire to scratch it. Then she needed to sneeze. A group of rowdy people, traders and whores, ambled past the entrance to the alley where the two lads were concealed. The women shrieked with laughter at a bawdy comment from one of the men. She used the opportunity to let loose two sneezes with her mouth covered by her sleeve.

They eventually left the cover of the alleyway and emerged, individually, into the approaching dusk. The heat of the day was diminishing slowly and Pretteen was glad to have donned her jerkin. She followed the youths for about a hundred yards until they eventually caught each other up and strode together, jostling the occasional passer-by. Pretteen shadowed them about thirty to forty yards behind until they passed through the barrier wall that separated the central city from the pauper's quarter. She took a deep breath of what would probably be the last clean air for a while and continued behind the youths.

She needn't have worried. The youths had barely paced thirty yards or so when they stopped at the door of a two-storey, pitch-covered, wooden building.

The older-looking lad rapped twice on the door and then, after a wait of about five heartbeats, twice more. It was opened by a large, blond-haired man with a short clipped beard. The two lads entered and the door was closed behind them.

...ooOoo...

Chapter 21

Boulaye and his team arrived just as dusk was falling. He was curious as to why Undar, Gandar and Harley were waiting by the corral gate.

"What's going on," asked Boulaye.

"It's Pretteen," said a creastfallen Undar. "She took herself off following a couple of kids who were following us. She's not back and we are concerned for her."

Rax looked annoyed. "Why in the name of the gods did she decide to do something so foolhardy? If you remember, we had decided that Hartimmer's spies were a problem, I could had already arraged for my own band of ne'er-do-wells to spy on any followers and we would have had no need for any of you to put your lives in danger."

"Does that mean that these boys were already spotted?"

"I don't know for certain. It is possible. We will keep an eye out for her," said Rax. "Get yourselves inside."

Each of the three teams explained their progress that day. Boulaye summarised their investigations. "Our teams' hopes now rely on just a few possibilities. My team has our hopes with the Temple of Diette for anything we can get on Karouche. The Temple of Cahuhl was a waste of time and they are now in profit to the amount of five silver coins. The Cleric of Diette did mention the Temple of Tarne so that is another option. Gandar, Olwetta?"

Gandar nodded to Olwetta.

"The Guild of Chroniclers seems to be our best way forward so far with a possible clue about the original Kashtillan's mother, Karouche's woman," she began.

"They may have been able to find something on Karouche too. The official at the City Assizes may have some information on Karouche so we will chase that route at the same time.

Boulaye nodded to Olwetta. "Good, that sounds promising. I don't imagine any of the other temples coming up with anything useful, but you never know. Now what about watchers? My team had no sign of anyone following but with the throng of citizens and children, we may not have noticed anything. Gandar?"

Gandar explained that DuPrenne had noticed that they were being watched by a pair of youths and that Pretteen had decided to follow them.

"Silly girl," gasped Boulaye. "What did she think she was doing?"

"Reckless but still very brave," responded Harley. "Perhaps we should listen to her story before we judge her."

"It had better be good!" grunted Boulaye. "Let us talk about our progress today. First, what about here at the corral? Undar?"

Undar began to speak but his emotion got the better of him. Tishia, who sat beside him, placed an arm around his shoulders.

Solarin, the bard, spoke instead. "Well, understandably, a few people 'ad taken interest in our wagons and 'orses and stuff. It weren't any surprise to 'em that guards were stationed outside our stable building. They asked if performances was being planned. Then one of our guards, Pallenne I think, notices a pair of onlookers loitering across the road from the corral but they ran off when we watched 'em back."

Pallenne raised a hand. "Tall, stocky, blond and scruffy-looking. With short sandy–coloured hair and beards."

"One of 'em came back in the afternoon and stood outside the tavern wiv an ale. It din't look like them Massbourgs though. I mean, it could've been them Massbourgs but they might 'ave cut off their long 'air. That's about it really."

"Very interesting," replied Boulaye. "We shall have to watch for them again."

Suddenly, the door to the stable swung open and Pretteen stood there, a huge smile on her face.

Undar rushed across and gathered her up in his arms, tears of relief coursing down his face.

"That was foolish and reckless, young lady!" exclaimed Boulaye. "Thank the gods you came back safely. We were worried sick about you."

"But we are immensely proud of you nonetheless," added Olwetta with a scowl at Boulaye.

There were murmurs of agreement from the company.

"Aye," agreed Boulaye softly. "We are that, Pretteen. Forgive me for my outburst; it was tinged with fear for your safety. Would you like to share with us where you went, what you did and what you found out?"

"I followed those two boys right past here," she explained breathlessly. "They didn't see me, not once. I changed how I look and hid my hair. It is too long. I think I should cut some of it off. Do you think I should?" She stopped to draw breath. "I think I know where Hartimmer is," she whispered.

...ooOoo...

Dawn was barely breaking when Harley and Riette rose from their blankets on the straw bedding in the stall. A blanket had been tacked over the front of their stall, similar to those across some of the other stalls, to afford

276

the occupants some privacy. Harley had told her that he did not intend to accompany the group this morning, saying only that he had other business to conduct.

The previous evening, when Pretteen had spoken of her adventure, Harley had taken Boulaye aside from the others and quietly explained his plan. Boulaye had objected at first.

This morning, Riette was concerned. "Where will you be?" she asked, anxiety showing clearly on her face.

"Keep it to yourself, beautiful girl, but I shall be looking around to see if I can find out who is watching us. Tell nobody yet that I have left." He loaded a small, wooden case into his backpack and a number of other items.

"I love it when you call me that. Stay safe, my love, I shall fret," she whispered tremulously. "Come back so you can call me that again."

"I shall be back before dark." He kissed her on the cheek, held her trembling hand and crept towards the rear of the stables. A few days previously, Undar and he had loosened some planks so that they could be swung aside allowing passage of a slim person out of the building.

I dearly hope so, she thought. *I have something on which I need to speak with Lady Olwetta first though.*

...oo O oo...

He crossed the narrow street behind the back of the corral. There was still enough darkness for him to melt into the deep shadows in between a blacksmith's forge and an armourer's workshop. The streets and alleyways were virtually deserted and Harley moved swiftly and unseen in a wide arc around the corral.

Casting his gaze around in the approaching dawn,

he noticed a narrow store shed lodged in between a hardware store and a Guild house. Harley could not tell from where he was which guild the building belonged to. He studied the front of the store shed and came to a decision. He waited for an ox-cart to trundle past before crossing the street in its wake.

He found a narrow passageway running down the side of the hardware store and slipped down it. A pile of wooden crates and planks of timber were stacked up against the back wall of the shed.

He immediately got to work, determined to finish his task before the sun rose.

Ideal, he thought, as he stepped back to admire his handiwork.

...o o O o o...

"Hail, and I welcome you!"

Boulaye had rushed the Company through their morning feast and, despite numerous questions as to Harley's whereabouts, he ushered them out of the stable with the instruction to watch out for followers and keep tightly together.

His last piece of advice came with a glare at Pretteen.

Boulaye and his team had returned to the Temple of Diette. Tolladin, the young acolyte door warden had once again greeted them in the customary fashion and led them up to the steps to Jeellan's chamber.

Jeellan intoned his greeting once again. The disorder on his desk, the jumble of ancient, yellowed parchment, vellum and papyrus scrolls had been cleared. A neat row of scrolls had now replaced them.

This morning, however, it was Jeellan that looked in disarray. Dark rings encircled his eyes and his hair was scruffy and untended.

"Hail, and, um. Ah. Now, the written records of the Temple of Diette did not go back to the time of the first god-wars." He stifled a yawn. "I have had some measure of success in that there was a cleric of the god, er, Clamberhan was it? Aye, God of Literacy and Literature, Glyphs and Images and the like. Forgive me, I have not slept because I wanted to complete my search for you this morning."

"I, you did not, er –" stammered Boulaye. "It wasn't necessary to work through the night. We could have returned again tomorrow. But you do have my, er, our gratitude. What have you discovered?"

"That a Cleric of Clamberhan, by the name of Kashtillan, did appear in the old records of Diette but this was about a decade after the infamous first God-war. However, it appears that a subsequent Kashtillan, this one now a cleric of Diette, attended the funeral of his grandmother, with the family name of Caroche, at the Temple of Cahuhl. As you can imagine, it did not go well with the clergy of Diette. There is a record of the belongings of the old woman having been given to this Temple."

Boulaye's eyebrows shot up at the name of Caroche. "Was the location of the woman's domicile recorded?"

Jeellan shook his head. "It was not, I am sorry to say."

"Did you find anything on Karouche?" asked Jetti.

"Aye. 'Tis the name Caroche again, spelt thus." He scratched the spelling on a scrap of parchment. "So it may be the same man, it may not. It seems this Caroche was a serious miscreant who escaped gaol and probable execution by paying a large sum of money to the authorities. It does not specify the exact amount."

"It does seem to be the same person," murmured Jetti.

The cleric looked up at her. "I really should

recommend that you try the Temple of Tarne. He is the God of Justice, Law, Bravery and protection. You know this of course. That temple took on the contents of many of the greatest libraries of the time, particularly those of the Temples of Clamberhan."

"Clamberhan?" asked Boulaye. "I must admit to having been remiss at my knowledge of the Pantheon. You mentioned that name earlier."

Jeellan smiled and shook his head slowly. "He is the God of learning, knowledge and Invention. Some of His temple libraries are vast and priests of many other denominations will journey to His temples to learn, even those of the dark gods. Documents and tomes on astronomy, history, mathematics, science, healing, alchemy and herbology, survival, warfare, agriculture and even magic are collected, archived and studied."

Boulaye thanked Jeellan and placed a gold crown in his hand.

Jetti cleared her throat to get her husband's attention. "Hartimmer's gang, dear?"

"Ah, aye. I have an important point to discuss with you," Boulaye added. "There are other people also searching for this information. I have to inform you that they are fugitives from the justice of Grappina. The group is led by one Traviss Hartimmer, a renegade town councillor of the city. He tortured the descendant of the cleric you were looking though the archives for; this poor man is also a cleric."

A shocked and pained expression crossed the cleric's face. "Rest assured, Goodsir Boulaye, that this man will receive little help from this temple."

Boulaye described the man. "It would be appreciated also if you could send word to us in the stable opposite the Star of Caspar Tavern."

The old priest nodded and beamed as Boulaye handed him another gold crown and ushered the team out.

"Where to, boss?" asked Tishia. She habitually raised her hand to her face when she spoke to hide her uneven and broken teeth; it often made her sound as if she was mumbling.

...o o O o o...

The same officious man sat at the desk in the lobby of the Guild of Chroniclers suddenly deflated as Olwetta led the group into the Guild house. He took off his seeing lenses with trembling hands as Olwetta strode purposefully towards him and fumbled with them in an effort to clean them.

"Ah, Ma'am. You, er, We, um!"

"Underling! Did you have success with your search for Karouche or the cleric Kashtillan?" she asked assertively. She turned her head to one side and stifled a laugh as the man scrabbled to replace his lenses. Fortunately, her long, wavy hair hid her face from the official.

"We, ah, I searched for information on the name Karouche first. Th-there were some records from City Watch archives. We could only find something on a Madame Caroche, a woman of unethical character who ran foul of the law by running a bawdy house. Strangely, her son was one Kashtillan who studied to be a cleric of Clamberhan before the first of the god-wars. That is all we have."

"Did you find where this Madame Caroche ran her business?" enquired Gandar.

The administrator shuffled through a small pile of scrolls, unrolled one of them and read slowly through the flamboyant writing.

"No, there is no mention of the whereabouts of her, um, er, business."

"And nothing more on Kashtillan or where he lived?" asked Olwetta.

"Nay. He would probably have lived in the temple."

"Aye, of course." Gandar paused for a second and rubbed his beard. "Have you seen anything of the other people who are searching for this information? Kamann, was it?"

"Nay, he has yet to return."

Gandar exchanged a glance with Olwetta and Ragdan and turned back to the official. He took out a silver piece and handed it to the man who, glancing surreptitiously about the lobby, slipped the coin into a belt purse that was half-hidden in the folds of his robe. He led the group out of the Guild onto the street.

"We have a watcher again," Carerre whispered to Gandar. "Do not look. Same two as yesterday. Down the street with pipes of smokeweed."

"Make certain Pretteen does not see them," chuckled Gandar.

"Too late; she already has. Look!"

Pretteen was almost jumping up and down with exhilaration. "It's them, Olwetta. Look, over there!"

"Do not stare at them, Pretteen," hissed Olwetta. "They are not making much effort to hide which probably means they know we can see them. Ignore them and this time stay with us! Do not follow them otherwise I will tie you up and put you in a sack over my shoulder, and believe me, I can do this, girl!"

Gandar brought everyone together. "I want to see if we can lose these two brats," he said.

"Leave it to Carerre and me," said DuPrenne. "Just up the street, down the far side of that store shed, is a passageway that winds left and right. Take the group down there and wait at the far end. We will hold up the boys."

"You aren't going to hurt them, are you,"

complained Pretteen.

"Nay," laughed DuPrenne. "We will encourage them to stay where they are for a while."

Duprenne led the team along the narrow alleyway. It ran in a straight line between the storage shed and an adjacent timber shed. The overhanging eaves of the buildings cast dark shadows along the length of the alley. A pair of townspeople also walked through the alley, chatting, laughing and virtually oblivious to Gandar and the team as they made their way past them.

As they reached the back of the storage shed the alley turned sharp right. Duprenne stepped back into the corner to allow Gandar, Olwetta, Ragdan and Pretteen to file past. They turned right once again and then reached the street at the end of the passage. Their two guards were not with them.

... o o O o o ...

Harley crouched low on the roof of the store shed. As dawn broke, he watched as the town began to wake up. Traders and workers strode by below him. After a while common folk and children also filled the streets. An hour after sunrise, a figure dressed in a black, studded jerkin and dark grey leggings tucked into tall black riding boots strode past the front of the shed and stood in the shadow of a narrow alley.

Harley watched with interest as the figure gazed attentively at the corral. From his vantage point Harley could clearly see Rax and Merrello as they patrolled the corral. He saw the figure stiffen as Undar emerged from the Stable. Undar briefly spoke with Rax and then re-entered the stable, closing the large door behind him.

Harley crawled to the rear of the shed and slowly climbed down to the ground. He reached into a belt pouch and withdrew a phial and a piece of cloth. He

283

pulled on a leather glove, pulled the waxed cork out of the phial and emptied some of the contents onto the pad of fabric. The noxious fumes immediately assaulted his nostrils and, knowing the lethal power of the fluid, he held it at arm's length. He crept down the side of the shed in the gloomy shadows.

...ooOoo...

"What did you do with them?" asked Olwetta.

"With who?" asked Carerre, a cheeky grin on his face.

"With the two youths, you dimwit!"

"Ah, them," answered DuPrenne. "They are in a warehouse. Well, you see, they got a bit tangled up in a length of rope. We tied them together in such a way that would make their parents doubt their sexual preferences."

"What?" Olwetta looked stunned. "Nay, do not say any more."

Ragdan and Gandar laughed. Pretteen looked puzzled until realisation dawned across her lovely face.

"We also told them that they would not see another sunrise if we caught them in this section of the city again."

"Did you release them?" asked Pretteen.

Carerre gave a small chuckle. "Their cries for help will attract someone very soon by which time, once their rescuers have stopped laughing, we will be miles away. By the way, where *are* we going now?"

They entered the City Assizes and the Assize manager, Meena Kandar, waved cheerily to them.

"I have studied the archived court records held in the citadel and I have good news but not a lot of it. I found some information on your renowned seafaring brigand by the name Caroche or Carouche. Both

284

spellings were used in the court proceedings. He bought his freedom with a veritable sum of twenty five thousand gold crowns."

Gandar was scratching his head. "Um, were there any other details of his woman? Was there a wife of the Pirate King? It is the same name, or near enough, after all."

"Actually, there is some detail of his woman. There is no record that they were wed but she was referred to as Madame Caroche. It is rumoured that the Pirate King bought his woman a property of substance somewhere on the cliffs on the west side of the city. I would suggest that over the centuries it has been long gone. That is all I could find. Probably, there may be other records but I would have to conduct a search that may take days or even months. It would cost you a lot of money."

"Have there been other people asking for this information?" enquired Pretten.

"Ah, you mean Hartimmer. No, dear. Nobody else has appeared. I have told the Citadel that Hartimmer and his gang are in the locality. They are putting out search parties but have not raised a hue and cry mayhap he would go to ground."

...o o O o o...

He dragged the body through the shadows to the rear of the shed. Under cover of the noise from the street and the shadows of the passage, he had moved silently up behind the figure. He had to hold the fluid-soaked wad at arm's length to avoid breathing in the lethal fumes.

Harley had reached around the man's chest with one hand, his left, gripping the tunic in his fist and forcing the man back enough to break his balance. With his right, he yanked the head sharply back with the cloth in

285

place over the man's mouth. The man dropped to the ground within a few heartbeats.

He had already cleared a space in the heap of timber and dug out a shallow trench with a piece of wood. Constantly checking that he wasn't being observed, he dragged the body round to the cleared space and dumped it into the trench. He piled the loose soil over the body and trod it down. Then he covered the mound over with the timber until it looked as it had before he had prepared it. The body would probably not be found for some time unless an inquisitive dog began to dig.

His expression was grim as he surveyed his achievement. He returned to the roof of the shed and continued his watch.

...ooOoo...

Chapter 22

The Temple of Tarne looked like a stone fortress. A great device bearing a silver helm, the symbol of Tarne, was mounted above the entrance. A twenty-foot high iron-bound wooden door was its only access. It stood open but was guarded by two door-wardens dressed in the manner of knights, complete with impeccably shining armour breast plates and helms and armed with longswords and gleaming pikes. They were Clerics of Tarne commonly seen about the city.

Boulaye and his team were formally challenged by one of the door-wardens, referred to as the *Blessed Knights of Tarne*.

"State how the Temple of Tarne may be of service to you," greeted one.

"We have come to request information and knowledge from the one who holds your historical archives," replied Boulaye.

The other Blessed Knight called inside and a young priest emerged to greet them at the great door. "Welcome visitors," he declared. "State your needs. I shall give assistance where I may. I am Blssed Knight Acolyte Kord." He was dressed similarly to the door-wardens although without a helm and with a lighter weight armour chest-plate.

Boulaye repeated his request and the priest gestured for them to follow him through the door.

Beyond was a large grass parade ground where a squad of priests were being drilled by drill-sergeants. In a corner of the parade ground, a number of priests practised swordsmanship.

The mantra revered by the Priesthood adorned the walls: "Courage, Justice, Loyalty, Conflict, Protection and Heroism" along with their most beloved prayer

"Verse Twelve: If Death in a Just Cause is Inevitable, Let It be Costly to Your Enemies – Do Your Utmost for a Courageous Passing."

Kord smiled at them. "Goodsir, I have the honour to tell you that we do indeed hold records, ancient and modern, associated with this city. I can ask a *Holy Knight* to escort you to one who will give you assistance, our *Holy Knight Custodian*. She is the curator of historical records and is said to have more archived information than the Guild of Chroniclers I shall have to request that you deposit your weapons, and magical accoutrements, in an ante-room that will be held secure for you."

"N – Nay, I cannot possibly," gasped Riette.

Boulaye's companions glanced at each other then agreed that only Boulaye and Jetti would enter. The others would stay outside with LeDuc and Capalle.

Kord led the pair through the quadrangle and into a large keep-like structure. Inside, the hallway floor was of highly-polished hardwood. The acolyte led them down a spiral staircase, along a short passage and into a great library. He led them over to a middle-aged woman sitting at a great table. Her grey hair was tied back in a tail. She wore a tabard bearing the holy symbol of the temple and grey leggings tucked into short highly-polished boots. Boulaye noticed a well-used sheathed longsword standing against the end of the table.

Kord introduced them to the woman. "This is Holy Knight Custodian Lyssa Tranta. I shall leave you now. When your business is complete please make your own way back to your companions."

"Welcome visitors," Lyssa Tranta declared in a strong and confident voice. "State your needs. I shall give assistance where I may." *Obviously a standard statement,* thought Boulaye but he repeated his request once more.

"Karouche, you say," she mused. "I know the name Ignacia Karouche, of course. He called himself the Pirate King and he eventually fell into the hands of the city authorities. It is said he bargained for his life by paying a fortune, twenty-five thousand gold crowns I believe. Then he left and sailed away, so it is said."

"It is also said he had a woman here in the city," prompted Jetti. "Do you have anything on her?"

"Give me a short while," Lyssa said. She went straight to a shelf and sorted through a pile of journals and scrolls. With "Ahhs" and "Hmms," she soon selected a single heavy journal.

"There was indeed a woman. Oh, and there was a son too." She followed a passage of writings, her lips moving as she read quietly. "A Madame Caroche. It does not name the boy or give his age. These records detail a residence as being a domicile of uncouth standing above the cliffs near the docks region of the city. It seems to have been a whorehouse run by a Madame Caroche. Shall I write it for you?"

Boulaye nodded. She added the address on the piece of parchment next to the names of those he had been probing.

"It is now a dark, rundown building on the edge the city," she explained. "Find the Street of Talismans to its end and turn right onto the cobbled road that leads to the harbour. At the dock gate there is an old road, unused now, that leads to the old house over the cliffs. The large house stands by itself. It is said to be haunted by the ghosts of wicked scallywags; seafarers and pirates it seems. People keep away from there nowadays."

...o o O o o...

It was soon after noon when another figure appeared at the alley by the side of the wood shed. This man, tall and lean with a vivid red scar from the left side of his temple down to his jaw, was dressed almost identically to the one that Harley had recently despatched. Within a few moments he was joined by a man that looked very familiar to Harley. The hair had been crudely chopped short as had the beard but the size and bulk was undoubtedly that of a Massbourg.

"Where is that bastard brother of yours?" growled the Massbourg. "He was told to be here and wait for us."

"Might be taking a piss round the back, Drent," suggested the other. "I'll have a look for him."

The scar-faced man casually strode round to the rear of the shed. It was to be the last walk he ever made.

The Massbourg brother continued the watch for a short while but then his curiosity got the better of him. He followed in the footsteps of the scar-faced man round the back of the shed. Neither of the former Grappina city watchmen was to be seen. He grasped the hilt of his sword and backed down the alley towards the street. Once there he trotted back towards the poor district and Hartimmer's lodgings.

From his vantage point on top of the shed, Harley watched the Massbourg brother disappear off into the distance. The body of the scar-faced man shared the roof with Harley. He would keep it there for now. He dropped to the ground, satisfied with his day's work.

...ooOoo...

The Company gathered together later in the afternoon and discussed their day. They sat in a circle on the bales of straw and drunk ale and wine from earthenware mugs. Arnan Ben-Harami, the owner of the Star of Caspar Tavern, across the street from the corral, had provided a barrel of ale and a good spread of food for the afternoon.

"So, we have the whereabouts of Madame Caroche's old whorehouse," laughed Boulaye. His expression turned more serious as he continued. "We just have to find it without Hartimmer's gang watching us look for it."

"Well, with luck, he has lost a couple of allies with those two youngsters being scared off," responded Rax jovially.

"What were you doing today, Harley lad?" asked Gandar. "We did notice that you were already here sleeping when we returned."

"Lazy ass," murmured Undar. "He dozed off in his stall without a word to any of us."

"Ah, aye. I was busy but, enough to say, that Hartimmer will be wondering where two of his men have gone."

"Why? What have you –" began Riette.

"You have taken some out, haven't you?" cried Gandar.

"Er, aye!" nodded Harley.

"The Massbourgs?" gasped Boulaye.

"Nay. There was one but he was too cautious. Watch for them. They have probably chopped their hair and beards but they still look mean and dress the same as before. Calfskins and rawhide mainly."

"Disguising themselves, are they?" commented Undar. "Think we won't recognise them? You can disguise a pig but they will still be a pig!"

"And smell like a pig," added Solarin.

"But the Massbourgs still have long sharp tusks," said Olwetta. "They are still dangerous."

"Probably more so now they are two more men down. The Massbourgs are probably still mad after I took out one of them." Harley folded his arms behind his head and looked up towards the roof of the stable. "After this, they may go on the offensive."

"Perhaps dispatching those two today was not such a good idea after all," muttered Jetti.

"Perhaps *we* should go on the offensive!" exclaimed Gandar. "There's a lot of us especially with Rax and his men."

"That is if Rax is happy for him and his men to join us," said Boulaye.

Rax looked at those of his men who were still inside the livery stable. "For myself, I will join you but I expect to be paid. My men will want paying for it too. Some of them have families, Boulaye. I will say fifty gold per man and a hundred to the family if me or one of them should die."

Except for the shuffling of feet and Solarin coughing around the stem of his pipe, a silence fell on the stable.

"You and your men do not come cheap," murmured Boulaye.

"Aye, Boulaye. We do not but we will be at the forefront of the assault. We shall take the brunt of the fighting. What say you? What say you all?"

"Money well spent, say I," responded Ragdan as he stroked his short beard. "I will be there too."

Harley raised a hand. "As shall I."

Gandar raised a hand. "And I."

Undar raised his hand too. Olwetta also.

"Who will go and who will stay?" asked Harley. "We cannot leave this place undefended."

After much discussion and argument it was decided that Jetti, Tinnisse and her husband Balari, Riette, Solarin, Tishia and Pretteen would stay to defend the stable. They would be supported by one of Rax's warriors, Merrello, he being a man with an ever increasing family.

"One final question," said Olwetta. "When do we do it?"

...o o O o o ...

Hartimmer was indeed in a fearful rage.

"Two of them have gone missing?" He screamed at the top of his voice. Saliva sprayed from his lips has he yelled. He paced back and forth, waving his arms and stamping his feet, stopping only to punctuate his tirade by slamming his hand, palm down, on the table. Flagons of watered ale jumped precariously with each slam. "Where? So they've cut and run have they?"

The third ex-watchman shrugged his shoulders. "I assure you I knew nothing of this, boss."

"Boss? I remind you young man that I may be on the run from the Grappina rule of law but I still hold a title as an aristocrat. You do not, *ever*, refer to me as *Boss*! Is that damned well clear enough for you?" His voice raised in pitch until he coughed with the strain. He stepped over to his chair and dropped into it, grabbing at a mug of ale. The chair creaked although Hartimmer was not portly by any means.

One of the Massbourgs cleared his throat. "M'Lord. There is another possab–, er, possbil–. Er, maybe they been killed. And those two young boys didn't come back, neither. Maybe they been killed as well."

"Yer Lordship," grunted the ex-watchman. "I think he's right. I don't think they ran off 'cause they was waiting to get their money from you an' wouldn't have gone off like that. They would have said something to me, I'm certain of it."

Hartimmer leapt to his feet again, nudging his thighs against the table and causing the flagons to jump again. "So, then you would have gone off with them too, I suppose!" His mug rolled off the table and smashed onto the floor, ale and pieces of pottery spreading across the wooden planks.

"Nay, M'Lord. I'm not like that. Gods, we've all stuck by you through this, have we not? Nay, they are dead, I am sure of it."

"Then, where are their bodies, doom brain?" retorted Hartimmer.

"Hidden, surely," responded one of the Massbourgs. "Prob'ly buried behind the stable."

Hartimmer calmed down and paused for a few moments. "Perhaps we need to take the initiative then, fight back then, like for like."

Each of the Massbourgs looked about them and broke into a grin. They knew they had a personal score to settle, especially with that young harlequin.

"What's your plan, Bo –, er, M'Lord?" asked the ex-watchman.

The slip of the man's tongue did not go unnoticed by Hartimmer and he glared across the table at the man.

...ooOoo...

It was an hour before dawn when Harley left the stable through the gap in the back wall. Keeping to the darkness, he sped past buildings, sheds and market stalls. A few people, mostly workers, were striding about, many of them the worse off for ale, and didn't notice Harley as he flitted from places of concealment.

He had dressed in his black harlequin's outfit although he did carry his favoured blade, the rapier his father had presented to him so many years before. Although it hung from his belt, he held the tip of the scabbard in his left hand to avoid it striking against buildings and hard objects.

He gradually made his way around the corral until

he could see all the building fronts, including the shed that he had hidden on top of, all the way up to the tavern. After a few minutes of covert searching, he was satisfied they were not being observed.

Harley raised two fingers to his mouth and gave three short whistles.

...o o **O** o o...

The armed group left the stable. They trotted out through the corral gate as Merrello shut the stable door.

Harley led the group through the city towards the impoverished area using the directions given by Pretteen. She had begged to accompany them but Undar had forcefully objected, instead saying her skills were needed to protect those others left behind.

The group passed through the gate and into the ramshackle huts and hovels, stepping through, or over, the filth of the paths and streets. They avoided using the main streets until they drew up close to the dark building Harley knew to be that in which Hartimmer and his men would be found.

The group gathered together in a dark passageway opposite the building and discussed the next move.

...o o **O** o o...

Hartimmer sat at the table, his head fuzzy with the effects of the ale he had consumed during the night.

One of the Massbourgs, he didn't know which one neither did he care, sat in a chair at the other end of the table. The thug drew a whetstone down the length of a battered sword. It would need a lot more sharpening before he was satisfied with it. One of his brothers, Ambry, continually criticized his lack of care with the weapon.

The other two brothers and the ex-watchman were out. Their mission was to pick off the two guards who would be outside of the stable and if anyone came out to investigate the noise, if there was one, they would attempt to take them as well before making a quick escape. Each of them was armed with a crossbow in addition to their blades.

Banta, the brother left behind, felt cheated and had sworn profusely but Hartimmer had become, well, insistent.

Hartimmer dozed off. Banta Massbourg flexed his aching fingers and shook his hand. It had been a long time since he had spent such an inordinate amount of time and his hand was getting painful.

He started at a creak on the stairs outside the door. *Damn, they were quick! Back already.*

He was beginning to rise from his chair when the door crashed open and a gigantic barbarian charged in through the door.

...o o O o o...

Merrello noticed the three figures standing in the shadows just as three crossbow bolts struck his chest. One glanced harmlessly off his steel armour breastplate and another buried itself in the armour just deep enough to graze his skin at the bottom of his breastbone. The head of the third however, passed much deeper through. Merrello's last act was to stagger backwards and slam his fist into the door of the stable while emitting a ragged yell. His lifeless body collapsed to the ground.

The Two Massbourgs and the ex-watchman rushed through the corral gate towards the stable. They stopped to grasp a wooden bench and went to the door.

Inside the stable there was a flurry of activity as the

occupants rushed to cover or to arm themselves. Solarin and Balari readied their short-swords which looked large in their Halfling hands. Riette began chanting and carrying out complex hand gestures; both her hands began to glow. Pretteen flexed her crossbow and loaded a bolt onto it. Tinnisse made ready with iron balls. Jetti uncoiled a drovers' whip. Tishia held a shortbow with trembling hands. Fear etched every one of their faces.

The large door reverberated under the force of a tremendous crash.

Two more crashes came but the door held firm with the great bar that was placed across it.

It gave at the fourth heavy blow and the door, with some of its timbers broken, hurtled open.

Three screaming figures rushed in.

...o o O o o...

The Massbourg brother swung his sword at the great barbarian but caught the tip in the back of the seat. His hand, numb from whetting his blade, caused him to lose precious moments fumbling with the weapon.

This was all the opportunity Ragdan needed. He slammed his great-axe, sliced its blade down through the thug's head and almost down to the heart. A shower of blood, bone, brains and gore splattered across the room.

Hartimmer, horror-struck and screaming, backed away from the table and held his hands forward to show he had no weapons. His mouth gaped open and his head shook from side to side.

"Where are the others?" growled Rax but Hartimmer merely gibbered.

"Spread out around the building and find 'em!" ordered Boulaye. "Watch for them. Tear the place apart. We shall put it to the torch if need be!" He advanced on Hartimmer with his sword extended.

"No! Nonono!" gasped Hartimmer at last. "They are not here. They have gone. The stable." He fell to his knees. "Do not hurt me! I shall pay you well. Gold! Jewells! All I have."

"Stable? Our stable?" cried Rax. Then he yelled at the top of his voice. "Boulaye!"

...ooOoo...

Rax had left LeDuc and Capalle with Hartimmer while the rest of them tore through the gate into the city. A few traders, those going to their place of work early to set up for their day, leapt aside as the group of warriors charges recklessly through them, yelling for a clear path.

Harley was yards out in front of the others. None of them knew how many foes they would encounter or what damage would have been done when they got there. They feared the worst.

The corral was in sight. Suddenly, two horses, with riders, burst through the corral gates and sped off in the opposite direction. It was too dark for them to identify the riders.

With sword in hand, Harley sped through the gate and was first to reach the stable door. It was wide open. The sight that greeted him was one of devastation.

Riette lay on the floor screaming; Harley rushed across to her. Jetti crouched over the form of Solarin Fleet, the Halfling bard. He was not moving. Pretteen looked unharmed but was weeping. Balari held Tinnisse but his head was a mass of blood. His legs buckled and he slumped to the ground. Another figure, dressed in black hose and studded jerkin, the like of which Harley had seen recently, lay on the ground. It was oddly smoking.

"Riette!" cried Harley. "What have they done to you?"

"It hurts, Har – Harley!" she gasped. Her arms were tight across her stomack but blood oozed through.

"A priest!" screamed Harley. "Get a priest! A healer!" He lifted her arms although she resisted, her stomach was soaked with her blood. Harley took off his black harlequin shirt, bundled it into a ball and pushed it into her belly. She screamed in agony but Harley held her close. "A priest!" he repeated.

"A priest is on his way already," called Rax. "The owner of the tavern sent someone to the closest temple to fetch one as soon as he saw Merrello lying on the ground outside."

Boulaye knelt next to Jetti. Solarin was dead, a sword thrust to the throat had seen to that.

A man, panting and sweating profusely, burst in through the doorway. "I am a priest of Haeman!" he announced. "I have four more behind me. Stand aside!"

"Here!" cried Harley. "Help her. She has a stomach wound." His eyes ran with tears. Olwetta strode over to him and placed her great arm around his shoulder.

"Let the priests do everything they can, Harley," she murmured. "She is in the best of hands. There are three priests with her. Another with Balari and another with Pretteen. Come, we shall all sit together and see what happened."

...o o O o o...

They sat together on the circle of bales. Harley hung his head in silence and accasionally glanced over to where Riette was being administered by the Priests of Haeman. Tears ran down his nose and dripped to the floor. He made no effort to wipe his face.

"It looks like they killed Merrello and then stormed

the door," stated Boulaye. "Three crossbow bolts from a place of concealment."

"Cowardly bastards," grated Carerre.

"What happened next?"

"The one in black was the first one through," said Jetti. "Riette blasted him with a fire and it tore into his chest."

"He – he s–screamed!" stammered Pretteen. "'Twas horrible. Like an animal."

Undar pulled her head onto his chest and stroked her hair. "They are godsdamned animals," he muttered.

"Then the other two men went mad and attacked us," said Jetti. "I took the skin off the face of one of them as he went for Riette. I am so sorry, Harley, it did not save her. I am so sorry." She dissolved into tears and buried her head into her husband's shoulder.

"You did well, my lady," said Boulaye.

There was a chorus of "Aye!" from the gathering.

"The other one attacked Solarin," continued Tinisse. "But he cut that man on his leg as he went down. It was deep and did that man much hurt. He fell to the ground and bellowed."

"He died well," said Ragdan.

"Aye, he did that," added Gandar.

Tinisse continued. "Preteen shot the other with an arrow from her crossbow. It went in his shoulder. You did, Pretteen. It was good shooting because it made him scream too."

There were murmurs of approval from all those sitting on the straw bales.

"Good lass!" said Gandar softly.

"Aye, you are, my lovely girl!" exclaimed Undar.

"What happened next?" prompted Boulaye.

This time Pretteen spoke, having gained much encouragement from the praise. "They went outside and we could hear them trying to take two of our horses. It took them a while but they rode off. Then you came." Her shoulders shuddered as she sobbed into Undar's shoulder.

Boulaye rose to his feet. "I want some of you to go back to Hartimmer's house and help LeDuc and Capalle bring Hartimmer here. Tie the bastard and drag him if need be."

"Why here?" asked Gandar. "You said there was to be a hue and cry and a search for him. Just hand him in to the authorities."

"You are right," agreed Boulaye, sitting back on the bale. "However, there is probably a sizeable bounty on him and I think it only fair that we collect on it. Dawn is only just upon us and we probably have a wait before we can hand him in."

Rax offered to ride with Duprenne and Carerre to the impoverished area. "The people there will be getting out onto the streets; it will not be safe. We know our way around." They left just as the sun began to rise over the buildings.

Balari joined the others by the circle of straw bales. "'Allo," he greeted them. "I needs a sit down!" A grey bandage was wrapped about his head but he seemed stronger now after his collapse at his wife's feet. Tinnisse stood next to him and hugged him.

"Welcome back to us, Balari," said Boulaye, relief showing on his face. He moved to one side to allow Balari and Tinnisse room to sit together on the bales.

"What shall we do with Hartimmer, dear?" asked Jetti.

Boulaye thought for a moment. "Keep him secure in one of the stalls and then some of us can take him in the back of a covered wagon over to the city watch-house. But before that perhaps I should go over there to see whether or not Hartimmer is actually a wanted man. What do you think, Harley?"

Harley, however, was standing outside the stall where Riette lay, with the three priests still in attendance. Healers' cases lay open and their contents were being sorted through by one of the priests. The other two, meanwhile, chanted in a monotonous drone, their hands glowed a faint blue and hovered above her stomach. Olwetta stood beside him, her face lined with worry and her comforting arm still across Harley's shoulders.

"He needs some space to be near his lady," muttered Undar.

"It is not good for you to go alone to the city watch, Boulaye," said Ragdan. "The Massbourgs may be waiting nearby to ambush us. There may be others with them."

"Aye. You are quite right." He agreed. "I should have thought of that."

"Why do you need to go to the city watch first," asked Balari. "Why can we not just drag 'im there?"

"Because if he is not yet a wanted man here at Casparsport, they may release him. If they do that he will cause more mischief and will still be a danger to us."

"And if he is not wanted by the authorities?" asked Jetti. "Does that mean we have to keep him here or do we take him back to Grappina?"

Boulaye rose to his feet and stepped over to the door. He pulled it open and, cautiously, looked outside. Carerre, DuPrenne and Pallenne were patrolling outside. He closed the door and faced the gathering.

"We have another option," he said. "We can speak with Arnan Ben-Harami – the owner of the Star of Caspar Tavern opposite and tell him what we know. He is a member of the City Council. Perhaps he can use his influence with the city watch commander."

"Sounds like a good plan," replied Olwetta. She had

stepped over from Harley's side and placed her hands on the shoulders of Ragdan.

"How is Riette?" asked Pretteen. Her voice tremored.

"Not good, but she is improving. She lost a lot of blood but the priests are hopeful. They are resting; it has been very taxing for them. Harley is with her now."

...ooOoo...

Riette looked up at him, an expression of anguish on her pale face.

"The priests say you will improve well," Harley whispered. "I have been so worried."

"Harley, I lost it," she said weakly.

"Nay, beautiful girl. You are getting well. You did well with your magic."

"I lost our baby, Harley," she whispered.

"What? Ba–, er, baby? B–but, I, er!"

"I spoke to Olwetta last night. I was not sure of the signs. She told me. I wanted to tell you today but everything went wrong."

"But she said nothing to me, my lovely."

"Of course not! It was for me to tell you. But our baby is lost!" She burst into tears. "Are you angry with me?"

He kissed her forehead. It felt cold and clammy. "Nay, my lovely. Not at all. But I *am* angry with the Massbourgs. They did this to you. To us. And damned Hartimmer for they will have done this at his bidding. I heard the others speaking. They are bringing Hartimmer here. I shall slit him!"

"Harley! That will make you as bad as him."

"Aye, lass. You're right, as usual! I shall watch every move he makes though."

"Just hug me, Harley." Her eyes closed.

A priest knelt beside her and put his ear above her face. "She is sleeping. Have no fears for now. We shall stay here until tomorrow."

...ooOoo...

The company was alerted to the sound of horse's hooves in the corral. Boulaye rose from his bale and paced over to the door. It burst open before he got there.

Rax and Duprenne carried a limp figure between them. Carerre carried another over his shoulders.

"It's LeDuc and Capalle," panted Rax. "They are sorely wounded. Are the priests still here?"

"Aye," replied Boulaye. "Bring them over there." He indicated the stalls and the wounded men were carried there. The others crowded around but Boulaye shooed them away.

Hey, you people. Give the priests space!"

"Rax!" called Boulaye. "What happened? Where is Hartimmer?"

"The Massbourgs came back, even with their injuries," replied Rax. "They had three thugs with them. They overwhelmed Duprenne and Carerre but not without loss. One of the thugs is dead and the other soon will be. He has lost an arm. The arm is there but not the man. The place was awash with blood. Hartimmer was gone too."

"Well," mused Boulaye, "that solves the problem of what we will do with Hartimmer. But it now raises the problem that he can still make mischief against us. We shall have to redouble our guard."

Gandar leaned forwards and smiled. "One good thing though, Boulaye. We won't have to split up into small groups any longer, will we?"

"Only two groups now, one to guard here and care

for the wounded and the other to continue the search," Boulaye replied. "Unless we want to stop all this and move on."

There was a clamour of protest. Rax spoke up. "I believe I speak for all of us when I say that we have made sacrifices in getting what we have so far. My men and I will continue with this, if only to raise some money for Merrello's family."

"Aye," said Balari. "Solarin died defending those 'e loved. Aye, 'e did. 'E might have been grumpy but 'e was fond of us all. We don't want his sac – sacraf – er, death to count for nothin', do we?"

This time the clamour was one of agreement. Boulaye smiled. "Just what I wanted to hear! Now, let us see to Duprenne and Carerre."

...o o O o o...

PART 4

SEARCH

Chapter 23

"We are going to find the City Repository," said Boulaye. "There is a slight chance that the Karouche family or someone by the name of Kashtillan may have left something in the vaults for all time. They often have treasures held there that go back generations waiting for descendants to come and claim them."

"That may not help," responded Olwetta. "Surely only a family member will be able to take out something that is lodged there."

"Perhaps a member of the city council can be of help. Perhaps s couple of us can go over to the tavern and ask Arnan Ben-Harami if he can help. Regardless, I want to give him our thanks for fetching the priests and to pay him what we owe for the food and ale he sends over."

"Don't go alone then," advised Harley. He had appeared suddenly from the stalls.

There was a chorus of greetings and "How is Riette?" from the Company.

"She will recover, thank you, but it will take a long time. She, er, she got a blow from a kick and a cut to her belly which, er, is being mended by the priests." He lowered his head for a few moments."

"The priests' divine magic is good though, aye?" asked Gandar.

"Look everyone. There was more. Riette said I could tell you." He lowered his voice. "But please do not speak with her about it. She was carrying my baby."

Olwetta stood up, wide eyed and dread showing on her face. "Was, Harley?"

"Aye. It is lost. The priests said it was so." Tears ran down his face, making tracks through the dust.

Pretteen ran over to him, wrapping her arms around him as his shoulders shook. "Oh, Harley."

"Another opportunity will arise," said Undar.

"Something will," added Tishia with a nervous giggle.

"Perhaps sometime if the gods see fit," he added. "What about this visit to the tavern. I shall go too while Riette is sleeping."

A general call of "And me!" came from the Company.

"I shall take three with me," declared Boulaye, "and I shall choose. Harley, Olwetta and Balari. We are not going for ale; just to speak with Arnan Ben-Harami. The rest of you will have an opportunity for ales and wine soon, I promise you. Meanwhile, I shall have another plan to discuss with you all. Perhaps this evening. Meanwhile, I need to speak with Ben-Harami urgently. Let us go!"

...ooOoo...

Boulaye led the group into the Star of Caspar Tavern. They chose a table in a quiet corner and Harley called over a barman.

"Ales and one wine," he instructed. The barrnan soon returned. "I wish to speak with your master as soon as possible," Boulaye requested.

"I shall see if he is willing to speak with you, Goodsir. What business do you want to discuss with him?"

"City council business," replied Boulaye. "Ah, and to pay monies owing."

The barman strode off and went through a door behind the bar.

"Let me do the speaking when he comes out," instructed Boulaye.

Harley leaned across the table and whispered to the others. "Do not turn your heads to look. Behind the bar, next to the door, is a little square window. There is a curtain across it, dark blue, which is twitching. I think that we are being watched by Arnan Ben-Harami."

No sooner had Harley finished his whisper than the door opened and the massive bulk of Ben-Harami waddled out and struggled towards them. Two of his flunkies brought out a large chair for him to sit on.

"My friends!" he wheezed. "It is so good to see you. I heard that you had suffered casualties today."

Boulaye stood and greeted the tavern owner.

"Sit! Please sit," replied Ben-Harami as he patted his sweating brow with a silk 'kerchief. "More ales, ah, and a wine too. This is a little treat from me."

Boulaye said "I must offer my gratitude for your promptness in calling for the priests. They saved one of us from certain death and three others from nasty wounds."

"Who was it that attacked you?" asked the huge man.

"They were thugs in the service of one Traviss Hartimmer."

"Hartimmer? Ah, the errant aristocratic Town Councillor from Grappina?"

"Aye. The very one. He is now a renegade and is on the run from the Grappina authorities. We have been hunting him to return him to Grappina but he has so far evaded us. We almost had him last night. We discovered his lair but as we were storming his building, his men stormed ours. We lost one guard and our bard and four more were injured, one very badly."

"Ah, I had heard rumours that Hartimmer was on the run but the Council has yet to receive official notification from Grappina. Without that there is little we can do. We would be contravening our own laws if we were to capture him because he has done nothing wrong in Casparsport, as far as we know. But what I can do is raise a silent order for him to be located and watched. If you like, I shall send word to you of his whereabouts but I must ask you to remember that you will not have heard that from me."

"That is more than we could have asked of you," said Boulaye. "Again, you have our gratitude."

"Tell me, exactly what is he doing here?" asked Ben-Harami.

"He is seeking the mythical treasure of the Pirate King, Ignacia Karouche. We are trying to stop him doing that."

"Karouche? I know the name. What is all this about?"

"Hartimmer had a cleric of Diette tortured to get information about the treasure. The cleric appears to be a direct descendant of Karouche and, after the torture, we have agreed he is entitled to do with the treasure what he considers is best."

Ben-Harami laughed, his chins and huge belly wobbling. "You did say *fabled*; how right you were. You do realise that the treasure has been hunted for centuries, do you not? It has never been found. There is no clue as to what the treasure actually is. It may be gold and jewels, it may be scrolls and books on knowledge, it may be art or it may be religious or magical items. You may be embarking on a fool's errand."

Olwetta shook her head. "You may well be right. We are looking and, having been attacked by these thugs, we think there is something behind this. We all consider it best to continue the search."

Boulaye continued. "Perhaps the temptation will be too much for Hartimmer and we will have an opportunity to apprehend him. There may even be a bounty for his capture."

Ben-Harami's face became serious. "If items of value are found, I must advise you that it is all to be declared to the city council, preferably direct to me. Some taxation will be payable to the city as I am sure you will know. I do request that you be honest with all of your dealings."

"I assure you, Goodsir, we shall be honest," Boulaye earnestly assured him. "I do, however, have other business to discuss with you."

"You do? Please continue." He called for more drinks.

"I wish to make a formal request to the city depository for anything they may hold relating to the Karouche or Caroche family or under the name of Kashtillan. They may have held items for some centuries. I would like to merely take a look, not remove anything from the depository. Would you be able to give me authorisation to do that?"

"I can do but this is most irregular. I insist that one of my Council officials accompanies you. Is that acceptable?"

"Aye, it is," replied Boulaye.

"Then I shall write a missive and include my Council seal. When do you want to do this?"

"In the morning."

He sighed. "So soon? I shall have a parchment available for you and my minor official will bring it to your livery stable an hour after dawn tomorrow. What else can I help with?"

"Firstly, we have a financial account to settle with you."

"Speak to my head barrnan. He has been keeping a tally. You said firstly. Is there something more?"

"Aye. We have an amount of jewels that we would like valued sometime. Could you recommend a reputable dealer?"

Ben-Harami placed his hands across his ample belly and smiled broadly. "Why, of course I can. Take them to the city depository when you go tomorrow. Not only will they value it but you can deposit them there. Now, if that concludes our business I have some of my own to complete. I bid you a good day and I do hope your injured comrades continue to improve."

Ben-Harami struggled out of the chair and clicked his fingers. His two flunkies immediately trotted over and followed him with the chair.

Boulaye strode over to the bar and chatted with the head barrnan. He handed over a large pile of gold coins. The delighted barrnan put them into a small bag and took them through the door.

The group followed Boulaye out of the tavern and back to the stable, their eyes scanning their surroundings with every step.

...o o O o o...

Harley spent the night dozing sitting half upright in the corner of the stall. Riette slept sporadically and each sound or movement brought Harley awake. Although the three Priests of Haeman were on hand, they were not needed.

Next morning, he rose and kissed Riette lightly on the cheek. She stirred slightly and a faint smile crossed her lips. Harley was relieved that she was not so cold and sweaty and obviously not in so much pain.

The council official appeared on a grey pony at the corral soon after dawn and LeDuc escorted her into the stable.

"Good morning," she greeted them. "I am Hollissa Tranti. I am here to represent the city council. Well, actually, Arnan Ben-Harami asked me to accompany you to the city depository."

Gandar held his breath. She was very attractive with olive skin, high cheekbones and dark eyes. Her black hair was unusually short, barely reaching her shoulders. She was quite short and had a stocky physique. The first feature that Gandar noticed was her smile; it lit up her face.

Olwetta returned the greeting and introduced the visitor to the members of the Company.

"Oh dear," she laughed. "I do not think I shall remember all of your names. I have seen you perform your skills, although that was last year. I enjoyed it so much. Will you be performing again soon?"

Gandar offered for Hollissa to sit on the straw bales and she sat between him and Boulaye.

"I do not think we will for a while yet, Hollissa. You see, we have lost one of our performers, our bard Solarin, and one other is very badly injured. We also lost a valuable guard and two more have also been injured but not badly. It will take us a while to recover from that attack."

"Aye, Ben-Harami did say that you had suffered from this attack. I must ask if I will be in any danger."

"Fear not, Hollissa. We shall take care of you to our best ability."

"That is a relief. So you have lost your bard? I remember him. He spoke to me when I told him that I have been singing and playing my lute and flute in my local tavern. He gave me a lot of encouragement and suggested that I learn the histories of the western lands and the songs associated with that. And so I did. I am so sad that he is gone."

Gandar nudged Boulaye. Boulaye winked back. "Not now!" he mouthed.

Barmen from the tavern appeared a short while later with probably the best dawn-feast they had ever had.

Hollissa was invited to join with them. And so she did, with much enthusiasm.

While they ate and drank the mulled wine and watered ale, Boulaye, Harley and Olwetta, gave Hollissa some details of what they were doing and the reason they were going to the city depository.

"A treasure hunt? Really? Oh, how exciting. Look, I should not really be telling you this but Ben-Harami told me to get you to let me accompany you on the treasure hunt too. I think he believes that you will try to cheat the city council out of their portion of the treasure. They do expect up to half of the value. That really sounds like a lot, do you not think so? I do."

Her own enthusiasm was infectious and many of them could hardly resist laughing. Gandar hadn't taken his eyes off Hollissa since she arrived.

"Half?" he gasped. "Is that how much they take?"

She nodded.

"Yes, it is a lot. I do agree," replied Boulaye. "Perhaps tomorrow, Hollissa, you could sing some of your songs or tell us some tales."

"Oh, I would be so nervous. I really am not that good. You might laugh. I would love to though, but my instruments are in my lodgings."

"Oh Falarr, dearest, that is so unfair of you to ask her like that," countered Jetti.

Boulaye winced. He hated it when she called him by his first name. It usually meant she was prickly with him. He turned back to Hollissa.

"No matter. We will chat about that later if you like."

"No, I would love to, I think!" laughed Hollissa. "As long as you know that I am not really that good."

...ooOoo...

Boulaye, Harley, Jetti, Olwetta, Pretteen, Rax, Pallenne and LeDuc, with Hollissa in tow, made their way through the mercantile area of the city. Hollissa directed them to the city depository.

They carefully scanned every alley, every building and open door and window as they walked through the busy streets. Occasionally, a threat would be pointed out and their two guards would rush over to investigate. Hollissa was intrigued.

"We have a couple of thugs called the Massbourgs out there somewhere who may try to waylay us," explained Harley. "There were four of them but now there are only two left."

"This really *is* exciting!" she gasped breathlessly. "The chief administrator of the depository is expecting us but will probably only allow a few of us to go through to the vaults."

"That will be me, Olwetta, Harley and you, Hollissa. You others had better wait in the entrance hall. Keep a sharp watch for the Massbourgs or anyone else who might be taking an interest."

Hollissa asked the desk official to speak with the chief administrator. The others followed as she was led to a large chamber. A small man, dressed in grey business clothing of wide leggings, a doublet and a long cape, walked forward to greet them, his arm outstretched. He greeted Hollissa like an old friend, even kissing her on the cheek.

"Hello Uncle Toll," she said. "Everybody, this is Toll Tranti. These are Boulaye, Olwetta and Harley. They are members of the Blue Sky Spectacular Company but they are on official business for the city council I have here a letter from Arnan Ben-Harami, the Justice Councillor."

"I have been expecting you, my dear. Are you still performing at the Flying Bat tavern?"

"I am Uncle. I don't make enough money to do it as a job of work unfortunately. Perhaps one day."

Boulaye winked at Harley. Olwetta, catching the gesture, raised a questioning eyebrow as she loomed over them all. Boulaye shook his head imperceptibly.

"I have been expecting you. I shall send some cool drinks to your colleagues in the lobby."

Toll Tranti read the letter and nodded his head. "There is one name here, Karouche. Is that the infamous Pirate King of old?"

Boulaye nodded. "There are other names too that may be connected with this. Shall I scribe them for you?"

Tranti handed him a piece of parchment and a stick of charcoal. Boulaye wrote down the names Karouche, Carouche, Caroche and Kashtillan and handed it over.

Tranti looked at the names and read through a large, ancient leather-bound ledger. He spent a while flipping through pages and stopped at an entry.

"We have an unclaimed deposit in one of our vaults under the name of Caroche. Let me look further. Aha! Kashtillan. There is another deposit for you to look at." He wrote two numbers on the parchment and closed the ledger. "Good. Come with me."

They followed Tranti to a steel door which was guarded by two heavily-armed, burly men. Tranti unlocked the door and beckoned the others through. He closed the door, relocked it and led them down two long flights of steps. He unlocked a heavy iron grill and led them through. Once again, he locked the grill behind them. He sat them at a table and went behind a curtain. He reappeared a few moments later with one large, rusting iron box on a wheeled trolley. He went back though the curtain and again brought out an iron box, this one much smaller, under his arm. He placed it at one end of the table.

"Help me lift this onto the table," he said, indicating the large chest. Harley held a handle at one end and Boulaye at the other. Together, they hefted it up.

"The large chest is that of one Caroche and the small is of Kashtillan," said Tranti. "Strangely, both ledger entries bore similar writings and personal signs which means they may have been lodged by the same person. Which would you like to open first?"

"The large one," replied Boulaye.

Tranti produced a large key. It was crude and Harley reckoned, quietly, that he could have opened the chest with a rusty dagger. Tranti handed the key to Boulaye.

"I am not permitted to see the contents," he said. "I shall go back beyond the curtain. Please remember that you must not take any items out of this vault."

"Aye, we are aware of that," replied Boulaye.

They opened the chest. It appeared to be full of clothing. Olwetta took items out one at a time and held them up.

"These are costumes," she said. "Many of them have a symbol. Ah! This symbol looks like a scroll and a quill."

Hollissa wrinkled her nose at the mustiness of the contents. "Be careful if you touch them, Olwetta; they look old and may be very fragile."

"Aye, they are," Olwetta replied.

"Wait! I know what these are!" exclaimed Hollissa, almost dancing with eagerness. "They are the ancient vestments for a Priest of Clamberhan. I am sure you know this god is known as the Lord of Knowledge, Inspiration and was also the Patron of Bards. The scroll and quill pen was His holy symbol. It is different now; a bound book. I have read that the Church of Clamberhan in Kambria used the harlequin's mask as its symbol." She smiled widely and appeared very pleased with herself.

Olwetta held up light blue shirts and trousers and then a vest of black with gold brocade. Although the shirt sleeves were wide, they were tied at the wrists. Similarly, the bottoms of the trouser legs would have been tied at the ankles. The vest portrayed numerous runes, glyphs and symbols of both divine and magical power, the meanings behind most having been lost in time. These had been sewn on, probably by its owner, using gold braid. There were also a blue and a crimson vest each showing a simple scroll and quill sewn in silver thread on the back. A small, round hat, similarly decorated to the black and gold vest, was lifted out and then a matching pair of slippers.

"What is that on the bottom of the box?" asked Harley.

Olwetta reached in and picked up an object. It was a metal disc on a chain. "I think it is copper, no, it is brass, but it is very badly tarnished." She turned it over and looked closely. "It is the holy symbol of the scroll. Oh, it feels warm! There are no other marks on it."

Boulaye looked inside the chest but there was nothing else to be seen. "Put everything back now, Olwetta."

She took the hat, looking inside it, and placed it on the bottom of the chest. She looked closely at the slippers. Inside each was a sheet of soft lining. She pulled each out but one of them was too brittle and tore.

"Oh, what is this?" she whispered, holding her fingertips to her mouth in a gesture of silence. She withdrew a small piece of parchment and handed it to Boulaye.

"Hide it!" mouthed Hollissa. "Quickly!"

Boulaye's eyes opened wide with surprise but he complied nonetheless. He slipped it inside a belt pouch.

Olwetta replaced all of the clothing as it had been when they had first opened it.

Boulaye relocked the chest and called in Tranti.

"May we open the other chest, Uncle?" Hollissa asked, an expression of mild disappointment etched on her face.

Tranti gave her a small key, took the large key from Boulaye and went back out behind the curtain.

She opened the box and lifted the lid. Inside was a single item wrapped in a small square of black velvet lined with blue silk – a grey pewter goblet. It was quite plain with no markings whatsoever.

Boulaye handed the goblet to Olwetta. She turned it around and examined it. Finding nothing, she handed it to Harley. He studied it, shook his head and gave it to Hollissa. She quickly looked over it and then shook it.

"It has a rattle," she whispered. She examined it again and twisted the stem. It came apart after she briefly wrestled with it. A small roll of yellowed parchment slipped out of the stem. She picked it up, held a finger to her lips and gave it to Boulaye. He slipped it inside the belt pouch along with the first find.

Hollissa reassembled the goblet and replaced it into the box. "There is nothing in there except this old goblet," she said as she locked the box. "Uncle Toll," she called.

Tranti returned.

"Who would be able to reclaim the contents of these chests?" asked Boulaye.

Tranti considered the question for a moment. "Any person who could prove that they are descendants of the previous owners. They would need documents to prove who they are such as a paper written by a city official, signed and sealed, of course. Can you assure me that you took nothing of value from the boxes?"

"Uncle," stated Hollissa. "I swear to you that no item of value has been removed from the chests."

He nodded led them back to the lobby. Boulaye

slipped off his small backpack and requested a private discussion with Toll Tranti. He was led into a small chamber that had two chairs and a small table.

"How can I help you?" asked Tranti.

"I have a number of precious stones that I would like valued," he explained. He dropped a fist-sized bag into Tranti's hand.

The chief administrator emptied the contents onto a small table and stared at them. His eyes widened at the sight.

"I have rarely seen better," he stated. "I can give you a valuation in a short while if you wait here."

He strode out and was back about half an hour later. He handed the bag back to Boulaye.

"These are white, yellow and blue diamonds," Tranti explained. "They are flawless and of the highest quality I have ever seen. We have analysed and weighed them."

He paused as if considering his next words.

"Can you tell me what you believe they are worth?"

"Aye, I can. Ben-Harami has left word that you are to be given the highest of consideration for your dealings with me here at the city depository. A recommendation such as that is always favourable where our business clients are concerned. I am pleased to inform you that the stones, together, are valued at seven thousand and two hundred gold crowns."

Boulaye felt the breath sucked from his chest.

Tranti continued. "The city depository will be prepared to purchase them from you although we shall ask for a payment of five one-hundredths of their value."

Boulaye carried out a calculation in his head. "That, Cityman Tranti, I believe, comes to three hundred and sixty gold crowns leaving use with, um, six thousand, eight hundred and forty."

"You are, of course, correct. Now, if you accept these terms, we can provide you with a promissory note for that value which will be valid in any major city depository in the north-western realms. The note can be made out to only those in your group who could utter a coded word so that, should it fall into the wrong hands, it would be worthless."

"But how would those in another city know that codeword?"

"Ah, that would be surreptitiously contained within the promissory note itself."

"In that case, I accept!" stated Boulaye.

"I expected that you would," replied Tranti. "I have already produced the document. If you just provide me with the names of those of your group to include in it, I shall complete it, sign it and attach the seal. At least two of those named will have to be present when presenting the document at the depository."

He gave the full names of himself, Gandar and Olwetta. He realised that he had never known Harley's full name or even if Harley used his real name. He would have to have a chat with that young man.

Tranti rolled the document, placed it inside a simple scroll-case and handed it to Boulaye. Together they left the chamber and rejoined the others.

"You were gone awhile," stated Olwetta. "We were getting quite concerned."

"I'll tell you about it later," Boulaye replied.

Tranti kissed Hollissa on the cheek again. He bade farewell to them and Boulaye led his companions out onto the street and back to the stable.

...ooOoo...

Instead of taking them through the gate and into the stable, Boulaye asked Rax to take Pretteen, Jetti,

Pallenne and LeDuc back to the stable.

"I need to speak with Harley, Olwetta and Hollissa before we return," Boulaye explained. Jetti gave him a sour look but said nothing.

He led them straight into the Star of Caspar tavern. He strode through the taproom with the others in his wake, sat down at a remote table and shouted for three ales and mead.

"If the mead is for me, I would prefer an ale if it is acceptable with you," said Hollissa.

Boulaye revised the request.

Boulaye looked straight at Hollissa. "Why did you do that, young lady?" he asked.

"Because I prefer ale," she replied, shrugging her shoulders. "I am not keen on –"

Boulaye took a deep breath. "I mean, why did you ask me to hide the two pieces of parchment?"

"Look, I do not like to be manipulated or used as a spy. That is what Ben-Harami of the city council is expecting me to do. I have only known you all today but, strangely, I believe in what you are doing. Perhaps I am being naive, but I hope I am not. Anyway, I have always wanted to be part of an adventure. I believe this could well be the only chance I will ever have. What do you think?"

Boulaye leaned back in his chair, linked his hands and put them behind his head. Then he relaxed, reached into his belt pouch and withdrew a pipe and smoke weed. He loaded the pipe and lit it from his tinderbox. The others sat quietly.

"Lass, you have done well. Show me how well you can perform and, with the blessing of the others, you could well be our new bard, a member of the Blue Sky Spectacular Company. Now you tell me what *you* think!"

"I, er, I – will not let you down, Boulaye." Then she

laughed.

Olwetta reached across and placed her hand over Hollissa's shaking hands. "You will do well. Try something raunchy; that will be popular in the stable.

"Before we go back," Boulaye began and then he let out a long belch. "I want us to have a look at those pieces of parchment."

"Have a care," warned Harley. "They may be brittle."

Boulaye wiped a small area of the table top with his sleeve and placed the parchments down. One had been folded and the other was rolled. They would both need careful handling.

"Here, let me try the folded one," offered Hollissa. "I am used to working with old parchment."

Boulaye nodded.

A small pocket-knife appeared in her hand. She carefully inserted the thin little blade between the folds and prised it open. She looked up at Boulaye and let out a breath of air. She repeated the process and opened the parchment flat. This time, a little piece of the parchment broke away.

Harley read the first parchment: "It says 'The welthe of the kinge is welle hyd'. I wonder what that means. It is written in an old style or the writer could not spell in the common tongue."

"We need to put that somewhere safe then," said Boulaye. "Other eyes may look for it if we do not keep its existence a secret. Let us have a look at the other piece."

Hollissa took a deep breath. "This will be more difficult because it is so tightly rolled. I will do my best but I am sure it will break."

Once again she carefully inserted the knife blade and a small piece immediately broke away.

"Damn!" she cursed. "I was too hasty. Keep that by.

We may have to put pieces together again."

It took almost an hour for her to unroll the little fragment and by the time she finished it was in four pieces.

Harley read the writing on the parchment: "It says 'The blade of the sworde shows the way to the hoarde.' It sounds obvious because it is what we like swords to do."

"It tells us nothing," murmured Boulaye.

"Or it tells us everything we need to know," responded Olwetta. "We just have to work it out for ourselves. Now, what were you up to with Hollissa's uncle?"

Boulaye smiled. "Hmm. When we left the Graban Hills way station a few weeks ago, we had in our possession a bag of jewels. I showed it to you recently. I have just been given a promissory note to the value of six thousand, eight hundred and forty gold crowns."

There was a stunned silence.

"What shall we do with all that wealth?" asked Olwetta.

"We need to discuss that as a company. It belongs to us all. Drink up," he ordered. "Back to the stable. Remember, we must keep the scraps of parchment to ourselves for now. What the others do not know, they cannot inadvertently give away in careless talk. They'll still benefit from what is found just as much as we ourselves do. We cannot afford to have the scraps ending up in Hartimmer's hands."

...ooOoo...

"What did you find out?" asked Gandar as they entered the stable.

Carerre and Undar had been on watch when Boulaye and the group entered the stable, Undar

326

followed them in and DuPrenne took over his watch. Harley had gone straight over to Riette's stall and was encouraged to see her sitting up, propped against a thick cushion of straw.

Meanwhile, Boulaye sat on the straw bale in the circle and reached for the mug of ale that Jetti offered him. "There are a couple of clues which may help but I don't know how," he sighed, taking a long drink of the ale.

"What are these clues?" pressed Gandar. "Perhaps we can work them out between us."

"Aye, we can but try, Gandar." He took another swig of ale, finishing the mug and gave a large belch. "Needed that," he gasped, then belched again.

"Well?" persisted Gandar, holding his hands to the sides of his head in exasperation.

Boulaye huffed. "Impatient bugger! Very well. There were two notes written in the contents of some chests. One said that the wealth of the king was well hidden and another said that the blade of the sword shows the way to the hoard"

There was silence around the stable.

"Well hidden?" cried Undar. "That is obvious. It would have been found if it had not been. Also obvious is the wealth of the king being that of the Pirate King."

"So it seems," said Balari, his voice hoarse from smoking his pipe almost continually since suffering his injury. "What about the sword?"

"The blade of the sword shows the way to the hoard," echoed Pretteen. "It is a rhyme."

"Perhaps that is hidden too," suggested Ragdan. "Maybe in such a way that the direction of the blade points to where the treasure is."

"Good idea, beloved!" exclaimed Olwetta.

"We just have to find a sword," said Boulaye softly.

"We know roughly where the old house of Madame

327

Caroche is to be found," said Harley. "That is a good place to start looking."

"It is said to be the haunt of ghosts and ghouls," laughed Tinnisse.

"I could keep a watch for a day or two," Harley suggested. "Leave it to me."

...ooOoo...

Hartimmer paced back and forth. It had taken him all day to make contact with the two surviving Massbourg's. As he suspected they had been in a healing house just inside the Impoverished Section of the city. One brother had a vivid red slash mark across his face and his right arm was tucked inside his jerkin. The other was walking with a pronounced limp, the result of a leg injury.

He eventually caught up with them in the corner of a small corral where they had left their horses many days previously. They were both drinking from an earthenware jug. They were reeling, obviously drunk.

"So, we are all that is left," gasped Hartimmer. "I suppose you know there is a general hue and cry out for us. People here in this shit-covered area will be looking for us as a quick way of making big money. We can assume people in the Mercantile City will be looking for us too. And all you idiots can do is to bring attention to yourselves by getting drunk on dwarf-liquor!"

"Are we riding out, boss?" asked one brother.

"I told you, I am not *boss*. I have a –"

"Now lookit, *boss*," growled the other brother. "We have sacrificed a lot for your scheme. We done what you asked. We lost two brothers, Banta and Crand. So perhaps it's time *we* decided what is happening next."

"Have I not paid you well for your work? You did

not complain when I showered you with gold coins. We have a chance to find a fortune. This treasure will now be split three ways instead of six. Use your imagination, limited though it may be."

The Massbourgs exchanged glances and one of them shrugged.

"What do you want us to do, boss?"

Hartimmer let that last epithet go without remark.

...o o O o o...

Chapter 24

Harley slipped out the back of the stable about two hours before sunrise. The city was quiet except for occasional pairs of watchmen who checked on doors and windows, alleys and corners. They roused drunks and sent them on their way with a cuff on the ears.

He moved cautiously using every bit of cover to help him. His black harlequin costume ensured he moved unseen.

He moved swiftly along the main city street, passing the city depository and then, half a mile beyond, the citadel walls. A quarter of a mile further on, he found the Street of Talismans. He sprinted to its end and turned right onto the cobbled road that led to the harbour. At the dock gate he searched in the dark for an old, unused road. Its entrance was through a thicket of bushes that had long been untended. He used his blade to hack a narrow passage through. After a difficult trek along the long disused track he saw the house. It stood alone and, judging by the lack of ground features and the smell of the sea, it stood close to the coast.

Now he needed a vantage point from which he could keep a watch on the house for a day.

He spotted one that would suit his needs. It looked like a ramshackle barn or stable. It stood about thirty paces across the track from the old house. He trotted towards it and, twenty yards from it, he dropped into a crouch and listened. He moved forward carefully and listened again. Nothing. Creeping to the opening, he looked inside. The double doors had long since dropped to the ground and were decaying where they lay. He crept inside.

He waited for his eyes to adjust. It would be dawn soon. There was a faint smell of horse and dung; the barn had been used fairly recently. He searched the floor and soon found horse dung. It was cold and dry but whole.

A ladder led up to an upper floor, probably the old hayloft. It was about seven feet above him. Harley tested the first rung; it held. The second and third did not. Clearly, nobody had used the ladder in a long time. He dropped back to the floor and dragged the ladder aside. It shattered as it fell.

He took off his backpack. Inside was a water-skin, some bread, cheese and fruit. He swung it up into the void above him and was rewarded with a shower of dust from the floorboards. He walked over a large wooden crate and checked it weight. It seemed empty. He dragged it just below the void and climbed onto it, reached up and pulled himself into the hayloft. *Ideal*, he thought. He picked up his pack and gingerly walked across the boards to a window opening that faced the old house. The boards creaked alarmingly and twice his foot almost went right through. Despite this, they held his weight.

It would be a long day. He settled down to wait.

... o o O o o...

Dawn broke and the Company began to stir in the stable. Pretteen brought fruit and water to Riette and was delighted to see Riette looking better. A priest of Haeman had visited each morning to check on the young mage's progress.

"Where is Harley?" Pretteen asked.

"He left early this morning on one of his sneaky walks," Riette replied. "I think he is looking at the house where the Caroche woman used to live."

"Let us hope he takes care. Do you think you can walk yet?"

331

"Probably, with some help. It aches though."

Five minutes later, Olwetta and Pretteen helped Riette sit on the bales. The others gathered around dutifully. A barrman from the tavern arrived with a trolley of food and drink.

"A new day, everyone," called Boulaye. "We are staying in here today so if any of you want to spend a while in the tavern, you will get your chance. Do not drink too much and definitely don't get drunk. Hartimmer is still out there with two of the Massbourgs and they will not be happy with us. They may strike at us from ambush."

"Where is Harley, Boulaye?" asked Ragdan.

"He went out during the night to look at the old house. He will be watching it and will be back before tomorrow morning."

"Why does he do this," murmured Riette. "He puts himself in danger all the time." Her eyes brimmed with tears and she wrung her hands in her lap.

Pretteen put her arms around Riette's shoulders. "He always comes back though, doesn't he?"

Riette nodded.

"He is very good at what he does," said Boulaye. "I have a plan that I want to discuss with you all. It involves this livery stable. We need a winter base here in this fair city, somewhere to rest and recover after our eight months of travelling each year. Up until now, we have dispersed into a variety of taverns and boarding houses around the city and taken what premises we can find for our horses and wagons."

"You want to buy this place?" asked Balari.

"This is my plan. I would like us to purchase this stable and corral."

"Us?" asked Gandar. "What with? It's a great idea but what money do we each have?"

"I shall get to that," Boulaye replied. "As I

suggested, I would like us to buy this livery stable and the corral. But more than that. If we could then build a taller wall around the corral with proper gates that may be locked on the inside. This structure is tall so we could build a floor above us with chambers so that we can all have our privacy. Lastly, we build a second structure to house the wagons and Company's equipment."

"This is madness!" gasped Undar. "And how shall we fund this?"

"With the proceeds of the treasure that we brought with us from the way-station at Graban Hills when we were on our way down towards Grappina. If you remember, it was part of a hoard collected by one Hanuta who plundered it from travellers and who was then murdered by his own men."

"This venture of yours will cost a vast amount," stated Gandar. "How much is that treasure worth?"

Boulaye smiled. "It will be easily sufficient for us to provide this place as our base here and another similar at Northwald City for our summer break. It will repair our wagons, provide us with new and better performance equipment and still leave enough money for a share for each of us. What say you all?"

Undar was unsure and looked to his brother, Gandar, for guidance.

Gandar smiled at him and then both he and Undar said "Aye!"

"Is there any person here that does not agree? Speak out freely or raise your hands," Boulaye called.

No words of dissent were spoken and, one by one, hands were raised and *Ayes* were called.

"I have already had the treasure valued," he said. "I shall employ the services of carpenters and craftsmen and have the work valued soon. After that, we shall know what our shares are worth."

"Equal shares?" asked Undar.

"Of course," replied Olwetta, glancing at Boulaye.

He nodded in agreement.

"But we have our present tasks to complete before that happens," advised Olwetta. "Oh, and perhaps some entertainment this afternoon if I can separate her from Gandar!"

Hollissa, who had been leaning against Gandar's shoulder, flushed, extricated herself, smiled and took a deep breath.

...o o O o o...

Soon after sundown, Harley awoke, crept across to the window and looked out. Moonlight gave the early night an eerie translucence. The large house looked ghostly grey, its open windows just black rectangles.

Suddenly he stiffened, every sense focussed. His hands gripped the bottom rail of the opening frame but it crumbled away to dust in his hands. There were voices. Laughing! They were faint at first, distant and thin. Then a curse! Then more laughing.

He heard speech in a language he did not understand. Then there was more laughing and a sharp statement in the common tongue. "Silence, fool!"

Three grey figures abruptly flitted from the direction of the harbour towards the old house. Two of them wrestled with a very large box, a handle at each end, although, to Harley's eyes, their struggles were caused by the size of the box, not its weight.

"It weell be a much more havvy when we comin' back."

"Shhh, keep it down!" the apparent leader hissed. "Ballaron is bringing a pack-'orse!"

"Needin' it now!"

The other translated for the third who responded

with a single word. They both laughed.

The trio made their way down the far left side of the house. Although they were now out of sight, Harley could still hear their banter.

Ghosts indeed! he thought.

A short while later he heard the sound of clumping and a snort. A figure appeared leading a mule. The beast resisted, tugging on its lead rope and rearing its head in indignation. The man responded by viciously goading it with a long cane.

Harley slowly shook his head as the man led the mule down the side in the wake of his three associates.

Harley grabbed his sword and eased over to the gap in the floorboards. He placed his blade across one corner and climbed down onto the crate below. Reaching up, he took down the sword and strapped it on. He carried the crate back to its original position and cautiously crept out of the stable.

Keeping his profile low behind shrubs and bushes in front of the stable, he moved towards the left side of the house using the tall grass for cover. Glancing around the corner he could just see the mule tied to a small bush, despite the shadow caused by the house in the moonlight.. He thanked the Gods for the inky darkness which helped to give him total cover in his close-fitting black costume.

There must be a door somewhere along there, he thought.

With his senses finely tuned, he eased around the corner. He froze as the mule stamped and snorted.

He hadn't realised that he was holding his breath. He released it slowly and breathed quietly. He stepped forward again, dislodging a small pebble and brushing through a clump of weeds. He froze again, all his nerves jangling and his blood pumping in his ears as he held his breath once again.

A thump sounded from inside the building. There was a scream. Light spilled out from a door being opened about halfway down the side of the house. A figure stepped out.

Harley dropped into a crouch and huddled against the wall.

The figure went back to the door and called inside. "Bring out the box!"

There was a response from inside as one of the men muttered in the strange tongue, probably translating the instruction. A crash sounded from inside. The muleteer, Ballaron, huffed and re-entered. Harley backed up and slid around the corner to the front of the house and waited.

He watched covertly as the muleteer reappeared holding a lantern. Behind him, the two others struggled with the large box as their leader watched and cajoled them. The crate seemed very heavy this time. All four men went back in and brought out a second, slightly smaller, box. From the way they struggled with it, it also looked heavy. The two thugs dumped it on top of the first box, flexed their arms and went back inside once more.

Harley watched all of this with interest. Once Boulaye and the Company finished searching inside the house perhaps they would inform the City authorities. *There might even be a reward,* he thought to himself. A smile crossed his lips.

The two men came out with a light pack saddle for the mule. They eventually managed to place it on the defiant animal, amid curses and threats from Ballaron and their leader.

"Did you do 'em?" asked the leader.

"Aye, Cap'n. We finashed 'em," replied another. "Den dead. Dey in the cellar wiv de odder two."

"Good. Tie up the crates. Lock the doors. We go

now. Back here in two nights."

More curses accompanied the lifting of the boxes onto the load-rests on the pack saddle. They tied these on, testing the ropes. The leader extinguished the lamps and closed the door. The four figures moved off towards the harbour and melted into the night.

Harley kept watch on the house for a long while. A chill breeze blew in from the sea while he remained crouched by the corner of the house. Eventually, he made his way to the side door and tested it. Surprisingly, the door was locked given its state of decay.

Idiots! he thought *I would have replaced the door.* He assumed that the tales of ghosts would keep people away from the building.

He entered through the door but it was so dark inside he was unable to see anything at all. He didn't think it was wise to light a lantern in case the gang turned up again or were watching. Flies were thick as he felt his way along a short passage. His outstretched right hand touched a door on the side of the passage. He turned and his left foot slipped on a slick, oily substance. He gripped the door frame and steadied himself.

He walked back down the passage to the entrance and left through the door, closing it behind him. He returned to the old stable, retrieved his pack and began his long walk back to the Company's stable.

...ooOoo...

Harley had entered unseen through the back of the livery stable a little before midnight. He appeared on the periphery of the ring of straw bales. Ragdan was the first to see him. The barbarian nudged Olwetta and she in turn prodded Riette.

"Harley!" she yelled, then winced and put her hand on her stomach. But she didn't stop smiling.

He sat next to her and places an arm across her shoulders. "I was so worried about you," she whispered. "Everyone was saying that you were doing something dangerous – again!"

"Nothing dangerous, I assure you. I was hiding in an old stable. I'll tell everybody all about it in a moment. But first –"

He leaned over to kiss her. It was a few moments before he was able to relate his story to the assembled Company.

"You feel hot, lovely girl. How do you feel now?"

"Better but a little tired," she answered.

He rose to his feet and sat on one of the straw bales.

"We have two days," stressed Harley as he took possession of a mug of ale from Balari. The Halfling moved gingerly because of his injuries.

Harley took a long draft and then continued. "It seems to me they are smugglers or something similar anyway. They were definitely moving something out in some large boxes. They sounded like they came from far abroad, probably the eastern lands. They may have been seamen because one referred to another as *Cap'n.*"

Boulaye smiled. "So perhaps the old house is not haunted after all then. What did these people look like?"

Harley took another deep draught from his ale mug. "They were dressed in grey, perhaps to give the impression that they were ghostly. Even their mule was grey. But they weren't disciplined at all with their laughing and talking. But their leader did ask the others if they had 'done them'. They said that they finished them and put them in the cellar with the other two. Now I don't know what this means but it does not sound good, does it?"

"Seems to me they killed a couple of people," suggested Riette. "That's what it sounds like anyway." As always, she lifted her hand to cover the scars on her face when she spoke.

"That may explain the huge number of flies that were buzzing around the passageway," pondered Harley.

"What are we to do then," asked Gandar.

"I think I can help," replied Hollissa. "If we search the building and see what is there then we can report it all back to Arnan Ben-Harami. He should then send in a squad of city watchmen to take these smugglers in or keep a watch or whatever. What do you think?"

"A good idea," nodded Boulaye after a few moments. "If we were to bring them in ourselves instead we might pick up a sizeable bounty."

There were murmurs of approval from around the circle.

"Of course, we will have to be well concealed and ready for them to appear at the house," Olwetta warned them.

"In that case, the sooner we get there the better," stated Boulaye. "We can search during today, stay over in the stable block in the night and carry on searching the next day. We can then lie in wait for the gang of smugglers, if that is what they are, and overpower them."

"Then perhaps a large number of us should get there before dawn this morning," responded Harley. He looked down at Riette. "But an equally large number must remain here."

Riette slumped her shoulders and hung her head.

"You are going again," she whispered.

"Not for long, beloved."

Boulaye called for silence. "By the way, we have all

agreed that Hollissa will become our new bard. Her rendition of *The Three Foul Maids of Casparsport* was hilarious. I have not heard that sung for many years. If Harley is happy then let us get a few hours sleep, about four hours to be exact."

...o o O o o...

Harley led them past the gates to the harbour and through the narrow gap in the bushes. Boulaye, Gandar, Undar, Jetti, Hollissa, Rax, Pretteen, LeDuc and Capelle stumbled along in the darkness behind him. Apart from their weapons, each of them carried a backpack with small tools, food, water and a blanket.

The faint glow of dawn was beginning to appear as they reached the house. They gathered around the front entrance. Gandar tried the handle and was rewarded by a grating sound, but the door was locked.

"It is old but I don't think the lock is as ancient as the house," remarked Gandar. "It's locked tight although the door is rotten. Kicking the bugger in will make it too obvious, won't it?"

"Then I shall unlock it," said Harley. He dipped his hand inside his pack and brought out a black leather roll. He unrolled it and sorted through its contents. He selected two shining rods, each with a hooked end.

"What tools have you got there?" asked Boulaye.

"Don't ask," replied Harley. "Give me some space," he hissed. "Gandar, I want you to push the handle down when I tell you to."

Gandar nodded and placed his hand on the handle. Harley inserted the two tools into the escutcheon and turned them but there was too much resistance.

"I need oil," he whispered. "Wait here." He rushed around the corner of the house and came back a few moments later holding a lantern. He removed the wooden stopper from the oil reservoir and poured some of its contents through the key hole.

"It will be getting light in a short while," Boulaye reminded them. "We need to get inside quickly."

Harley nodded to Gandar and inserted the two tools into the escutcheon once again. This time when he twisted them, he felt them move.

"Now," he said.

Gandar pushed down on the handle and the door opened a couple of inches. Harley pushed it and they all trooped inside. He pulled the door shut behind them.

"So where did you get those tools?" hissed Boulaye. "You know they are illegal in almost every country in these lands. If you are caught with them it's you who will be under lock and key."

"Just some of the tools of my trade, Boulaye. No less than my sword and dagger. I don't use them for illegal purposes, you know that."

"Aye lad, I do. Now for our morning feast and then we start the search when it is light enough."

"One more thing," suggested Harley. "We need to post a sentry up in a high window at the front of the house."

"Perhaps the girls can take it in turns."

"They are amateurs, Boulaye, and may not spot somebody moving from one hiding place to another or recognise a dangerous situation like you, or me, or Rax's guards maybe. Besides they may be of better use searching. Ladies always seem better at finding things. I remember my mother –". The words seemed to catch in his throat and he cast his head downwards.

"Aye. Jetti is the same with me, lad. Sometimes I can't find my own rump with both hands."

"At last you admit it," laughed Jetti. "Let's eat. Everyone will be hungry."

"There is a garderobe out here!" called Gandar from

341

a passage leading to the back of the house.

"A what?" replied Hollissa.

"It is a place where you do your toilet and it goes down into the ground down a shaft."

"Aye," agreed Rax. "You just throw down a bucket of water to stop the smells."

"There is a bucket in there and a hand water pump," called Gandar. "I don't know if it works. The handle is rusted and it won't move without effort."

"Try some of that oil from the lantern," suggested Harley.

They strode through the house; it was a maze of chambers, rooms and passages. Most doors had fallen from their hinges and lay rotting on the floors. Many of the floorboards were also rotting and gave way when they stepped on them. Most of the rooms had been virtually stripped of timber from the floors and ceilings.

"Treasure hunters," muttered Rax as he picked up a rusted jemmy from between floor joists. "I wonder if it is the same upstairs."

"The stairs seem sound enough," Boulaye added. "LeDuc and Capelle went up there to look for a sentry point although a few of the treads are potentially dangerous. I'll have a look around up there myself later."

"Hmm. Have a care, keep to the edges and keep your hands on the rails."

Suddenly, Harley stiffened. He held his hands up for silence. "What's that?" he hissed. "Listen!"

Neither of the others had heard anything at first but then a faint moan caused each of them to catch their breath. A cold shiver ran down their backs. Harley felt the short hairs rise on the back of his neck.

Then the moan stopped.

"Oh shit!" exclaimed Boulay. "I think I need to relieve myself!"

Gandar, Undar, Hollissa and Pretteen came running into the room through one door. LeDuc and Cappelle tore in through another, their swords at the ready.

"What was it?" quavered Hollissa, her voice pitched high with fright.

"Whatever it is, it is somewhere up the main stairs," gasped Capelle, breathlessly. "We were just on our way up."

"It sounded like more than one," whispered Undar as he felt his arm being gripped by Pretteen.

"I feel cold," Hollissa whispered.

"Aye, me too!" murmured Rax.

The moan started again but this time increased in its intensity. Pretteen stood wide-eyed and shaking as her fingers dug in to Undar's arm. He winced but said nothing. Other blades were drawn as the frightening howl rose and fell.

Suddenly, Rax grabbed Harley's shoulder and yelled "Come with me!" He saw Harley falter. "Now! Quickly lad!" He ran out of the room towards the main staircase with Harley close behind.

"Use the edge of the stairs!" called Rax as he leapt up them two at a time.

At the top, a corridor stretched to the rear of the building. Rax led Harley down it to a door at the end. Floorboards, rotten with age, cracked and splintered under their feet.

The wailing howl was much louder now and the hairs rose again on the back of Harley's neck. Rax launched his foot at the door, a few inches below the latch, expecting it to burst open. Instead, his foot went straight through it. He lost his balance as his boot became caught in the disintegrating timbers of the door.

Harley caught him just before he crashed to the floor and helped him extricate his foot. He reached for the latch and the door swung forwards. Now the howl was almost a shriek. His heart beet so furiously that he thought it might burst through his chest.

Rax pushed his way past him and they stood in a small chamber. In the window hung three copper pipes. Each emitted a shriek.

"I thought so," laughed Rax as he ripped the pipes down from the window. "These are your ghosts! Wind pipes! We used to use them when we were deep in the forests hiding from the Goblin armies in Cascant. The drones used to scare them; even they were scared shitless by the possibility of ghosts."

"I know just how they feel!" gasped Harley. His hands were shaking as he returned his sword to its scabbard.

They took one of the pipes, with its long cord hanging from it, and returned to the main chamber below.

"Do you know what a ghost can do to you?" roared Boulaye as the laughing pair strode onto the room. "One touch is all it takes for you to be sent mad, or worse. We do not have the means to fight –"

Rax whirled the pipe around his head and it emitted the shrieking wail they had heard earlier. The others shrank away until Rax dropped the pipe onto the floor and stamped on it.

"There," he said, a huge evil grin across his face and his single eye glinting. "One dead ghost. We killed another two like it."

Boulaye persisted however. "That was foolish, nonetheless. Brave, aye, but foolish."

Rax waved a hand, palm outwards. "Nay, it was neither foolish nor brave. I have heard these before. I recognised them for what they were. As I told Harley, we used them when we were deep in the forests hiding from the goblins. It scared them away thinking them to be banshees."

They continued searching on the ground floor through the rest of the day until dusk began to fall. The dust, having been set swirling by the occasional frenzied movement of the searchers, irritated their eyes and found its way into their mouths and noses.

"We need some water," said Boulaye. "This dust is getting everywhere. I don't suppose anyone has got the pump working."

"I'll see to it," volunteered Hollissa. "I'll need some help if it is jammed solid." She looked pointedly at Gandar.

Harley had left the lantern earlier by the front entrance.

"I think we should stay together in this room tonight," advised Boulaye. "No lanterns though."

"Why not?" asked Hollissa.

"Because we do not want to alert the gang to our presence here," replied Pretteen. "We may scare them off and lose the chance of capturing them."

Undar put his hands on her shoulders. "You have learned well, my lass," he spoke softly. She smiled up at him.

"Aye, that is quite right, Pretteen," agreed Boulaye. "We also need to keep the noise down. No shouting or raised voices for they carry far in the night when everywhere else is in silence. Use the garderobe if you need to do what, er, you need to do."

"With luck the pump will work," responded Rax. "The water will probably be filthy with old dirt and rust but it will fill the bucket to wash away the waste."

...o o O o o...

Harley, Gandar, Undar and Rax took over the watch during the night from LeDuc and Capelle. The night was quiet with no eeriness as might have been expected if they had heeded the stories of ghosts, or worse. This did little to stop them sleeping restlessly though. Neither did any of the night watch wish to be in the upper windows alone. Two would watch while the other pair slept. In the large room the others were also fitful. Each creak and groan of the old timbers brought them awake.

LeDuc and Capelle resumed their watch in the morning and the tired night watchers rejoined the bleary-eyed group.

Boulaye was stretching, rubbing his aching posterior and complaining about the hard floor. "I will not be protesting about our livery stable when we get back there," he said.

They continued their search on the upper storey. If anything, there was little to be found. A small cache of ancient silver and copper coins was discovered beneath the floorboards in one room. The coins had once been in a leather bag but it had perished so badly the coins had fallen out. Jetti counted them out, fourteen silver and eight copper, and put them away for safekeeping.

The group had laughed saying that this was probably Karouche's hoard.

"There must be more, though," grunted Boulaye. "Keep searching."

It was mid-afternoon when they agreed there was nothing to be found in the upper chambers.

"There is the cellar where the flies were buzzing," suggested Harley.

This was the one place that Boulaye had been putting off until the end of the day.

Boulaye sighed. "Very well. Let us get down there. Me, Harley and you, Rax."

...o o O o o...

346

Harley pushed the door open and was immediately assaulted by a swarm of flies. Beyond was darkness but there was sufficient light for them to see steps leading down.

It was the smell, however, that overwhelmed their noses. It was the reek of corpses.

Rax passed Harley a lantern and he used it to light his way down the steps, followed by Boulaye. Harley baulked at the sight of four bodies, two of them with their throats slit, that were propped in a corner. One of the bodies was that of a woman. Boxes and chests were stacked in the centre of the cellar.

"Karouche's treasure hoard?" gasped Boulaye.

"Nay, these boxes are too new," replied Harley. "These are what the gang were moving in and out of the cellar. I would guess they are stuffed full of contraband. Boulaye, can you see any place that may hold a clue to the sword of Karouche?"

"Thought I was boss here!" muttered Boulaye. Like Harley, he held his sleeve up across his mouth and nose in a vain attempt to filter out the reek of the corpses.

"Nay," he said. "The floor and the walls are of solid dressed stone. Nothing will have been buried here. I feel sick with this stench. Perhaps we should open the boxes when we have finished with the gang later."

"We can try one of them," agreed Rax. "Have you got your special tools, lad?"

"Aye, I have. We could leave the others for the city watch and the officials to dispose of," said Harley wryly. "If there is anything of value, it will soon go missing though. It is the way of city watchmen everywhere. I have an idea though."

...o o O o o...

Meanwhile, as soon as Boulaye, Harley and Rax had

347

disappeared along the maze of passages, Gandar and Undar continued searching in some smaller rooms along another corridor near the back of the house. Jetti watched fixedly as Hollisa and Pretteen tried to strip a panel from the wainscot around the room.

Pretteen huffed. "The woodwork in this house may be rotting but these panels are hard as rock."

"Probably because they are made from mahogany or something like that," suggested Hollissa.

"Wait! I've just had a thought!" called Jetti. "Instead of tearing it down, try knocking on it to see if it is hollow; listen for an echo."

Jetti, Pretteen and Hollissa rapped their knuckles against the wainscot. An occasional "Ouch!" sounded as knuckles collided with edges and splinters. Pretteen sucked at a knuckle to stem bleeding.

They had tapped and knocked on the panels as high as they could reach and virtually all the way around the room.

"Well, it seemed like a good plan at the time," sighed Jetti.

"We should try the higher panels," proposed Hollissa. "It could be up there somewhere."

"We need something to stand on," said Pretteen. "A box or a table or something."

"There is a table," said Jetti. "I have seen it."

"In the cooking chamber, er, kitchens," cried Pretteen.

They rushed out. Between them, they dragged the heavy oak table to the great room and with great effort managed to bring it through the doorway. They set it up against the wall and, with Pretteen, being the tallest of them, standing upon it they gradually moved it around the room.

Pretteen was soon rewarded with a hollow echo when she stretched higher up on the wainscot. She pulled her little dagger and used it to lever the panel away from the wall. There was a twang.

"Oh no!" she cried. "I have broken my knife." Her face was crestfallen.

Jetti handed her another, hilt first. It was much more substantial than Pretteen's own.

The wooden panel clattered to the floor, a piece broke away from it. Pretteen looked inside a fissure between two upright beams.

"There is something in here," she gasped. "It's in a tall gap between the wood plank things. It's wrapped in a bit of canvas and leaning against the wall. Wait a bit, I'll pull it out."

She stretched up and withdrew the object, letting out a whoop. She handed it down to Jetti's reaching hands and then climbed down to the floor. A piece of fabric fell away and drifted to the floor.

"It's a rusty old sword!" gasped Jetti as she laid it on the table.

"The one we are searching for!" gasped Hollissa.

A heavily-rusted, narrow-bladed sword, partly wrapped in the desiccated, dusty piece of hessian sacking, had been hidden there for centuries. None of them spoke. They realised that they were probably the first people to look upon it since Karouche, the Pirate King, had hidden it there. Jetti reached down to grip the sacking but it tore away in her hand. She gripped the old weapon and lifted it up.

The sword hilt's leather grip was black with age. It was extremely delicate and Jetti advised against touching it. The wide cross-guard and the protective basket hand-guard had lost most of their original gilt coating to tarnish. Although the whole weapon was black with rust, the blade itself, as well as its hilt and cross-guard seemed sound.

"Surely this is not the treasure of Karouche, is it?"

asked Hollissa.

...ooOoo...

"What *is* this idea of yours, lad?" asked Boulaye.

"Oh, I just thought about emptying the contents of the crates and replacing them with rubbish. Then we can hide the contents until we decide together what to do with it."

"Harley, you're not as daft as you look, are you lad?" laughed Boulaye.

"Nobody could be that daft," answered Rax with a snigger.

"We need to get a couple of others down here to help," advised Harley, smiling wryly at their humour. "We won't be able to manage it on our own."

"I'll bring Capelle and LeDuc down," said Rax. "They've got the stomach for this sort of thing."

"Wait," ordered Boulaye, holding his hand up, palm outwards. "We shall need them to be up there later just in case the gang gets here sooner than we expect."

...ooOoo...

Gandar and Undar came trotting into the room, swords in hand with a warlike yell. They stopped sharply on seeing the expressions on the faces of the three women.

"What is all this noise?" asked Gandar. "We could hear you down the passage. We feared something was amiss."

"We have found it!" cried Hollissa. "Karouche's sword, look!"

Gandar stooped over the table to look at the sword. "Give Boulaye and the others a shout, will you Undar?"

"Will do, brother." He trotted off.

Boulaye, Rax and Harley were there within minutes.

They all looked at the sword and Boulaye carefully picked it up. He held it by the hilt, tiny pieces dropping from the perishing leather cover, and hefted it in his hand. "Fine balance," he said softly. "The pommel stone is perfectly weighted."

He passed it to Gandar who lifted it. "Aye. 'Tis good indeed!" he agreed and handed it back to Boulaye who studied it closer. "I cannot make out any markings in this low light. Where did it lay?"

Pretteen pointed at the alcove in the wainscoting. "'Twas in there."

"Which way up was it?"

"Blade pointing down. Why?"

Boulaye paused for a moment and placed the sword back down on the table top.

"The blade of the sword shows the way to the hoard, so it was written. If the sword was blade downwards then perhaps we should be looking below it in the wall or beneath the floor."

"We should do that before darkness comes," suggested Jetti.

"Aye, but time is running away with us," replied Boulaye. "We have other tasks to do which outweigh the search for now. Me, Rax and Harley need some assistance at the top of the cellar while we refill the boxes. We have emptied them of their contents and need to replace it all with any crap we can put in them. Heavy stuff."

"What stuff," asked Hollissa.

"Pieces of wood, rocks, dirt, anything will do. It is to give the gang the impression that they are full of their contraband."

"So when they are carrying the boxes out of the house we will have them," finished Harley. "It is worth saying that there are four bodies are in the cellar and the reek is foul. I suggest that only the three of us venture down there with the pieces of rubbish that the rest of you can collect for us."

The sun was beginning to sink down on the western horizon when they returned the boxes to their original positions. Harley relocked the mechanisms. Many of them had gagged at the stench emitting from the cellar. Pretteen had thrown up outside the building.

"Oh, sorry," she groaned. She was leaning against the side of the building coughing.

Harley was concerned. "The smell of that vomit might alert the gang when they get here."

"Out of curiosity, what did you do with all the contents?" asked Gandar.

"What? Of Pretteen's stomach?" laughed Harley. "I shall cover it with sand and soil."

Gandar rolled his eyes. "No, you idiot! The contents of the chests and crates."

"It's under the bodies."

"Ughh!" said Pretteen and started to gag once more. Jetti and Hollissa led her back into the house. The others followed behind.

"It all looks the same as we found it. It's getting dark now. The gang will be back here very soon. To your places, everyone."

"He sounds like he's setting us up for one of our performances," Harley whispered to Jetti.

...ooOoo...

"Shh!" Boulaye used his foot to nudge Harley who, in turn clamped his hand over a sleeping Gandar's mouth. The latter awoke with a start, instantly wide awake.

They carefully inched over to the aperture in the floor. Harley dropped through onto the large crate below. He helped Boulaye find his footing and together the pair helped Gandar down. They crept to the entrance and collected their weapons.

Gandar murmured "Where are they, Harley?"

Harley had earlier advised them that a soft murmur would not carry as far as a whisper at night. Furthermore there were low background sounds coming from the harbour area and, more faintly, from the city. A breeze from the sea was rustling the long grass and the small bushes dotted around the space between the stable and the house.

"Two minutes," he replied.

"Hope the others are ready," said Boulaye.

They heard voices and raucous laughter well before a group of six figures wandered into view. They were making no effort to conceal themselves or to keep quiet. Surprisingly, the figures continued walking along past the front of the large house and down the old road towards the harbour gates. After a while they were out of earshot.

"Wonder who they were," whispered Gandar.

"Probably a few seafarers going into town for ale and a good meal," offered Harley. "Avoiding the main harbour gates so nobody notices them going out."

Boulaye, however, had another idea. "They may have been checking the place out to see there is anyone here. Thank the gods that the others didn't attack."

They sank back into the shadows and sat on the old crates in silence. Around them they could hear the skittering of small animals.

"I hate rats!" hissed Boulaye after a long while. "I hope they are not rats. There was one in our stable the other day. Almost crapped my –"

"Shh!" Harley's warning quietened him.

They crept back to the old stable's entrance.

"One minute," muttered Harley. "I think I can see 'em."

Three grey figures soon walked into view. They

were moving in silence towards the side door of the house. Harley immediately recognised them as the men he had seen two nights previously. They were all armed with swords, cutlasses or similar, and all lingered outside presumably waiting for the muleteer.

They didn't have to wait long. This time two men, each with a mule, arrived from the direction of the harbour, leading the mules to the side of the house.

Harley nodded to Boulaye and Gandar and, keeping their profiles low, the three of them flitted between the patches of undergrowth to the front of the house. Harley crept to the corner and peered round.

The two mules already had their pack saddles on them. The muleteers had hitched them to a bush. Harley immediately recognised one of them as Ballaron, the muleteer he had seen previously.

Harley held up two fingers and indicated around the corner. He then held up three fingers and pointed downwards. The others nodded in understanding. Boulaye held out his hands palms down and murmured "Wait."

A moment later, the three other gang members appeared carrying crates from the cellar.

"Stinks a shit donn dare," said one. "Dose dead mans goin' bad."

"Quiet, fool," hissed Ballaron. "Load up and bring up the other three chests, quickly!"

Harley watched as the three men disappeared down into the cellar once more then he nodded to Boulaye and Gandar. Boulaye put two fingers in his mouth and whistled. Suddenly there was a flurry of movement as LeDuc, Capalle, Rax and Undar burst out from behind a thicket of hawthorns, bushes and undergrowth.

The muleteers immediately drew their swords and knives. A melee ensued as the four warriors rushed in and engaged them.

Harley and his two companions had rushed to the side door but flattened themselves against the wall either side of the entrance. Not a moment later the three heavies rushed out brandishing their old, battered naval cutlasses.

"Drop your weapons!" yelled Rax. "You are outnumbered!"

His command fell on deaf ears, however. The muleteers were already fighting furiously with LeDuc and Rax while Capalle waited by, thrusting with his sword when an opportunity arose. The three thugs gazed upon the fight with the muleteers and were about to leap in when Harley jumped out from behind them.

"Drop your swords, boys!" he yelled. "Now!"

The three whirled and immediately began swinging their swords.

In the meantime, Ballaron parried a thrust from Capalle and lashed out with his long knife. Capalle barely avoided the attack and countered with a vicious slash with his longsword. The stroke whistled over Ballaron's head and the man laughed. He lunged forward and thrust his knife once more at Capalle who retaliated with a punch with his free hand across the muleteer's jaw. The man dropped to the ground, his knife and sword clattering to the ground.

Harley's conflict with one of the thugs lasted no more than a few heartbeats. His rapier flashed too quickly for the man to see in the darkness. The man was completely outclassed and with his chest spurting blood, fell dead at Harley's feet.

The second muleteer fared less badly. Both Rax and LeDuc scored small injuries to the man before he dropped to his knees, throwing down his sword and dagger.

"I yielding," he pleaded. "Do kill me not!"

Undar, meanwhile, dashed over to where Harley,

Boulaye and Gandar dealt with the last two heavies. These two noticed the surrendering muleteer and their dead colleague and threw down their swords, similarly dropping to their knees.

"Where is Ballaron?" asked Harley. "The other muleteer."

"I knocked him cold," replied Capalle. "He is there." He turned to indicate but then stood there with his mouth agape.

Ballaron had gone.

...o o **O** o o...

Chapter 25

Boulaye was furious. He stomped back and forth waving his arms in frustration. "Where in the nine hells of the Void did he go, dammit?"

"Only the gods know!" answered Capalle. "Likely flown back to the harbour. I did hear a cracking sound and a quiet sort of call."

"You struck him down, man! You should have watched him," roared Boulaye. "There was enough of us!"

"Steady, Boulaye," said Rax. "There was still fighting going on and it was dark. My men have worked damned well for you. Do not ignore that."

Boulaye stopped his ranting and breathed out. "Aye, they have indeed." His thoughts went back to the demise of Merello. "That is fair enough, Rax. I spoke in haste. I apologise to you, Capalle."

"We must consider what we do next," said Harley as he kicked gravel at one of the fidgeting captives. "It is probable that the rogue will go back to the gang and alert them that they have been uncovered. They will either disband or flee, probably both."

Rax stepped forward. "There is another possibility," he said softly. "They will come here in force and try to slaughter us."

Undar stepped beside his brother. "Aye. That means they could come here at any moment. We have no knowledge on what their numbers could be. We have just six men."

"Hey! And three feisty women," called Jetti from the shadows of the front corner of the house.

"We can wield bows, crossbows and daggers," added Hollissa.

Pretteen giggled. "We can also throw stones," she

offered. "And we can use clubs if necess'ry."

"Heh heh! Hopefully, it won't be," laughed Boulaye.

"Right then," rumbled Rax. "We have about three hours to dawn. We need to act quickly now!"

Boulaye despatched the brothers, Gandar and Undar, to the top of the house to watch out; Undar to the front, Gandar to the back.

"We must sort out the contraband," suggested Harley. "We have two willing volunteers here." He indicated the captives.

Harley, Capalle and LeDuc coerced the muleteer and the thug at sword-point into emptying the crates and refilling them with the contraband from beneath the bodies. They dragged the crates and chests up the steps and outside the house. They were carried across into the old stable, LeDuc slapping the brigands with the flat of his sword blade.

"Tie 'em up and secure 'em in the stable," said Rax gruffly. "Keep a watch on 'em through the rest of the night. Keep 'em watered but no food. We don't have enough. If they make a noise you can gag 'em. If they look like they're going to yell out warnings then knock 'em on the head or slice their throats."

The eyes of their captives opened wide with fear.

"That Ballaron may come back with the rest of the gang," warned Boulaye. "If they do not, we resume our search at dawn. After that we take the captives and the contraband to the city watch commander. We will need to inform Arnan Ben-Harami and let the city watch commander know that we will be doing so. What now, Harley?"

"Three of us into the stable with the mules," responded Harley. "The rest back into the house."

They took the crates and chests into the house and led the mules into the stable. Rax, LeDuc and Capalle went into the stable to watch over the captives and the contraband.

"If we get unwelcome visitors you'll be able to come up behind them and stick it up 'em," laughed Boulaye. "Where will you be, young 'un?"

"I'll be around," replied Harley. "Somewhere outside."

"Watch your step. Riette will rip my danglers off if anything happens to you!'"

. . . o o O o o . . .

The first light of dawn appeared in the eastern sky. Gulls shrieked over the cliffs and wheeled above the old house. A sea mist was beginning to drift slowly across the coast.

There was barely a breath of wind as Harley stood outside the front of the house chatting with Rax. Boulaye stepped outside and breathed in the cool morning air.

"That front door is almost off its hinges," he muttered. "Looks like a fog coming in. The gang didn't appear then."

"Nor will they," replied Harley. "I've found Ballaron."

"What? Where is he?" asked Rax.

"At the bottom of a deep pit over there." Harley pointed beyond the left of the house. "The pit, an old well I think, was blocked by a wooden cover. It was rotten and Ballaron fell straight through it when he fled."

"Hah!" huffed Boulaye. "That was the sound that Capalle heard when Ballaron bravely ran off."

Harley cleared his throat. "It is possible that the rest of the gang will still come here looking for those who are missing. We still need to bury the dead ones."

"Throw them down the pit too," suggested Rax. "They will be well rid of and will remain hidden there. It will save us some hard work. Show us the pit, Harley."

Together, they trudged through the long grass and thick weed in between the acacia trees. Harley indicated the position of the pit.

"Have a care," he warned. "The timber cover is now mostly gone down along with Ballaron."

They cautiously leaned over and peered down. In the misty slowly growing light, they could make out nothing down there.

"It was a well, long ago," said Rax. "Look here." He pointed at some rotten timbers that protruded from the weed next to the pit.

"It is a grave now," responded Boulaye. "We can throw the bodies down there later. Let us get back to the house."

...o o O o o...

As daylight grew, Boulaye brought the sword of Karouche outside. They gathered around and Boulaye studied the hilt and the blade. Seeing nothing, he handed it to Harley.

Harley turned the sword over and held it up towards the sun. Despite the thickening mist he could see detail quite clearly. "Wait!" he exclaimed. "Look at the blade. This is not rust; it is some sort of hard, black clay."

Rax and Boulaye leaned over towards Harley to gaze over his shoulder.

"Can you chip it off?" enquired Rax.

Harley took out his dagger and struck the sword blade with the butt of the knife's hilt. Small pieces of clay broke away and fell to the ground. He continued to batter the sword until most of the shining blade was clear. It had taken him quite a while.

He turned the blade to catch the light. "There is some faint writing scratched on it," he said excitedly. "Erm, let me see. It says '*The water is nowe dust and hydes the fruites of mine years of labours.*'"

Boulaye scratched his head and sighed. "Now we just need to work out what it means. Water is now dust? Very cryptic, I must say. It tells us nothing. Is there more? What about the other side?"

Harley turned the blade over. "Aye, there is. It says '*Take oute the stone then looke benethe*'."

"Perhaps we need to search beneath the place where the sword was concealed just as we planned."

Suddenly, Harley straightened up and slapped a hand to his forehead. "Hah! I know where the treasure is!" he exclaimed. "I am sure of it."

"What?" cried Boulaye. "Where?"

"It was you, Rax, that gave us the clue. One note said something about the sword pointing the way to the hoard. Boulaye, what did the other note say? The one with the chalice."

"The treasure was well hidden."

"It said that it was '*welle hyd*' I believe." Harley spelled the two words."

"The well!" called Rax. "'Tis hidden down the well! It looks like Ballaron found it for us!"

...o o **O** o o...

As the sun rose higher in the sky, so the fog began to dissipate. By mid-morning Boulaye, Harley, Gandar and Undar had secured one end of a hastily-constructed rope ladder to an anchor-point adjacent to the well-head. The rest of the group was providing a careful watch. Earlier, they had used the rope to measure the depth of the well. They estimated twenty-three feet. The ladder itself was a single-core of rope with loops a foot apart along its length.

"I'm not going down it," grunted Boulaye. "I'm too big!"

"Me too!" muttered Gandar, shaking his head. "I'm too big too."

"I'm not either," agreed Undar with a laugh. "Too scared!"

"So that leaves just me, does it?" sighed Harley with a wry smile on his face.

"Well, the rope *was* made by you," said Boulaye. "It is only right that you should be the one to use it."

"Very well, but I get extra treasure."

"It was *my* rope," gasped Undar. "Good quality hempen rope, that was! Cost me a fortune, it did!"

"Let us just get on with it," growled an exasperated Gandar, "instead of bickering about it."

"Remember, there are twenty loops," advised Boulaye. "Count them as you go. The last loop is a big one in which you should be able to put both feet.""It will make it too tight for both feet though. I probably won't bother."

With Gandar holding onto his shoulders, Harley eased himself over the edge of the well lip and searched for the first loop with his right foot. He located it surprisingly easily.

"One!" he called.

"We'll lower the lamp down when you say," called Gandar.

"Look at the walls as well as down on the floor," called Boulaye.

The next few loops did not come so easily to him, especially as the darkness of the well increased. He counted each one aloud as his foot search and found the loop.

"Six. I need the lamp now," he called up.

An ancient lamp, with a spluttering candle inside it, came down level with his head. It provided a little light. *Oil would have been better*, Harley thought. He used his dagger to probe the walls. The old stone bricks seemed sound.

"Take it down another five feet," he called up.

As his eyes adjusted to the gloom, the candle-light seemed to be more beneficial. He could make out the next few loops below him.

"Ten! Bring the lamp down a bit more." The lamp lowered. "That is enough."

He counted down a few more loops, searching as he went.

"Fourteen!" It had taken him almost an hour. His feet hurt from the strain of the rope loops and his hands ached from gripping the rope.

"Have you seen anything yet," called Boulaye.

"Do you think I would not say if I had?" replied Harley angrily. He relaxed a little, his legs also aching from the climb. "No, nothing yet. How many was my last count?"

"Thirteen," replied Boulaye. "Or was it fifteen?"

"It was fourteen," called Undar.

"Are you sure?" asked Harley.

"Aye, fourteen," insisted Undar. "At least I think so."

"Hope you're right," called Harley. The echoes seemed louder in his ears. *But I am sure I took another.*

He found a couple more loops but then the next proved impossible for him to locate with his foot.

"Bring the lamp down about six feet."

The he saw the loop. It had snagged on a protruding brick. *Strange*, he thought. He kicked it away. "Nineteen!"

"Are you faring well, lad?" called Boulaye.

"Aye, I am. But there is a brick sticking out down here. I need to get a bit lower to see why that is."

He stepped down to the last loop. There wasn't one.

"Shit! I must have miscounted," he called up. "I am on the last loop." The echo was almost deafening.

The jutting brick was just below hip-height.

"Bring the lamp down a little more," he called, not so loudly. He could see the body of Ballaron just below him. The head was twisted at a grotesque angle and showed signs of a severe amount of bloody damage to the forehead. Large pieces of wood were scattered around the body. The floor was about four feet below the last loop, an easy drop for him although he knew that stepping back up onto the bottom loop would not be so straightforward. *There will be a way*, he thought. *I'll just step on Ballaron!*

He replaced his dagger and gripped the rope with both hands. He withdrew his feet from the loops and dropped to the floor.

"I am on the floor," he called to those above.

"What can you see?" called Boulaye.

"Ballaron is keeping me company but he is asleep; permanently! Chunks of rotten timber all over. It stinks down here. Pull the lamp up a little bit. That's better. The sticky-out brick is at head-height and it is covered with bits of Ballaron's head!"

"Very nice!" boomed Gandar.

"Not so loud, it echoes down here! I am going to try to move the brick now."

He moved himself a little to one side to allow a little more light from the lantern and gripped the large brick with both hands. He pushed it hard left and then right. There was no movement. He tried once again, this time with his full bodyweight. *Was that movement?*

He repeated the swing from side to side and this time he felt a slight rocking of the brick. His arms were

364

already aching from the climb down and he stopped for a moment, shaking his arms.

He tried again, this time a little more frantically. The brick moved more noticeably now, and a little fine rubble dropped to the floor. He rocked and pulled at the brick until, at last, it came loose and fell to the floor. Harley only just dodged out of the way in time; it narrowly missed his left foot.

"What was that?" called Boulaye.

"The brick is out," Harley replied. "It fell to the floor."

"Is there anything in the hole?"

"Wait! I am looking."

He moved the lamp, pulled out his dagger again and probed the hole. Loose rubble and a pebble fell to the floor. He bent down and picked the pebble up. *I wonder*, he pondered.

"Lower a bag on a line," he called.

It was quite a few moments before a soft leather bag appeared by his shoulder. He placed the pebble inside it and called for Boulaye to pull it up.

"Harley!" gasped Boulaye. "By the gods! It is an uncut ruby. Are there more?"

...o o O o o...

Two hours later, Harley climbed out of the well. He was soaked in sweat and his face and hands were covered in grime and dust. But he was smiling broadly.

"There are more than two hundred stones here," said Boulaye. "I have never heard of such riches, such a treasure, let alone held them in my hands."

"I kept digging the wall and removed a couple more stones. There is nothing more in there. What now?" He splashed some water over his face and hands from a waterskin proffered by Undar.

"We get out of here with the treasure, the prisoners and the contraband. Everyone is ready. Let's go."

...ooOoo...

Boulaye, Harley and Gandar walked through the tavern towards Arnan Ben-Harami's chamber. Undar, Rax and Capelle waited outside the Star of Caspar tavern with the two loaded pack-mules and the three hostages while LeDuc escorted Jetti, Hollissa and Pretteen back to their livery stable in the corral.

Ben-Harami met them at his door and ushered them inside. He clapped his hands twice and one of his lackeys rushed over. "Refreshments for my honoured guests," he said. The barman hurried off.

"Please be seated," he wheezed. "To what do I owe the pleasure of your visit?"

Boulaye smiled. "We have something for you, Councillor," he replied. "Three captive smugglers, some chests of their contraband goods and some articles we found that were once the property of one self-styled Pirate King."

He rose to his feet, grinned and rubbed his hands together. "By the gods! This is marvellous! Tell me more about these smugglers, firstly." He sat back down on his chair.

"We were at the old house atop the cliffs nearby to the harbour gates. The Temple of Tarne described it as having long been rumoured to be the haunt of the ghosts of seafarers. These ghosts turned out to be a gang of cutthroat smugglers bringing in silks, thus avoiding the import taxes imposed by the Casparsport authorities."

Ben-Harami's mouth fell open. "You mean that you tackled them and caught them at their nefarious activities?"

"Aye," replied Harley. "I watched them one night soon after they had killed four people and thrown their bodies into the cellar. I spoke with Boulaye and the rest of our company and we decided to see if we could catch them with their smuggled goods."

There was a knock at the door. Ben-Harami ordered "Enter!" and the flunkey stepped in pushing a trolley loaded with jugs of ale, wine and mead.

"I want you to rush to the headquarters of the city watch," he directed the man. "Ask him to report here immediately with half a dozen men."

"Aye, Excellency." The man rushed out once again, closing the door behind him.

"Ha ha! I am not royalty or aristocratic in any way but my men do occasionally refer to me by the epithet Excellency. I find it humorous and I don't correct them. Perhaps I should one day, when I tire of it, hahaha! Tell me more of what you have learned of their activities."

Boulaye had been about to drink from a cup of mead. He replaced the cup on the table. "Apart from bringing in silks, these people also smuggled out copper, tin, silver and semi-precious stones, much of which is loaded into the chests outside. They were also dealing in liquor, like elven sour-honey wine and dwarven bloodwine. There is a chest of this outside too."

"Ah, our laws forbid its dealing and making available this liquor in Casparsport. It causes the imbiber to suffer badly when it is drunk to the slightest excess. We have occasionally kept the old house under observation but have seen nothing. Yet we know that smuggling is constantly going on."

"Perhaps your observers were seen." offered Gandar.

"Perhaps the smugglers were alerted to the fact that the house was to be watched," suggested Harley.

Ben-Harami looked aghast. "You mean by an informant? Somebody within the city watch?"

"We can't say, of course, but it is possible, is it not?" asked Boulaye. "Perhaps you need to use outsiders to do your observing and tell only the minimum of people necessary. If the smugglers are still alerted it will be all the easier to find out who their informant is."

Ben-Harami considered this for a moment. "I shall give this some thought. Now, what about Karouche's treasure? I assume that is what you alluded to when you spoke of articles that were once his property?"

Boulaye placed a leather sack, tied at the neck by a thong, on the table. He pulled on the drawstrings and the bag opened. He dug his hand inside and withdrew and handful of its contents. A number of small stones, of different colours but dull in colour, sat in the palm of his hand. They ranged in size from small beads to almost the size of hens' eggs.

"Uncut stones," said Boulaye. "There's rubies, diamonds, sapphires, emeralds, topaz, garnets and more besides."

"By the gods!" Ben-Harami exclaimed once more. "Was there anything else?" Boulaye shook his head. Ben-Harami asked. "Where were they?"

"They were hidden in the wall down the well by the old house," replied Harley. "The only other item down there was the body of one of the smugglers who fell down the well while running away from us."

"Can you describe the people you found in the cellar?"

Harley straightened up and rested his head on his hands. "One was a woman, tall and stocky with brown hair in braids. One of the men had his black hair cropped short and a clipped beard. The other two were fair-haired, probably from northern realms. All of them had their throats cut."

Ben-Harami rose to his feet again "Ah. Oh dear," he said sadly. "They were my agents. I sent them out some time ago to infiltrate the smugglers' organisation. For a while I had occasional reports from them but that stopped a couple of weeks ago. I feared the worst and now those fears have been confirmed." He sat back down again. "Are you happy that I take your stones to the city depository for valuation? They will give you the best rates. I have to tell you that the city will take half the value. You may have the remainder. It will, no doubt, take a few days for this to happen. I shall discuss with the city council the terms of reward for your efforts. I shall make no promises however."

Boulaye nodded after first looking at Harley and Gandar. "Aye, that is acceptable," he replied.

With effort, Ben-Harami rose again from his chair. The others followed. Boulaye led Harley and Gandar back outside to where Undar, Rax and Capelle waited outside. The city watchmen had just arrived and took responsibility for the captive smugglers and the pack-mules. The city watch commander stepped inside the tavern where Ben-Harami was waiting for him.

It was early in the afternoon when Boulaye and the others returned to the livery stable.

...ooOoo...

Harley stepped through the livery stable door and was immediately met by Olwetta.

"She is in the stall yonder," she said. "She is most unwell."

He rushed straight over to Riette and dropped to his knees beside her. She was mumbling incoherently. An elderly Priest of Haeman administered a salve to the vivid suppurating injury on her stomach. She was

369

soaked in sweat and very flushed, her damp hair sticking to her face. "She is very unwell," he said gently. "She has been delirious."

"What has happened to her?" asked Harley. Fear and worry were etched on his face.

The priest took him gently by the elbow and led him away from Riette's stall. Olwetta and Jetti strode over and stood beside Harley.

"The wound to her stomach was worse, er, deeper than we thought and it has become badly infected. I am doing all I can to save her. I wish I could do more but the healing I am able to give is very limited. I shall continue to try to keep her alive but I have to tell you that her condition is slowly worsening. I am so sorry to bear this bad news."

Harley opened his mouth to speak but no words came. He looked over to Riette's stall and a tear ran down his face.

"No," he gasped. "She was getting well two days ago. She will recover, won't she?"

Olwetta placed a comforting arm around his shoulder but he angrily shook it off.

"I will do all I can," the priest repeated. He walked back down the passage to attend to Riette. Harley, in a daze, followed after him.

The stable was quiet.

Riette woke up a short while later. Harley lay down beside her and held her hands in his.

"I love you, beautiful girl," he whispered. "I always will."

"I know. I love you too, my handsome boy," she replied.

She passed away an hour later. Harley held her body tightly against his and sobbed.

Chapter 26

The old priest took her body away on his small wagon a while later, promising to ensure that she would be given an honourable funeral by the Temple of Cahuhl, as was customary in the city.

Harley sat in the stall all night, occasionally dozing for short periods. His moods switched from despair, to anger, and to deep sadness. Olwetta came by once to give him some food and water but he didn't touch them.

Boulaye entered during the late evening and squatted down in front of him without a word being said. It was a long moment before Harley raised his head.

"Damned Hartimmer!" breathed Harley. "And damned Massbourg." He curled his right hand into a fist and beat the straw bale.

"They will pay, Harley. They will pay for Riette, for Solarin Fleet and for Merrello too. They will pay."

"I need some time alone, Boulaye. Just tonight."

Boulaye rose to his feet. "There is not one of us here who wouldn't hesitate to do anything for you, lad."

"Aye, I know that."

Boulaye pulled the blanket across the stall and joined the company. The remainder of the evening continued quietly.

...ooOoo...

Duprenne stepped in through the livery stable door. "Arnan Ben-Harami requests the pleasure of your company in his chambers, Boulaye. A morning feast will be arranged for you and four others of your choice within the hour."

Boulaye nodded his thanks and Duprenne resumed his watch. Boulaye glanced through the door and could see that it was quite light outside. He pulled the door shut and turned around.

Who shall I take? he posed to himself.

He went over to Harley's stall. The young man was sitting on a straw bale, much as he was when Boulaye left him last night.

"Have you slept, lad?"

Harley looked up at Boulaye. He looked pallid. "Some."

"Ben-Harami wants to speak with some of us in a few moments. I would like you to accompany us."

"I am not sure I want to."

Boulaye sighed. "I need you with me, lad."

Harley coughed and realised he had been holding Riette's backpack. He put it down and stood up. "I need to wash my face. I shall come. Who else?"

Boulaye rubbed his chin. "I have not asked anyone else yet. Your stall was the first I passed. I shall ask Olwetta, Ragdan and Balari. It would be beneficial for them to have experience of formalities."

"Not Hollissa?"

Boulaye shook his head. "It may not go down well with Ben-Harami. She is supposed to be working for the city council. Instead she has become one of our company members."

"But she *is* still reporting to the city council," Harley confirmed. "I agree with you that she should not go at this time. You should speak with her though, to make sure she has informed the council, or that she intends to do so."

"Aye, lad. I shall."

"There is no need to ask me," said a voice. Hollissa poked her head through the curtain. "I was walking past and I heard your voices. Look, I have yet to tell Ben-

372

Harami. I have intended to tell him as soon as I take in my next report."

"When is that?" Boulaye asked.

"Today. Now that you discovered the jewels and the contraband, I just have to confirm that what you found is what you handed over to the authorities yesterday."

"What will your report say?" asked Harley.

"It will confirm everything. It is just the sword of Karouche. What will you do with that?"

Boulaye thought for a moment and then shrugged his shoulders. "I had given that no thought at all," he replied. "It is there in mine and Jetti's stall, beneath a bale. I shall take it with us. I suppose you should come over there with us this morning after all."

"Aye, I would like to. If I may."

Boulaye, Harley, Hollissa, Ragdan and Balari left the livery stable. Olwetta offered to stay behind. Rax, Capalle and Duprenne escorted them to the tavern and returned to the corral to await their reappearance. Rax and Boulaye still insisted that no chances would be taken with their safety.

...o o O o o...

As they approached the door to the tavern; one of Ben-Harami's flunkies was ready and waiting for them. He led them to Ben-Harami's chamber and opened the door.

"The master will meet with you momentarily," he drawled. "Please make yourselves comfortable."

The large table was already groaning under the weight of an array of breads, meats, cheese, chutneys and spiced fruits, hot mutton tea, mulled wine and mead.

They sat down at the table, tactfully avoiding the heavy, wide chair at the table's head, but immediately rose again as their host wheezed in through the door. He shuffled over to his chair and collapsed into it.

"Welcome to my humble chambers," he announced in his almost falsetto voice. "Sit, dear people. Sit! Do not stand on ceremony here." He wiped his brow with a silk kerchief. "Please, eat and drink. It is a warm day already, is it not?"

Boulaye introduced Balari, their host having already met the others.

"My goodness, there is such a diversity of races in your company," he panted, again wiping his brow.

They filled platters and, except for Harley, ate hungrily. Their host crammed his platter with a pile of food and started eating voraciously. Harley however, merely picked at slices of mutton although he did drink a sizeable quantity of mulled wine.

"I see you are accompanied by the Lady Hollissa Tranti," said Ben-Harami. "I hear rumours that she will be leaving the employ of the city. Is this true, lady?"

"That is indeed true, Councillor," replied Hollissa. She had flushed as he spoke and quickly glanced at Boulaye. "I have been intending to inform you of that today. I am a little surprised that you know for I have told no person outside of the Company."

Ben-Harami laughed, his rolls of fat shaking like a jelly. "Ahh. I must admit to misleading you. It was, shall I say, a shrewd guess based on what I know of your prowess with the lute, the flute and storytelling. I knew that the lure of the travelling performer troupe might prove a challenge for you to resist. You must do what your heart dictates. I shall not think badly of you. You shall be much missed by the council though. You have proven yourself tenacious and worthy."

The group sat in silence apart from the sound of food being eaten.

"Mmph, I am devastated, of course, to hear your sad

news," mumbled Ben-Harami around a mouthful of meat. He chewed the remainder of his mouthful and swallowed it. He looked across the table to where Harley sat picking at a small piece of bread crust. "I understand, young man, that she was very special to you."

Harley looked up. "Aye, she was that. They took my unborn child from her and then they took Riette from me." His head dropped and he was silent.

"This leads me to why I called you all here," continued Ben-Harami. "You are searching for one Traviss Hartimmer and two henchmen by the name of Massbourg."

Harley's head snapped up. "Aye, we are!" he hissed. The others nodded.

"While you were engaged in searching for the Pirate King's treasure I instigated a general city-wide hunt for him for three days. I believe we have run him to ground in a disused shack on the edge of the deprived area's shanty town. It is barely half a mile from where you found him before."

"I want to see where it is," growled Harley.

"What would you do with that information?" asked Ben-Harami.

"I hope the city authorities would turn a blind eye," Boulaye cut in. "Just this once."

Ben-Harami thought for a moment. "I have not told you a word about the possibility of someone who may be called Hartimmer having been found. You have said nothing to me regarding any intentions you may have regarding that person. My man will call at your premises to take a couple of you on a guided tour of the city later, soon after dusk. He will provide the necessary, er, clothing. Will that suffice?"

Boulaye looked over at Harley who nodded back to him. "Aye!" he replied.

"Then please finish this sumptuous meal. Is there anything I can be of assistance with for you?"

"Aye, if you please," replied Harley. "There are a number of items that are difficult for me to buy because I am unable to venture out safely."

Harley listed a number of items, and quantities. "I shall reimburse you for your trouble," he added.

"There will be no trouble, I assure you, and consider this a gift from the city council. I have an inkling of what you will need some of these for. My compliments to you for the apparent skill you have. My man will have them delivered to you by about midday. I shall now take my leave."

The councillor hauled his massive frame out of his chair and waddled out through the door. The others followed a short while later.

Balari released a long belch. "I've been needin' to do that for ages!" he exclaimed.

Boulaye took Hollissa by the elbow as they stepped out onto the street. "*Lady* Hollissa Tranti?" he asked. "You are an aristocrat?"

Balari stepped up. "Aye, what was that all about?"

Hollissa took a deep breath. "Very well, I shall tell you. I wasn't going to. You remember my uncle, Toll Tranti, is the chief administrator in the city depository? He is my father's younger brother. Well, my father has died, at the end of last year's massive heat-wave, but he was Lord Tranti, one of the three City Lords. Therefore as he was a widower, my mother having died when I was very young, I then became Lady Tranti. Uncle Toll is just about to inherit the title of City Lord and when he dies I expect it will pass on to me provided that Uncle Toll has no children. He is sixty-four and has no spouse so it is unlikely, unless he has been dallying about in his younger days and left an heir that nobody knows about! I don't usually tell people about this so

376

please keep it to just those of us in the company."

"I doubt I could remember all of this anyway," laughed Boulaye. "You're secret will be safe with us, *Lady* Hollissa!"

Rax, Capalle and Duprenne were waiting by the corral gate and escorted the group back into the stable.

... o o O o o ...

Two of Ben-Harami's lackeys arrived just after midday, each carrying a large, heavy wooden crate.

"What is all this?" Boulaye enquired as Harley prised the lids off.

"It will be a little gift for Hartimmer and the two remaining Massbourgs!" grunted Harley. "I intend to spread their rear ends all across the city. I really need a space out of sight and away from this stable. I don't want this going up too."

"Spread their rear ends?" gasped Boulaye. "Going up? What do you mean? This all sounds a bit vague to me. Finding you a space should be easy enough though. Leave it to me. What do you need?"

Working together, the Company manhandled three wagons to form a square enclosure across the open end of which was hung a tarpaulin. Gandar set a wooden table with a stone paving slab placed upon it. Helped by Boulaye and Gandar, Harley unpacked and arranged the small barrels and linen bags of substances provided by Ben-Harami.

"What have you got in the barrels and bags?" asked Gandar.

Harley looked up at him and then over at Boulaye. "Observe and I shall explain it all to you as I go," he sighed. "First, I have saltpetre, sulphur and charcoal. I grind each separately like this."

Using a hand-sized flat stone, he slowly ground

each of the components into a fine powder, sweeping each of them into separate earthenware bowls. He placed a large bowl in the centre of the stone slab.

"I put lots of measures of saltpetre into this bowl," he murmured, "then some of sulphur and some of charcoal." He measured out precise quantities of each using a large spoon, combining them in the bowl.

"I don't understand what it is that you are making," whispered Boulaye as he wrinkled his nose at the small of the sulphur.

Harley looked up at him with an almost insane smile on his face. "I am making a blasting powder from these chemical components that Ben-Harami obtained for me. I have to mix it thoroughly otherwise it may not work properly. Sometimes it helps to slightly dampen the mixture. When it is ignited it burns rapidly and makes an explosion. Watch this! You better step back a pace."

Harley moved his small bowls and the apparatus onto the ground, placed a small heap of the mixed powder in the middle of the slab and, using a flint and tinder, lit a taper. He touched the burning end of the taper to the powder. There was a whoosh, a bright flash and a cloud of thick, grey smoke.

Boulaye leapt back and coughed. "Gods!" he exclaimed, a look of shock on his face. "But how can this aid us?"

"Simple. When packed into a small enclosure it behaves a little differently. What we need is tube. A thick bamboo pole is ideal or even a scroll case. If I pack the blasting powder inside it, add a taper that I shall make especially and seal it tight, the blast will be quite destructive, I assure you. One the size of a scroll case can bring down our stable building and kill just about everyone in it."

"What?" gasped Boulaye. "Where did you learn this

stuff?"

"Why did you learn this stuff?" laughed Gandar.

Harley paused for a moment. "I was taught this art by a great man," he sighed. "Now, by mixing the blasting powder with certain metal filings and salts it can have some interesting effects such as thick smoke that can obscure me or aid my escape, or it can produce a bright flash that will blind my enemies for a few moments."

"Olwetta has always said that there's more to you than meets the eye," huffed Boulaye. "I wonder if this powder could have some benefits in our performance."

"Aye, we could do but in small quantities," nodded Harley. "We do not want to frighten our audiences. But I guess it can make for interesting effects for our performances with different colours."

"Will your blast really cause that much damage?" asked Boulaye.

"Probably but there are other things I can put in it that will make it more potent. Do not ask what. Can you get me a couple of small scroll cases?"

"Aye," replied Boulaye. "I believe Olwetta has some. I'll ask her now."

He strode off and appeared a short while later with two scroll cases, one of leather and the other of ox thigh bone.

Harley looked up and gave a wan smile of appreciation.

"Have you finished?" asked Gandar.

"Not yet."

Harley opened a small metal cylinder inside which was a black glutinous substance. Both Gandar and Boulaye turned their faces away at the acrid smell.

"Is that pitch," Boulaye asked.

"Aye, it is."

Gandar looked puzzled. "What are you concocting

now?"

"Something nasty," replied Harley with a blank expression. "They are called pitch grenades."

Boulaye and Gandar watched intently as Harley worked with the strange chemicals. He combined saltpeter and sulphur and mixed it into a small quantity of pitch. He divided the thick black substance into two and rolled each of them into a ball. He took a short length of cord, cut it into two lengths about three inches long. He rubbed a little of the mixture of saltpeter and sulphur into the cords in between the strands, made a small hole in the balls and inserted a cord into each of the black spheres. Lastly, he used two of the linen bags to wrap each of the balls.

"They look interesting, young 'un" muttered Boulaye. "What are you going to do with them? Are they, um, blasting balls?"

"Nay, when lit, they burn slowly but with an intense heat to produce a stinking smoke. They will continue to burn in water to produce a thick poisonous fume. In a confined space it will confuse, disorient and choke an adversary causing them to want to get out of their hiding-hole. I have some ideas for these! If you wait in the stable I shall finish up here and be with you in a while."

"But we can help," protested Gandar.

"Please! I insist," urged Harley.

An hour later, Harley strode into the stable and carefully dropped the two scroll cases and the pitch grenades onto Boulaye's lap. Boulaye almost jumped clear off the straw bale. The scroll cases each had a short cord protruding from one end. Each end was sealed with the thick, black pitch-like substance that was still sticky.

"Keep those well away from any flame source," warned Harley as he walked to the stall that he had shared with Riette. The others looked on, puzzled at Harley's actions. Despite questions from the company, Harley, Boulaye and Gandar gave no explanation or said anything further.

...ooOoo...

Duprenne pushed his head through the stable door. "A visitor," he called. "Looks like a city watchman. He came in on a small wagon."

"Send him in!" replied Boulaye. "Somebody give Harley a shake."

A tall, athletically-built man with cropped, black hair and a trimmed dark beard stepped inside. He was dressed in the standard watchman's uniform of dark blue hose and tunic over which he wore a heavy studded-leather armour.

"Greetings to you all," stated the watchman. "I am Sword-man Reever, sent to you by His Excellency Arnan Ben-Harami. I gather you are expecting me?"

"Aye, we are," replied Boulaye. "I understand you are giving us a tour around the city."

"Aye, part of it at least. I am instructed to provide up to four of you with suitable attire. It is all on my mule-cart outside."

The clothing proved to be watchman uniforms similar to that worn by Reever. He also produced four short-swords and two city watchman's pikes. He laughed as he watched their expressions.

Harley stepped out of his stall and joined them. He yawned as Gandar handed him one of the uniform packs. He raised an eyebrow as he looked at the weapons.

Harley, Boulaye, Gandar and Undar followed as Reever led them out of the corral. They turned left at the corral gate and walked in file along the street.

Boulaye and Undar carried the pikes over their left shoulders.

Harley was surprised at how the folk shrank away from them as they swiftly marched in silence through the city towards the deprivation district. He recognised the area from a seven-day of week earlier when they had first encountered Hartimmer and the Massbourgs. Now they were on their way to hunt them again. His face was grim, as were those of the others, as they marched in step. This time, he was determined that his quarry would not escape *his* justice. They would be destroyed. He would have vengeance.

"Did you bring your toys with you?" Boulaye asked out of the corner of his mouth.

Harley shook his head. "I'll bring 'em later."

"Quiet in the ranks!" growled Reever.

"He's taking this a bit seriously!" whispered Gandar.

"We have to look convincing," hissed Boulaye.

Harley's face returned to its scowl as he concentrated on remembering the route they were taking.

With Reever calling the pace, they passed through a checkpoint that led out of the mercantile city and out into the shanties of the pauper's area.

He was prepared for the stench and filth, the ankle-deep horse dung, rotten vegetation and the carcasses of dead dogs and birds that covered the street. He was disgusted by the vermin that freely roamed the streets. Despite the darkness, braziers burned only on street corners, children still ran through the decrepit wooden buildings and hurled crude insults at what they believed to be the group of watchmen. Although the men, mostly roguish drunks by the look of them, gave the group surly expressions they kept clear.

A pair of drunks, jostling with each other with their

382

arms flailing, stopped their aggression to piss in the centre of the street. As Reever's group passed by one of the men directed his stream towards them, laughing coarsely. Reever jerked his whip from his belt and without uncoiling it viciously slashed the thug across the face. The brute fell backwards into the foul street.

Reever led them a little further and turned to the right. He raised a hand to quietly bring them to a halt. The street, little more than a wide passage, was quiet and relatively unspoilt by filth. They could clearly see that the road was cobbled although many stones were missing.

Reever pointed to a dark, wooden building on the left, about forty paces down the street and standing on its own. A dim light glowed through gaps in the planking. They moved over to the right side of the passage.

"You might find that shed interesting," he mumbled. "Seen enough?"

"Shed?" responded Boulaye. "It is not a disused stockroom at all but an old watermill. Wait! Listen! I can hear the water beneath it. Aye, I've seen enough. You, Harley?"

Boulaye's whisper had sounded lke a yell in the quiet darkness despite the raucous noise from revellers a few streets away.

Harley stood rock still, glaring at the mill. He crept forwards a couple of paces. "I want to take a closer look," he murmured. Without waiting for a response he trotted down the street keeping close to a low wall to the left.

"Wha–! Get back!" Reever gasped, giving an exasperated wave of his arms and Boulaye just shrugged. Harley was gone and was soon out of sight.

Harley was back within a few moments. "I seen enough," he whispered.

They marched through the muck-laden streets back to the mercantile city and the livery stable. Reever retrieved his uniforms and weapons and led his wagon out of the corral. A pair of Ben-Harami's barmen had already provided their evening feast.

"Where's Harley?" asked Boulaye as the company gathered around the circle of straw bales.

"Back in his stall," replied Gandar. "He's hardly spoken a word."

Olwetta was about to bite a piece off a lump of cheese. "He really should have something to eat," she said.

"E's grievin'," mumbled Balari. "Give 'im a bit o' space, 'e'll be alright in a few days."

A while later Olwetta looked up from her platter. "Somebody give Harley a call please," she called. "He should have water at least."

Hollissa rose from the bale and strode through to the stalls. She was back within moments.

"He's not there!" she cried.

"Oh gods!" exclaimed Boulaye. "What's he doing?"

"No need to guess," replied Ragdan in his baritone voice. "He has gone to destroy Hartimmer and the last Massbourgs."

...ooOoo...

Chapter 27

While the others enjoyed their feast, mulled ale and mead, Harley had quickly and quietly dressed in his black costume; Tishia had washed it the previous day to clean it of Riette's blood. He blacked his hands and the exposed part of his face with a mixture of oil and soot.

Using the darkness to his advantage, he silently made his way from the opening at the rear of the stable, out through the back of the corral and out into the dark streets of the mercantile area of the city. His small belt pack softly bumped against his right hip as he darted from one place of concealment to another. His dagger sat at his left hip and he carried his precious rapier in his hand to avoid it knocking against obstacles.

Despite his grief, he felt alive, excited. He was doing what he had trained hard for. His heart beat was fast and the adrenaline flowed through his body enhancing his senses and energy. He was impatient to get on with this task but aware that he had a two-mile hike to complete in total concealment.

The streets were busy despite the lateness of the hour and Harley was forced to lay low for a long time. From his hiding place he could see the front of the company's livery stable and the corral. He witnessed Capalle and Pallenne handing over the watch to LeDuc and Carerre and was relieved to see that none of the others had come out to find him or to determine what had become of him. He had no doubt that he was missed by now. He took the time to consider the lair of Hartimmer and his sidekicks, the Massbourgs. An old watermill; from his earlier search he knew this would be ideally suited to his own needs.

A light rain began to fall. It was warm but nonetheless refreshing after so many weeks of hot, throat-parching dryness. It was almost two hours before he felt it sufficiently safe for him to continue by which time the rain had became a little heavier.

After waiting for an ideal opportunity, he crossed through the checkpoint in the dividing wall by concealing himself between the rear wheels of an ox-drawn wagon that trundled slowly through. The mounted escort guards had no idea that he was there, neither did the bored checkpoint watchmen. This way he entered the stench-filled poor quarter of the city.

Another hour passed before he was in deep shadows at the entry to the wide passage leading to the watermill. The rain had kept the bedraggled crowds away from these streets which suited him well. The persistent rain was soaking through his clothing but it did little to interfere with his determination. The sounds of revelry in a nearby drinking hole had reduced to little more than ribald singing interspersed with belligerence and cheering. Harley strained to listen during the quieter moments and then tuned his ears to the sound of running water.

He noticed, through the rain and the misty steam that rose ghost-like from the warm ground, that the dim light he had seen earlier glinting through cracks in the wooden planks was still there. The raindrops were quite large and he hoped they would be drumming sufficiently on the wooden roof of the building to cover any sound that he might make when he approached the mill. Harley estimated that it was now well after midnight as he eased himself out from behind the broken piece of fencing that leaned against the wall of a burned-out wooden shack. He trotted towards the mill, keeping a low crouch close to a squat wooden stockyard wall. He promptly reached the mill and flattened himself against the dark wall.

He let out his breath in relief and tuned his senses to

filter out the noises from the patter of the rain and from the nearby hostelry, enabling him to listen through to the inside of the mill. He could hear the soft sounds of footfall and occasional voices from inside and surmised that most of the sound seemed to emanate from the bottom of the building.

Ideal, he thought.

He cautiously made his way to the left and rounded the corner to the rear, stopping himself just in time to avoid falling into the stream. Now he could clearly hear the voices inside.

...ooOoo...

"How in the Hells of the Void can I sleep with your damned snoring?"

"I friggin' well don't friggin' snore!"

Hartimmer strode across the floor of the mill, narrowly missing the large gap in the floor that had once held a large water wheel. Water still flowed beneath but the smell that rose up through the floor was almost unbearable. He had tasked the Massbourgs with ripping down some boards from elsewhere in the mill to cover the gap but so far the idle thug had avoided doing so. The second brother, Drent, slept soundly but quietly.

"I do not like your attitude, Massbourg. With your damned big mouth, your damned snoring and that damned hole in the floor, I am just about sick to my back teeth with it all. The treasure has been found, so it seems, which means that the travelling clowns will be carrying their share next time they get on the road. Tomorrow I meet with a contact with whom we will get us some professional help. But until then I need to sleep. To that end, you moron, I need some peace from your incessant snoring." The last few words came out as a yell.

Things had gone awry with the disappearances and probable deaths of Hartimmer's henchmen. Two of the Massbourg brothers had been killed along with three hired ex-watchmen from the Grappina city watch. Hartimmer was convinced that one or more members of the travelling performers were to blame, particularly one of them. A young, athletic-looking lad by the name of Harley, had caught his eye when the troupe were performing in Grappina. The Massbourgs had seen him practising with a weapon and had remarked on how formidable he had looked. Then one of the Massbourgs had looked on, from a distance, when the young fighter had killed one of the brothers out in the wilderness on the long ride down to Casparsport.

The surviving brothers had a score to settle. It ate at them like a chancre.

"I'll move over there, boss!" Ambry Massbourg indicated a corner a dozen paces away from Hartimmer's sleeping-cot.

Massbourg rose to his feet and sniffed the air. Although the small oil lamp gave some light in the main mill room, suddenly he couldn't see Hartimmer.

"Boss?"

He heard Hartimmer coughing and then retching. He smelt the first acrid stink and immediately thought that the candles had fallen to the floor. Then he heard the clatter of an object hitting the floor near to Hartimmer. *Something is wrong!* he thought. Another clatter as something bounced onto the floor and he launched himself, shoulder-first, at the rickety wall.

Then the world erupted in flame and shock.

...ooOoo...

Harley had lit a taper, a length of cord impregnated

with saltpeter and sulphur, and used it to light the corresponding tapers protruding from the two pitch grenades. He tossed them both into the stream just below the point where he estimated the opening to be that would have once housed the mill wheel.

He watched as the resulting cloud of smoke poured upwards and, hopefully, into the mill and was soon rewarded by a fit of coughing from inside.

Harley stood up, used his glowing taper to light one of the blasting devices and looked up at a high window. It was just a couple of feet above his head. He tossed the device inside.

He then rushed round to the front of the mill, lit his second device and tossed it through a large window, about ten feet above him.

Then he ran, quickly, down the wide passage to the burned-out shack, reaching it just as his devices exploded. The first blast came, a bright flash and a loud *crack*, followed by what looked like the rear of the mill being blown away from the main structure. A wave of pressure and heat hit him. Within a few heartbeats the second device exploded with similar results except this time the complete mill structure collapsed to the ground. Large and small pieces of wood and debris clattered and crashed around him and a cloud of smoke and dust surrounded the area of the explosions.

He cried out in agony as one large piece of planking caught him on the side of his head and his shoulder. He swooned but the retained his consciousness.

Harley smiled despite the pain. *Nobody could survive that,* he thought. *That's their arses spread across the city!*

He heard the sounds of shouting men, barking dogs and shrieking seagulls as he surreptitiously made his way back towards the checkpoint onto the mercantile city.

Boulaye and Gandar were awake in the very early hours. They were startled by the thunderous sounds of the double boom which echoed across the city.

"By the hells of the Void!" exclaimed Gandar. "Is that what I think It is?"

"Harley!" retorted Boulaye. He smiled dryly and shook his head.

LeDuc was on watch outside the stable. He inched the door open. "A flash and blasts from across the city," he reported. "It might be in the shanty town." He ducked outside again and shut the door.

Ragdan burst out into the ring of bales with his axe across his shoulder. "What was that?" he gasped. "It sounds like someone is breaking into the stable."

Boulaye laughed. "Hopefully, it is the sound of one Traviss Hartimmer and his sidekicks learning the error of their ways."

Rax appeared and rushed over to the door but Gandar stopped him.

Tinnisse nervously stepped out and stood beside Ragdan. The little Halfling looked even tinier against the massive frame of the barbarian. "Was that Harley's blasting thing?" she asked.

"Aye, Tinnisse. That it was. We had best ensure we keep this a secret between us just in case any innocent people were caught up in the blast."

"Innocent?" laughed Ragdan. "In the poor quarter?" His laughter sounded like a deep rumble.

...ooOoo...

The steady rain had now turned into a tropical downpour as LeDuc observed as a black figure stagger into the muddy corral. He was instantly alert with his

390

great-sword at the ready as the figure lurched towards him. It dropped to one knee, uttered an oath, pushed itself back onto its feet and staggered a few steps towards LeDuc. Then the figure collapsed.

LeDuc rapped the stable door hard with his fist and swung it open. "I need someone out here now!" he yelled.

He pulled the door closed and rushed over to where the figure was now laying on its side. He turned the face upwards, the rain having washed some of the blackening away. There was something else, Something slick. Blood?

"Harley? Gods, boy! What have you been doing? Is that blood on your head?"

LeDuc put an arm under Harley's shoulder to sit him up and was rewarded with an almost maniacal laughter coming from the young man's lips. Gandar and Olwetta had rushed out of the stable, swords in hand.

"Hold there!" cried LeDuc. "'Tis Harley. He is sorely wounded I think."

Olwetta passed her enormous sword to Gandar who, surprised at its weight, almost buckled. The barbarian woman easily scooped Harley up in her arms and, with Gandar close behind, rushed back into the stable.

Most of the Company was awake by now and gathering around the ring of bales. Many of them were armed, not knowing what to make of LeDuc's call.

"What's happened? Is that Harley?" Boulaye cried as he shouldered his way past Undar, Tinnisse, Pretteen and Tishia. Jetti followed close behind.

"Aye. It's Harley," called Hollissa.

"Make way for him," yelled Olwetta. "I need to lay him on the bales. He is losing blood. I think he has passed out. He needs a healer. Jetti?"

Boulaye held up an oil lantern, despite his rule that

they should not be held over the straw bales. "I need to speak with him as soon as he is back with us," he grunted.

Jetti, assisted by Olwetta and Tishia, attended to Harley until dawn. Boulaye hovered close by throughout. Tishia, her face ashen by the sight of Harley's wounds and with her hand shaking, passed a stake of wood, about a foot in length, to Boulaye. One end was pointed and covered with blood.

"This was impaled in Harley's shoulder," she said. "Jetti has sewn his shoulder up and applied a salve. He got a nasty cut on the side of his head too, and has a lump there the size of a chicken's egg. Jetti says he should have a healer take a look."

Boulaye despatched Rax and Ragdan to the Temple of Haeman.

...ooOoo...

Harley was still unconscious when the priest, a confident and pleasant young woman named Emay Deerhunter, washed her hands and prepared to leave. She was tall and moved with an athletic grace. Her long copper-coloured hair was coiled in a thick braid. She was dressed in common travelling garb and the only sign of her profession was a copper symbol of her Temple on a chain about her neck and a dark blue cape which hung at the corner of the stall.

"What is his condition?" asked Olwetta.

"He will be well," replied Emay. "Mistress Jetti did everything skillfully. The young man's wound will heal but the bump on his head is a different matter. I believe he may have cracked his skull but not seriously. He is to have at least two days of rest on his bed. He must lie still. I shall return in a couple of days to check upon him once I return from my duties about the shanty town. He should regain consciousness in a few hours. If his condition worsens then send someone to the temple. Oh, and if his bandages become dirty or blood-soaked then remove them carefully, spread this honey thinly across the new bandages and wrap them around. Only if the bandages he wears becomes dirty though."

Olwetta thanked her and promised to send a donation to the Temple. She escorted Emay to the corral where a donkey was tied to a hitching rail.

"I admire your courage, Emay," Olwetta said. "Very few women would risk going alone into that quarter of the city."

"I shall be perfectly safe, Mistress Olwetta," Emay replied. "It is something I have been doing regularly for almost a year. The people there know me and trust me. I shall soon be travelling the lands providing spiritual and healing comfort to people in the western lands. That will be a much more challenging task."

Olwetta looked shocked. "How will you travel? Alone?"

Emay shook her head. "Nay," she said. "Not necessarily. I would travel with traders and groups of other travellers."

"In that case, I would suggest you call in on us for in a few weeks we shall be going north again. It would do members of our company the world of good to have some spiritual guidance."

"My thanks, Mistress Olwetta. I shall bear that in mind." She unhitched her donkey turned back to Olwetta and waved a farewell.

Olwetta stepped inside the livery stable and almost collided with a bleary-eyed Boulaye.

"What was that conversation all about?" he asked.

Olwetta told him all that was said. She repeated Emay's advice on caring for Harley and mentioned the priest's plans on travelling north.

"She certainly travels well-armed," Boulaye mused. "A long-sword, a short-bow and a small war-hammer. Could be a good asset for our journey."

"I shall keep watch over Harley," said Olwetta. "Hollissa will help and so shall Tishia. The others will be catching up on sleep. You should too, you look exhausted."

Boulaye rose to his feet and nodded at her. "I thank you for that. Please send someone to wake me as soon as Harley wakens."

An hour later Boulaye was roused again. Jetti had shaken him awake in response to Tishia's call from outside their stall. He rubbed his temples and shook his head. He immediately regretted it; the pain of a headache immediately coursing through it. He greedily drank from his waterskin and began to feel a little better. He walked out into the ring of bales.

He was surprised to see Arnan Ben-Harami standing there flanked by a pair of city officials. The two were dressed in the customary dark blue formal clothing of wide leggings, a doublet and a long cape. Their wide-brimmed hats were also of the same colour and each carried a short baton adorned with a small silver orb.

"Welcome, Councillor Ben-Harami. Welcome Goodsirs," said Boulaye. "May I offer you refreshments?" He fervently hoped that he was observing the correct protocol and was rewarded with a smile from the councillor.

"Thank you but that will not be necessary," wheezed Ben-Harami. He lowered himself down onto a bale and waved for his two officials to do the likewise.

"I shall not stay more than a few moments," he continued. "I have some news about an, er, incident that occurred in the poor quarter last night."

Boulaye stiffened imperceptibly. "Some of us were awakened by a loud crashing sound," he ventured. "We thought it was a storm. What has it to do with us?"

"Ah, it concerned a certain traitorous politician from Grappina, one Traviss Hartimmer. I believe he was one that had caused you some problems and was personally responsible for the deaths of three of your comrades."

"Aye. Hartimmer. What has he been doing now?"

"An old shack, a mill I believe, was blasted to by a large explosion. We had learned that it was the hiding place of Hartimmer and two of his henchmen, the Massbourgs. My watchmen report that the explosion may have been caused by a magical blast. I sent a squad to search the remains of the place and they found charred parts of a single body and another body some yards away."

Boulaye stammered "P-parts of –"

"The burnt head with the shoulder and half of an arm was not with it. That had crashed through the roof of a shack a short distance away. A drunken woman and her husband were disturbed while –. Well, the rest I shall leave to your imagination!"

"Whose body was it?" asked Boulaye.

Ben-Harami wiped his sweating brow with a silk 'kerchief. "It was Hartimmer, of that we are certain. The torso had a gold chain, very expensive, embedded in the charred flesh.

"So one Massbourg still lives!" gasped Boulaye. "The threat still remains."

Ben-Harami waved a hand. "Perhaps not," he said. "He will probably be on the run now."

"I doubt that," said a gruff voice from the passage leading to the stalls. Harley's head and shoulder were wrapped in white bandages through which some blood had seeped.

Hollissa stood behind him with an exasperated expression. She shrugged her shoulders. "I couldn't keep him in his stall," she sighed.

"Harley!" cried Boulaye. "You are supposed to be resting."

"Aye, I shall," he responded. "I do not believe the last Massbourg escaped without injury. This, um, blast must have hurt him badly, surely. Search the nearby healers' houses."

Olwetta's voice came from behind him. "Harley, off to bed with you, now!"

"Aye, Lady Olwetta. Straight away." He shuffled back to his stall.

"I would imagine Massbourg will have gone to ground somewhere in the shanty town," wheezed Ben-Harami. "Now, to other matters. I am pleased to say that your Company has just been awarded a bounty of six hundred gold crowns for your part in the apprehension of the smuggling ring. I would imagine that would go a long way towards your Company's future."

Boulaye was stunned. "Aye, Councillor. That it will."

Ben-Harami smiled and wiped his brow again. "One of my companions has some news for you." He turned towards the man standing at his left shoulder. "Cityman Clanta?"

Clanta, a young man barely out of his teens, stood up and bowed curtly towards Ben-Harami. He looked at the faces around him and cleared his throat nervously. He then glanced at Hollissa and reddened. " I, um, I can arrange for a p-promissory note to cover the value of Karouche's jewels, er –"

"Promissory note?" queried Olwetta.

"The, er, the note would be given to you which can be redeemed at the city depository of any major city in the western lands. All you would need to be able to do is quote a pre, er, pre-arranged code word. It would instantly be recognisable by the establishment."

Olwetta leaned forwards. "So should the promissory note fall into the wrong hands, it is worthless to them?"

"Of course."

"If it should be stolen from us, how do we reclaim our money?"

Clanta paused and considered the implications. "Only by reporting the theft directly to the city depository that issued it. Then I believe there is a twelve-month wait while all city depositories are approached to ensure the money has not been claimed."

Boulaye sat quietly for a few moments, saw the slight nod from Olwetta then nodded to Clanta. "Aye. We shall accept your proposals but the reward for caturing the gansters we should like in coinage if you please. I do need to share that among the Company."

"That is satisfactory," agreed Clanta. "I shall arrange that today."

"What of Karouche's treasure?" asked Olwetta. "Has this been values yet?"

"Ah, that is the next piece of good news," beamed Ben-Harami. "Cityman Bontay?"

Unlike Clanta, Bontay was tall, confident and quite elderly. He rose, bowed curtly to Ben-Harami and turned towards Boulaye, occasionally glancing at Olwetta.

"There were two-hundred and twelve stones, a large variety indeed." He unrolled a piece of parchment and read out a list. "There were two hundred and twenty-two stones in total, every one of them uncut. One-hundred and sixty-seven were precious and the remainder, fifty-five, were semi precious. Now, there were –"

"What is the value?" interrupted Boulaye.

Bontay glared at him. "I shall get there momentarily!" he huffed. "As I was saying, there were seventeen diamonds of varying sizes but perfect purity.

These I valued at twenty-hundred and forty gold crowns in total. Next were twenty-one sapphires of varying size. These I valued at sixteen-hundred and eighty gold crowns. Next came forty-six rubies, most of which were uncommonly large. I valued them at sixty-four hundred and forty gold crowns. Following them are thirty-one emeralds of various size, some of which were large. These are valued at thirty-one hundred gold crowns exactly. Lastly are fifty-two garnets, again of varying size. These I have valued at thirty-hundred and sixty gold crowns."

Boulaye looked open-mouthed at Bontay. He said nothing. Olwetta looked stunned but smiled faintly.

Bontay wiped his face with a red 'kerchief. "Now for the remaining semi-precious stones," he continued. "Thirty-one amethysts I valued at four-hundred and sixty-five gold crowns. Finally, there were twenty-four rather large opals which I valued at five-hundred and seventy-six gold crowns."

Bontay cleared his throat and wiped his face once more. "Now, the total value is seventeen-thousand, three-hundred and sixty-one gold crowns."

An incredulous silence descended.

Bontay continued again. "I must remind you that a portion of this is payable to the city council in the form of tax. The council has agreed that the percentage be forty-one-hundredths of the full amount, that is sixty-nine hundred and forty-five gold crowns which leaves you ten-thousand, six-hundred and eighty-six gold crowns. Will you want to arrange a promissory note? The terms of this are as my colleague explained earlier."

With effort, Ben-Harami rose to his feet and was about to bid a farewell to Boulaye. "What has stricken your young man Harley?" he enquired.

"Ah, an injury sustained during the night," replied

Boulaye.

"Of course, I shall ask no more," laughed Ben-Harami pausing only to cough into his 'kerchief. "Advise him to watch his back. Farewell."

With silence now descending on the stable, Boulaye turned back towards his stall.

...ooOoo...

Chapter 28

Ambry Massbourg was in pain.

This was no ordinary pain. He had burst, shoulder-first, through the flimsy wall of the mill. Some sixth sense had prompted him to do it when he had lost sight of Hartimmer in the choking smoke and something had clattered through the open windows. The fragile timber had shattered easily enough and just as he ploughed through a great blast of noise, pressure and heat had lifted him off his feet and thrown him through the air.

He had landed not on the ground but against a timber wall of a building that was thirty, or more, paces away from the mill. He fell to the ground. That was when the pain started.

His clothing was on fire, he could not hear a thing and he was screaming in extreme agony. He rolled on the wet ground in an attempt to put out the flames. He could feel the rough ground as it made direct contact with his skin, even through the agony.

The coolness of grass was strangely soothing but only temporarily. Small fires and debris were all around him.

He began to feel searing agony on the back of his head. He put up a hand to touch it and felt a sticky, warm wetness that worried him. He screamed again with the new agony.

Oddly, he could hear his own screams. Then faces appeared in the darkness. They flickered with red and orange colour as if on fire. The faces spoke to him but all he could hear was a faint, unintelligible murmur.

Then darkness overwhelmed him.

...ooOoo...

Later that morning Boulaye assembled the Company around him. Although Harley was looking a little improved, he was forbidden to attend by Jetti and Olwetta. The Company was advised to raise their voices so Harley could hear the discussions.

"Every person in the Company will receive fifty gold crowns to keep for themselves," began Boulaye. "In addition, there are your usual earnings. It is just as well that we have come into money because we have taken little in recent weeks and funds were running short. We have become very wealthy, as a Company. It now remains to be seen what we each decide is to be our future. We must make some provision for the cleric, Tyson Kashtillan."

"Fifty gold crowns will hardly change my life, Boulaye," grunted Balari Lightfoot.

There were murmurs of agreement from around the Company.

"How would a further six-hundred gold crowns change your life?" asked Olwetta.

The silence was so complete that they could hear the movement of horses, carts and people outside on the streets.

She rose to her feet and looked at each person in turn. "That is each person's share of the gems we, er, liberated from the Graban Hills way station and from Karouche's treasure hoard." She sat down on the bale again.

"What does our leader say to this?" asked Gandar. "Is this your plan, Boulaye."

"She has just told you," Boulaye replied. "I think it is time, Olwetta."

"Time for what, Olwetta?" enquired Undar. "What is this about?"

"All will be made clear," she replied. "Let us eat and drink first. It is midday and we all need time to

401

reflect on things that have happened."

...ooOoo...

He woke up lying on his left side on a bed. The straw mattress did little to give him comfort. Somebody was giving him a cooling, soothing treatment on the back of his head. He cried out in pain once again. He heard a voice telling him to keep calm and relax. He could hear!

He kept still while a bandage was wrapped around his head. What had happened? A magical fire spell? What else could cause that searing, agonising, powerful blast? His brother had killed that mage bitch in the stable. Her bastard man was behind this for certain.

I'll have 'im, he thought quietly, *as soon as this bitch healer woman has finished with me. And if she causes me more pain while tending to me I'll finish her too!*

The healer woman helped him into a sitting position. He cried in anger out as pain coursed through his back, the drying injuries to his back stretching with his movement despite the salve she had spread across it.

"Bitch!" he yelled as he picked up a cutting-blade from the priestess' healing pack. Then a strike to the uninjured side of his head laid him out cold.

...ooOoo...

Olwetta stood up and paced to and fro behind the seated Company. She towered above the others and stopped to rest her hands on Ragdan's shoulders.

"As some of you know," she began, "the Company was formed some years ago. In that time, we were all just a fledgling group of individuals who had been recruited by Boulaye and Jetti to form the Blue Sky Spectacular Company. Ragdan and I were the first. I should say that it was I who engaged Boulaye and Jetti, not the other way around."

"But Boulaye has always been our leader," insisted Gandar. "I am right, am I not, Boulaye?"

"Nay, Gandar," responded Boulaye. "I led your practises and your rehearsals; I directed the performances and provided training. However, it has always been Olwetta who led the Company. You remember me speaking of my aspirations some days ago? They were Olwetta's, not mine. But I was fully supportive of her and I still am."

"Aye, they were mine," she replied. "I believed the Company would have benefitted from a winter base here in the south and a summer base in the north. We could become stronger, perhaps larger and with more fame. But things are about to change, I believe. I am now fully expecting you may all have other plans now you have wealth. I do urge you all to consider a future with the Blue Sky Spectacular Company though."

"I don't understand," blurted Undar. "Why did you pretend that Boulaye was our leader?"

Olwetta looked down at her spouse, Ragdan. He looked up, smiled, nodded and winked at her.

"It was important that Ragdan and I kept our identities out of the public eye, so to speak. With increasing numbers of our people from the northern plains travelling through the western lands we did not wish to draw attention to ourselves."

"Why not?" asked Gandar. "What is that about? It sounds as if you are being hunted or you are on the run."

"We are. Or at least I am. I am outcast from my tribe in the north." A look of sadness passed across her face. Ragdan looked up at her and smiled again. She put her arms around his shoulders and rested her head lovingly against his. "If it weren't for Ragdan, I would have been murdered too. My husband, Eganrick, was our Ildarran, the tribal leader. Being one of two brothers he had inherited the leadership by birthright. His brother, Galenrick, was older but his mother was not the rightful consort of my father. He had been plotting so it now seems. Eganrick was called upon to quell a drunken brawl and was set upon in the night. Eganrick was killed although his bodyguard survived. This was Ragdan."

"Gods!" exclaimed Undar. "A predicament indeed."

Once again she looked down at Ragdan. "Galenrick swore to hunt down the perpetrators and he falsely named me as their ringleader. I had no choice but to go on the run. I had one only who believed me and helped me in my predicament, as you correctly described it, Undar. It was Ragdan who helped me to retrieve what weapons, money and personal items I could find and together we fled west then south for many months, so leaving our lives and our identities behind us. The names Olwetta and Ragdan are not our own. Even our physical appearances have been changed slightly and time has also contributed. It has been ten winters since we fled."

"Eleven!" rumbled Ragdan.

Olwetta nodded. "Is it, beloved? Aye. How time has flown by," she mused.

"So what would happen to you if you were found?" asked Pretteen.

"Ah, probably nothing now, but I would probably have to defend myself, by arbitration or even physically."

"I would fight alongside you, my lady," said Ragdan, his deep voice as intensive as his expression.

"I know that, dearest," she said. "You know, Harley

has been very perceptive. He seems to have recognised something about me, calling me Lady Olwetta occasionally. I wonder how he is."

"I can hear you," called a voice from the stalls. "I am feeling better. Laying here without ale is very depressing!"

"It is mid-morning; too early for ale," called Jetti.

"Ale will probably help him sleep," giggled Tishia.

"Aye, it would. Keep the noise down so I can sleep then," Harley responded.

After a flurry of laughter, silence descended once again.

Olwetta sighed. "I still think we should come to a decision about our future," she said quietly.

Murmurs and objections flooded across the circle.

Olwetta walked around Ragdan and stepped into the centre. She held up her hands, palms forward. The hubbub reduced. "Wait, wait," she said. "Let us sleep on it and discuss it another day. Tomorrow perhaps."

Heads nodded in agreement.

...ooOoo...

One of Ben-Harami's flunkies was escorted into the livery stable next morning a couple of hours after dawn. He delivered the daily morning feast on a wheeled trolley and requested an audience with the Company's leaders. The flunky had removed his wet cloak and handed it to DuPrenne. Boulaye and Olwetta sat with him on the circle of bales. Harley shuffled out, coughed and pulled a blanket around his shoulders. There was a chill in the air this morning due to the rain that had fallen overnight and continued to fall albeit lightly.

"I have been instructed by my master to convey some information," the man began. "After the, shall I say, incident in the shanty town, the surviving rebel, one Massbourg, was taken by a couple of locals to a healing house. Unfortunately for him, he was rejected by the wicca woman there. We heard that a Priestess of Haeman then tended to him in the Grunting Sow Tavern, an establishment of very ill reputation and commonly frequented by some very iniquitous and foul people indeed. It has been reported that he attempted to stab her with her own healing instrument for her troubles in the early hours of this morning. She actually knocked him cold!"

Olwetta's head jerked up. "A Priestess of Haeman, you say? Was her name Emay Deerhunter by any chance?"

"Aye, it was so. She is well known to us as being a priestess with renowned skill as a healer and a fearsome fighting reputation by all accounts. Despite Massbourg's burns he has made good his escape. That is all I can tell you. The proprietor of the Grunting Sow is one Chanda Braak, a monster of a human who is rumoured to have more than a little goblin blood in his veins. Actually, he is on occasion prone to feeding information back to the city council that allows us to apprehend the most wanted villains. That is something I divulge to you in confidence."

"Does anybody know where Massbourg went?" asked Harley.

"Nay, although Chandra Braak may know more than he originally admitted. My master has let it be known that there is a reward out for his capture, alive or dead. The sum is one-hundred gold crowns. I shall take my leave of you now. Farewell."

The manservant was led out of the stable. Gradually the rest of the Company had been gathering around the periphery of the circle of bales and every one of them was silent.

Olwetta broke the silence. "We shall be deciding on the future of the Company today, Harley," she stated.

"I shall not be a part of that future for a while," he replied.

Boulaye's head snapped up and he stared at Harley. "You are not going after him, are you?" he gasped.

"I have to," Harley replied. "I have to find him before he finds me. If I stay here, others of you may be in danger. He has lost three brothers and was sorely wounded. He has also lost his boss and will be needing money. He knows we all have it and may look for hostage. He will never give up."

"He is just one man and badly hurt," Olwetta said. "I do not think he will be that much of a threat to us now."

"I shall hunt him nevertheless."

"Will you rejoin us afterwards, Harley?" Jetti asked.

"I cannot promise that but I shall attempt to meet you all on your summer journey to the north. I have to go to see my employers and then visit my sister and father. I have much to do but I promise I shall find you."

"If we are still all together," muttered Boulaye. "When do you leave?"

"Today. I shall need a pair of good horses, some food and some money, Boulaye, er, Lady Olwetta."

"You are still unwell, Harley," Jetti said. "For the sake of the gods, give it another day at least. The priestess said she will call in on you. That will be today or tomorrow. Let her look at your injuries first."

"I agree," responded Olwetta. "In fact, Harley, on this I insist."

"The ladies are right, you know," Boulaye added. "It is still raining too. I need to get you some money so it will take most of the day for me to do that. You know we are right, don't you?"

"Aye, you are," Harley relented. "Another day."

"And you will not crawl out through the back of the stable either, will you?" Olwetta warned him. "We are boarding it up this morning."

Harley laughed. For the first time in a while he sat with them and ate heartily, despite the pain of his wounds.

Emay Deerhunter, the Priestess of Haeman, appeared later that morning. She looked at Harley's wounds, changed the bandages and declared him improving. He still had a lot of difficulty turning his head and moving his left shoulder. Olwetta and Jetti looked on as Emay gave him advice. Olwetta crouched to look over Jetti's head at Harley's shoulder injury.

"It will take a week or two to improve," Emay said. "Continue to rest your shoulder and exercise it gently throughout the day."

"Bah!" exclaimed Jetti. "He is riding out of here in the morning, tomorrow, on a manhunt."

The priestess was horrified. "Nay! I forbid it!" she exclaimed. "You are not ready. What is this manhunt?"

Olwetta rose to her full height. "It is the very man you were attacked by in the shanty town this morning," she replied. "It was Harley who gave the beast those injuries."

"How did you manage to do that? The man had bad skin burns on his back and head. I am told that the building he was in was totally destroyed by a blast. It will have taken magic or something to do that. You do not look like a mage."

Harley looked up shyly. "I used, er, alchemy."

Emay looked a little confused. "I have heard of blasting substance that the people of the eastern lands use. Is that what you mean? The easterners guard their secrets closely."

"I used something like that," he conceded, desperate

to change the subject. "I do have to travel. Massbourg is dangerous in spite of his injuries. He will hunt me if I don't find him first. I have to be out of here by the morning."

"In which case, I shall make a bargain with you," Emay stated. "I also wish to travel north. If you are happy, I could accompany you. In that way you will be able to escort and guide me and I shall ensure your injuries are treated daily and do my share of night watches."

Harley thought on this for many moments. "Aye," he replied. "But you ride into danger if you are with me. The man may attack from a place of concealment, without warning and without mercy. Are you prepared to risk that?"

She looked at him for a few moments without her gaze wavering from his eyes. "I am no wilting girl," she replied earnestly. "I bested him once. The man is an oaf with little sense. Besides, two pairs of eyes are better than one, particularly at night."

At that moment, neither of them realised just how prophetic her statement was.

...o o O o o...

"Two?" replied Harley.

"Aye, two warhorses," repeated Boulaye. "You will need 'em, lad."

"Look after your saddle, too," suggested Gandar, indicating an old, slightly battered saddle that was sitting across a rail. "It is the best one you have ever had, believe me."

Harley looked closely at it. It looked no different to any other military-style riding saddle. He shrugged his shoulders. "It looks like cra–, very well-used. Have you got some money for me?" he asked.

Boulaye handed over a leather bag the size of Ragdan's clenched fist.

Harley released the thong and looked inside. "It looks a little light to me, Boulaye."

Boulaye laughed. "It is indeed. You have fifty gold crowns there. Tell 'im. Gandar."

Gandar smiled. "Olwetta, Hollissa, Pretteen and Tishia have been up all night. You might have noticed their absence this morning."

"What are you telling me?" prompted Harley.

"I told you that your saddle was the best you have ever had. You have a thousand gold crowns sewn inside it. We selected a rough saddle that would be unlikely to attract attention. Now you know why you'll need a heavy horse! That saddle weighs a ton! It will take two of you to put it up on the horse."

Harley breathed in and let it out slowly. "So the priestess is still intending to come with me then." It was a statement rather than a question.

Boulaye turned to face him squarely. "Lad, Just look at you. You cannot stand up straight. You can barely raise your arm above chest height. You will need help getting up on horseback. And look at your face! Apart from being an ugly toad, you are pallid. You will need help with hunting and cooking. So I don't want to hear any more protests about someone riding with you. She is a healer and a damn good fighting woman by all accounts. Besides, you will benefit from pious guidance. She's a lovely girl, Harley."

"I don't really need a lov –"

Olwetta appeared from her stall and cut him off short. "Emay is outside," she called from the door. "She is on her horse and has another in tow."

The whole Company gathered as Harley loaded his personal equipment onto his horses and saddle. He nodded a greeting to Emay who nodded back.

Olwetta stepped up to Harley and put her arm across his shoulders. "We shall all be thinking of you, Harley. Your grief will lessen with time so do not cut yourself off from other people. Remember Riette as a bright star and keep that memory safe in your heart. Other stars will shine in time, other opportunities, other loves."

Harley smiled wanly. "Thank you, Lady Olwetta, for your kind words. Look after the others. Will you all travel north together?"

"Ah, we all spoke on this while you were preparing to leave. Everybody has voiced their commitment to continuing with the Company. While we are travelling north in a few days, the stable will undergo a transformation. It will become our base during the winter months and we shall call it Winterhome. I hope you shall see it in the future, Harley."

"Will you also build in the north?"

"Aye, we shall. In Northwald City we shall build our base too."

"And call it Summerhome?"

Olwetta laughed. "Aye, I expect we shall."

With effort and help from Gandar, Harley climbed atop his great horse. He adjusted his sword so it hung conveniently behind his left thigh and within easy reach of his right hand.

Boulaye held the horse's bridle as Harley bade farewell to the Company. "Where shall you go first, lad?"

"Direct to the Grunting Sow to speak with Chanda Braak. I want to find out where Massbourg may have gone. Then I shall ride after him."

"Take care, lad. Trust in Emay too."

Emay eased her mount over to Harley. "I can lead you to the Grunting Sow. Chanda Braak will speak to me for he knows and trusts me."

Harley nodded and reined his mounts towards the

411

gate. He didn't look back as he rode through. Emay followed behind but overtook him on the road towards the shanty town.

The Company was in sombre mood as they filed back into the stable. Rax and his five men were also to leave in the afternoon, their pockets filled with gold crowns.

With the Company sitting around the ring of bales, Boulaye rose to his feet to speak to them. "Life will now return to normality," he stated. "We start our performance preparations tomorrow. This is the first time we have been in safety for a long time so I think we can celebrate by having a drink or two in the Star of Caspar Tavern. I will remind you that work will go on in the morning regardless of hangovers."

"Wait!" Hollissa cried out, her voice shrill and excited. She leapt to her feet and jumped into the centre of the floor.

"What?" exclaimed Boulaye, shocked at the interruption. "What is it?"

"Boulaye," cried Hollissa. "Let me see that sword again. Karouche's sword. We have missed something, I am certain."

"What do you mean, lass? Forgotten something?"

"The sword, Boulaye," gasped Hollissa. "Please."

"Go fetch it, Falarr," ordered Jetti.

As always, he cringed when she called him by his given name but be stamped out to his stall nonetheless. He reappeared holding the sword in front of him as if it were made of glass. He handed it to Hollissa.

She took it gingerly and turned it to look at one face of the blade and then the other. "Here it is," she said, her voice rising in excitement. It says '*Take oute the stone then looke benethe*'."

"We did that and found the precious stones."

"Aye, Harley looked *behind* the stone and found the

412

gems. But he did not *then* look beneath. I think there is more treasure down there."

Gandar rose from his bale. "You mean that there could be more treasure behind a stone lower down the wall," he said slowly.

Hollissa smiled. "Either that or it is buried in the floor of the well. If you inform Ben-Harami. He will send his own team of men to search the well. If there is anything down there and they find it, the treasure will all go to the city."

Boulaye let out a breath and leaned backwards. "Perhaps we can delay the rehearsals," he said softly. "We had better ask Rax and his men to stay with us for a few days more."

...o o O o o...

They rode through the squalor and filth of the shanty town attracting quite a lot of attention. Filthy children, mostly dressed in rags or, if they were more fortunate in poorly-fitting clothes, begged for food and coppers. Emay tossed them a few coins occasionally. Harley had noticed some older siblings and even adults encouraging this beging by the little ones but, if Emay had also noticed, she gave no sign of it.

Emay reined in her mount in front of what to Harley's eyes was the most decrepit structure he had ever seen. This was the Grunting Sow tavern, illustrated by a rough hand-painted sign showing a black and white pig. The wooden building was square and seemed to have been constructed from pieces of timber that had been salvaged from the remains of other buildings, fences, wagons and even logs. There were no windows that he could see from the front.

The only obvious door was guarded by two burly-looking thugs. He guessed that each of them had more goblin blood in them than human. Their lower jaws jutted forward of their faces and porcine tusks could just be seen despite having probably been filed down to the level of their lower lips. Although tall, almost seven feet, they were squat with short legs and were powerfully-built across the shoulders. Each of them leaned on a heavy cudgel but Harley suspected that their fists would have been equally capable of dealing damage to a miscreant.

The guards watched them suspiciously as Harley, with difficulty, and Emay dismounted. Three teenagers stood nearby. One of them stepped up.

"Watch yer 'orses for yer, chief?" he offered.

Emay was about to object but Harley stepped forward.

"Aye," he said. "A silver for you now and one more and one each for your two friends when we come out. A deal?"

The youth grinned. "A deal," he replied, spitting into his hand and holding it out.

Harley spat in his own hand and grasped that of the lad. He passed a coin to the youngster and turned to enter the tavern.

Emay trotted up to him. "What are you doing?" she asked earnestly. "They will run off or rob the horses."

"No they won't," Harley replied. "We made a deal and shook on it. The other two lads will not allow him to run off because they will lose the promise of silver coins. Let us go inside. Drink nothing, if you do it will probably give you the shits."

"But –"

It took Harley a few moments for his eyesight to become accustomed to the gloom. The air was thick with acrid pipe smoke and the stench of vomit, sweat, urine and poor ale. He strode straight to the bar and demanded to see Chanda Braak.

"You's talkin' to 'im," replied a huge man. "Dat's me. What you's wantin'? Hey, dat you Emay?"

"Aye, Braak, 'tis me," she replied. "Good to see you again."

"Aye. Dis man wid you?"

"Aye, he is."

"You's drinkin'?"

"Just talking," replied Harley. He lowered his voice. "I am Harley, a friend of Ben-Harami. We are in haste. I need your help."

Braak spat in an earthenware ale mug and wiped it with a filthy cloth.

"Ben-Harami. Hmm. You talk," he said. "Mabbe I talk after. Mabbe a gold coin helpin'!"

Harley had been fingering a coin in his hand. He flicked it up and Braak laughed as his hand shot out to seize it.

"That is fastest I movin' today, friend Harley. Aye, I help you. What you talkin'?"

Harley gave a mirthless grin. "I speak to you of the Massbourg man who was here two nights back."

"De burned man? He try killin' friend Priest Emay, don't 'e? All town speakin' o' de great burnin'. What you wantin' me speakin'?"

"Where did he go, friend Braak?"

"He run. De folk of shanty town speakin' o' big reward for de catchin' de bad burnt man. Dey chasin' 'im an' dey catchin' 'im. Aye. But 'e killin' one an' lop arm off anodder and stealin' 'orse. Den 'e bleedin' all over an' dyin' also, was de man wid arm off. De folk chasin' 'im to de Nort' Way but 'e ridin' 'ard and de folk, dey givin' up de chasin'. Dey comin' back wid de dead mans."

He tossed Braak another gold crown, nodded his thanks and grasped Emay by the shoulder.

"We leave now!" he said. "The North Way."

He handed the youth outside three silver coins. Emay helped Harley to mount up and they raced out of the shanty town. They dashed eastwards out through the outer city gates and within the hour they were galloping east and then northwards.

...ooOoo...

Chapter 29

They rode hard until nightfall, and then they stopped only to rest the horses and sleep for a couple of hours. They had been asking questions of other travellers, mostly traders and merchants.

Only once had a rider resembling Massbourg been noticed. A pair of peddlers had rested on the roadside. The horseman had left his own mount, almost having had its heart bursting from its chest, and had demanded a fresh horse from them. This was done at the point of his sword which lay across the throat of one of the traders. The horseman had then ridden northwards.

"We were lucky to escape with our lives," the man had said.

Harley and Emay continued their ride, albeit at a slower pace, about two hours after midnight. Soon after dawn five days later, they passed a three-wagon merchant's caravan that was travelling in the same direction as themselves. One of its two outriders drew his sword as Harley approached but Harley kept his hands clear of his own weapons.

"I mean no harm," he called. "I would like to speak with your master."

The outrider indicated the caravan owner, a far-southerner dressed opulently in a gold turban and a multi-coloured silk gown around which was wound a gold cloth sash. A long, curved dagger was tucked into the sash.

"I am Kalesh," the merchant said. "How can I be of service to you?"

"I am called Harley. I hunt a rider, tall, blond and carrying burn injuries."

"Aye. A man stopped us not one hour back and begged our healer for succour from some terrible injuries. Out healer asked for a donation for the salve and bandages he had used but, I am angered to say, all the horseman did to show his appreciation was to strike our healer to the ground. Now it is our healer that needs healing care."

Harley called Emay and she eased her mount over to him.

"The healer here needs help," he stated. "If you can stay here and attend to him, I shall continue on."

"No, you cannot ride alone," protested Emay. "Wait for a couple of hours, I implore you. You are not strong enough."

Kalesh interrupted them. "There is a way station about three hours horse ride ahead," he said. "Leave one of your mounts with us. We shall care for it and meet you there before nightfall."

"Ride with care, Harley," called Emay as he spurred his mount on the road. "Watch your back."

...o o O o o...

Harley rode at the canter for an hour. Small stands of trees, with shrubs and bushes in between, were on either side of the road. He scanned each area as he rode past expecting the impact of an arrow at any moment. *You could conceal an army in there,* he thought.

The terrain was hilly and as he crested each rise he would rein in his mount and search ahead. The road stretched as straight as an arrow for at least two leagues before him. He had looked behind him and could see two riders galloping towards him less than a mile away. He was certain he had seen a rider about half a mile ahead but, apart from those, there were few travellers on the road this day. He rushed past a few of them without stopping or even checking his pace and continued this way for another half hour. His horse was straining and Harley knew he would have to stop very soon. He slowed his mount to a steady trot for a while before picking up speed again.

Suddenly, as he galloped down a slope and through a stand of trees and thick undergrowth, he came across a lone brown horse, its head hanging with fatigue. It was saddled and a bedroll lay on the ground beside it. Harley glanced about him, his senses heightened, but there was no sign of a rider.

He continued to look about him, suspicious and wary. He struggled to dismount, pain shooting through his left shoulder. He realised he had taken no drink since before dawn. He had allowed his horse to take water from streams as he rode along but had neglected to do the same for himself. This would have earned him a disciplinary rebuke during his years of training.

He drew his rapier but his left arm was still too weak for him to wield his dagger too. He stepped forwards slowly, cautiously approaching the horse. It raised its head in alarm and snorted but, with the reins dangling from the bridle, it made no attempt to move.

Without warning, a vicious blow on the back of his head felled him face down onto the ground. His forehead struck a log hard enough to cause sufficient dizziness to almost overwhelm him. Dazed and nauseous, he rolled onto his back.

A large shape loomed above him, blocking out the sunlight. A heavy weight descended onto his midriff and a powerful hand gripped both of his wrists above his head. He felt acrid breath on his face as the man head hovered a few inches above his.

Where is my damned sword? Harley thought as he began to try struggling free.

His head swam; he couldn't seem to concentrate.

...o o O o o...

419

Ambry Massbourg had seen the rider behind him and, despite the agony on the back of his head, he had hatched a desperate plan. He had jumped down from his tired horse leaving the reins dangling. He had then leapt behind a thicket of blackthorn picking up a heavy stone on the way.

He waited patiently until the rider came close. He nodded with surprise, tinged with satisfaction, as he recognised the rider. *That damned boy, the jester!* He would be a dead jester damned soon.

As the young man crept vigilantly towards the horse, Massbourg launched the rock hard. He had perfected the technique over many years when despatching rats and other vermin on the family farm. He grunted as the pain of his stretched muscles aggravated his burns but then almost leapt with satisfaction as the rock caught the youth on the back of his head.

Massbourg leapt forward and crashed down onto the body of the youth as he turned onto his back. Luckily for Massbourg, the brat had reached both hands behind his head, probably to explore an injury. He grasped the kid's wrists and pulled out his hunting knife with his other hand. He leaned forwards and lowered the blade down towards his victim's exposed neck. Blood oozed from a deep cut on the young man's forehead. This moment would be worth savouring; he would take his time.

That would prove to be a costly mistake.

...o o O o o...

Harley's head began to clear. His hands were still pinned above his head and despite his own contortions he could neither release his arms nor dislodge Massbourg. Pain lanced through his shoulder causing

420

him to cry out.

Then he felt the edge of a blade across his throat.

"You're gonna die, bastard," grunted Massbourg. "I lost three brothers to you an' you're gonna pay. I'll make it slow. Now, nod your head if I get my question right."

As the thug's spittle splashed onto his face, Harley knew he would die out here in the wilderness. The only thought to enter his head was that he would soon be with Riette. He found that strangely comforting. He smiled.

A piece of dark grey metal suddenly came out of Massbourg's mouth. It was like a steel tongue. A shadow appeared behind Massbourg and Harley could now make out the thug's features. Surprise was etched on Massbourg's face and his eyes bulged.

The metal tongue twisted around and Harley's own face was suddenly covered with the hot blood gushing from Massbourg's mouth. The pressure of the blade across his throat lessened. Despite the hot, sticky blood on his face, Harley found the idea of a steel tongue somewhat amusing.

Harley laughed. Dizziness returned despite his agony and it seemed to Harley that it was getting dark. *It is hours before dusk,* he thought. *So tired.*

The steel tongue disappeared back inside Massbourg's mouth. Massbourg's body weight eased sideways off Harley's midriff.

A voice said "Hello, Tamm DuHan. Or is it still Harley?"

Harley swooned and sank into unconsciousness.

. . . o o O o o . . .

Harley surfaced from his state of oblivion a number of times. Shapes seemed to swim about and voices

421

sounded faint, distant, and then he would return to the unconscious comfort that gave him relief from the pain in his shoulder and both the back and front of his head.

He awoke in the night. It was quiet and he could hear the sounds of muted revelry close by. He was having difficulties trying to remember the recent events. Someone had held him down; someone with a metal tongue had then released him. A metal tongue? *Nay, that was impossible.*

He retruned to his state of unconsciousness. He woke up later not knowing if he had been asleep for hours or days. Or years.

Where in the name of the Gods, am I? he asked himself, over and over again. He was in a bed. His searching fingers felt a blanket on top of him. It wasn't enough; he was damnably cold!

But more than that, he was terribly thirsty. He remembered he hadn't drunk anything since the early hours this morning. He shivered violently. *Gods, I'm so cold!*

He heard a snuffle. Someone else was in the chamber with him; sleeping. He drifted back into unconsciousness before he had a chance to get the attention of the sleeping person.

He woke up. He was not so cold. A throbbing pain in his neck and shoulder.

Someone was holding him, keeping him warm. *Riette!*

Nay, not Riette. But who? He searched his memory. *Emay?*

Somebody called my name as I fainted.

But it was his old name. Tamm DuHan. But nobody else knows it; not even Boulaye or the Lady Olwetta. His tongue felt like leather and his lips were dry and sore. *So thirsty!*

He turned his head to try to see who was beside him.

It was too dark but there was a lot of hair. *Who in the hells of the Void can it be?* Pain lanced through him at the movement and he cried out.

The figure beside him was instantly awake.

"Ah, you are back once again!" It was a statement, not a question. The voice was female, soft and compassionate.

He tried to respond with "Aye!" but it came out as a croak. He tried again. "Aye! Water!"

The figure rose from the bed and Harley heard the sound of fluid being poured into a vessel.

An arm gently lifted his head and once again, pain shot through his head, neck and shoulder. He grunted but decided to bear the agony if it meant he could drink.

"Take the cup," the voice said. It was slightly familiar but he couldn't place its owner.

He reached for the cup and eagerly drank its contents. It was water but had an underlying bitter taste. He gagged.

"It will help relieve your suffering," the voice said, softly again. "Drink it slowly or you will throw it back up. Then I will be mad at you."

I know that voice from somewhere, he thought. He sipped the fluid and slowly began to feel better. The woman lowered his head slowly. He still shivered but closed his eyes and felt the woman climb onto the bed beside him, put her arms around him and warm him with the heat of her own body. He was asleep within a few heartbeats.

...o o O o o...

Harley awoke. Shafts of sunlight shone through gaps in the hessian that hung at the window. He felt warmth and heard the singing of songbirds. He was alone in the bed. *Who was she?* he wondered.

He exercised his left arm and shoulder, and despite a dull ache, it felt much improved. Gingerly, he raised his right hand to the back of his neck. It was still bandaged but did not seem painful.

Somewhat reassured, he pulled himself up into a sitting position and looked about him. Although gloomy, he saw a small table in front of the window, upon which was a grey bowl and water pitcher. A large chair sat to the left side of the bed and had been adjusted to face him. Upon it were a few plump cushions to give the watcher some comfort. Another chair, smaller and plain, sat to his right in the far corner. His clothing had been neatly folded and placed on it.

My clothing? He glanced down and saw that he was naked. Beneath the blankets he was wearing undergarments but not his own. *Oh gods! That means – !* These garments were clean and fresh.

His backpack and weapons were on the floor beside the chair. The door to the room was by his right shoulder.

His head ached still and his mouth was parched. He was also hungry.

He heard footfalls on the wooden floor outside his chamber. He listened intently. The footsteps stopped outside his door. He pulled the blanket higher around him.

The door opened and a tall, slim woman entered, walked across the room, her hair shrouding her face, and pulled back the hessian at the window. Sunlight flooded the room. She turned towards him and smiled.

"Good morning, Harley," she greeted him. "Welcome to the world of the living."

He was speechless for a few moments.

"D – Dellie?" he spluttered. He searched through his

memories. "Er, Soren-ko should I say?"

She laughed a tinkling, joyous sound that made him forget his aches, anguish and troubles. "We were fortunate to find you when we did," she said.

"We? Who, er, what –?" He was confused.

"I wasn't alone. There were two of us. Wait, shall I call my travelling companion. Just a moment, Harley."

She left through the door but was back within a few heartbeats. She held the door open. A shorter, stocky, young woman with brown hair walked in.

"Hello Tamm," she murmured. It was a face he knew and recognised immediately. It was his sister in the travelling garb of a Priestess of the God, Haeman.

Harley fely light-headed. "Hanni, by the gods. You both found me? Were you looking for me?"

"The Magelords of Westron Seaport asked the Guild of Protectors for help in locating you in the southern lands. We have searched for two months."

"Who were the Magelords?" he asked, knowing she would not be able to provide an answer. It was a stupid question.

"He did not identify himself. We were both summoned to the palace, separately though. He referred to himself as –"

"The *Commander*!" Harley interrupted.

"Ah you know him then."

"Aye, very well indeed," he replied. "He tasked me to investigate the corruption in the Grappina City Council. I did that and sent a message to the Westron Seaport Palace. The troubles took me to Casparsport. I should have tried to send word to Westron Seaport but the means to do that was increasingly difficult."

"We went to Grappina," explained Hanni. "A city councillor called Niebelittin Bellpealer, what a nice man, explained what you had been up to with a group of performers. He said you were engaged in a manhunt and a treasure hunt."

Harley looked pained and anguished as he recounted the long chain of events that ended with the attack on him by the last surviving Massbourg brother. He told her how he had met and formed a friendship with Rax Starwatcher, her father. He choked when telling her of Riette.

Soren-ko sat beside him and put her arm around his shoulder. "Your own travelling companion, Emay Deerhunter, told us some of what happened while you were at Casparsport. She told us about Riette, Harley. She also said that you killed the ringleader who was responsible for her murder."

"The bastards killed my unborn child and then Riette. Alright, it was not Massbourg directly but things became personal between him and me. I killed one of his brothers. How did you find me?"

"We were travelling south with a merchant's caravan," explained Soren-ko. "We had camped to one side of the road when a rider rushed past us at dawn. An hour or so later you rode past at the canter. We mounted up and gave chase but kept a short distance behind you. We overtook you by riding round the hills and lay in wait."

Hanni took up the story. "We observed the rider get down off his horse. We crept up and when you arrived we saw him throw a rock at you. Lucky we were there, Tamm. Dellie, I mean Soren-ko, pushed her sword through the back of his neck. You really should have been more careful, big brother!"

Soren-ko also reprimanded him. "She is right, you know," she said, wagging her finger at him. Have you forgotten your training?"

He sighed and shook his head. "I was wounded, angry and was seeking revenge. It clouded my judgement."

Hanni frowned at him. "Poor Emay was dreadfully upset when she turned up here with a merchant's caravan. She blames herself, you know. She was tearful for days."

"Days?" Harley gasped. "I have only been here a day, surely!"

"Four nights, Tamm!" exclaimed Hanni.

"You were very ill," said Soren-ko. "You were so cold. I kept you warm during the nights."

"Ah, that was you? But I was undressed."

"Oh dear, silly boy," she teased him. "I have seen you undressed before."

He blushed and Hanni giggled.

"I will be continuing north to Westron Seaport soon," he said, intentionally changing the subject. "I have to report to the Palace at Westron Seaport. Then I think I will go and see our father, Hanni."

"Then we shall all ride together," replied Soren-ko. "The three of us and Emay. It is two-hundred leagues, a thirty-day ride, probably. But it is essential that you spend a couple more days here."

Hanni again reprimanded him. "You have recovery to finish, big brother. Emay and I shall care for you during the day."

Soren-ko gave a mischievous smile. "And I can keep you warm during the nights," she said.

"I am not sure," replied Harley after a few moments. "It is too soon."

"When you feel ready, then," she answered.

"I am tired though," he said. "Dusk falls and I do feel somewhat cold!"

...o o O o o...

427

EPILOGUE

The Star of Caspar Tavern, Casparsport

Boulaye, Olwetta, Gandar, Hollissa and Rax were in a quiet corner of the Star of Caspar tavern discussing the wisdom of starting a new search at the cliff-top house. The tavern was busy in the early evening and the smoke from many pipes of smoke weed was beginning to get quite thick. It was supplemented by Boulaye, Gandar and Rax who had also lit their own pipes.

"We must inform Councillor Ben-Harami," insisted Hollissa quietly. "If we were to go there and be seen digging up the well, we would be in gaol before we had time to break wind and belch!"

"Break –" gasped Boulaye. He began to laugh.

Olwetta grinned. "Boulaye, shush!" she urged. "The image is disturbing, I must admit! But you are right, Hollissa. We must inform him."

"Wait a bit!" Gandar chuckled. Somehow, Hollissa's description of their potential arrest had made him laugh almost uncontrollably. When he regained his composure he continued, whispering. "We don't have to tell him we are searching for treasure, do we? We just let him know we are interested in buying the old place to use for ourselves."

"It may not be for sale," Rax reminded them. "Who owns it?"

"It may belong to the descendants of Madame Caroche," replied Boulaye. "That would be Tyson Kashtillan, the Priest of Diette's Temple in Grappina who was tortured by, oh, what was his name?"

Gandar's head nodded. "That was Zheulin the dwarf," he replied. "Harley saw the end of him. He was working with the town hall guard commander, Tron."

"Who would know if Kashtillan is the rightful heir of the house?" asked Rax.

Hollissa placed her elbows on the table and clasped her hands together. "We could ask Councillor Ben-Harami to find out for us," she suggested. "We need to talk to him but we must be careful not to let slip our true purpose."

They finished their drinks and Boulaye rose, slightly unsteadily, from his seat. He strode between the busy tables to the bar and leaned across to speak to the barman. The man nodded at Boulaye and slipped through the door behind the bar. He was back after a few moments and spoke briefly with Boulaye who then returned to his companions.

"The barman will call me in a while," he said. "Me and Olwetta will go through to speak with Ben-Harami. Meanwhile, the barman will bring us more ale."

It was a couple of hours before midnight when the group returned to the livery stable. Great stacks of timber were arranged in the corral. The Company was seated around the ring of straw bales where Balari and Undar had been telling bawdy tales, much to the amusement of the ladies in the Company.

"Listen everybody," called Boulaye. "Olwetta and me have suggested to Ben-Harami that we are interested in buying Madame Caroche's old house on the cliffs if it is of a habitable state. He himself suggested that we go up there to look around it carefully as soon as we like. So we reckon that some of us should go up there in the morning."

There was a hubbub of conversation that Olwetta quietened with a wave of her hand. "Ben-Harami looked surprised and a little suspicious," she said. "He did suggest that we go ahead but warned us that if we are still searching for treasure we still remain bound by the agreement to inform the city council of everything we find."

Before dawn next morning, Boulaye, Olwetta, Hollissa, Undar, Balari and Rax prepared to return to the house. LeDuc and Carerre had constructed a rope ladder during the night and had equipped two horses to use as pack-mules. Two large, empty packs hung from the saddles.

They were at the house soon after dawn and began their search immediately. One end of the rope ladder was secured to the ground using two stout iron stakes. Olwetta descended into the well taking with her a pick and a shovel. An oil lamp was lowered just below her as she descended. The first she noted was that the body of the muleteer has already been removed.

She started digging. The ground was compacted and hard but she loosened the rubble little by little, putting the spoil into a large canvas bucket that was lifted to the surface and emptied by those above.

After an hour her pick struck against a metallic object. It took almost another hour for her to free a large, very weighty, iron-bound wooden chest. She called for those above to lower one end of a stout rope which she tied about the chest.

"Pull it up," she called, the ear-splitting echoes reverberating off the walls of the well. "Take care not to release it. If you do it will fall on me and I will be crushed."

Above her, Boulaye, Hollissa, Rax and Undar hauled it to the surface with Balari anchoring the rope by winding it around the iron stakes holding the rope ladder. They dragged the chest away from the lip of the well and called Olwetta to climb up.

Together, they took the chest into the house and forced it open.

What they saw left them breathless.

"Even if the city takes a share and we give Tyson Kashtillan a generous share, we should still have enough to build proper playhouses," gasped Boulaye.

"What is all this treasure?" croaked Balari. His mouth was dry and his hands ached from securing the rope as he gathered it in.

"I can tell you exactly what this is," said Hollissa, slowly. "It is the legendary royal treasure of the house of Bu'Qann to the far south. The royal city was repeatedly attacked by pirates and raiders until it was finally sacked and burned. This treasure has long been thought lost."

Olwetta gasped and sat back on the edge of a table. "So it was Ignacia Karouche, the Pirate King, who took it and hid it here."

"Aye, it was," agreed Hollissa. "This was probably why he gave himself that nickname. I wonder why he did not take it with him when he sailed away."

"Probably because he was escorted to his ship when he left these shores," replied Gandar. "I reckon he intended to to return one day to retrieve it."

"The reward for finding this will be immense," said Hollissa excitedly. "The Bu'Qann royalty was re-established a couple of centuries ago. They will be extremely pleased to know their royal treasure has been recovered. We will not be able to hide this from Ben-Harami. This is what the piece of parchment meant when it said the wealth of the king being well hid."

"We have much to do and much ahead of us," said Olwetta. "I do hope we meet up with Harley again. I have a feeling we will need his unique skills."

THE END

www.ingramcontent.com/pod-product-compliance
Lightning Source LLC
Chambersburg PA
CBHW030547020726
47494CB00005B/1508